P9-CDX-621

MICHELLE GAGNON

"*Boneyard* is a winner!
A compelling page-turner that pays due attention to the human heart. It'll keep you up all night."
—Jeffery Deaver, *New York Times* bestselling author

"A stellar work of mounting suspense and terror.
Ritual murder, ancient magic and buried secrets all blend seamlessly in this debut mystery by a major new talent. Not to be missed!"
—James Rollins, *New York Times* bestselling author, on *The Tunnels*

"I defy anyone to read the first chapter of *Boneyard* and put the book down.
With a cast of deftly drawn characters and a beautifully resonant setting, *Boneyard* is pure reading pleasure—creepy, terrifying and utterly believable.
I recommend it with great enthusiasm."
—Douglas Preston, *New York Times* bestselling author

"*The Tunnels* starts out scary and only gets worse, or—if you like frightening thrillers—better.
Michelle Gagnon is a fresh and confident new voice in crime fiction. An auspicious debut."
—John Lescroart, *New York Times* bestselling author

"Gagnon's plot is fast-paced, appropriately detailed in its forensic depictions, and reveals an attention to authentic FBI detection procedures that lets the reader know that the author has done her homework...an engaging and quick read."
—*Library Journal* on *Boneyard*

Praise for

"Michelle Gagnon's stellar debut is an edge-of-your-seat story of suspense and intrigue. With a deftly crafted plot and a winning protagonist, Gagnon spins a fast-moving yarn that is certain to keep you up late. We will hear more from this talented newcomer. Highly recommended."
—Sheldon Siegel, *New York Times* bestselling author, on *The Tunnels*

"Michelle Gagnon has written a tremendously fine debut novel that's as dark, twisty, and thrilling as the tunnels she so hauntingly describes therein. Expect to sleep with the lights on for at least a week after you've relished the final page."
—Cornelia Read, author of *The Crazy School*, on *The Tunnels*

"A great read. Scarily good. *The Tunnels* takes you into some very dark places, as a bright new talent takes on old-world horrors and scares the living daylights out of you. It's *The Wicker Man* meets *Silence of the Lambs*."
—Tony Broadbent, author of *The Smoke* and *Spectres in the Smoke*

"A fast-paced novel that taps into primal fears as it unfolds in real tunnels as well as in the labyrinth of the human mind. Things go down fast, decisions have to be made, and Michelle Gagnon has written characters who are up to it. Don't read this one when you're alone in the house."
—Kirk Russell, author of *Deadgame*, on *The Tunnels*

MICHELLE GAGNON

THE GATEKEEPER

MIRA®

If you purchased this book without a cover you should be aware that this book is stolen property. It was reported as "unsold and destroyed" to the publisher, and neither the author nor the publisher has received any payment for this "stripped book."

Recycling programs
for this product may
not exist in your area.

ISBN-13: 978-0-7783-2672-4

THE GATEKEEPER

Copyright © 2009 by Michelle Gagnon.

All rights reserved. Except for use in any review, the reproduction or utilization of this work in whole or in part in any form by any electronic, mechanical or other means, now known or hereafter invented, including xerography, photocopying and recording, or in any information storage or retrieval system, is forbidden without the written permission of the publisher, MIRA Books, 225 Duncan Mill Road, Don Mills, Ontario, Canada M3B 3K9.

This is a work of fiction. Names, characters, places and incidents are either the product of the author's imagination or are used fictitiously, and any resemblance to actual persons, living or dead, business establishments, events or locales is entirely coincidental.

MIRA and the Star Colophon are trademarks used under license and registered in Australia, New Zealand, Philippines, United States Patent and Trademark Office and in other countries.

www.MIRABooks.com

Printed in U.S.A.

For Kate

"Invictus"
(Unconquered)

Out of the night that covers me,
Black as the Pit from pole to pole,
I thank whatever gods may be
For my unconquerable soul.

In the fell clutch of circumstance
I have not winced nor cried aloud.
Under the bludgeonings of chance
My head is bloody, but unbowed.

Beyond this place of wrath and tears
Looms but the horror of the shade,
And yet the menace of the years
Finds, and shall find me, unafraid.

It matters not how strait the gate,
How charged with punishments the scroll,
I am the master of my fate;
I am the captain of my soul.
                    —William Ernest Henley (1849–1903)

JUNE 25

One

Madison Grant leaned over the sink, careful not to get her jeans wet as she applied another coat of gloss. She rubbed her lips together, smacked them once, then dabbed the excess with her fingertip. She examined the resulting pink sheen critically—perfect. Stepping back, she tossed the wand into her purse. It was actually her sister's knockoff Fendi. Bree would totally flip when she realized it was gone. Hopefully that would distract her from checking for other things that had gone missing, like her driver's license and social security card. Of course by that time the shit would have hit the fan anyway. Their mom would be so freaked out that Bree's complaints about a stolen purse would fall on deaf ears. At least that's what Madison was hoping.

She shrugged on the purse and grabbed the handle of her carry-on. It was their fault for basically ignoring her. Ever since the divorce, Dad was only a voice on the phone, and Mom spent most of the day in her room, shades drawn. And Bree was so busy with her friends, she barely bothered to talk to Madison. No, the only person who really cared about her now was Shane.

Madison flushed at the thought of him. They'd only known each other a few weeks, but she could already tell this was it, her one true love. They'd met online and instantly hit it off. She lived for the sweet texts he sent while she sat in class, bored out of her skull. They had these long, intense IM sessions where they talked about everything: what they wanted to be when they grew up, what their families were like. He was the only person Madison had confided in about how shitty things had gotten since the divorce, how awful it was to be dumped in a new city across the country, how she hated school and everyone in it.

Shane was older, nineteen, in his first year of college at San Francisco State. But he said the age difference didn't matter since girls were more mature, and he was totally right. Madison was a lot older than sixteen in her mind. And with Bree's license and social security card, she could get a job. Shane had offered to let her crash with him for as long as she needed to. He hinted that since they'd be spending the rest of their lives together anyway, they might as well get started. When he sent the plane ticket she got so excited, dancing around her bedroom. Then she swiped some of the cash her mom hid around the house and lied about staying with a friend for the weekend. That gave her a few days before they'd realize she was missing. And now she had finally arrived.

It was hard to believe she was about to meet Shane in person. It was going to be perfect, just like in the movies. They'd kiss, he'd look into her eyes and tell her he loved her. She'd work at a cool café in the city while he finished school. Maybe she'd take some classes herself, then eventually they'd get married. They'd have two kids, a boy named Max and a girl named Penelope. Someday she might even call her parents to tell them what a great job she'd done with her life. They'd forgive her for leaving, and everything would turn out the way it should have been all along.

On the other side of the security gate, a guy wearing a cap held a sign that read GRANT. Madison's jaw almost dropped. Shane must have some serious cash—first the plane ticket, now a limo? Maybe his family was rich. He was probably keeping it a secret to see if she liked him for who he was, like in that movie where the prince pretended to be a normal guy. Which was silly, she'd love Shane even if he was totally poor. But she had to admit, the thought of living in a huge house was definitely appealing. Better yet she might not have to get a job, she could just hang out all day. Madison repressed a giggle, trying to look serious and adult as she approached the driver.

"Hi. Are you here for me?"

The chauffeur eyed her, and she drew herself up to her full five-seven. "Madison Grant?"

"Yeah. I mean, yes, that's me."

The chauffeur motioned for her bag. She followed him to a Lincoln Town Car. He popped the trunk, tucked the suitcase inside, then opened the passenger door. Madison climbed in, impressed by the plush surroundings. There was even a bottle of sparkling water in the cup caddy. She unscrewed the cap and took a swig, then belted herself in. The car eased into the steady stream of traffic leaving the terminal, and Madison settled back against the seat.

"You know where we're going, right?" she asked after a minute.

The driver didn't turn his head, just nodded.

Madison was self-conscious. She'd never been in a limo before, but thought there was supposed to be one of those panels between them. Without one, she felt obligated to make small talk.

"So where are you from?" She asked after a short pause.

The driver didn't respond, and she figured his English wasn't very good. He looked Russian, at least around the eyes. Madison sipped more of the water. It had a funny metallic aftertaste, probably because it was from France. Her eyelids drooped. The flight had only been six hours, but she'd spent the whole time amped up in what Dad called her "condensed matter" state. It wouldn't hurt to take a little nap, she decided. After all, she didn't want to be sleepy the first time she met Shane.

When she awoke it was dark. Madison felt drowsy, disoriented. She wasn't in the car anymore, and wondered if they'd arrived and the driver hadn't bothered waking her. If she had been asleep when Shane first saw her that would be totally embarrassing, she realized, mortification jolting her from a stupor. She was on some sort of bed, there was a rough blanket beneath her. Was she in his dorm room? She stood and felt her way across. It was pitch-black, cold, and she shivered in her light sweater. Shane had warned her to pack layers, but she'd wanted to look cute so she'd kept her fleece jacket in her suitcase. She groped until she reached the wall. It was freezing and felt like metal. She rapped on it once, tentatively, then worked her way along it to a door. There was a handle but it was huge, also metal, and didn't respond to her tugs. Madison bit her lower lip, experiencing a tremor of fear. Something was seriously wrong.

"Shane?" She called out hesitantly. Her voice sounded squeaky. She tried to inject more assurance as she repeated, "Hey, Shane, are you out there? I think I'm stuck!"

There was no response. Madison felt a tear trickle down her face, followed quickly by another. As she slid to the floor and clasped her knees to her chest, she began sobbing in earnest. She was all alone, and no one even knew she was missing.

JUNE 28

Two

Jake Riley leaned back in his chair, crossing his feet on top of his new desk. It was solid oak, and according to the antiques dealer had once belonged to George Steinbrenner. Even if that was bullshit, it was a nice desk, he decided. And the Steinbrenner story would probably impress potential clients.

His office was still filled with boxes. It had taken longer than expected to find a suitable space, commercial rents in New York were through the roof. Even with the exorbitant severance package from Jake's previous employer, the new company would have to secure some contracts soon. But they'd made the right choice, he thought, gazing through the floor to ceiling windows. After searching the entire borough for an office with room to expand, they'd finally settled in one of the new skyscrapers jutting up around Columbus Circle. Central Park was across the street, and Jake was looking forward to eating lunch there, maybe strapping on his running shoes for a jog on slow days. Although hopefully there wouldn't be many of those.

He ignored the needling voice that questioned the

decision to branch out on his own. Sure, Dmitri Christou had paid him well, but for the first time in his life he was his own boss. And hell, they'd be doing good work along the way. They'd decided to name the company The Longhorn Group, a nod to the fact that both he and his partner originally hailed from Texas. If Jake had his say, The Longhorn Group would quickly become the go-to company for K&R insurers.

K&R was shorthand for "Kidnap and Ransom." In recent years there had been a sharp uptick in the number of kidnappings of American executives abroad, some figures estimated as high as twenty percent. To secure the release of abducted employees, many companies hired private firms to either negotiate with kidnappers or, failing that, attempt a rescue. South American countries, particularly Colombia, were the most notorious for kidnappings, but plenty took place stateside. They just weren't widely publicized, since no corporation wanted to put ideas in someone's head. And despite the increased number of companies signing on for K&R insurance, most operatives trained in negotiation and recovery were busy working security details in the Middle East. Jake was hoping The Longhorn Group would fill that void.

Eventually Kelly might come on board, and they'd be able to work together again. It was a nice thought. Jake picked up the sole item on his desk, a framed photo of her, and gazed at it. It showed her in profile, sitting on a beach, red hair reflecting the setting sun. She always griped about the angle, but then she hated every photo of herself. He thought it captured a side of her that was usually hidden—there was a vulnerability in the way she held her knees that always got him. He set the picture back on the desk. They were officially engaged now, had been for months, but hadn't set a date. She said work was keeping her too busy, but he knew better. Still, he didn't mind. She was worth waiting for.

He glanced up at a knock on his door. His new partner, Syd, stood grinning at him. Looking at her, compact in a well-tailored navy suit, every blond hair in place, you'd never guess she had single-handedly brought down one of the most dangerous terrorist cells in Yemen a few years back. Even though she was only in her mid-thirties, she'd been one of the CIA's best operatives. Lucky for him she'd become so disenchanted with the amoral aspects of Agency work, she jumped at his offer to partner up.

"I think we've got something," she said. Like him, over the years she'd managed to shed her drawl.

"Seriously?" They had just begun meeting with insurers to secure contracts. "That's great! Did Tennant Risk Services get back to us?"

Syd plopped down on the wing chair opposite his desk. "Nope, not yet. This is a private client." She paused a beat before continuing. "Actually, it's kind of a favor for a friend."

"Uh-oh. We talked about that."

Syd sighed and wound a strand of hair around her finger. "I know, I know. But this could be a good case to build on. He's a physicist for a lab that does Department of Defense work. It's worth considering, anyway."

"That sounds suspiciously like a pro bono job."

"He'll pay us what he can afford. Probably not much, but it'll be something. Besides, it'll give us a chance to double-check our operations. Kind of like the soft opening of a restaurant."

"Uh-huh." Jake examined her closely. "Just how good a friend is this guy?"

"That's a long story." Syd kicked off her heels and set her bare feet on the desk opposite his, settling back in the chair.

"No nylons?" he teased.

She tossed a paper clip at him. "That's the main reason I'm doing this, so I won't have to stuff my legs in sausage casings anymore."

"Benefit of being the boss," Jake said. In spite of himself, his eyes trailed up to where the navy hem rode above her knees. He forced his focus back up to find her grinning.

Syd wiggled her toes. "See something you like?"

"I wasn't aware we had a dress code," he said, gesturing to her suit. Even he could tell it was pricey, Chanel or something like it.

"One of us has to dress like a grown-up, on the off chance that a client comes calling."

"You kidding? These are my good jeans. And I have it on authority that Bono wears the same T-shirt."

"I'll bet. But then, Bono isn't exactly the first guy you call when a loved one goes missing."

"Speaking of which." Jake tapped his finger on the desk. "What's the story with this guy?"

"His name's Randall Grant. We met at a conference before I left the Agency."

Jake frowned. "You're dating him?"

"*Dating* is a strong word. Let's just say, we see each other when we can. Anyway, his kid got taken."

"His kid? Sounds like an FBI case to me."

"He can't call the FBI. Whoever took her wants information on his work."

"What's he do?"

"I don't know specifically, something high clearance. Nuclear stuff."

Jake let out a low whistle.

"Exactly," Syd said. "So you can see why he doesn't want the FBI riding in and screwing things up, Ruby Ridge-style."

Jake raised an eyebrow at her last comment. She

waved it off. "No offense. I'm sure your fiancée is great at her job. But you worked for the Bureau, you know how ass-backwards they can be. Bottom line, they care more about the secrets than the kid. And Randall doesn't trust them with her life."

"But he trusts us?"

Syd shrugged. "He trusts me."

Jake examined the ceiling, considering. His gut was saying this was a bad idea, and he knew better than to question that. Getting involved in a case where you had personal ties was always a mistake. Still, it was a job, and after months of inactivity he was itching to do something besides choosing office furniture.

"Get him on the phone," Jake finally responded.

"You sure?"

"Let's hear what he has to say. But he's got to give us more information, security clearance or not," he warned her. "And the minute I get a bad feeling, we pull out. Deal?"

"Deal," Syd said, tucking her feet back in her pumps. "You're a prince, Jake."

"Don't I know it." He grinned back at her. "Now let's call your boyfriend."

Kelly frowned as she took in the scene. Directly in front of her was a memorial to Arizona peace officers lost in the line of duty. The artist had made some interesting choices. The kneeling figure was straight out of a spaghetti western: neckerchief in place of a tie, hat in one hand, revolver at his side. The metal base he perched on jutted out into the points of a star. And on each point rested a different piece of Senator Duke Morris.

A few smears of blood marred the base, but other than that it was clean. Police tape cordoned off the area. Stairs led from the small platform to the State Capitol building, which currently housed a museum. A sign described it as neoclassical with Spanish influences, which explained the shade of salmon rarely seen on government facilities. At the top, a copper dome was dominated by a statue called *Winged Victory.* It was a strange choice for a body dump site.

As she waited for the crime scene techs to finish, Kelly pivoted. The capitol complex was sprawling. The statue was dead center in the middle of a pavilion, surrounded by modern buildings that currently housed the seat of power. Wide concrete paths penned in browning grass and scraggly bushes, all fighting to survive the onslaught of the desert sun. Late June, and at 10:00 a.m. it was already a hundred degrees. Kelly raised her arm, wiping a bead of sweat from her brow, and wished for the umpteenth time that the FBI dress code allowed shorts.

Agent Danny Rodriguez appeared at her elbow. "They're still canvassing, but so far no one saw anything. The locals set up a tip line for information, they're already flooded with people blaming everyone from the president to bin Laden."

"Great," Kelly sighed. A high profile murder always drew the crazies. "What about cameras? State Capitol building, there should be a surveillance net."

"You'd think so, but thanks to budget cuts security was axed. They've got cameras focused on the main buildings, but nothing on the plaza. Guess they figured vandals were their biggest threat."

"They figured wrong." Kelly squinted against the glare. A two lane road marked by a center divider faced the pavilion. On the opposite side, a park stretched off into the distance. Too much to hope for an ATM or liquor store camera nearby. "Where were the guards?"

"They got two guys, but the Diamondbacks were playing the Yankees." Rodriguez shrugged.

"So what, they were busy watching baseball?" Kelly eyed him. She was less than thrilled with her new partner. Rodriguez was just four years out of the Academy, young to have been assigned to the elite Behavioral Science Unit. Rumor had it his career was fast-tracked after he ratted out a former partner to OPR, the FBI's internal affairs division. And Kelly had a sneaking suspicion he'd been assigned to spy on her. Ten months earlier one of her cases had turned into a debacle, and she knew some of the Bureau higher-ups were screaming for her head. Her boss had stood by her, so far at least. Being stuck with Rodriguez reminded her she was on shaky ground.

"Hey, don't take it out on me. I'm a Mets fan," Rodriguez joked. He shrunk slightly under her stare. "So what next, chief?"

Kelly watched the medical examiner gingerly lift one of Morris's legs off the base of the statue. Senator Morris was popular in Arizona, but best known outside it for his draconian ideas about immigration reform. She'd seen him on the talk show circuit last week, railing about how America's borders needed to be closed entirely. The cop that led her past the tape mentioned that Morris had a good shot at president, then mumbled something about wetbacks before she cut him off. A man like that had probably made a few enemies over the years. And by gruesomely displaying his remains, someone was clearly sending a message.

The leg slipped from the ME's grasp and bounced along the ground as he fumbled for it. Kelly repressed the urge to roll her eyes. "Family has already been notified, right?"

Rodriguez nodded.

"Let's go ask them who hated the senator enough to hack him up with a machete."

Three

Madison shivered. The thin blanket they'd left her barely made a dent in the chill, and she swore it grew colder by the hour. She had no idea how long she'd been here. She usually told time by her cell phone but that had been taken along with everything else. She hoped it was already Monday, and that her family had realized she wasn't at Cassidy's house. A tear snaked down her face as she berated herself again for being such an idiot. Everyone knew that creepy older guys had MySpace pages; people weren't always who they claimed to be. But she'd fallen for the whole Shane thing like a total moron. And now something horrible was going to happen to her.

The worst part was the waiting. She'd screamed for a while, becoming increasingly hysterical until the door had suddenly been thrown open. It was the driver, now dressed in jeans and a filthy sweatshirt. Madison hushed as he approached, shrinking back against the wall. She expected him to start tearing her clothes off, or worse, but he'd just injected her with something that knocked her out again. She'd learned pretty quickly that screaming brought the needle.

Madison couldn't figure out what they were waiting for. So far no one had hurt her. In fact they brought her food and water regularly, and cleaned out the bucket as soon as she used it. And they'd left her a blanket. Though the light only changed slightly, she could now differentiate between night and day, the room brightened enough that she could make out the dim edges of her surroundings by sight, and the rest by touch.

She was in a ship of some sort, military judging by the dull gray paint job. The room was a steel box, ten-by-ten, with a cot in one corner and a bucket in the other. Other than that there was no rug, chair, or other decoration. She guessed she was being held in the bowels of the ship, she could hear the occasional slap of a wave against the hull. They didn't appear to be moving, which she took as a hopeful sign. Maybe it was one of those white slavery rings, and they were planning to ship her off to Saudi Arabia. Madison shuddered at the thought. If she was lucky, they'd kidnapped her for ransom, confusing her with the daughter of someone rich. Maybe they'd realize the error and let her go—she'd only seen one guy's face, and she'd promise not to tell if they just let her go home.

She had tried to pry the door open, hauling the cot frame across the room to use as a lever. But the minute she exerted some force, the sound of a chair scraping against the floor on the other side sent her scampering back. A moment later the door creaked open. The driver came in and glanced at the cot on its side, shook his head and gave her another shot. She hadn't tried again. Escape was clearly hopeless: there were no windows, and a guard was stationed at the only exit. She was screwed.

The door suddenly banged open. The driver still didn't speak, but something about the way he looked at her made Madison recoil. She protested as he crossed the room. Without breaking stride he yanked her up and flung her on the cot. She shrieked and clawed at him, "No, oh please God no…" then paused when he didn't do anything.

He was holding something inches from her face. A flash, then he left the room.

She sat up, puzzled. He'd taken her photo, so maybe this was about ransom. She couldn't decide if that made the situation better or worse. Madison pictured her parents' reaction to the photo, and in spite of herself felt a spark of something like satisfaction. Served them right, the way they'd been ignoring her. If she ended up dying some sort of horrible death, it would be their fault.

She dropped back on the cot and crossed her hands behind her head. There would probably be a huge funeral if she didn't make it out of here. Even her former best friend Jamie, who had totally screwed her over last year, would probably cry. Chris Dinsmore would be completely devastated that he'd never asked her out. They'd get a choir to sing "Ave Maria," and hundreds of sobbing people would follow the casket through the streets. They'd all regret how they'd treated her.

But she really might not make it out of here. The guy had let her see his face, which wasn't a good sign. And her parents didn't have any money. The whole divorce had been a joke with them fighting over air miles; it wasn't like they had a fortune hidden somewhere. And once the kidnappers realized that…she'd watched enough cop shows to know what would happen. At the thought she started to shake, teeth chattering. Madison drew the blanket up to her neck and tucked the corners under her heels so her whole body was covered. But it did nothing to stop the uncontrollable shivering.

* * *

Jake rolled his head to work out a kink in his neck. He didn't generally mind flying, but the only seat available on such short notice had been in coach, and his body wasn't designed for middle seats at the rear of the plane. His knees were jammed against the seat back in front of him, high enough that they prevented him from lowering the tray table. He'd tried to work on his laptop, but the kid on the aisle was playing a handheld video game that bleated nonstop, and the woman in the window seat issued a heavy sigh every few minutes. Another kid hung over the seat in front of him, staring at him while she picked her nose. All in all, the experience was making him seriously reconsider starting a family. Maybe he and Kelly could get a puppy and call it quits.

As they taxied to the gate, the flight attendant announced information for connecting flights, and the woman beside him grumbled something unintelligible. Jake hunched over, waiting for the slow file off the plane to proceed far enough for him to grab his carry-on. Once out of the Jetway he glanced at his watch and flipped open his cell phone.

"Frank? Yeah, sorry about that. My connecting flight at O'Hare was delayed. Where am I meeting you?"

Five minutes later, Jake was stationed in front of a bank of monitors. Frank, an old Agency buddy of Syd's, shifted nervously at his elbow. Apparently he'd done something bad enough to get shuffled down the ranks of Homeland Security to airport detail. Jake couldn't imagine what kind of heinous act would result in such a reassignment. Screwing the president's dog, maybe. Hard to believe anything less would matter to the CIA.

"I can give you a few more minutes, man, but that's

it." Frank's eyes shifted from the screens to the door in a constant cadence, like he was watching a tennis match. "Shift change is in a half hour, and I got plans tonight."

Jake jabbed a finger at the screen. "That's her right there. Pause and rewind five minutes, then go forward slowly."

Frank obliged, working the elaborate controls. A few other men were scattered around the room. After their initial appraisal they'd pointedly ignored Jake, which was fine by him. *Although it didn't instill much faith in airport security,* he thought, watching them peck away at phones and BlackBerries, periodically casting a token glance at the monitors.

They watched in silence as Madison Grant made her way from a restroom near the gate to baggage claim. The angle changed as Frank shifted from camera to camera. Jake had to admit, he was good at this. Had the tapes cued up and ready to go when he arrived, and despite the employees, the technology itself was state-of-the-art, HD quality.

"Pretty girl," Frank said. "What'd she do?"

Jake eyed him, not liking his tone. Maybe that's what the CIA had found so offensive. Syd had fed Frank some backstory about a CI they were tracking. Not very plausible, but then Frank obviously wasn't the type to ask questions when enough money changed hands. That level of pliability was also not a good sign for air travel, Jake thought. Maybe he should take the train home.

"Zoom in," Jake said, as Madison approached someone. Big guy, looked yoked even from this angle, six-five easy. A cap obscured his eyes, and the hands holding the sign were large and meaty. Jake frowned as they exchanged a few words, then watched Madison follow him out of the building. The film switched to a line of cars stacked at the curb. Madison climbed into the rear of a sedan. Jake frowned as it drove off.

"Can you get me a printout of that guy, and of the plate?"

Frank shrugged. "Yeah, no problem. Technology is a beautiful thing."

Jake didn't respond. He leaned back against an empty console as Frank shuffled to the printer. So Madison Grant hadn't been snatched, she'd been lured. Not surprising, he'd done plenty of dumb shit himself at that age. And whoever she was meeting must have money, curbside limo service didn't come cheap. He'd have Syd run the plates, but he doubted that would give them anything. This smelled professional. Someone had spent enough time developing a relationship with the girl that she didn't hesitate to jump on a plane. And if Syd was right about the dad's job, there were high stakes involved. Jake shook his head. He was liking this less and less by the minute.

"Here you go." Frank handed over a stack of pictures.

Jake flipped through them quickly. It didn't look like there was enough of the guy's face to run through facial recognition software, but there was a nice close-up of Madison. She was a pretty girl, light hair, big smile. She appeared sweet and trusting and more than a little naive. And right now, she was probably in some shit-hole, scared to death.

"Crap," Jake said, shifting the photo to the bottom.

"What?" Frank asked.

"Nothing. Thanks for your help." They shook hands and Jake walked out, blinking in the fluorescent glare. Even without looking at it he could still picture the photo. It was as if Madison was challenging him to try and forget about her. Jake tucked the stack into the outside pocket of his carry-on and headed for the car rental courtesy shuttle. He already knew there was no walking away from those eyes.

Four

Kelly adjusted the surgical mask over her mouth. Rod-riguez was growing progressively paler as the medical examiner peeled the skin back from the senator's face. And she had to admit, she was enjoying his discomfort. Kelly had sat in on more autopsies than she could count. It wasn't the sort of thing you got used to, exactly, but she'd developed coping mechanisms. Plus this wasn't a victim that inspired the warm fuzzies. Kids were still tough, she preferred to come in at the end for those results. But this guy, the more she found out about him the less she liked. Not that he deserved to be hacked up, but Duke Morris didn't inspire a lot of sympathy.

The ME had arranged him on the table like a jigsaw puzzle. Morris's feet were splayed out, arms and legs canted at angles that would have been impossible were his skeleton intact. A disassembled mannequin, Kelly thought. And an ugly one at that.

Under the glare of the overhead lights his skin was pale, suggesting he spent more time on the Beltway than in his home state. A protruding gut attested to plenty of pricey dinners, and his body was covered with an alarming amount of hair. His eyes and mouth were closed, and the hair plugs along his forehead stood out in stark relief. Kelly flipped open the file. On top was a professionally taken photo of Morris in front of an American flag, robust and strong, grinning obsequiously at his constituents. He possessed that air of smug satisfaction common to men who took money and power for granted.

"So officially, gunshot wounds were the cause of death?" Kelly finally asked. Over the years she'd learned that MEs came in all shapes, sizes and levels of ability. This one didn't seem half-bad, but whether it was the pressure of working on such a high-profile corpse or his own habitual pace, this autopsy was taking a hell of a long time. She pulled back the sleeve of her surgical smock to check her watch: nearly 5:00 p.m. Her stomach growled, reminding her that they'd missed lunch.

The ME peered up at her. "Yes, I'd say so. Two to the back of the head, fired at a downward angle."

"Execution style," Rodriguez noted faintly.

"Any way to tell how long they waited before using the machete?" Kelly asked.

The ME shook his head. "No blood around those wounds, so he was definitely dead. That would put it anywhere from a few minutes after his heart stopped beating to several hours. Time of death was around midnight last night."

Kelly nodded. That matched what they knew about the senator's schedule. He'd attended a fundraising dinner at the Hilton in downtown Phoenix. His wife thought that afterward he'd gone to a private men's club, but according to his credit card receipts Morris had actually whiled away those hours with a blonde from a local escort service. And not for the first time, according to both the lovely, gum-snapping Trixie and a trail of charges on his government-issue card. Kelly repressed a sigh—politicians, always so predictable. Apparently stamina wasn't one of Morris's strong suits. After spending less than half an hour in the room, hotel cameras captured him strolling out the lobby doors while adjusting his tie.

If the ME was right, Morris had been waylaid somewhere between the hotel lobby and the lot where his Cadillac was parked. And the next time he was seen, it was in pieces in front of the capitol building.

"I voted for him," the ME said contemplatively as he draped the sheet over Morris's body.

Kelly closed the file. "I hear he was a real pillar of the community. When will you have the full report?"

He shrugged. "A few hours. Initial tox screen shows he'd had a few drinks, but no illegal substances or anything that points to him being drugged."

"Make sure to scan for everything and fax the results to this number." Kelly handed him a card and left the room, tossing her mask and gloves in a bin.

"I'm kind of surprised you let the hooker go," Rodriguez grumbled as they strolled back out to the lot.

"Why?" Kelly asked.

"She might have been in on it."

Kelly tilted her head to the side. "But then why not drug him in the room and take him out the back stairs? No cameras there, and it would have been easier than trying to grab him on the street."

Rodriguez shrugged noncommittally. "I'm just saying," he said. "She smelled funny to me."

"She's a prostitute, they don't usually smell very good," Kelly replied wryly. She slid into the driver's seat and glanced at him across the interior. Rodriguez's face was still too round for his body, definitely a former fat kid who'd worked off the residual pudge in the gym. A few more years would probably take care of that. He wasn't much taller than her, maybe five-nine, and his high cheekbones and light eyes pegged him as closer to a Spanish-Mexican lineage than a Mayan one. Based on his file she knew he was twenty-seven years old, had entered the Academy straight out of Princeton, and spent his childhood in Los Angeles. Aside from that, not much there. Which lent further credence to the OPR rumors. His constant second-guessing of her decisions was irritating. Plus, every time he called her *chief* it was getting harder not to smack him.

"So what next, chief?" he asked casually.

Kelly gritted her teeth. "Don't call me chief."

"You prefer *boss?*"

Kelly decided not to get drawn into a pissing match, dinner was coming up and she didn't want to lose her appetite. "You make any progress on those gang files?"

Rodriguez shrugged. "The machete thing has been popular in L.A. for a few years, originally started by the Salvadoran gangs like MS-13. But then it caught on with everyone else—there have been incidents with immigrants from Sierra Leone, Somalia, Mexico. It's a cheap weapon, and chopping someone into bits sends a pretty strong message. There weren't any tags near the bodies, and according to the local Gang Task Force no specific group or gang is claiming responsibility. Which is kind of weird. Something high profile like this, you'd figure folks would be coming out of the woodwork to build their street cred."

Kelly shook her head. "Probably not with something this big. A mayor, maybe, but a senator? They'd have to know the government would throw their whole weight behind this one. Death penalty for sure." Which made her wonder again why she'd been assigned such an important case. Either the brass had more faith in her skills than they'd let on, or they knew this was a stinker. Still, it gave her a team of fifty agents doing everything from running down Morris's staff history to canvassing door-to-door. With that kind of man power, she wasn't complaining.

"Maybe ballistics will turn something up."

"Doubtful. Shot with a .45, no casings, and you heard the ME—the bullets ricocheted around his skull, they're a mess. If we find the gun we might get a match, but I'd be surprised if it turned up." Surprisingly clean for a gang hit, Kelly mused, unless they were well organized or got extremely lucky. Now that they had a rough idea where Morris had been snatched, Kelly had a team of agents combing through video surveillance footage from 10:00 p.m. to midnight. That was their best shot, to get a grainy image of a license plate, anything that would provide a lead. Barring that, without a specific group claiming responsibility, her list of suspects ranged from environmentalists to illegals to single parents, all of whom Morris had recently managed to piss off.

Rodriguez's cell buzzed an electronic version of some pop song. He flipped it open and barked, "Rodriguez!"

Kelly shifted irritably, waiting for him to finish. Until they got reports from the ME and the tape squad, there wasn't much more they could do. Time to call it a night. She repressed a yawn and idly wondered whether room service would be available at the hotel. She'd love some Mexican food—she could almost taste a burrito dripping with cheese and guacamole.

Rodriguez snapped his phone shut, a triumphant expression on his face. "We got the gun."

"What?" Kelly snapped awake.

"Phoenix P.D. got an anonymous tip today about a

local MS-13 stash house. They raided it, turned up a stack of weapons. And one of them is a .45."

"There are a lot of .45s out there. How do they know it was used in our killing?"

"Because it had Duke Morris's name right on it."

"What, literally? We inventoried his guns, everything was accounted for." And what an armory it had been: the entire wall of Morris's study was a display case with everything from handguns to paramilitary weapons. All registered legally, his wife hastened to point out, and licenses backed that up. Had the fighting ever gone house to house, Duke Morris would have been ready.

Rodriguez shook his head. "Not this one. Gift from a grateful lobbyist. It's a beautiful 1911, bone handle with his name carved in it. Phoenix P.D. already checked with the wife, she said he probably hadn't gotten around to registering it yet."

"Yeah, I'm sure it just slipped his mind. And he was in the habit of taking it to fancy dinners?"

"This is Arizona, Agent Jones." Rodriguez looked bemused. "Carrying concealed is considered a God-given right in these parts."

"Remind me never to move here. Jesus." Kelly furrowed her brow. And they wondered why the gun fatality rate was through the roof. "So whoever snatched him shot him with his own gun?"

"And then that gun turned up in an MS-13 stash house," Rodriguez concluded. "MS-13 loves machetes. They're questioning the gang members downtown, said we could observe if we like. Looks like this case might be open-and-shut after all."

"Looks like it," Kelly said. She punched the Phoenix Police Department's address into their GPS and silently kissed her burrito goodbye. While she waited for the machine to calibrate their course, she nudged away the feeling that something was off. Hell, she was due for an easy one, Kelly reminded herself. And the less time wasted on a scumbag like Morris the better, as far as she was concerned. It made sense: a gang composed primarily of illegal immigrants targeted a loudmouth who was making their lives difficult. Still, she'd feel a lot better with a confession, or footage of them hauling an overweight senator into a van.

Randall Grant was clearly having a bad day, Jake thought as he took the man in. Honestly, he was having a hard time understanding what Syd saw in the guy. Tall and thin, slightly gawky-looking. Maybe under normal circumstances he had a sparkling personality.

But these were obviously not normal circumstances. He looked hollowed out, shoulders slumped, bags under his eyes, the portrait of the tormented father. They sat across from each other in a nondescript café on the outskirts of Livermore. Initially Jake was glad they weren't meeting in one of the coffee franchises that dominated the Bay Area, but after a sip of espresso he'd changed his mind. *Say what you will about Starbucks,* he thought. *At least they were consistent.*

"So why don't you want to get the FBI involved?" Jake asked. Randall had spent the first ten minutes rambling on about his daughter, including too much information about his divorce and the dance classes she used to take. None of it had direct bearing on the case, but he seemed unable to help himself. Jake wondered whose brilliant idea it was to trust Randall with government secrets, if he spilled this much personal information over a cappuccino.

Randall shook his head violently. "Can't do it. The people who took her said they had someone high up in the Bureau, that they'd know if I called in outside help. And the minute I did, they'd kill her."

"And you believed them?" Jake asked, skeptical. It sounded like an idle threat. What better way to keep parents from calling the authorities than to sow distrust of them?

"Did you ever hear of Operation Snow White?" Randall asked.

Jake shook his head. "Nope. Some sort of poisoned apple scheme?"

Randall glared at him through red-rimmed eyes. "I was hoping Syd would be here."

"I'm sure you were. Unfortunately, I'm the one who needs convincing before we agree to help you." Jake raised an eyebrow.

Randall sank an inch lower in his chair. "Operation Snow White was initiated by the Church of Scientology back in the seventies. They wanted to purge any records that cast them or L. Ron Hubbard in a bad light. By the time it was discovered, they'd placed operatives in over a hundred government agencies in more than thirty countries. It was the single largest infiltration of the U.S. government in history. They denied it, but I have it on good authority that the FBI was one of those agencies."

"So, what? Scientologists took your daughter?" Jake had to fight an urge to laugh, he had a sudden mental image of Tom Cruise and John Travolta carting off a struggling girl in a duffel bag.

"Don't be ridiculous. I'm just saying, such a thing isn't outside the realm of possibility."

"Background checks are a lot more intensive post 9/11," Jake pointed out. "It's a whole different ball game now."

Randall shrugged. "Who says their guy wasn't already inside? Anyway, I couldn't risk it."

"And what exactly do they want from you, in exchange for her life?"

Randall rubbed his eyes with one hand. His jaw was stubbled with at least a day's worth of growth. "I can't tell you. It's classified."

"You're considering handing whatever it is over to the kidnappers. So I don't see the harm in telling me what they're looking for."

"Does it really matter?" Randall met his eyes sharply. "Would knowing help you find her?"

Jake shrugged. "Hard to say. I just don't like going into a case blind. I'm kind of puzzled that they didn't just snatch you. If you've got what they need, why take your daughter instead?"

"Because it's not like I have it in my head. They need me to requisition things, pinpoint certain…materials…then gain access to transport records. And they want it done over a period of time."

"So whatever they're after, they want a lot of it, is what you're telling me."

"Essentially, yes."

"But you can't say what."

Randall shook his head. Jake tilted back in his chair and eyed him. He couldn't put his finger on it, but there was something off about this. "Remind me which department you're with?"

Randall smiled slightly. "Advanced Defense Capabilities. But Syd would have told you that."

"Right, Advanced Defense. Any chance that has something to do with nuclear defense? Or are you folks still working on Star Wars?"

"Like I said, Mr. Riley…"

"Right, I know, you really can't say. And you did your postgrad work in physics?" Randall didn't answer, dropping his gaze to the table. Jake watched him closely. "What makes you so sure that Madison was abducted? Maybe she ran off with this Shane guy she was e-mailing."

Randall pushed a photo across the table, keeping his eyes averted. Jake held it up for a better look. It was a close-up shot of Madison Grant, eyes wide and terrified, printed off a JPG onto regular computer paper. She was lying down against a nondescript gray background.

"When did this come in?" Jake looked up sharply.

"This morning. It was in my work account." Dr. Grant buried his face in his hands and rubbed his cheeks hard. "No one outside the facility has that e-mail address. And I mean no one, any personal exchanges are strictly forbidden."

"But they had it. And that got you even more spooked," Jake said. "I need you to forward this to me." He considered for a moment before continuing, "This isn't proof of life, you know."

"What?" Randall looked puzzled.

"Proof of life. Usually in a kidnapping, they have the victim hold up a newspaper so we know they're still alive, or were on the day the photo was taken."

"So you're saying what, that Madison might already be dead?" The anger in Randall's voice was overlaid by fatigue.

"Not necessarily. But we need to push for that on the next contact. How have they been getting in touch with you?"

"They sent me a phone." He fumbled in his pocket and dug out a generic cell, the disposable kind available in any drugstore.

Jake flipped it and pulled off the back panel: no SIM card, which meant it would be nearly impossible to clone. Someone was being very careful. "Funny they didn't just text you the photo," Jake mused, handing the phone back.

"And I'm guessing hitting the call return button doesn't work."

"The number is blocked. I even had one of the lab guys see if they could trace it, but nothing. Maybe the phone company…"

Jake shrugged. "I'll give it a shot, but chances are they're calling you from the exact same thing, a prepaid cell that gets tossed when the minutes are gone. And if they're really smart, they paid cash for it. Tough to even triangulate those."

Randall slumped lower in his seat. *One more bit of bad news and he'd be on the floor,* Jake thought.

"So you're saying there's nothing you can do," Randall mumbled.

"Nope, not saying that at all. But it sure as hell won't be easy. And not knowing what they're after doesn't help." Randall started to speak, but Jake waved him quiet. "We'll leave that for now. What's our time frame?"

"They said it would be in stages. I'm supposed to go to work, pretend everything is normal, and get them the information."

"How do you get it out of the lab?"

"Flash drive." A pained expression crossed Randall's face. "To get it out undetected, I have to—"

Jake cut him off. "Trust me, that sounds like 'need to know,' and I'm not feeling the need right now. So you're getting them something this week?"

"It might be information, or it could involve rescheduling some…things. They haven't told me yet."

Jake eyed Randall coldly. The guy was scratching at some ketchup that had congealed on the surface of the table. "So tell me, Doc. You're a smart guy. Say you do everything they ask you to. I'm guessing you've got a pretty good idea what the end result would be, right?"

Randall paused, then nodded without lifting his eyes.

"All right. So what are we talking here? How bad could it be?"

Randall waited a long time before responding. His eyes swept the room, taking in all the people with their cardboard cups, laptops and cell phones. He slowly shook his head. "It depends."

"Depends on what?"

"Let's just say they could do a lot of things with what I give them. All of which could result in significant loss of life."

"What, hundreds of people?" When Randall didn't respond, Jake raised his eyebrows and asked, "Thousands?"

"Maybe. That's why you need to find Madison soon. Because I can't allow them to get their hands on what they're looking for. No matter what."

In spite of himself Jake was shaken by the finality in Randall's eyes. If it came down to it, he was willing to sacrifice his daughter. And the only thing standing between him and that outcome was Jake and Syd. Bad odds, any way you looked at it. Jake cleared his throat. "So. Looks like I better get to work, huh?"

Dante Parrish ran a hand over his bald scalp, the stubble reassuring against his palm. No need to be nervous, everything was going better than expected. Still, he always had to gather himself before opening the large mahogany door. Most people would find that surprising: at six-five, two-fifty, Dante wasn't easily intimidated. But Jackson Burke could make him quake.

Dante rapped twice with his huge knuckles, then turned the knob. Inside was the kind of office he used to think only existed in movies: plush carpets, fancy paintings on the walls, sweeping views of downtown Phoenix. An enormous desk dominated the room, mahogany, like the door. Aside from that and two small armchairs, there were no other furnishings. As always, Dante was momentarily awed by the fact that somehow he had ended up here. His reflection was cut short when the man behind the desk slammed down the phone. In spite of himself, Dante jumped.

Jackson's cheeks were flushed, although it was hard to tell whether he was angry or excited. In Dante's opinion, the most remarkable thing about him was that until he opened his mouth, you wouldn't look twice at him. Brown hair, gray eyes, just under six feet tall. Completely average-looking. But then he started talking. Jackson had one of those voices that could "charm a cat off a fish wagon," as Dante's mother used to say. Within ten minutes of meeting him, Dante had been willing to lay down his life for the man.

"So how are things on the front?" Jackson swung around the desk, propping himself on the edge as he motioned for Dante to take a seat.

"All good so far, sir," Dante said, picking his words carefully. He'd never made it past eighth grade, and every time they spoke he felt that disparity keenly. Not that he was stupid, just a different kind of smart. The kind of smart Jackson could use, like he always said.

"Excellent. Saw the news today, looks like our ducks are falling in a row." Jackson raised his hands and mimicked firing a gun, then bellowed a laugh. Dante joined him.

Jackson cut it off abruptly. "Did you see the new census reports?"

Dante shook his head, and Jackson looked mildly disappointed. He tossed a folded paper across the desk and pointed at a headline halfway down the page. "See? Says right there that there haven't been this many illegals since the 1920s. And back then they were mostly white. Ten more years of this, Spanish will be our first language. Not on my watch, no way no how."

Dante nodded in agreement. "We won't let it happen, sir."

"Damn straight we won't. So I want you to personally stay on top of this Grant thing, make sure there are no screwups. I'm counting on you, Dante. Don't let me down, boy."

Dante saluted. Jackson acknowledged it with a nod, then turned to face the view. Dante was halfway to the door when Jackson spoke again. Without glancing back, he said, "Never forget, this is a war we're fighting."

"I won't forget, sir."

Five

Kelly gazed through the glass wall of the observation room. Four MS-13 gang members were arrested in the house raid. Despite the fact they'd been armed to the teeth, SWAT managed to extract them without any bloodshed. Kelly pictured the four of them scattered through the house, three on the couch, one in the kitchen making nachos in a surprisingly domestic gesture. The confusion and disarray as flash bang grenades followed battering rams through both front and back doors. The four of them on the ground, eyes blinded, ears ringing, hands being cuffed. She almost envied the SWAT team. Their goal was simple: get in, get your guys, get out. What she dealt with was much messier.

She examined the putative leader of the gang, Marco Guzman. He was older than she'd expected, maybe late twenties, a testament to his survival skills. Gang tats rode up his neck and down his arms, framing a carefully buttoned blue-and-white shirt. Close-cropped hair and a face marked by a trim goatee and hooded eyes. Clearly Guzman was no stranger to interrogation rooms, he looked right at home.

His lawyer sat beside him. Despite the fact that he looked like a teenager, according to the local cops he'd developed a reputation for himself as the local MS-13 consigliere.

Kelly gathered herself. A successful outcome for this interview was highly unlikely. She was dealing with a seasoned criminal and an adept lawyer. Three hours of grilling by Phoenix P.D., and Guzman had only admitted to knowing there were steak knives in the house. The stacks of guns had apparently escaped his attention. Still, she had to give it a shot.

She entered with Rodriguez at her heels. She wasn't crazy about having him sit in, but he spoke Spanish, which would come in handy.

"Good evening, Mr. Guzman."

"Call me Psycho," he said. His voice was different from what she'd been expecting, smooth with a slight trace of an accent.

Rodriguez rattled something off in Spanish. Guzman leered at him and shot back a response.

"Let's stick to one language, shall we?" Kelly said.

"He was asking what my momma was thinking, naming me that," Guzman said, smiling at her. He had probing eyes, and Kelly leveled her gaze to meet his. "I warned him not to mention my momma again, or—"

The lawyer said something sharp. Guzman clammed up, sucking his teeth loudly.

"It says here your momma named you Marco," Kelly said, one eyebrow raised. "Seems like a perfectly good name."

Guzman shrugged. "So call me that. Don't make no difference to me, *Roja*."

Kelly fought a flush over his reference to her red hair. "I'm FBI Special Agent Jones, this is Agent Rodriguez. We have some questions about one of the items found in your house."

Guzman shrugged. "Not my house, *Agent* Jones."

Without glancing up from his BlackBerry the lawyer said, "As my client informed the police, he was visiting that house today solely to watch a baseball game. He has no knowledge of any weapons being stored there."

"No? Hard to believe, when there were handguns on the table behind him in the living room."

"You know what's psycho, is you showing up," Guzman said. His lawyer threw him a hard glance, but he ignored it. "ATF, sure, but you got no business with guns."

"This one, we do." Kelly slid a photo of Duke Morris's gun across the table.

He glanced at it. "Looks like a *chica*'s. Yours?"

Kelly shook her head. "No, Mr. Guzman. That gun belonged to a murder victim."

He shoved the photo back across the table. "Never seen it."

"You sure? Because it was used to kill a U.S. senator this morning," Rodriguez said.

The lawyer's head snapped up, as if he were a retriever who had just caught a scent.

Kelly tried to conceal her irritation. She had hoped to lull Guzman into complacency, so he might slip up and say more than he should. Now that Rodriguez had revealed their endgame, there was no way he would give them anything. "Got your attention now?" Kelly asked.

"I'd like a minute to confer with my client." The lawyer said with finality.

She tried anyway. "Mr. Guzman, Senator Duke Morris was murdered late last night. Ballistics indicate that his own gun, this gun, was used in the killing. And then it turned up in your stash house."

Guzman just shook his head. His eyes had cloaked

over, dark and impenetrable. Shark eyes. "Don't know what you're on about, *Roja*. I was watching a game."

"MS-13 likes to use machetes, don't they, Marco? That's your calling card. Morris was hacked to bits—"

"This interview is officially over." The young lawyer stood, pushing his chair back so violently it tipped over. The noise was loud in the small room.

Kelly and Rodriguez exchanged a glance. The lawyer couldn't force them to leave, but chances were he'd put a muzzle on his client and they wouldn't get anything regardless. Kelly gathered up the file and motioned for Rodriguez to follow her.

"Well, that was a waste of time," he grunted as the door closed behind them.

Kelly threw him a look. She wouldn't chew Rodriguez out with a suspect in hearing range, but once they were alone he was in for it. She shrugged and said, "I wasn't expecting much."

"Shame they couldn't pull any prints off the weapon."

Kelly didn't answer, her eyes still fixed on the door. The lack of forensic evidence bothered her. She didn't have a lot of experience dealing with gangs, but assumed they weren't generally known for their attention to detail. "Did they track the tip about the stash house?"

Rodriguez cocked his head. "I don't know. Why would they?"

"It would be good to know if it came in from a concerned citizen, a rival gang, or someone else. Maybe even a former member who's currently on the outs. Someone like that could prove helpful."

"Yeah, maybe." Rodriguez looked dubious. "I heard the only way out of MS-13 is a casket. But I could ask around."

"Great." Kelly looked at him pointedly. "The sooner the better, I'm thinking."

"What, now?"

"No time like the present."

"What about this?" He jerked his head toward the interview room.

"I've got this under control," Kelly said. "Like you said, not much here anyway."

"All right," Rodriguez grumbled. "I'll try to track it down."

"Keep me posted." She watched Rodriguez slump away. Kelly had worked with a motley assortment of partners over the years. Based on his bad attitude and lack of initiative, she was consigning Rodriguez firmly to the bottom of the pile.

Of course, when they first worked together it took time for Kelly to trust Jake, so maybe there was hope for Rodriguez yet. Although Jake's weakness was a cavalier attitude coupled with reckless disregard for authority. Rodriguez seemed just plain lazy.

Kelly realized she was fingering her engagement ring. She bit back a smile, picturing Jake on one knee in their hotel room, cobbling together a proposal after she accidentally discovered the ring. She hadn't seen him in a few weeks. He was busy moving into his new office space, and she'd been tied up by a case in Florida. If this lead panned out, they might be able to spend the holiday weekend together. Kelly spun the ring around her finger with her thumb. It still felt oddly heavy, strange that after ten months she hadn't adjusted to the weight of it.

The door to the interview room opened and Kelly quickly tucked her hand in her pocket. The lawyer poked his head out, saw her standing there and ducked back inside. After directing some final instructions in Spanish at Guzman, he stepped out and closed the door.

"So I guess we're done in there," Kelly said.

The lawyer's eyes flicked to her. He was slight, maybe five-six. His suit was well cut but not flashy. Aside from a simple watch with a ragged leather band, he wore no jewelry. Whatever the gang was paying him, he didn't spend it on clothes and accessories. He saw her examining him and grinned. "You like the watch? It was my father's."

He held it out. The battered face was so stained by time it was hard to distinguish the numbers.

"Nice," she said.

He laughed. "You're so polite, Agent Jones. It's a piece of junk. But it helps me remember why he came here, why so many still come every day. Reminds me there's nothing back there for me but junk."

"Oh." Kelly wasn't sure how to respond, the intimacy in his tone made her uncomfortable.

He leaned in and said, "Here's the thing about Guzman. He's no genius, but a gun that killed a senator? Even he isn't stupid enough to leave something like that lying around."

"And yet he did," she pointed out. "Unless you expect me to believe they were just enjoying the big-screen TV."

The lawyer's mouth twisted in a smile. "I have no comment on that, outside of what I've already told you. But the gun you mentioned is something of a special case."

"Really," Kelly said drily.

"Hypothetically, let's say that particular weapon was brought in by someone else."

"Who?"

"Some wannabe named Emilio. They tolerate him as an errand boy, but he's not Salvadoran, so…" The lawyer shrugged, puckering the shoulder fabric of his suit.

"And he gave them Morris's gun? Am I supposed to believe he shot him, too?"

The lawyer shrugged. "Maybe he thought it would get him initiated."

Kelly narrowed her eyes. "Or maybe your client clued in to how serious this is, and he's trying to deflect the blame on someone outside the gang."

"Yeah, but a senator?"

"A senator who was avidly anti-immigration and was raising a lot of fuss in the media about closing the borders. That wouldn't be good for their business, if I'm not mistaken." Kelly knew that the gangs' lifeblood was the stream of guns and drugs from the south. More stringent legislation might have made smuggling trickier.

The lawyer shrugged again. "Hey, I'd be skeptical, too. But I gotta say, I know these guys." He leaned closer, and Kelly smelled onion and something spicy on his breath. "They'll go to the mats if they think another gang is infringing on their territory, but getting political? They're not big CNN fans, you know? I bet half of them couldn't name the president, never mind some senator."

"Maybe they were under orders from someone else. MS-13 is a national organization, right?"

The lawyer shifted his briefcase to the other hand. "I wouldn't know about that," he said carefully. "But if it was, most groups would probably be individual cells. Kind of like al Qaeda. Crediting them with a national mission statement, something on this organizational level…" He flicked his eyes down the hall as a sheriff approached, then back to Kelly. "Let's just say if that's the case, what you're dealing with is something entirely new." He lowered his voice and said, "And I haven't heard anything about it. Trust me, I would have." He flashed a smile and shook her hand. "Adios, Agent Jones. Hopefully next time we meet under cheerier circumstances."

Kelly watched him stroll away before turning back to

the interrogation room. Through the small window she watched Guzman carve his name on the underside of the table with a ballpoint pen. The lawyer was right; "Psycho" didn't appear to be a criminal mastermind. Which didn't eliminate the possibility that someone else was pulling the strings.

She headed back to the squad room. On the way Kelly wondered who might have gotten an MS-13 "cell" involved in a killing like this, and what they hoped to accomplish. If anything, this worked against their goals. In the wake of Morris's death, anti-immigration groups were organizing rallies and right-wing talk show hosts were treating it like Christmas and the Rapture all tied up in one. If someone had done this to shut Duke Morris up, they'd made a terrible error. Dead, his voice was carrying louder than ever.

JUNE 29

FOUND 29

Six

Randall Grant hunched over the steering wheel, drawing deep breaths to steady himself. These past few days had been hell, starting with the frantic, incoherent phone call from Audrey, drunk as usual. He could hear Bree yelling in the background and assumed it was one of their usual fights, that he was being called in to arbitrate. But when he'd finally puzzled out what she meant, her broken voice wailing, "She's gone!" over and over, a cold ball settled in his stomach. They'd carried through on their threat, snatching the most vulnerable member of his family.

The impotence was the worst part. After hanging up he'd stormed around the apartment in a rage, fantasizing about bursting into rooms and mowing down the people who took his little girl. By midnight he'd come to his senses and sat down to weigh his options. His division answered directly to the Department of Homeland Security, one call to them and the full resources of the U.S. government would have been mustered. The problem was, in that scenario he'd be placed on full lockdown. Every conversation would be monitored, and no movement would go unnoticed. In the grand scheme of things, it was in the DHS's best interest to protect what he knew. The loss of a teenage girl would be tragic, but not their first priority. He'd be hauled off to a safe location while Madison had a gun to her head. With Syd, at least they had a shot at recovering her, before…

Randall stopped himself from picturing her broken and dead and God knows what else. And it would be his fault, her blood on his hands forever. He could still see Madison's stricken expression when he explained that she'd be relocating to New York, and he'd see her when he could. Which hadn't been as frequently as he'd hoped, not after the promotion. It had been over a month since his last visit, and that one had been disastrous. For a long, awkward weekend they all barely spoke. He'd chosen activities that were far too young for them, he realized belatedly, trips to the Museum of Natural History and the *USS Intrepid*. He'd lost touch with what teenage girls enjoyed. On Sunday night he'd secretly been relieved to drop them off. Randall cringed at the memory.

He was such an idiot. He should have stuck it out, just a few more years and both girls would have been in college. Then he and Audrey could have gone their separate ways without all this drama. But it was far too late for that.

Randall squared his shoulders and climbed out of the car carrying the travel mug. All his work materials were on-site. After a spying debacle a few years ago, the facility had increased security measures exponentially. Now anyone with access to highly classified material was forced to work in two-man teams. Not only were they supposed to keep an eye on each other's computers and filing systems, they were actually expected to take a piss together. Fortunately the scientist he was paired with had a prostate problem. After a few awkward weeks at the urinals, Barry asked if Randall would mind ignoring that particular rule. Which made acquiring the first part of what the kidnappers wanted much easier than it should have been. It was probably why they targeted him in the first place.

The lab complex was sprawled across acres, dozens of nondescript buildings painted a muted brown that melded into the barren landscape. It was a desolate section of the East Bay. The town proper had sprung up to service the facility, rows of coffee shops and cafés that closed at night-fall, leaving only a few neon-lit bars blinking desolately in the darkness. Randall had accepted a job here straight out of MIT, back when he and Audrey were newlyweds. The salary had been far above what any university was offering, the work promised to be groundbreaking with nearly limit-less funding, and they could afford a house nearby. At the time it had been a no-brainer. Looking back, he wished to God he'd accepted that position at Berkeley, where at worst he'd be responsible for the lives of a few lab rats.

At the entrance to the facility Randall nodded to the guard and held his ID card up to the scanner. After a brief pause it buzzed, and he strode down a long fluorescent hallway. The security became progressively tighter—to get into the inner sanctum, as people jokingly referred to it, he'd have to pass palm and retinal scans. Rumor had it that one of the other departments was working on a blood analysis machine. Randall hoped he wouldn't still be here when going to work involved a daily needle prick.

Once in his office he relaxed. Barry wasn't there, but an identical travel mug on his desk issued steam. Which meant he was already taking bathroom break number one, of dozens to come. *A guy with prostate problems should cut out the caffeine,* Randall thought as he waited for his computer to boot up.

A stream of numbers flew on-screen, coordinates pin-pointing the location of loose nuclear fissile material worldwide. He and Barry had spent months cataloging this data as the U.S. government belatedly dealt with the fallout from the collapse of the Soviet Union, as well as the mass amounts of radioactive waste produced by everything from medical equipment to offshore drilling. It was staggering that no one had recognized this potential threat until 9/11 jarred everyone's consciousness. And now Randall was part of a team that tracked radioactive waste, ensuring that it ended up at the appropriate facility, either to be safely disposed of or reutilized. Which in reality made him a glorified administrator with a Ph.D. in radiation physics.

Randall shook his head, unscrewed the base of the coffee mug, and removed the flash drive. He hit a few buttons to call up the data.

Initially there had been a fuss over the mugs, too. A memo had gone out insisting that everyone consume company coffee from the canteen. Based on the outcry that followed, they might as well have suggested drinking tainted Kool-Aid. Getting between scientists and their espresso was a fatal error, and in the end the brass made a concession: as long as everyone brought in standardized, company-issued mugs, outside coffee was fine. Mugs that apparently had been all too easy for someone to manipulate.

Randall glanced over his shoulder before popping the flash drive in the port. The download would only take a minute, but he was antsy. There had been a close call yesterday, and he got the feeling Barry knew something was up. He'd been struggling to act normal, but it was just that, a struggle. He'd blamed it on lack of sleep due to residual stress from the divorce. A lifelong bachelor like Barry didn't question that.

An icon popped up. Randall quickly slipped the flash drive out, inserting it into the mug's base just as the door clicked open.

Barry squinted myopically at him. "Everything okay?" he asked hesitantly. His stringy hair was wet where he'd combed it over his bald spot, and his sweater had a mustard stain near the collar.

"Fine, Barry. Just didn't sleep well again."

"Oh. Sorry to hear it." Barry shuffled to the desk beside his. In a space that small it was like being crammed in a cockpit together. "Did you see they moved up the date of the Texas shipment?"

Randall's ears pricked up. "I didn't have time to look at it yet. Any idea why?"

Barry shrugged. "Dunno. Maybe there's another storm coming."

"Hurricanes are usually in the late summer and fall, Barry. It's June."

"Right, right," Barry mumbled, staring at his monitor.

Randall had to fight the urge to throttle him: an IQ of 165, and he was useless unless you were discussing primordial radionuclides. Sometimes Randall suspected they were both being punished for some transgression. Initially, he'd taken this assignment as a break from researching, to give himself time to recover from the divorce. They'd given him a big speech, too, about serving his country, blah, blah, blah…

Thankfully they had almost finished laying the groundwork, and once that was accomplished the day-to-day monitoring would be handled by computers. Of course, there was a good chance he'd be under arrest for high treason by then.

Randall tapped some keys and a map of the United States appeared, with different-colored dots identifying which materials were being stored where. He zeroed in on the spots off the Gulf Coast, offshore drilling rigs that used radiography cameras to analyze lengths of pipe. As newer cameras came online, older ones were retired, along with their low level radioactive source material. As he watched them blink, the ball in his stomach sunk an inch lower. This was just what the kidnappers were looking for, the right materials in the correct amount. And they were due to be transported imminently. Suddenly their timing made sense; they had known, somehow, that this shipment was coming. It was too much of a coincidence otherwise, and as a scientist he eschewed belief in chance.

Randall chewed his lip. Part of his job involved overseeing the transit of loose materials from one facility to another. He was in charge of constructing a safe route skirting all densely populated areas and providing the most defensible means of transportation. The kidnappers wanted him to change that route at the last minute to divert iridium-192 sources. Randall gritted his teeth as the dots flickered at him. He'd have to pray that Madison was found before the shipment was set in motion.

Madison struggled with the back of the console, prying it open as carefully as possible. She'd managed to work loose a metal coil from her cot, fashioning it into a makeshift screwdriver. But the tiny screws were proving tricky to undo, and she was panicked by the possibility of stripping one. For this to work, she needed the console more or less intact.

After repeated sessions of begging, she had finally convinced Lurch (as she'd christened the driver) to dig through her luggage for a fleece jacket, her face medication, and her Nintendo DS Lite. Madison now understood why prisoners went nuts in isolation. She almost looked forward to when Lurch cracked the door and slid in a tray of food, or came to empty her bucket. If she wasn't mistaken he was lingering, too, and by her calculation there had been two straight days without a shot. When he opened the door she jabbered at him, a steady stream of information about her life, her old friends, her parents, anything to get him to stay an extra minute. Despite the fact he still hadn't spoken to her, Madison was pretty sure he understood English. Maybe she was flattering herself, but if he was forced to kill her, now at least he might feel badly about it.

But Madison wasn't counting on his generosity continuing. A few times she'd heard a low murmur outside the door, Lurch talking to at least one other person. He definitely wasn't the brains behind this operation. And if whoever was in charge found out about the DS Lite, chances were it would be snatched back and the needle would return.

The final screw popped loose and rolled away. She scrambled after it, trapping it with her palm. There was a bang on the other side of the door, then the bolt scraped. Lurch jutted his head in, a frown marring his features.

Madison held the console in both palms, leaning back against the end of the cot. She cocked an eyebrow at him. "What? Did you miss me?"

He scanned the room, paying particular attention to the floor. After a minute, he grunted and closed the door. As the bolt slid back into place, Madison released a sigh. The screws were digging into her palms, and she tucked them in her jeans pocket. If she'd known she was going to be in the same clothes for days on end, she would've worn a sweatsuit on the plane. These were her nicest pair of jeans, but nice didn't exactly equal comfort. She waited several beats, straining her ears. She knew Lurch was probably rethinking the decision to give her the console, and she needed to move quickly on the off chance he would take it back.

Unlike her father and Bree, she hadn't gotten the physics gene. Every time she tried to wrap her head around certain theories, it felt like she was being sucked into a black hole. However, from a relatively early age it had been clear that she had exceptional mechanical skills. At six she'd been able to fix most of her friends' electronic toys when they stopped working, and every year she'd been the runaway winner of the state science fair.

Madison and her father had even built a robot once. She'd been the youngest participant ever in Robot Wars, a series of steel cage matches between remote-controlled robots that ended when there was only one left in the ring. The two of them drove to San Francisco for the competition. They'd named their entry "Maxwell's Law" (her father's idea). They had to settle for second place after their robot's rotary saw fell off in the final round. But her father had been so proud, he told everyone that his daughter had built the machine herself out of scrap metal, he'd hardly been involved.

Madison was startled to find a tear slipping down her cheek. She wiped it away, agitated, and focused on the task at hand. She'd almost left the console at home, not wanting Shane to know that she was secretly hooked on "The Legend of Zelda." Thank God she'd decided there was only so much a person could sacrifice for true love. She wondered if Lurch had been the one e-mailing her, pretending to be Shane. At the thought she started cracking up, and bit her lip to stifle the giggles. She didn't want him poking his nose back in, not now.

Handheld consoles had come a long way from when

she got her first Game Boy. Thankfully, Lurch didn't appear to know that. This particular model had been a birthday gift from her dad, a next generation prototype that wouldn't even be on the market for another year. Like all the newer systems, it had Wi-Fi capabilities for multiplayer online games. Of course, an accessible wireless network had been too much to hope for. She'd done a search immediately, but the only one in radius was secured and she was no hacker. She'd made a halfhearted stab at passwords to amuse herself, typing in *Addams Family, Lurch,* and, with a pang, *Shane's girl.* No luck, she'd need the proverbial million monkeys tapping away for years to crack it. And she didn't have that kind of time.

Fortunately, there was one more feature of the unit that Lurch had overlooked: a GPS transmitter. It was an add-on that worked by comparing the signals received from several satellites, then running a complex set of computations to triangulate the results and produce a set of coordinates. Unfortunately, the thick metal hull of the ship prevented access to most satellite signals. Luckily Madison had spent the past few months studying an alternative.

In 2006, when GPS devices started glutting the commercial market, the U.S. government became concerned that military receivers might be lost in the barrage of white noise. The military relied upon a GPS system for navigation and targeting, and any compromise of that system could prove catastrophic. To protect themselves they launched new satellites, with "boosted" signals that were only available to the Department of Defense. Madison's last science fair project had been disqualified, thanks to her claims to have tapped into the new satellite systems. At a conference with the school principal, her father had explained that scientifically speaking there was no way she could have done it, and her mother had grounded her for a month. The principal still gave her funny looks whenever she passed him in the hall. They all thought she was trying to get attention, still reacting to the divorce.

Well, yeah, maybe she had been. But that didn't mean she hadn't done it. After conducting experiments with her iPhone all over the city, Madison discovered a rogue signal. Honestly it hadn't been all that hard, just time-consuming. And once she had that signature down, all she had to do was find it again.

If she could tap into it and recalibrate her DS Lite's GPS to send a signal rather than receive it, maybe someone would be able to track her down. She just hoped one of her moron family members remembered the console.

Her tongue jutted out the side of her mouth as she concentrated, squinting in the dim light, carefully manipulating the interior components. Madison was careful to touch the plastic exterior each time to ground it. She'd have to reconfigure the power settings, too—it would be a race against battery life at the end. She just hoped someone out there would be listening.

Seven

Jake forced himself to tear off a bite of turkey sandwich. He was trying to eat healthier these days, a losing battle for a guy reared on steak and lots of it. All those months of setting up the new business had kept him out of the gym, and he recently realized with alarm that his six-pack was morphing into a two-pack. Kelly had teased him, grabbing his middle and riffing about the slow march of time and declining metabolisms. Well, screw that. Jake Riley wasn't giving in without a fight. Even if that meant switching to light beer and turkey.

He was in one of the ubiquitous sandwich factories lining the Berkeley campus, trying to get his mouth around a sandwich so stuffed with sprouts they should have named it the "Colon-Cleanser." The place buzzed with students grabbing a bite between classes. Their tie-dyed shirts and Birkenstocks reminded him of when he first met Kelly, during an ugly case at a university. At least in the end something good had come out of it.

As he took in the fresh faces he experienced a pang: Madison Grant wasn't much younger than these kids, another two years and she might have been among this crowd. He hoped to God she'd still get the chance, but based on the day he'd had so far, things were looking bleak.

The pressure was compounded by the fact that if Randall was telling the truth, more than just Madison's life hung in the balance. Jake preferred to think he was just blowing smoke up their asses, trying to make sure they did everything possible to find his daughter. But a small voice in the back of his head argued that Randall was scared enough to risk his job and reputation by trusting them rather than Homeland Security. The lab he was working in had produced most of the major advances in military hardware in the past century, along with bio-chemical weapons that could wipe out civilization as we know it. And whoever had stolen Madison Grant was a pro: not only were they good at covering their tracks, there were almost none to speak of.

Syd and what he referred to as her "shadow network" had diligently run down every lead, no matter how tenuous. There was a moment of excitement when the license plate trace turned up a limo company based in South San Francisco. But that died down fifteen minutes later, when Syd got a faxed copy of the stolen car report. And ten minutes after that they learned that the final destination of the Lincoln Town Car had been a chop shop in Oakland. It was currently being returned to the limo company owner in pieces.

Jake had immediately headed over to the chop shop, driving through a section of Oakland that closely resembled war-torn Beirut. A few guys were hard at work on an Escalade. It took a few hundred to convince them he wasn't a cop, and a few hundred more to find out where they got the car. If they were telling the truth, when they showed up at work three nights ago it was sitting in front of their garage, keys in the ignition, like a gift from the gods. And they knew better than to question it.

Syd had considered calling in a favor, trying to get the remaining parts dusted for prints, but Jake convinced her otherwise. They'd probably end up with the oily imprints of a few grand theft auto felons. Whoever possessed the car before them was too careful to be that sloppy, it had probably been detailed inside and out before materializing in Oakland. Syd was running a background check on everyone at the limo company in case it was an inside job, but so far they'd turned up clean. So he was sitting here choking down a sandwich while he waited for Syd to call.

Jake rubbed his face. They had two leads left to follow: the shadowy image of the driver's face, and the mythical Shane's e-mail account. At the moment he wasn't holding out much hope for either. Facial recognition software was notoriously unreliable even when you had a good image to work with, and good didn't describe what they had. As for the e-mail address, computers weren't his thing, but he knew that any hacker worth his salt could bounce messages through dozens of servers worldwide, rendering them untraceable.

Jake's phone buzzed and he tossed the sandwich back on its biodegradable plate, strewing a comet trail of sprouts. "Hey, Syd. What have you got?"

There was a pause before she replied, "Not much, I'm afraid. All the texts trace back to a disposable phone. I managed to track down its batch number. It was sold to a Walgreens distributor in the Bay Area, but from there it could have gone to a dozen different stores. And whoever purchased it probably paid cash."

"So the number kept switching?" Jake asked. "Why wouldn't that make Madison suspicious?"

He could almost see her shrugging. "Don't know.

She's a bright girl—according to Randall she's some sort of mechanical genius—but he must have given her a rational explanation."

"What about the e-mails?"

"Same deal. Bounced all over the damned place, last location we got was somewhere on the Caspian coast."

"Which country?"

"Turkmenistan."

Jake's brow furrowed. Could this be the link? Maybe some foreign power stole the kid to force Randall to share intel. It would certainly explain the level of organization, and the deep pockets. Syd's voice interrupted his train of thought. "What're you thinking?"

"You worked that part of the world, right?"

There was a lengthy pause. Officially they'd decided not to discuss past cases unless absolutely necessary. As far as Jake was concerned, this was the exception to that rule. Apparently Syd agreed, because after a moment she said, "I was stationed in Tbilisi for a few months."

"That's a little off the grid, isn't it?"

"Way off the grid. Officially we were afraid that some of the decommissioned nuclear arms weren't being appropriately monitored and might fall into the hands of rogue nations. Unofficially, I was being punished for not sleeping with my boss when he asked me to."

Jake decided to ignore that last part. "What do you think? Any chance we're dealing with a group that's trying to get hold of some nukes?"

Syd went so long without saying anything, Jake was concerned he'd lost the connection. "Hello?"

"I'm still here. I'm just thinking."

"Ah, Christ. You know something," Jake said. "What the hell, Syd—"

"Nothing specific, I just…I've got some idea what

Randall has been working on these past few months. And it might tie in with that."

An image of the driver's face flashed through Jake's mind. Big white guy, could definitely be Slavic. "Great. I agreed to take this case, against my better instincts, as a favor to you. And you keep me in the dark. That's it." He resolutely pushed his chair back from the table and stood. "Call Randall, tell him I'm getting on a plane. You want to help him, come out here yourself."

"Jake, wait—"

"Nope. I'm done, Syd."

"All right."

Jake paused at the door to the sandwich shop, rental car keys in hand. It wasn't like Syd to give in so easily. "Bullshit."

"What?"

"I don't believe for a minute you're letting me off the hook."

"No, you're right. I promised that the minute it smelled bad, you could back down. Besides, if this Turkmenistan thing is the real deal, I can follow up just as well from here. The Bay Area part of this operation seems dead in the water anyway. Just because she got off a plane there doesn't mean anything, she could be on a container ship halfway to China by now."

Jake had thought the same thing, but there was something about her tone he didn't trust. Besides, if they'd wanted Madison on a container ship, it would have been just as easy to yank her from the East Coast. Even easier, maybe. The truth was that despite his posturing, he wasn't ready to ditch Madison Grant yet. He walked to the car, as if physically calling Syd's bluff. "Okay. So I'll head to the airport."

"Perfect. Oh, one thing…"

Jake grinned. He knew it wouldn't be that easy. "Yeah?"

"Randall's getting nervous, he's starting to think she might already be dead."

"Yeah, well. He has a point."

"Right, I know. I was just wondering if you could stop by his place and talk him down from the ledge. Give him some tips on what to say next time, how to ask for proof of life. That sort of thing."

Jake repressed a snort at the thought of Randall Grant attempting to negotiate proof of life on his own. "You're a piece of work, you know that, Syd?"

"What?" she asked innocently.

"I'll hang around to make sure Randall doesn't screw this up. But if I get the sense that either of you is jerking me around again, that's it."

"Yeah, yeah," Syd said smugly. "You're out of there, I know."

"Next time I'll mean it."

"Sure you will. Oh, and Jake? Give Randall a big kiss for me."

"Go to hell. And keep running that facial recognition software. All that bragging about your tentacles extending everywhere, and so far you've given me a crappy chop house."

"Hey," Syd said, wounded. "That was a good lead. I had to pay off a slew of people for that one."

"A name, Syd. We need something to go on."

"Gotcha. The shadow network is on it."

Jake hung up. Shadows was right. He felt like that was all he'd done so far, chase Madison's shadow. He glanced back at the sandwich shop and considered grabbing another turkey club for the road, then decided against it. He'd seen an In-N-Out near Randall's house, and if anything could help clarify his thought process, it was a one hundred percent all-beef American burger. Sprouts weren't going to cut it on a case like this. Better save the diet for later, he decided.

Kelly skidded to a halt, breathing hard. On the other side of a six-foot-high fence a dog barked frantically. She jumped up and caught a glimpse of a Doberman chained to a pole, lunging at flannel and ragged jean shorts. She skirted the edge of the house, yelling into her radio, "Rodriguez! He's back on Van Buren Street!"

Her breath was loud as she ran. Turning the corner, she caught a glimpse of Emilio Torres tearing across the street, stopping a cab short. Jesus, he was fast. No more than twelve or thirteen by her estimate, and small for his age. It didn't help that he knew this neighborhood like the back of his hand. He could probably dodge them for days in here.

Kelly tore after him. After a morning of paperwork she'd decided to investigate "Psycho's" claim that a hanger-on gave them the gun. The lawyer had provided Emilio Torres's name and address. She didn't expect the lead to pan out, but eliminating it would strengthen the prosecution's case against the gang at trial. So after lunch she and Rodriguez knocked on Torres's door, only to have the kid bolt at the sight of them. If Kelly knew she'd be dealing with a runner, she wouldn't have ordered the grande burrito.

They'd been chasing Emilio for over ten minutes, from the back of his grandmother's house down countless streets and alleys. Every time they thought they'd lost him, he'd pop up again. On the plus side, he didn't appear smart enough to go to ground and stay there.

He bowled over a guy walking his pit bull and sent a Chinese food delivery man flying in a tangle of spokes and handlebars. Kelly almost sprawled on top of them. She vaulted over with a gasped apology and continued running.

Emilio glanced over his shoulder and saw her gaining. She caught a look of panic in his eyes. Kelly was ten feet behind him now, the beginnings of a cramp in her calf muscle. Sweat poured down her back, it had to be over a hundred degrees and she was getting dizzy. Emilio's blue-checked flannel shirt trailed behind him as he sharply changed direction, turning right. She was hard on his heels, halfway up the block when a dark form hurtled out of the alley. It slammed into the kid hard. Both figures flew into the street. The screech of brakes pierced the air as an old Buick jerked to a halt. Kelly edged around it, slowing her pace, ignoring the tirade spilling out of the driver's open windows. Rodriguez and Emilio lay in a tangle on the ground.

"Jesus, Rodriguez," she said, grabbing the kid's hands. He'd risen to his knees, prepared to bolt again. With one smooth gesture she knocked him flat and cuffed him. "You both could've been killed."

"Little son of a bitch would've deserved it," Rodriguez said, standing slowly and brushing himself off. The knees of his trousers were torn, and he raised his hands in supplication. "Christ, look what he did to my pants!"

"I didn't do nothing, fool," Emilio spat as Kelly yanked him to his feet. He was tiny, just over five feet, wearing baggy jean shorts, an enormous flannel shirt over a white undershirt and a blue-and-white Colts hat cocked to the side.

"Shut up, you little punk," Rodriguez grunted.

"Agent Rodriguez," Kelly said warningly. "Save it."

"I got nothing to say to you," Emilio sulked.

Kelly looked him over: too young to even be shaving. She repressed a sigh. "Your grandma seems like a nice lady, let's have her join us. We need an adult present to question you anyway."

"I ain't answering no questions, bitch. I don't disrespect the colors." He jerked a thumb at his baseball cap.

Rodriguez rattled off something in Spanish, and Emilio responded with a tirade, struggling against the cuffs to get in Rodriguez's face. Kelly pulled him back.

"Stop it, both of you," she said sharply. "Not another word until we get him back to the house." She cast a warning glance at Rodriguez. Anything said by a minor without a legal guardian present would be inadmissible. And she was hoping the grandmother might prove helpful. The woman had been shocked to find them on her doorstep, and judging by the way she called for Emilio, she didn't tolerate back talk. With any luck her presence would cut down on his posturing.

In silence they proceeded down the street. The guy with the pit bull had righted himself, and as they passed by he muttered something. Emilio paled noticeably and jerked sideways as the pit bull growled. Kelly pursed her lips and wished for the hundredth time that she'd opted for Spanish instead of French in high school.

Dante fidgeted. His crew had been stuck in the warehouse for three days, and they were becoming increasingly restless. All twelve sat around a table playing endless games of five-card stud. They were almost indistinguishable, a solid mass of shaved heads and prison tats, clad in identical uniforms of black T-shirts and jeans.

Composed of three four-man teams, each was only privy to part of the plan. He was the only one holding all the proverbial cards. They knew enough, though, to potentially make it rain down cops and Feds. For that reason Jackson wanted them kept in complete isolation, to prevent a screwup on the magnitude of the KKK one in 1997. Back then a small group of Klansmen almost succeeded in torching a natural gas processing plant in north Texas. It would have been spectacular if they'd succeeded, could've taken out thousands and brought a lot of attention to the cause. But one of the morons got cold feet, and in swept the FBI. Jackson was too smart to allow something like that to happen.

One of the crew suddenly launched to his feet, scattering chips as he exploded in a stream of expletives. The guy he was yelling at stroked a knife clipped to his belt but remained seated. Dante frowned, debating whether or not to intervene. The other men tilted back in their chairs, watching with interest. One of them, Jimmy, glanced at Dante and raised an eyebrow.

When the first guy kicked back his chair, sending it skittering across the cement floor, Dante stood. They both caught the motion out of the corner of their eyes and paused. He approached the table slowly. These were hardened guys, between them they'd clocked decades in some of the country's toughest penitentiaries. But there was a clear pecking order in the Brotherhood, as respected as any military rank, and in this room he was king.

"Cut the shit," Dante said, voice low.

He eyed them, waiting. The second guy shrugged and muttered an apology that sounded more like a challenge. The troublemaker took longer to back down. Thanks to his enormous blond handlebar moustache he was nicknamed "Hulk," after the wrestler. A full minute passed before Hulk turned, retrieved the chair, and straddled it.

"It's been a long week," Dante said when they'd settled down. Murmurs of assent. One of the other guys had gathered up the cards and was shuffling them. "I'm thinking it's time to blow off a little steam."

"Thought you said we couldn't go anywhere," said Hulk.

"We can't." Dante held up a hand to stem the tide of groans. "But I got a few girls cleared by management. One phone call and they show up to party."

"No shit?" Hulk stroked his moustache. "How old? 'Cause I like 'em young."

No surprise there, Dante thought. "Young enough. You know the rules, though."

"No worries boss. I don't need her mouth for talking," someone chimed in, and everyone laughed.

Dante made the call. The girls were fresh meat, caught coming over the border by the local militia. They were supposed to report all illegals to Border Patrol without engaging. But this unit contained some of Jackson's most avid supporters, and they were happy to provide whatever was needed, whether that meant gathering up a few women or ignoring a duffel bag tossed over the wall. Dante wasn't really worried about the men talking—the language barrier would prevent that, and besides, the girls were headed to a pit in the desert afterward. They'd keep the boys occupied for a few days. And by then they should have their marching orders.

The thought reenergized him. It had taken years to set this thing in motion. Hard to believe that by this time next week, they'd be guiding the nation back on its true path.

Dante headed to the opposite end of the warehouse and ran a hand along the side of a truck. Two others just like it lined the back of the room, waiting to be called into commission. He allowed himself a small smile as a whoop from the card table signaled the arrival of the girls.

Eight

"It's not like that." Randall sighed. "I send a text when I've got something for them, and they respond with instructions on where to drop it off."

"So you've never spoken to an actual human?" Jake pressed. He'd persuaded Randall to leave work a few hours early so they could talk. Randall's apartment screamed bachelor pad. It was a small, cluttered one-bedroom. The walls were bare, and aside from the futon couch and a tiny TV on a rickety table, there was little in the way of decor. Clearly Randall didn't subscribe to any Martha Stewart publications.

"Once, when they first contacted me. I thought it was a joke at first." He paused, examining his hands. "It never occurred to me that my family might actually be in danger."

Jake thought that for a smart guy, at times Randall was staggeringly clueless. Maybe a bus driver could be nonchalant in the face of such threats, but it should've given a guy working at a top secret government lab pause. Still he nodded sympathetically. "Sure. What did he look like?"

"He was a big guy, white, bald. Wore a hat and sunglasses, so it's kind of hard to say. Lots of tattoos."

"Interesting." Eastern European gangsters mapped their entire criminal life on their bodies with tattoos. "Any accent?"

"He wasn't foreign, if that's what you're asking. Southern, I think, but I'm not sure which state."

"Okay." Jake paused to think. Maybe a foreign operative trained to mimic American accents. Or a mercenary who lived stateside. "You sent your ex and daughter off to stay with a relative, like we discussed?"

"Yes, they went yesterday."

"And didn't tell anyone where they were going, right?"

Randall nodded.

"So back to the million dollar question. Any idea who took Madison?"

"I told you—"

"Because now we think it might be someone from one of the former Soviet bloc countries." Jake watched him closely, but nothing seemed to register. "Turkmenistan, maybe."

"Turkmenistan? But that doesn't make any sense." Randall's brows furrowed.

"Look, Randall. I don't know much about your work, but I'm guessing it has something to do with nuclear materials." When Randall didn't respond, Jake had to fight the urge to throttle him. "Without getting too specific, you should at least be able to tell me that much. Otherwise how the hell am I supposed to figure out who took Madison?"

A shadow crossed Randall's features. Reluctantly, he nodded.

"So maybe an extremist group in Turkmenistan is trying to get hold of some for an attack against the United States," Jake concluded.

"I don't know," Randall said slowly. "There's more loose material over there, and it's less tightly monitored. Plus most of those groups want to target Russia proper."

"So a Muslim sect in one of those countries. Maybe one with links to al Qaeda."

"Possibly." Randall turned the thought over in his mind. "The thing is, port control here is one of the things we're doing right. Every single shipping container in and out of the U.S. undergoes a radiation scan. They'd need help from someone working Customs, not me."

Jake shrugged. "Maybe they've got that, too. Sure you can't tell me exactly what they're after?"

Randall considered carefully before speaking. "I think you're on the right track. Not necessarily with the Eastern European connection, but the other thing…yes."

"All right then, we're making progress." Jake clapped him on the shoulder. Randall smiled weakly in response. Jake pressed a little harder with his fingers and locked eyes with him. "And you have no other theories?"

Randall shrugged off his hand. "Nothing. Like I said, it could be anyone. I think they contacted me because I have access to what they need."

"How many others have the same access?" Randall's eyes shifted away again. "C'mon, Randall, I spent some time working for the government, I know what is and isn't a state secret. How many?"

"It's just so hard to trust anyone anymore," Randall mumbled. He examined his fingers. "Four people total. It's a small project."

"And what do you know about the other three?"

"Why?"

"Because whoever took Madison obviously knows about your access, and if you're right, only a handful of people in the facility are privy to that information. Going on that assumption, they selected you as the most likely to cave—nothing personal," he said, raising a hand to stifle Randall's protest, "but it's true. So we need to figure out why they targeted you in particular. Do the other guys not have families, or gambling debts, anything that could be used against them?"

Randall scratched at a spot on the couch. "I don't know. It's not a very social environment."

"Well, consider that your assignment. I want everything you can find out about the other guys in your department. Also, get me a list of everyone who has any idea what your work entails. If you're right, someone at the facility pointed them in your direction. We find that person, the trail could lead back to Madison."

"All right."

A hint of hope in his voice, for the first time in days. Jake hoped it wasn't misplaced. "When will you have what they're looking for?"

Randall shifted uncomfortably in his seat. "Soon. I already have most of what they'll need."

"And what are you supposed to do next?"

"Text them this code and wait for a response. I was about to do it when Syd called and said you'd be stopping by."

"What's the code?"

"I'm supposed to say everything is great." Randall's jaw tightened as he said, "Using the number eight. I suppose that's their little joke."

"Joke in what way?"

"In making me send something a teenager might write."

"It's smart, actually." Jake mulled it over, then said, "Okay, here's what we're going to do. Write, *Everything is ok*. They'll be forced to respond, and you demand to talk to someone."

"I'm not so sure—"

"You have to trust me, Randall. Remember, right now they need you. Unless they're idiots, they're not going to hurt your daughter until they get the information. And we're going to use that to buy ourselves some time."

"How?"

"There's this ancient Malaysian board game, men versus tigers. The men win if they can surround the tigers and block their movements. Right now, that's our game plan."

"Yeah?" Randall eyed him skeptically. "How do the tigers win?"

Jake pulled off his jacket. "Too many questions, Doc. Just pay attention while I go over everything."

Kelly winced as Emilio sustained another cuff to the head. He sullenly sank deeper into the chair as the middle-aged woman beside him let loose with another tirade. Kelly had no idea what was being said, but the tone was clear enough. Even Rodriguez looked mildly uncomfortable.

When they arrived at the door with Emilio in tow, still trying to jerk out of their grasp like a fish on a line, his grandmother grabbed him by the ear, dragged him to the couch, and launched into an impressive verbal assault. It was rare for someone under five feet tall to be intimidating, but Celia Torres was the exception to the rule. It took a few minutes to get a word in edgewise. When Kelly asked her to come down to the station, Celia's brow darkened with fury. She cast a menacing look at Emilio, snatched an enormous purse off the counter, and marched out to their bu-car. In the backseat en route to the station, Emilio had opened his mouth twice to speak. Each time he was silenced with a sharp look from Celia. Kelly was concerned that upon arrival they might discover that Celia had summoned a lawyer for her grandson.

But then they got into the interrogation room. Apparently Celia had more than a rudimentary understanding of how to play bad cop, along with a strong flair for theater, neither of which she was afraid to use. Whenever Emilio had the audacity to say something in his defense, she went so completely ballistic they almost had to call in assistance. And the minute Rodriguez mentioned a gang connection, Celia spent ten minutes threatening to do things to Emilio that apparently didn't bear translating.

After an hour of this, Emilio was a far cry from the posturing punk they'd chased down. His chin quivered, eyes filled with tears. Celia had switched tactics and was mumbling to him in Spanish. Rodriguez occasionally leaned over to translate. "She's saying he broke her heart," he mumbled. "Man, she's good."

Kelly had to agree, it was an Oscar-worthy performance. Clearly someone watched a few too many *telenovelas*. But it was having the desired effect on Emilio.

Celia finally sat back and said thickly, "He ready to answer your questions."

"Great." Kelly sighed, feeling like she'd been through the wringer herself. "So, Emilio. Where were you yesterday morning?"

"In school."

"School says you never showed. We called and checked."

A small growl from Celia. Emilio avoided her eyes. "Yeah, okay. I didn't go."

"Where were you?"

"*Sí*, Emilio. What was so important you miss school, break a promise to your *abuelita?*" Celia hissed.

"Nothing." Emilio shrugged. "I just…I didn't feel like going, yo."

Kelly held up a hand to stave off Celia's response. "Here's the thing, Emilio. There was a raid on an MS-13 house in your neighborhood yesterday. I'm guessing you heard about it?" He shrugged noncommittally. "One of the guns we found was used in a serious crime. And they're claiming that gun came from you."

Emilio paled visibly, and Celia sucked in her breath. "Guns! No no no, not my Emilito." She cuffed him across the head. "See the trouble? This why I tell you, stay away. But no, you want to wear everything *blanco* and *azul*." She shifted her attention back to Kelly. "These boys, the gang? Filthy Salvadorans. I always tell my Emilio to stay away."

"Well, Emilio didn't listen. We found his fingerprints inside the house. And on the weapon." Rodriguez threw a closed file on the table. It would be hours before forensic results came in, but they didn't have to know that.

"Where'd you get the gun, Emilio?" Kelly pressed.

"Stole it, bitch," he spat, recovering some of his bravado. Celia inhaled sharply, brought back her palm and slapped his face.

"Mrs. Torres! You need to control yourself. If you strike Emilio again I'll have to call in child services," Kelly said sharply. She really didn't want to do that, since with a caseworker sitting in they'd get far less compliance.

Celia nodded tersely.

Rodriguez leaned across the table. "Stole it from where?"

Emilio shrugged. Kelly caught a flash behind his eyes. Shame? Embarrassment? She leaned in. "See, Emilio, here's my problem. I've got a group of gang members who are going down anyway saying you brought them a gun. And that gun was used to kill someone."

"*Jesús Cristo.*" Celia whispered under her breath, crossing herself. Emilio's face went a shade paler.

"But I find it hard to believe you would be stupid enough to kill someone, then give that weapon to Guzman knowing it might shift the blame onto him. You understand what I'm saying, Emilio? Because that's how it would look. I bet that right now, they're thinking you set them up."

Emilio blanched completely. Sitting there, hair sticking out in tufts, he looked small and very young. And absolutely, completely terrified.

"You said you stole the gun, *rata*. Gotta arrest you on that." Rodriguez leaned across the table, balancing on his knuckles. "And since it was used in a murder, that sends you to intake, not Juvenile Detention. Guess who else is spending the night in intake?"

"Tell them, Emilito. Tell them it's not true." Celia was rigid, facing straight front. Tears snaked through the heavy powder on her cheeks.

"It's not true." Emilio said in a small voice.

"*Qué?*" Rodriguez held a hand to his ear. "Didn't hear you, Emilito."

"It's not true," Emilio said. "I didn't steal the gun. I found it."

"Where?" Kelly asked.

"Outside their house. I was there yesterday, hanging around." He glanced sidelong at Celia, who glared back. "Sometimes they give me stuff to do, but they were all still sleeping. I was sitting on the steps, and I saw it."

"Saw what?" Rodriguez asked.

"The gun, okay? I saw the handle sticking out from under the steps. Like someone tossed it there."

"Then you went inside and told them you stole a gun, and were giving it to them?" Kelly asked.

Emilio shrugged. "Yeah. I knows it wasn't theirs, since it was all fancy and shit. Figured it was worth some cash.

They always blowing me off, calling me a *naco*. Thought if they saw I was serious, they'd bring me in."

Kelly was tempted to cuff him herself. "What'd they say?"

Emilio colored. "They asked where I got such a bitch-ass gun. They kept it, though," he said defensively.

"Did you see anyone when you found the gun, or earlier? Someone who looked like they didn't belong there?"

Emilio cocked his head to the side. "What, like white people?"

"Anyone who looked out of place," Kelly said.

Emilio slowly shook his head. "Didn't see no one or nothing." His chin jutted out.

"What will happen to my Emilito?" Celia asked, lip quavering.

Kelly exchanged a glance with Rodriguez. "Hard to say. But I'd call a lawyer."

Jackson Burke gazed out his office window. Dusk was falling, sending shadows marching through downtown's glassy steel columns. The Phoenix skyline wasn't as impressive as New York or Dallas, but he intended to change that. Soon enough there would be plentiful opportunities for rebuilding.

He sighed. Getting to this point had demanded tremendous time and energy, not to mention financial resources. Thanks to a family fortune he'd multiplied a thousand-fold, cash flow wasn't an issue. That and a lack of vision were where so many operations had gone astray in the past. But in the end, all his efforts would be worth it. He'd seen the potential, realized what the growing numbers of converts could accomplish if their man power was properly harnessed, disparate groups united in one cause. Now, after more than a decade of planning, he was close to accomplishing that goal. He just needed the last few dominoes to fall into place.

The phone on his desk beeped, and Jackson frowned. His assistant knew he relished these few moments alone at the end of each day. For her to interrupt, something serious must have happened.

He lifted the receiver and listened for a moment before saying, "All right, put him through."

As Dante spoke, Jackson's expression hardened. He picked up a rock from the Zen garden on his desk and kneaded it between thumb and forefinger. "I see. And how did you respond?" Another burst of chatter. Jackson thought for a moment, then said, "It's time to make Grant understand the seriousness of the situation. Do whatever is necessary."

Nine

Madison awoke in the dark. Despite becoming some-what acclimated to her surroundings, the shock of waking in a strange place never failed to throw her. Every time she went to sleep, deep down she harbored the hope that perhaps this was one of those dreams within a dream, where you only thought you were awake. She always fell asleep hoping to open her eyes and see her bedroom.

Not this time. She drew the thin blanket up to her shoulders and tried to still her shivering. Wherever they'd taken her was cold for June, and for the millionth time she wondered where she was. Back home on the East Coast, summer was in full swing. Central Park was lush and overgrown, the grass still green after recent rains. It felt like forever since she was there. Madison had skipped the last day of school, and spent that Friday hanging out by the pond exchanging texts with Shane and tossing her lunch to the geese. How long ago was that now? One week? Two? She'd started tracking the days, it had been at least three since they took her. But considering how many times they'd injected her with drugs at the begin-ning, she could have been whacked out for weeks. She wondered what the hell they wanted, and why it was taking so long. And if anyone was ever going to clue in to her GPS transmitter.

She groped under the mattress and pulled out the DS Lite. Even on the lowest power setting, she was down to the last bar. Madison chewed her lip. Maybe she could ask Lurch to bring her the power cord, it was with the rest of her stuff. Or she could give it to him to charge. That was riskier—he might decide not to give it back. She didn't think he'd be able to tell it had been altered, but whoever was with him might be shrewder.

Suddenly, the groaning of metal indicated that the door was about to open. She hurriedly tucked the DS Lite back in its hiding place and flipped over to face the wall, regulating her breathing to mimic sleep. A shaft of light sliced the room, casting a silhouette on the wall facing her. Madison drew in her breath sharply. Whoever had come for her, it wasn't Lurch.

"I know you're not sleeping," he said. His voice was gravelly, like he was getting over a cold.

Madison's stomach clenched. Slowly, she rose to a seated position and turned. His face was cast in shadow, and she squinted in the light. "What time is it?" she asked.

He chuckled. "Time for us to get acquainted, kitten."

"Sorry, Kel, you're fading in and out. They've got crap reception here." Jake plugged an index finger in his opposite ear and squinted at the lights below. The sprawling lab facility was visible from Randall's small deck. Some buildings were floodlit, others hunched in the dark. Ironic that so close to the epicenter of the world's most cutting-edge technology, he couldn't get a cell signal to save his life. Maybe they had some sort of jamming apparatus.

"I said, I'm still in Arizona."

"Well hey, we're nearly on the same coast. Wanna meet for a late dinner in Bakersfield?"

"No way Bakersfield is the halfway point," Kelly snorted.

Jake could picture her nose crinkling as she said it. He smiled. "All right then, Denver."

"Wow, your grasp of geography is impressive," Kelly laughed.

"Hey, keep in mind I was living abroad for years. How much longer are you there?"

"Tough to say. Right now the chief is ready to call it, blaming everything on this street gang."

"But you're not buying it?"

There was a pause. "I don't know," she finally said. "These are bad guys, but this seems beyond them. Unless we come up with a more direct tie to the senator, they don't seem the type to be making a political statement, you know?"

"Yeah, it doesn't sound like it." Jake recognized the note of frustration in her voice. The Bureau always wanted high profile cases solved quickly, even if that meant arresting the wrong person.

Not Kelly, though. If that happened, it would eat at her. Even if this gang had been killing nuns and schoolkids on a daily basis, she'd hate to see them locked up for something they didn't do. It was one of the things he loved about her.

He caught himself hoping she'd be forced to compromise. Something like that would practically guarantee her departure from the FBI. Then the endless debates over her job and where they should live would be forced to a conclusion. He experienced a pang of guilt at the thought and forced some cheer into his voice. "Don't worry. It'll work out."

"Maybe." She sounded disconsolate.

"Rodriguez still riding you?"

"I feel like I'm babysitting."

"Yeah, but you felt that way about me, too, right?"

"I still do." Her voice brightened at the teasing.

"So should I be jealous?"

"Of a twenty-seven-year-old who's driving me nuts?" Kelly laughed. "Sure, go ahead. I think he has a fiancée, though. He mentioned something about getting married in the fall."

"Yeah? I love fall weddings."

There was a long pause before Kelly said, "How's everything going for you?"

"Wow, you're becoming the master of the segue."

"I can't handle wedding talk right now," she said. "Did you get any clients signed on? One of us deserved a good day at work."

Jake shifted uncomfortably. As a concession to Syd, he'd told Kelly he was scrounging up business with Silicon Valley venture capital firms. He hated lying to her, yet another reason why things would be easier if she joined The Longhorn Group. "Mine was okay, I guess. This is a lousy part of the state, nothing but strip malls and parking lots. I feel like I keep getting off the interstate in the same place."

"Drum up any business?"

"Maybe. Got some leads." He cleared his throat. "Listen, I've been thinking about heading to Costa Rica after this wraps up. Want to tag along?"

"A few weeks into a new job and already he needs a vacation." Kelly laughed. "Your work ethic is truly awe inspiring. Don't you have to be around in case any of these leads pan out?"

"Nah. Syd's a closer, she loves dealing with the clients. Besides, we still haven't taken a real vacation together."

"What about Vermont?"

"You mean that first weekend we went away together, two years ago?"

"It counts."

"It took almost the entire weekend just to get you in my room."

"I didn't hear you complaining at the time."

"That was only because—" Jake's call-waiting beeped. He glanced at the number: Syd. "Kelly, my love, I've gotta go. Syd's on the other line, it might be important."

"Okay."

She sounded despondent, and Jake's heart lurched. He hated that after all this time they still hadn't found a way to be together for more than a few days. "Costa Rica. Think about it."

"I will. Love you."

Jake clicked over to Syd's call. "Please tell me you've got something."

"Who's your favorite person?"

"Depends. Give me a reason."

"I got a match on the face."

"Really?" Jake straightened. "The driver?"

"Yep. The facial recognition software worked. We were lucky the shot was more or less head-on. And let me tell you, getting access to that database was a bitch."

"I'm sure." Jake considered asking how she'd done it, then figured he probably didn't want to know. Infiltrating government databases was definitely frowned upon. "Let me guess. Ukrainian."

"Not even close. You're going to love this. Winner of the creepy kidnapper prize of the month is Marcus Krex. 'Mack' to his friends."

"Krex doesn't sound Eastern European."

"Give the man a prize!" Syd sounded gleeful, and Jake was glad to hear it. This case had been beating them both up. "Born and bred in Stockton, California. Krex doesn't even have a passport, he's never left the country, at least not legally."

"So the e-mail router was meant to throw us off track."

"Apparently. But based on his sheet Mack isn't tech-savvy."

"Let's hear it."

"Petty crimes starting as a juvie, graduated to grand theft auto and burglary, closed out his career nicely with a stretch in Corcoran for armed robbery. Paroled less than a year ago."

"Jesus." It was nice to finally have a name to go on, but the fact that Madison was snatched by a hardened criminal wasn't the best news he'd heard all day. At least Krex hadn't been convicted of a sex crime—thank God for small favors. "How did this guy not qualify for the three strikes law?"

"Grandfathered out. But he will, if he's caught one more time."

"Where is he now?"

"Kept his nose clean, as far as I can tell. His parole officer said Krex was coming in every week, passed all the drug tests, seemed to be a model citizen. But he missed last week's appointment. He's been so good, the PO didn't worry. He was going to report him if he missed this week."

"When's his appointment?"

"Tomorrow morning, 8:00 a.m. His PO said he'd be happy to sit down and review the case file."

"I'll get on the road first thing tomorrow. Who knows, maybe Krex will even show."

"That would make our lives easier," Syd said drily. There was a long pause.

"Syd?"

"Yeah, I know you've gotta go. I was just wondering. How's Randall holding up?"

"You talked to him."

"Right, I did." She sighed. "I'm shit at this sort of thing."

"Shocking." Jake grinned. "Fortunately you've got a relationship master like me to ask for advice."

Syd barked a sharp laugh before asking, "You think we'll get her back?"

Jake gazed across the landscape. The moon hovered above the buildings, casting them in stark relief. "Maybe. But we're probably going to need more firepower. If we find out where they're keeping her, we should call in the cavalry."

She thought it over. "It might jeopardize the operation."

"I don't think we'll have a choice."

Jake clicked the phone shut and went back inside. Randall sat at the desk tucked in a corner of the living room, staring in horror at his computer monitor. The tinny speakers played a garbled soundtrack that sounded like pigs squealing.

"Jesus, Doc, what the hell are you watching?" Jake crossed the room in long strides. A video filled the screen. It was a close-up of Madison, eyes wide with terror, head whipping back and forth in torment as she screamed.

Kelly ran a hand through her hair as she hung up the phone. Jake had sounded unusually sketchy ever since he abruptly flew to California. There was no reason for him to stress over business meetings with executives, he thrived on that sort of thing. Then there was his Costa Rica suggestion, a prototypical Jake Riley reaction—when you're on a bad case, plan a trip. He clearly had no idea how predictable he was.

It bothered her that he felt the need to lie, she'd rather hear that he couldn't discuss the case. She could respect that, there were certainly details of her work she didn't share. Lying just fed her doubts. Kelly spent a good chunk of her day getting misled by people, the thought of facing the same at home was unbearable.

After the interview with Emilio, she and Rodriguez had spent a couple of hours going over the files to see if they'd missed anything. At 6:00 p.m. they met with the rest of the task force, who reported that the tip line and canvassing had produced the usual band of loonies and conspiracy theorists. Barring any new developments, they'd charge Psycho and his friends with the Morris murder in the next couple of days. Kelly sent everyone home, figuring they'd earned a good night's sleep.

At least they were in a decent hotel. She propped the pillows against the headboard and flipped through TV channels. All the local news stations were running elegiac montages of Duke Morris's career. A former exterminator-turned-public official, there were shots of him holding a rifle at an NRA meeting, glad-handing at a rally, practically spitting into a microphone as he gripped a podium. Kelly had the TV on Mute, but based on his demeanor she guessed he was ranting about his pet issue, immigration reform. Within a day or two something else would shove the Morris story off the national media's front pages. Arizona would hold out longer, but once arrests were made and the governor appointed a new senator, it would be over.

Kelly knew that her superiors were keeping a close eye on her work in this case. She'd be expected to toe the party line if they forged ahead with the MS-13 connection. Even if the gang was guilty, if she uncovered a real connection between them and Morris, her boss would want it buried. And then she'd have to decide what to do.

The camera cut to a studio anchor, one of those inter-changeable blondes with perfect hair. Kelly watched her lips move, and idly wondered how they always found a shade of lipstick that exactly matched their suits: hers was peach. The camera cut to a man. A banner at the bottom of the screen announced him as "Jackson Burke, lifelong friend of Senator Duke Morris." He looked vaguely familiar, although Kelly couldn't place him. She clicked the volume up to catch what he was saying.

"…the real tragedy here, Dawn, is that we lost a man who grasped the true threat our nation faces. Since 9/11, our government has spent so much time focused abroad, we've completely forgotten about the dangers right here at home. Our military is stretched to the limit, our debt is spiraling out of control, and we have thousands of illegals streaming over our borders every day. Some of those people come here looking for a better life. But others clearly intend to do us harm."

"What kind of harm, Mr. Burke?"

"We keep hearing about how al Qaeda is trying to sneak in a bomb, so they can destroy the democratic prin-ciples that this great nation was founded on. But the real threat is more insidious. I'm talking about cartels, mul-tinational gangs whose sole purpose is to flood our schools and streets with drugs. And God knows what else they're bringing over with them. Guns? Bombs? In Cali-fornia, felons get away with murder, literally, because of so-called Sanctuary laws. Just last week a young Honduran man was released from jail even though the au-thorities knew he wasn't here legally. Next day, he killed an entire family in a home invasion robbery."

"And what would you propose, Mr. Burke?"

"In honor of my good friend Duke Morris, I'm starting a new lobbying firm. We're going to put some pressure on those honchos in Washington, ask them to get the National Guard back here to do what they should have been doing all along—guarding our borders. Stem the tide, before natural-born Americans wake up to find that Spanish has become the first language and their kids are now the minority…"

Kelly turned it off with a snort. She'd grown up on the East Coast, and spent most of her adult life in New York and Washington, D.C. She knew that immigration reform was a major issue for a lot of Americans, but she lived at a remove from it. Here, it seemed to taint everything. The murder of Duke Morris by machete had inflamed passions. Editorials in the regions' papers screamed for ICE raids and mass deportations. Protests and counterprotests were sparking up everywhere. There was a sense that the whole region was about to explode in retaliatory violence.

Kelly's cell rang. She checked the number and frowned before answering. "Yes?"

"Jones, I've got some bad news. Emilio didn't make it."

"What?"

"The processing instructions got screwed up—instead of juvie he was sent to intake. Someone shivved him."

Kelly squeezed her eyes shut, an image of Celia's tear-streaked face flashing through her mind. "Jesus, Rodriguez. One of the MS-13s?"

"Nope, another guy. White. Guard said it was probably race-related. Tensions are high, with all the shit that's been going down."

"Crap." Kelly kneaded her forehead. "Have you told McLarty yet?"

"Technically, we had handed him over to Phoenix P.D., so…"

Kelly's eyes narrowed. "So, what?"

"So he wasn't our responsibility anymore."

Kelly was surprised at the coldness in his voice. Sure, Emilio had been a little punk, but he was just a kid. She wondered if this was residual rage over the chase earlier that day, or something deeper. "I doubt Celia will agree."

"Yeah, well. Maybe she should have kept better track of him."

Kelly was too tired to argue about it. "Anything else?"

"Nope. Just wanted you to know."

"Good night, Agent Rodriguez."

He'd already hung up. Kelly readjusted the pillows and lay down, reflecting on the day. Crazy that she lived in a world where a twelve-year-old dreamed of joining a gang. Crazier still that they might offer him the best prospects. Public schools were a mess, jobs were tight, and for a kid growing up in a tough neighborhood, chances of survival, never mind success, were slim. Maybe Emilio was just another casualty of the American Dream. The confluence of events that landed him in an interrogation room could be considered inevitable, based on statistics alone. If not today, maybe five or ten years down the line he would have found himself in the same situation, dying from a blade shoved in his gut.

Kelly felt responsible regardless. She picked up the phone and dialed. "This is Agent Jones, I'm part of the Morris task force. I'd like a copy of the processing papers for Emilio Torres on my desk tomorrow morning."

Madison was curled in a ball on top of the mattress. She'd never been in so much pain. The closest was when she'd broken her leg snowboarding, and they trundled her downhill on a sled that jolted over moguls. But that didn't even begin to compare to this.

She shuddered repeatedly as flashes of what happened

darted through her brain. His scary grin as he dragged her down the hall and into a different room, then tied her to the chair. His fumbling hands all over her, tugging at her shirt. She'd shied away, screaming, but he yanked out her bra straps and attached wires to them. Then the pain, so bad she blacked out. And Lurch in the background with a camera, recording it all.

It seemed to go on forever. It was still dark outside, and she wondered if she'd lost another day.

Madison felt like she'd been beaten all over, every limb, every joint ached. For the first time she confronted the full gravity of her situation. All along in the back of her mind she'd maintained this elaborate fantasy. Commandos storming in and putting a bullet through Lurch's brain. They'd tell her she was so smart, so brave. Deep down she never doubted that someone was coming to save her.

Now she could see how childish that fantasy was. Sometimes there was no happy ending. Sometimes people just died. She almost laughed aloud at how pathetic her GPS transmission was. Ridiculous, really— the world was full of signals now, a never-ending stream bouncing along every wavelength, a constant din. And yet she'd managed to convince herself that her little signal, from a DS Lite no less, would filter through. It was completely absurd.

Madison realized she was shuddering again. She drew a deep breath. No more imagining who would show up at her funeral, no more pretending this was a nightmare she would awaken from. She was done with all that. All she could do now was hope they never brought her in that awful room again.

JUNE 30

Ten

Jake lifted a corner of the mattress and grimaced at what was underneath. Mack Krex's living quarters redefined the term *hellhole*. A dank eight-by-ten-foot room in a boardinghouse so far on the wrong side of the tracks they weren't even visible in the distance. The only furnishings were a caved-in bed and a rickety pasteboard bureau propped against the wall. *Honestly, a cell would have been preferable,* Jake thought. At least it would've been clean.

"Pretty foul, huh?" Mack Krex's parole officer grinned at him, rocking back and forth on his heels. "No fast-food joint pays enough for a place without rats."

Jake wasn't in the mood to joke around. He hadn't been able to forget Madison's tortured face all morning. "I called the manager at Plucky Chicken. He said Krex quit a few months back."

"Yeah? Huh."

"But he's current on the rent here. Paid three months in advance."

The guy shrugged, and Jake narrowed his eyes at him. The PO stood about five-six, wearing a short-sleeved button-down shirt, skinny tie, cheap shoes. His scraggly goatee was a misguided attempt at trendiness, and the beginnings of a potbelly hung over his belt. He looked fifty but was probably closer to thirty-five.

"Doesn't bother you that Krex might have backslid?"

"Maybe he got a gig under the table, working the door at a club. Some of them do that, and Mack's a big guy." The PO held up a hand defensively. "You want to see my caseload? I can't babysit these guys 24/7. He showed for our meets, and his piss was clean. Far as I'm concerned he's a success story."

"So missing last week didn't faze you?"

"Hey, it's not like he was caught diddling kids. I got three of those right now, one of 'em keeps trying to move on to school property. Mack was small-time, supposed to be the muscle in a botched bank robbery. Got talked into it by some buddies, then took the fall when it went south."

"This time he might have abducted a sixteen-year-old girl."

The PO shrugged. "So I'll issue a warrant. Lots of fucked-up shit in the world. All I can do is try to swim through without drinking it."

"Nice analogy." Jake cast one last gaze around the room. "Bit of an accent there. Where you from?"

The guy hesitated before saying, "Mississippi."

"Yeah? You're a long way from home." Jake eyed him. "What brought you to Stockton?"

"The weather."

"Huh." Jake glanced out the window. Stockton was in California's Central Valley, a region that turned into a choking dust bowl each summer. It had to be a hundred degrees outside, convection-oven territory. "So you got any leads on Krex's known acquaintances?"

"Not much in the file, but I'll give you what I got. If you're done, I got a crap-load of paperwork to do."

Jake followed the PO out. Beating himself up didn't help matters, but he couldn't seem to stop. He was the one who told Randall to take a hard line, refusing to continue without proof of life. It was a dangerous dance, bartering over a person's well-being. What he'd recommended was Kidnap and Ransom 101, the baseline that any kidnapper should have recognized. Problem was, they were apparently engaged in a different tango.

The video clip was less than a minute long, shot so close it was impossible to tell what was happening to Madison. Nothing audible but her screams, nothing to show that it was filmed yesterday or a week ago. Jake hadn't pointed that out, figuring Randall was too rattled to handle it. He had to give him a serious pep talk before sending him off to work this morning. Randall drove away slowly, hands still shaking. Not that Jake blamed him. He couldn't even imagine watching your kid undergo that kind of pain.

A hulking guy passed them on the stairs, shaved head, lots of tattoos. He glared at Jake.

"One sec." Jake ducked down the dark hallway, past a pay phone to the door marked *Manager* in tarnished, crooked letters. Knocked once, and the guy who had let them into Mack's room opened it. He was holding a fresh bottle of Bud.

"Yeah?"

"You got a list of all the tenants?"

The guy squinted at him. Jake felt the PO peering over his shoulder. The manager glanced at him, then back at Jake. "What for?"

"Just curious."

"Don't you need a warrant or something?"

"Sure, I could get one of those," Jake bluffed. He had no idea what strings Syd had pulled to convince the PO that he was a federal marshal, but figured it was best to play along. "Or I could spend the day grilling every person who walks through that door. Maybe check some of the other rooms, see what I find. Up to you."

The manager grunted and scratched himself. Clearly Jake wasn't winning friends and influencing people in Stockton. Maybe it was outside his target demographic. Without another word the manager turned and shuffled off. A second later he returned with a smudged spreadsheet. "Here."

"Thanks." Jake tucked it under his arm, then strode down the hallway. The PO fell in step behind him. Maybe Jake was being paranoid, but he half expected to feel a knife in his back.

Alone in the car five minutes later, he rang Syd.

"Anything?" she asked, sounding breathless.

"Are you jumping rope back there?"

"Give me a break, I was across the office dealing with something. Any leads on Krex?"

"Not really. Just finished up at his place, now I'm headed to where he used to work. I got some names for you to run down." He read them off, made sure she had the right spelling. "Another thing. Get me background info on Krex's PO and find out who owns that boarding-house."

"Okay." The sound of typing in the background. "Am I looking for anything specific?"

Jake glanced back at the building, three ramshackle stories that in happier times had been painted bright yellow. "Something feels off here. The PO was too laid-back about Krex slipping off his radar, and there are a bunch of doppelgängers shacked up there, too."

"Not unusual. Can't imagine many places rent to ex-cons."

"I know, but still. Look into it. Might be nothing, but…"

"Hey, I'm not complaining, it's good to have something to do. I was down to arranging my pens by color."

"We only bought blue pens."

"You see my problem."

Jake grinned. "All right. I'll check in later."

"Later, partner."

Jake sat for a moment, drumming his fingers idly on the steering wheel. Mack Krex had slid off the grid, not unusual for an ex-con. But then he turned up at the airport as part of an elaborate plan to kidnap a sixteen-year-old girl in exchange for nuclear secrets. Someone was pulling the strings here, and he'd bet it wasn't a third-rate felon with an eighth grade education. He pressed Redial and waited for Syd to pick up. "Hey, can you get me in to see the warden at Corcoran? Maybe he knows more than the PO."

"Sure thing."

Jake hung up and shifted the car into Drive. The fast-food joint where Mack used to work was a mile away. Unless something shook loose there, they were pretty much back where they started. And Madison was running out of time.

Randall sipped nervously at his cappuccino, trying not to look as terrified as he felt. He had left work shortly after arriving, complaining of a stomach bug. Barry, no stranger to intestinal distress, agreed to cover for him. And the truth was he'd been nauseous ever since that awful video last night. He clenched his fists at the memory. Randall wished again that he was someone different, the kind of guy who would find the people responsible and wring their necks. Unfortunately, he had to rely on Syd and Jake to do that for him. And so far, they hadn't really helped.

He was sitting in a park on the outskirts of Concord, a patch of green etched out between office buildings. Like most of the East Bay, the town was a mix of strip malls, office parks and suburban neighborhoods wound around cul-de-sacs. To his immediate right a bronze memorial to 9/11 read, "Through blurred eyes we find the strength and courage to soar beyond the moment." Under the current circumstances, it struck him as particularly ironic.

Randall glanced at his watch again: 11:00 a.m. He'd arrived late, there was construction on the 680 and traffic had slowed to a crawl. A shadow blocked the light, and he squinted up. A man stood over him, head cocked to the side. He was white, medium-build, wiry-looking; not the same guy who first approached him. Dressed in jeans and a black long-sleeved shirt despite the weather, his features masked by aviator sunglasses and a Giants baseball cap. Randall's throat closed up with rage at the sight of him. He gripped the bench's armrest to prevent himself from doing something stupid.

"Dr. Grant, right?" His voice was a chain smoker's rasp. "You got something for me?"

Randall reached into his jacket pocket for the flash drive. The guy's hand clamped down on his wrist, stopping him. "Don't get cute, Grant."

"You tell that son of a bitch he fucked up by hurting my daughter," Randall said. "I told him I'd get it, I just needed more time…"

"You give us what we want when we ask for it. You knew that was part of the deal. Can't stall and expect nothing to happen."

"I want my daughter back."

"Behave yourself and we'll cut her loose this afternoon."

A woman approached with a stroller, the only other person to enter the park since Randall had arrived. The guy clasped his shoulder, guffawing as if Randall had said something hilarious. As he exerted pressure, Randall fought not to cry out.

Once the woman passed them, the guy said in a low voice, "We had a deal, Grant. And that deal included delivery dates." He released his grip.

Randall watched the young mother wheel the stroller away. Funny, sometimes it seemed like yesterday he was pushing the girls around in one of those. His mind flashed back to a day at the zoo when they were still tiny, the two of them hanging off the metal fence around the penguin compound, laughing, and his stomach seized up. Without a word, he dropped the flash drive in the man's hand.

"Good. Now get back to work, we need you there in case anything goes wrong."

"You said she'd be free this afternoon!" Randall protested.

The guy laughed. "Just fucking with you, Grant. Don't screw with us and we'll return her safe and sound."

Randall snorted. "I'll be lucky if there isn't an armed detail waiting at my desk."

"Yeah, that would be unlucky. For both of you." The guy drew a pack of gum from his pocket, peeled off a piece, and stuck it in his cheek. "Remember, we're watching you."

"Fuck you."

The guy grinned and sauntered away. Randall watched as he slid into the passenger seat of an SUV with tinted windows. As soon as it turned the corner he slumped and buried his head in his hands. He'd royally screwed everything up again.

* * *

Jackson Burke leveled the barrel. He nodded once, and the trainer released the dogs. They surged toward the cattails lining the pond. A dozen mallards exploded from the reeds, necks straining upward as their wings beat the air. He got one in his sights, led it, then squeezed the trigger. He lowered the rifle and watched, satisfied, as the mallard stopped dead before spiraling back down. Tails wagging, the dogs dove into the water to retrieve it.

Jackson tugged his hat brim up an inch.

"Not bad for an old man," his companion remarked.

Jackson grinned at him. "Not too old to whip your ass."

"Not in a fair fight."

"I always thought that was an oxymoron. A fight's a fight, the goal is to win." Jackson leaned against the bumper of their 4x4.

"Sorry to hear about Duke. He was one of a kind." The young man propped a rifle against his shoulder. They were both dressed in matching camouflage and waders.

"He surely was." Jackson nodded. "Terrible shame. But maybe some good will come of it. Woke some people up, made them realize the enemy is already inside our gates."

"Absolutely." The young man nodded and spit a long stream of tobacco juice out the corner of his mouth. "If they stay this angry, we might finally push that bill through in the next session."

"Oh, I believe you will." Jackson watched the trainers drop the lifeless birds into a cooler before loading the dogs back in their crates. "More trouble coming, you can bet on that."

"You think?" The young man squinted toward the setting sun. "Speaking of which, I heard a rumor the governor is naming you Morris's replacement. That true?"

Jackson smirked. "Little birdie tell you that?"

The other man laughed. "Fine, Jack, don't tell me. But we need more people like you up on the Hill. It'd help keep some focus on this border problem."

"Change is coming, boy. Trust me on that." Jackson settled back into the passenger seat with a grunt.

"Always an optimist."

"Hardly. An optimist hopes for the best. A pragmatist makes sure it happens." Jackson pulled the brim of his hat low over his eyes again and nudged the driver. "Let's get going. I'm fit to eat a horse."

"Celia, I'm so sorry."

Celia eyed her through the screen door. Less than twenty-four hours ago, Kelly had been standing on this exact spot asking for Emilio. And now the boy was dead.

"What you want?"

Kelly shifted awkwardly. It was a fair question, and one she wasn't sure she could answer. Rodriguez didn't know where she was—she'd slipped out of the task force room, figuring she'd come up with an excuse on her drive back. If McLarty knew she was here, he'd already be filing her termination papers. But she didn't care. A kid had been hurt on one of her cases last fall, and still hadn't fully recovered. Now she'd have Emilio's death weighing on her conscience as well.

"I wanted to make sure you were okay."

Celia glared at her. "*Mi* Emilito is dead."

"I know. Like I said, I—"

"You sorry." Celia snorted, then turned and shuffled away. Kelly took that as an invitation to follow and hesitantly opened the screen door. She glanced around. Yesterday she'd been so focused on Emilio, she hadn't taken note of the interior. It was small, two bedrooms, a kitchen, a living room. Shabby and filled with secondhand furniture, but clean.

Kelly followed Celia into the living room. On top of a bookshelf sat a small shrine. Votive candles burned in front of framed family photographs: sepia-toned ancestors, a school portrait of Emilio with his hair slicked back, a younger shot of him kneeling beside a soccer ball. A dime-store painting of the Virgin Mary hovered watchfully above. In one corner an ancient television perched on wooden legs, bunny ears askew. Celia dropped into an easy chair that released an anguished gasp. She gestured to the seat opposite her. *"Siéntate."*

Kelly perched on the edge of a love seat that bore the faded remains of a floral print. She crossed her hands in her lap. "I pulled the processing papers, and it looks like there was a mix-up at the sheriff's office. Someone stuck Emilio on the wrong bus. It was a mistake."

Celia snorted again. "No mistake."

"I believe it was. I spoke personally with the administrator who filed—"

Celia shook her head. "This gun *mi* Emilito find, that gun kill the senator, yes?"

Kelly shifted uncomfortably. It was only a matter of time before that detail was leaked to the media, but for the moment she preferred to keep it under wraps. "What makes you think that?"

"My English not so good, but I clean houses here for twenty years. I see things." Celia pointed to her eyes. "FBI involved, for a gun? Must be reason." Kelly started to respond, but Celia cut her off. "And I know this man who die."

"Know him how?"

"Always on television, Mexicans this, Mexicans that…" She waved a hand in the air to illustrate her point. "Then my Emilito is killed. Mix-up you say. A white man kill him."

"It happens in jail. There are a lot of…racial tensions."

"My friend Rosa see a van full of gringos, same day Emilito find the gun."

Kelly furrowed her brow. "Saw them where?"

"By that house, with *los Salvadoreños de perros.* Early, she saw them."

"So you're saying there's some connection between this van and the gun that we found?"

Celia stared her down without responding.

"Maybe they were workers," Kelly suggested.

"Aquí?" Celia rolled her eyes.

She had a point. In a predominantly Latino neighborhood, cheap labor was rarely provided by Caucasians. "They could have been lost."

"No. Rosa say she no like how they look."

"Did she see them get out of the van?"

"Rosa go to work, she must be there at seven or no more job." Celia pointed a finger at her. "But those men leave the gun. And they kill my Emilito."

Kelly didn't want to point out the flawed logic—the white man who shivved Emilio was in lockup, not driving around in a van. "Okay. Can I talk to your friend Rosa? Maybe she got a license plate number?"

"She no talk to police," Celia said with finality.

"Well, then." Kelly stood. "Thanks so much for your time, Celia. I'm so sorry again for your loss."

Celia's eyes filled with tears and she crossed herself.

Kelly let herself out. As she walked to her bu-car an Eldorado cruised past, filled with teenage boys who challenged her with their eyes. One of them whistled, and another laughed. Kelly ignored them, thinking that a van full of white men would definitely stick out like a sore thumb here. But there were any number of explanations, and a canvass of the neighborhood would probably only result in more slammed doors. Still, it was hard to shake the sense that she was missing something. Why would a group of white men kill Duke Morris, their purported champion, and stow the gun at an MS-13 stash house? Sure, it had stirred up considerable interest in their cause, but to commit murder for that reason seemed excessive.

She flipped open her phone and dialed.

"Where the hell are you? I thought—"

Kelly cut Rodriguez off. "Did you ever run down where the tip came from, for the raid?"

"What, on the MS-13 house?"

"Yes."

"Why?" He sounded irritated.

"Just do it, Rodriguez."

"You know, I'm not your assistant, I'm your partner."

"Fine. I'll get someone else on the task force to do it." Kelly gritted her teeth as she pulled away from the curb.

A pause. "You're thinking someone wanted us to find that gun, right?"

"Maybe. It's something we should follow up on."

"It's not a bad theory," he conceded. "All right, I'll check it out."

As Kelly drove back to the station she tried calling Jake, but he didn't answer. With any luck his day was going better than hers, she thought grimly as she hung up.

Eleven

Dante tapped a finger on his holstered gun. Chances were he wouldn't need it, but he wasn't a big believer in chance and preferred to hedge his bets. He glanced at the gate, legs jiggling nervously. Nearly time now. He was in a security booth at the entrance to a waste storage plant. One of hundreds in Texas that handled "low risk" radioactive materials, it had been mismanaged by an owner with a weakness for strippers and was currently stuck in bankruptcy court. They'd broken in the night before with a hacksaw and bolt cutters. Everything here had already been moved when the government belatedly consolidated hazardous materials at more secure facilities. There hadn't been a shipment here in months. Although hopefully the truck drivers wouldn't know that. And if they did, well, then it was their unlucky day.

It was a relief to finally have something to do. A few more days stuck in that warehouse and Dante would have gone out of his head. Despite the diversion provided by the girls, his men were increasingly hard to control. Things were close to combusting when the call came in.

Dante had a sixth sense for when shit was about to hit the fan, it was kind of his gift.

So far the plan was going off without a hitch. Of course, Jackson had taken everything into account, down to the most minor detail.

They'd brought a small TV set with them. Dante had it tuned to a baseball game to maintain the illusion of a bored security guard. The Sox were top of their division again. He never thought he'd see the day when that team became a goddamned dynasty. But given enough time, even the worst sometimes came out on top. Kind of like what was happening in the country today, he thought, lips pursing in a sneer.

The rumble of engines in the distance. Dante straightened in his chair. He could see them coming over the hill, three eighteen-wheelers towing flatbeds draped with tarps. Eleven o'clock, right on time. The first truck slowed as it approached. The driver rolled down his window and Dante left the booth, opening the gate to greet him. "Morning," he said, forcing a grin.

The driver was older, mid-fifties with a beard down to his chest. He craned his neck to see around Dante. "That the game?"

It took a second to realize what he was referring to, but Dante caught himself and said, "Sure is."

"Damn, wish I'd seen that triple. Listening to it just ain't the same." He squinted at the low line of buildings ahead. "Awful quiet around here today. Place used to be bustling."

Dante's hand crept to his holster, but he kept his smile wide. "You know how it is. Cutbacks. They laid off half the guys."

"Shame. Times are tough all over." The driver nodded toward the flatbed. "Where you want it?"

"Wheel it on back. They'll unhitch the trailer so you can get on your way."

"Sure would appreciate that. I gotta be back in Galveston by noon."

Dante waved him through and the other trucks followed, gears groaning as they lurched past with their payload. As he slid the gate shut behind them, his face split in a genuine grin. Easy as pie, just like Jackson promised. An inside man was changing the records to show the equipment landing a couple hundred miles farther west. Unless someone was paying real close attention, they were golden. And now that they had the raw materials, it was time to start phase two. Which meant their own personal D-day was less than a week away. Dante glanced down at his belt, checking the dosimeter clipped to it. None of the circles were tinted. Satisfied, he turned back to the Sox game and let out a whoop as a ball sailed clear of the stadium.

Panting, Madison forced herself through one more push-up before collapsing on the floor. Being stuck in this room with nothing to do for hours on end was driving her nuts. Finally she'd resorted to exercise, usually the bane of her existence. She spent a good chunk of each day performing half-remembered calisthenics from gym class—lunges, push-ups. She had a vision of herself as that ripped chick in *The Terminator* by the time she got out of here. Not that she would be getting out, but at least it kept her busy.

Madison forced that thought from her mind and started again. For a long stretch after they hurt her, she'd curled up in bed. Lurch had even added a piece of cake to her morning tray, but she didn't see the point in fighting the inevitable anymore. She decided that she'd stop eating and drinking. If she was going to die anyway, she might as well do it on her own terms.

But for some reason when she awoke again, she felt better. Maybe it was because even in this dark place she could smell a change in the air. For the first time the metal walls felt warm; summer had finally arrived wherever she was. She figured it was time to stop sulking and get back to her routine. She might only have a few days left to live, no point spending them in bed.

She was getting stronger, now she could get to eight without collapsing. Madison lay on her stomach for a minute, gasping, catching her breath. The face of the man who had come for her rose unbidden in her mind and her teeth clenched. She pictured slamming her fist in his mouth, clawing out his eyes, yanking that creepy smile off his face. Gritting her teeth, she pushed off the floor again and kept counting.

"Apparently Mack Krex was a model prisoner."

"Really? I find that surprising." Jake crossed his legs and sat back in the chair. The Corcoran prison warden faced him. He wasn't sure what he'd expected, but it definitely wasn't this glamorous woman in her fifties with a coiffed updo and manicured nails. She looked like someone who would be at home sipping martinis on the ninth hole. Yet here she was running a prison that harbored some of the most ruthless offenders, including Charles Manson and Juan Corona. Of course, when it was revealed a decade ago that guards were staging "Gladiator Days," orchestrating fights between inmates, the Department of Corrections had frantically attempted to burnish the prison's image. And appointing a woman like Elise Faulkner to run it was definitely a sea change. Despite her high society appearance, Jake sensed a steeliness that accounted for her success in such a testosterone-filled environment.

"It says here he had one or two incidents right after arriving, nothing too serious. We tend to see that sort of thing during the initial adjustment period." Warden Faulkner pushed her designer glasses up the bridge of her nose. "Hmm," she said, lips turning down as she read further. "Looks like he joined the Brotherhood."

"What, the Aryan gang?"

She glanced up sharply. "Gangs are a way of life here, Mr. Riley. I don't like it any more than you do, but I'd be hard-pressed to find a prisoner who didn't join one."

"Sure." Jake knew that gangs offered protection in what could generously be described as a difficult environment. Without that, chances of surviving a prison term were slim.

"And once he matched up with them, no more trouble. Early parole, thanks to overcrowding."

"Even for a violent offender?"

Warden Faulkner shrugged. "We only have so much room these days, Mr. Riley. And according to his record he never actually hurt anyone. The board would have taken that into consideration."

"Great." *So much for keeping the streets safe,* he thought.

"What's he done now?" she asked, setting down the file and crossing her hands on the desk.

"We're pretty sure he kidnapped a sixteen-year-old girl."

"Interesting. That doesn't match his priors." The warden pursed her lips.

"I'm thinking he's not the brains behind this. Someone else is pulling the strings."

"That would make sense. Based on his file Mack wasn't an initiator."

"So can you tell me who he answered to in here?"

The warden sighed and tapped her thumbs against each other. "How much do you know about the Brotherhood, Mr. Riley?"

He shrugged. "They're not fond of minorities and have a real thing for swastikas."

She smiled thinly. "True. But don't underestimate them. This is one of the most highly organized gangs in the entire country. Their methods of communication continually stump us, they've even managed to exchange information with inmates in solitary confinement. They have a whole system of hand signals that we've had no luck in deciphering, they pass coded messages with invisible ink created from their own urine. They make up one-tenth of the prison population, but they're responsible for nearly a quarter of the murders."

"Lovely," Jake said. "Jesus."

"Jesus, indeed. They're practically a mercenary army, even assigning military ranks to members. Once indoctrinated they're taught a very strict code, and they follow it or suffer the consequences. Chain of command, loyalty. You won't find a more devoted band of soldiers."

"And when they get out?"

Her eyes narrowed. "Excellent question. We, of course, don't track them." She leaned forward in her chair. "I will tell you something I've noticed personally. The rate of recidivism has dropped substantially in the past few years."

"Here at Corcoran?"

The warden shook her head. "Everywhere. At the last national conference on Corrections, there was a seminar about it. One of the hacks in charge of the prisoner reentry program claimed we're finally seeing the results of changes implemented years ago."

"You sound skeptical."

She leaned back in her chair and waved her hand. "I've been doing this a long time, Mr. Riley. And leopards never change their spots."

"So I'm guessing you've got a theory?"

Warden Faulkner eyed him. "I do. Just a pet one, but I'd like to know if it's correct. Which is why I agreed to speak with you, despite the fact that you have no legal right to the information I'm providing."

Jake tensed in his chair. Seeing his reaction, Warden Faulkner winked. "Relax, Mr. Riley. All I want from you is answers, if you happen to solve this little mystery of mine."

"So?" Jake shifted uncomfortably. For the past five years he'd worked for one of the most powerful men in the world, and before that an FBI badge always greased the skids. Now that he was in business for himself, he had no real authority anymore. He was beginning to grasp how much harder that made things. "What do you think is going on?"

The warden leaned forward, a glint in her eye. "Someone has finally organized them. Think about it, Mr. Riley. An entire army of violent men with a wide range of skills and few morals. All these years they've been focused on survival, eliminating immediate threats to themselves. But what if someone with vision managed to organize them?"

"Like who?"

"That's the real question here, isn't it?" She sat back and arched an eyebrow.

"Huh."

"You're looking at me like I should be committed," she noted. "All right, then. But keep it in the back of your mind. There might be a reason that men like Mack Krex are suddenly resurfacing, committing crimes outside their MO."

Jake had to admit she had a point. Who would have expected a Saudi to orchestrate a plot from the mountains of Afghanistan that would take out the World Trade Center and a good chunk of the Pentagon? "So can you give me any leads?"

She pushed another file toward him. Jake flipped to the mug shot. A large man with a shaved skull, goatee and hooded eyes stared back at him.

"Dante Parrish, the capo of the Brotherhood when Mack was here. Rumor has it his influence extended beyond Corcoran. Track down Dante, and you'll probably also find Mr. Krex. And a lot of other men, too. So be forewarned, Mr. Riley. These are the worst of the worst."

"Sounds like my last family barbecue."

"You have a robust sense of humor, Mr. Riley," Warden Faulkner said, extending a hand across the desk. "I hope no one sees fit to beat it out of you."

Rodriguez slid his bu-car into Park and left the engine idling. He squinted at the pay phone through the tinted windshield. He was in a section of downtown Phoenix where the sprawl edged the buildings away from each other, alleys gradually bloating into full parking lots. Everything looked empty and run-down: For Lease signs on the windows, trash in the gutters, relentless heat baking everything a cracked taupe. He tugged at his collar and considered loosening the top button. In a climate like this no one should have to wear a tie, ever.

The only place that showed signs of life was a bar on the corner. The pay phone was halfway down the block on the same side of the street. It was a long shot. Whoever called 911 to report the MS-13 stash house might have been passing through, stopping off to do a good deed. Or maybe they were involved, and foolishly opted for convenience. Either way, it was worth a shot. He was actually surprised to see a pay phone, he'd thought they'd gone the way of eight-tracks and VHS players. There was something reassuring about it.

Rodriguez chewed his lower lip. He should call Jones to share the info, but she'd been so pissy he figured he'd see if the lead panned out first. And if it did, he was damn sure taking credit for it. Solving the murder of a senator would be a huge boon for his career. He was no fool, he knew about the rumors swirling around his promotion. That he'd made it thanks to affirmative action and quotas, or worse, that he'd ratted out his partner. He'd caught Jones looking at him sideways a few times, knew she'd heard them, too. Well, screw her, she could believe what she wanted. Talk around the watercooler was that she was circling the bowl anyway, one more screwup and she'd be lucky to get a desk job. Not that he was on a mission to destroy her career, initially he'd even been excited to partner with her. Kelly Jones was still something of a legend at HQ. But the way she treated him was all too familiar. Truth was, most people liked having Mexicans clean their houses, mow their lawns and cook their food. But become their equal, and all bets were off.

He remembered Jones's tone as she basically ordered him to do her scut work, and a flush rose up his neck. Then she got all holier than thou about that Emilio punk, as if the murder was somehow his fault. Like she suddenly cared about a dead wetback, when a dozen kids like Emilio had probably been murdered that week.

Rodriguez could call in a team to dust for prints, but a public pay phone would prove a nightmare for any Crime Scene Unit. And he had a feeling about the bar. It was obvious, but the truth was most criminals weren't that smart. They made stupid decisions, they got caught, end of story. With any luck, he'd open the door and see someone sitting there with a machete. Or maybe he'd find a witness. You never knew.

Deciding, Rodriguez got out of the car and undid the top button of his shirt as he approached the bar. A faded sign on the door announced *Happy Hour: $2 Pitchers 4–6 p.m.* He pushed open the door with authority. It took a minute for his eyes to adjust to the dimly lit interior. And once they did, he realized that he'd just made one of the worst mistakes of his life.

Twelve

Syd's eyes widened as she tapped the keyboard. Dang, it had been a long time since she'd seen anything like this. And certainly never with a redneck yokel like Dante Parrish. He'd completely slipped off the grid. It was possible he was working somewhere under the table, paying rent in cash and steering clear of credit cards. After all, banks didn't generally give ex-cons a line of credit. But some sort of footprint usually remained. A postal address, e-mail account, cell phone. Hell, a video-store card.

Not here, though. If she had to guess, she'd say that someone erased Dante's existence from every system imaginable. It was the sort of thing the Agency did with operatives on a daily basis, but you never encountered it with civilians. Either Dante had moved to a self-sustaining commune somewhere in the wilderness, or he'd found someone powerful enough to cover his tracks.

Syd reached her arms overhead and stretched. For the millionth time she wondered whether or not she'd done the right thing pressuring Jake to take this case. The irony was that she had been on the verge of breaking up with

Randall. Not that they were even dating, their entire relationship consisted of a few random encounters when their paths crossed. She'd met him at an intelligence conference, and one thing led to another. He was so different from the rough-and-tumble guys she usually fell for, she found his geekiness oddly appealing. Neither of them was looking for anything serious, so it seemed like the perfect solution: occasional companionship without the usual muss and fuss.

Recently, though, Randall had become clingy. Late night weepy phone calls, showing up unexpectedly, demanding attention when she was knee-deep in the company launch. And Syd Clement was not one for commitments. She'd never been with anyone for more than a few months, and she was happy to keep it that way. She'd been composing the "Dear Randall" e-mail when he called pleading for help.

Syd surprised herself by pushing for this to be their first case. Madison's kidnapping was well outside the parameters of what they'd normally be doing. Beyond that, it involved the kind of messy personal connection that was usually the kiss of death. The whole time she'd been half wishing Jake would refuse. And though she hated to admit it, the worst part of her, the part that the Agency had fed and fanned until it threatened to consume her, was only hoping Madison would survive so that she wouldn't have to comfort Randall. Awful. But maybe knowing it was awful was a good first step toward reclaiming her humanity.

Syd tucked her feet beneath her and spun in the chair. Not finding Dante on any of the traditional servers was disheartening but not hopeless. Her network of people was bound to uncover something. Until then, all she could do was wait.

Unfortunately, waiting was never her strong suit. She'd thought that a desk job would be a nice change of pace. Lord knew she could use a break from the fray. The past few years had been hell, with the "War on Terror" whipping up small conflagrations throughout the globe. The best and worst times of her life, bouncing from Shanghai to Tbilisi to Tehran. Escaping by the skin of her teeth a few times, and by even less others.

And now here she was, sitting behind a desk, wearing pumps and pearls. You had to laugh.

The phone rang and she lunged for it. "The Longhorn Group."

A pause. "Is this Sydney?"

"Who's this?" Syd replied, dodging the question. First thing they taught you, knowledge is power. And she didn't recognize the voice offhand. Her pulse kicked up a notch and she felt that familiar rush. Old habits died hard.

"This is Audrey Grant."

Syd sank back into the chair. "Hello, Ms. Grant."

"I thought it was you." Audrey's tone indicated that she knew the exact nature of Syd's relationship with her ex-husband. Also, that she didn't appreciate being referred to as Ms. *Too bad,* Syd thought.

"Randall hasn't called recently. I was hoping—"

"We don't have any new information," Syd said. "But we're doing everything we can. We'll be in touch." She lowered the receiver. Small talk had never been her strong suit, and chatting with her current lover's ex-wife was too weird, even for her.

"The thing is—" the receiver bleated.

Syd repressed a sigh and raised it back to her ear. "Yes?"

"Bree remembered something. It's probably nothing, but Madison has one of those toys, the handheld video games. She's constantly playing it."

"And?" Syd knew she should probably be more sympathetic, after all, Audrey's kid was missing. But if half of what Randall said was true, she could end up spending an hour comforting a woman who was deep in her cups.

"Well, it has GPS. Isn't there some way to track her down with that?"

Sure, Syd wanted to say. *All we'd need is a Department of Defense supercomputer and a dozen analysts.* "Chances are she's probably not able to send a signal. But if you get me the serial number, I can look into it."

"My daughter is very bright, *Ms.* Clement. For her science project this year she boosted satellite signals, tapping into some sort of network. I didn't understand it, frankly, but if anyone could manage it, Madison could."

Syd noted the *Ms.*, decided to let it slide. "Like I said, I'll check it out."

"Fine." Another long pause. Syd itched to hang up the phone, just holding it made her feel dirty and she'd done nothing wrong. "I just want you to know, I was not in favor of hiring you. And if my daughter is not returned soon, I am going to the FBI."

"That would be a mistake."

"It's my daughter, Ms. Clement." Audrey's voice hardened as she said, "You have twenty-four hours. After that, I'm making the call."

Fantastic, Syd thought. Now she could add a pissed-off ex-wife to the list of people who loathed her.

Kelly pulled in behind Rodriguez's car. Son of a bitch had tried to follow up the lead without her; luckily, someone else had left a note on her desk with the 911 call information. Her eyes scanned the street, alighting on the bar. Obvious. Too obvious, in her opinion, but she knew that an unseasoned agent like Rodriguez would have assumed he could crack the case by leaning on a few barflies. And of course he hadn't called for backup, despite the fact that they knew nothing about the bar or the area.

Kelly radioed in. Dispatch placed a unit ten blocks away, said they could be there in five minutes. She settled back to wait. It was 4:00 p.m., and the air rose in waves off the pavement. She kept the air-conditioning blasting to counter it.

The bar was set on the corner, no windows, with an unlit neon sign that read: *Acme Lounge. Lounge was pushing it if the exterior was any indication,* Kelly thought. The windows were painted black and there were streaks where the paint had peeled away, like a giant cat had sharpened its claws against them.

As she watched, the door opened and a guy stepped out. He was huge, at least six-four, close to three hundred pounds. He glanced up and down the street, eyes lingering on her car. Something about his stance got her instincts jangling. After a decade with the Bureau, she knew the look of someone who was up to no good.

He ducked back inside. Kelly fought to quiet the alarm signals in her head, glancing at her watch. Backup was still two minutes out. Rodriguez had been unreachable for nearly two hours. She bit her lower lip, then got out of the car. Placed her hand on the hood of his bu-car: hot, but that could be from the sun. She unclipped her radio. "Dispatch, have backup meet me at Acme Lounge, same intersection."

"Copy that."

"And make sure they come in quiet, okay?"

The sirens in the distance cut off. It was probably an unnecessary precaution, but if something was going down she'd prefer the element of surprise. While she waited, she dug her bulletproof vest out of the trunk and strapped it on. Immediately her core body temperature shot up and her silk shirt was soaked with sweat. Kelly gritted her teeth. If Rodriguez was in there, she was holding him personally responsible for her dry cleaning bill.

Kelly decided to try the window, maybe some of the streaks were large enough to provide a view inside. She crossed the street, unclipping her holster and keeping her hand low, ready to draw quickly. Something about the whole scenario felt seriously off. She'd lost her partner a few cases back. No matter how she felt about Rodriguez, she didn't care to lose another.

Kelly edged along the window farthest from the door. One section of peeling paint was at shoulder height, and she ducked slightly to peer in. Newspaper was taped along the insides, blocking it.

A movement to her left. Kelly spun quickly, drawing her weapon. A Latina woman emerged from a doorway across the street, saw her, and did a double take. She was hauling a shopping cart filled with purses. She raised both hands and backed into the building, leaving the cart where it stood.

Great, a sweatshop, Kelly thought, releasing her breath slowly and tucking her gun away. The accidental killing of an illegal immigrant would pretty much guarantee her reassignment to Dubuque.

A police car approached. She motioned for it to slow and it eased to the curb, parking at an angle. Two young officers got out.

"Special Agent Kelly Jones," she said in a low voice. "Either of you know this place?"

They both shook their heads. "Not much happens over here. We cruise by every few days, but it's quiet. Our other sector is in an all-out gang war, so…" He shrugged.

"Okay. It might be nothing, but Agent Rodriguez's car is parked down the street and I have reason to believe he's inside. I need you to cover my back."

They looked skeptical, but nodded. Kelly could imagine what they were thinking: a female suit was afraid to enter a bar alone, so she dragged them away from where they were really needed. Didn't matter to her. Going in without backup was a recipe for disaster, and she couldn't afford the fallout.

She checked the straps on her vest. Felt the cops' impatience pouring over her like water on rocks. Took a deep breath and pushed open the door.

A roomful of eyes shifted in their direction. There was a line of fifteen men at the bar, all carbon copies of each other: large, bald, thick. Identical outfits, too: jeans, black tank tops, work boots. Each of them had a bottle of beer in his hand, she noted—bottles that could quickly become weapons, not a good sign.

Kelly paused on the threshold before stepping all the way inside. They watched as she entered, cops flanking her. No one said a word.

"I'm looking for another agent," she said, taking a step forward. The three of them against fifteen guys who looked recently paroled weren't her favorite odds. Worse yet if some of them were armed.

No one answered, and the tension in the room ratcheted up another notch. The men at the bar stared at her, motionless. Poised. Ready for the situation to get ugly, looking forward to it even, judging by their expressions. She should have called for more backup. Apparently one of the cops agreed. He unhooked his radio and said, "Dispatch, this is unit fourteen. We've got a Code 8."

"He ain't here," said the bartender, an enormous beard differentiating him from the others.

"Who said it was a he?" Kelly asked, drawing her Glock.

The bartender gazed at her for a long moment before replying, "Lucky guess."

"You should pick up a lotto ticket, I hear the pot is at twenty million." Kelly took another step forward, making sure there was no way for the exit to be cut off. One of the cops fell in next to her, the other stayed by the door. They seemed to have the same read of the situation, she noted with relief. Hopefully they'd know how to handle themselves if things went south.

"I'll do that." The bartender carefully polished the glass in his hand, although Kelly doubted cleanliness was the clientele's chief concern.

"Don't suppose you'd mind if I look around," Kelly said.

"I'd expect to see a warrant for that."

"I can have one here in ten minutes."

The bartender shrugged without answering.

They all heard it at the same time, a muffled grunt from behind a door marked *Employees* in crooked letters. Everyone froze. Kelly saw the cops pull their weapons, the guys straighten at their stools, the bartender setting the glass down, hard, then reaching for something behind the bar.

"Hands where I can see them!" she barked, aiming for his chest. He waited a beat before raising them.

"The rest of you drop the bottles and raise your hands. I want you to stand up and take a step back."

The guys on the stools exchanged glances. The bartender nodded slightly and they did as she asked, almost in unison. Kelly watched as the cops got them down on the floor, hands behind their heads. She hoped they had enough zip ties.

She kept her Glock steady on the bartender's chest. He

was watching her, calculating. Kelly got the sense he was waiting for something.

"I'd like to take a look behind that door. Now."

He shrugged. "Suit yourself."

He moved down the bar slowly. "Keep those hands up!" Kelly ordered as they started to drop. She was careful to stay out of arms' reach as he approached the door.

"Open it."

"I don't got a key."

"Bullshit. Open it now."

"I'm telling you, lady, no key. Locks from the inside."

Kelly examined the door. It looked cheap, plywood. She glanced quickly over her shoulder: both cops were still occupied, halfway down the line of prisoners. "Kick it in."

"What?"

"You look like a big strong guy. Kick it in."

He raised a boot halfheartedly, gave the door a tap.

She took another step forward until he could feel the Glock's barrel at the base of his skull. "I've got reason to believe there's a federal agent in there. I'm not fucking around with you."

"What, you going to shoot me?"

"Try me." She pressed the muzzle harder against his spine. He lifted his knee again and drove his heel into the door. It flew open with a splintering of wood.

Kelly slipped to the side, keeping him in her sights but out of direct line of the door. From her angle, she could see a foot.

The bartender suddenly dove into the room. Kelly followed on instinct, clearing the door frame. In a flash she saw Rodriguez in a chair, bloodied almost beyond recognition. Then the bartender whipped around, a twin-barrel shotgun in his hands.

Thirteen

Madison sat on the cot, one hand wrapped around her knees, the other holding her DS Lite. The screen was flickering with a low battery warning. She'd done everything she could to reconfigure it, but the last bit of juice was draining away. It would stop transmitting in a few hours, tops.

She dropped her head in frustration. She'd known it was a long shot, chances were no one would be searching for the signal, but still. She'd allowed herself to hope, which was probably a mistake. Her only choice now was to give up on the idea, or ask Lurch if he'd charge it for her. There was a chance he'd do it. Since that torture session he'd been gentler with her, almost paternal. Small gestures, like the cake, but she got the sense that he didn't want to hurt her. Unlike his partner.

She shuddered involuntarily. She'd ask Lurch. After all, it wasn't like she had anything to lose. Once the battery was dead, it was just a hunk of metal anyway.

The door to her room swung open and she glanced up. The other guy stood there, leering at her. She paled and reflexively skittered away from him.

"Time for some more fun," he hissed. His attention shifted to her hand. "Whatcha got there, kitten?"

Madison tucked it under her legs. He crossed the room in three long strides and caught her wrist, twisting until she yelped in pain. His eyes narrowed as he yanked the DS Lite from her grasp.

"Where'd you get that?"

"It's mine."

"Fuckin' moron," he swore. "Which model is this?" He checked the back, then spat, "I'll kill him."

Madison shrank away from him, feeling the cold steel of the wall through her shirt.

"So you like playing games, huh?" he said. "That all you been doing?"

"What are you talking about?"

"Don't talk down to me, princess, I'm not like that retard. This thing has a GPS receiver. But then, I'm guessing you knew that."

Madison's heart sank. Tears rose hot in her eyes and spilled over. "I don't…"

"Yeah, sure you don't. You and that smart daddy of yours." He tucked the DS Lite into the back pocket of his jeans and bent down. His breath was hot and smelled like old meat. "Rain check for today, sweetheart. I gotta go deal with our friend. But don't you worry, I'll be back before you know it."

The door slammed behind him. Madison hugged herself tightly in an effort to stop shaking.

Randall Grant ran a hand through his hair. It felt thick with grease—he couldn't remember the last time he'd washed it. Even Barry, whose hygiene was notoriously lax, had moved his chair away when he entered the office. Not that he gave a shit anymore.

Randall was sitting in a park a few blocks from the facility. Absurdly ugly brown blocks formed a fountain that hadn't produced a drop of water in all the years he'd been coming here. Benches stood in forlorn formations, shedding paint and broken boards like molting skeletons. There was always a foreboding aura to the place, as if something bad was imminent. His colleagues shunned it for that reason. Which was why he liked it.

Those monsters had his daughter and he was sitting here. He'd followed their orders and gone back to the office, ignoring Barry's raised eyebrows, saying he felt better and had work to do. They hadn't called, which meant they'd probably succeeded in getting what they were after. And he was responsible for whatever they did with it. He'd left work early, pleading a resurgence of the flu, and came here to think.

Randall shook his head hard. If they had anyone competent involved, and he had no reason to doubt that, then thousands were at risk, possibly more. All because he'd been a greedy asshole.

The first request, nearly a year ago, had been harmless enough. One day a man had approached him in this park. Randall had retreated there to eat in silence, mulling over the recent collapse of his marriage and trying to figure out how the hell he was going to pay his attorney. When the guy slid onto the bench next to him he'd stood, prepared to move away. The last thing he wanted was to engage in casual conversation when his life was crumbling. Audrey had packed up the girls the week before and driven away in a blur of accusations and hysterical tears. He'd spent the past six nights padding around the house in the dark, as if they might miraculously rematerialize.

The guy stopped him, saying his name and asking for a minute of his time. Against his better instincts, Randall listened. All they wanted was a minor piece of information, for which they'd pay extravagantly. In fact, they offered almost double what he'd need to pay off his lawyer, enough to keep him satisfied through the entire litigation. Randall had asked for time to think it over. Went back to the office and found what they were interested in: nothing serious, just some financial records. They weren't even kept in a secure section of the building, but were tucked in an unlocked filing cabinet in storage. He had no idea why those records would interest anyone, he read them through twice and found nothing of note. So after a few days of consideration, he'd copied them and handed them over. No harm, no foul, he figured. Hell, he'd given this facility his blood, sweat and tears for his entire adult life, and how had they repaid him? Long hours and promotions that amounted to demotions, all of which contributed to the dissolution of his marriage. No, it was time the company helped him for a change, and why not now when he most needed it?

Thinking back he berated himself for his stupidity. Of course they had only asked for something minor that wouldn't raise many moral qualms. That's how they'd hooked him. Then a few months later, when what they wanted was more sensitive and he balked, they reminded him that he'd already committed treason. There was a stack of photographs documenting the exchange, a tape recording of him discussing it…everything they needed to disgrace him forever and send him away for life. His daughters were already barely speaking to him. Imagine if they thought he was a traitor.

So he'd complied. A few items here, others there. Nothing that would be too damaging if a foreign power got their hands on it. At least, that's what he told himself.

But then they asked for access to low-level radioactive

materials. And finally, Randall put his foot down. Despite all their promises to the contrary, he realized they would never stop. They would milk him until he was dead, fired, arrested or all three. He'd stalled for a few weeks, trying to get his affairs in order, figuring out what to tell Syd, how to break the news to his daughters. He lay awake nights breathing in fast, panicky pants, the walls closing in as if a cell was already mounting around him.

And then Madison disappeared. He'd already ruined his life, and now he'd probably destroyed hers as well. In retrospect it all seemed so absurd. If he was honest, all along he'd secretly expected to outwit the situation. The downside of always being the smartest guy in the room is that occasionally it made you do stupid things.

Well, now he'd given whoever was behind this all the power they'd ever need. And in doing so, he'd probably condemned thousands of people to death, his daughter among them.

Randall stood and absentmindedly brushed off the legs of his pants. He was done. He'd given Syd her chance, and so far it had only caused Madison to suffer more. Hiring her and Jake had been one more stalling tactic designed to stave off the real authorities. Everyone wanted to believe that when faced with a terrible situation they'd rise above it, become the hero that lay hidden inside them. It was a shame when that moment arrived and you turned out to be a coward.

Randall barely looked up as he strolled back to the facility, headed for the parking garage. By now Barry would have gone home, along with the bulk of the staff. Randall squeezed the Post-it in his hand, the number of the San Francisco FBI field office scrawled on it. Thanks to the facility's jamming measures he needed to drive outside the gates for his cell phone to work. He'd call as he drove, making sure they started searching for Madison while he crossed the bridge to turn himself in. The FBI had the most experience handling kidnappings, and maybe he could strike up an agreement to get housed with a better class of criminal. He'd call Syd afterward, that way she wouldn't have an opportunity to talk him out of it.

He was still a block from the parking garage gate, digging in his pocket for his ID card, when the van rolled up beside him. Distracted, he barely registered it. At the sound of a door rolling open he snapped his head to the side. By the time his brain processed the arms reaching out for him, it was already too late.

"Shit!" Kelly hissed, leaping back behind the shelter of the door frame. A sharp report, then the thunk of dozens of pieces of shot sinking into wood.

"Agent Jones!" one of the cops yelled.

"I'm okay," she called back. "Get the rest of them secured." The sound of sirens in the distance. "Better come out," she yelled. "Hands where I can see them!"

"Fuck you," the bartender growled.

Kelly glanced down, noting the trail of blood out the door. "Is Agent Rodriguez still alive?"

There was a chuckle, then the bartender called out, "For now. Anyone else comes in, though, it's gonna get ugly."

Kelly closed her eyes. It was already ugly. And the fact that Rodriguez wasn't communicating was cause for concern. She hadn't noticed a gag, but then she'd only had a second to process the scene. "Backup is going to be here in a minute. As of right now, we don't have anything but assault on you."

"I'm a three-striker, lady. Doesn't matter."

"It will when you're facing federal prison time. Believe me, they're a hell of a lot worse."

He laughed again. "You don't got a prison that can scare me."

Kelly recognized the accent, southern Tennessee. "You don't want to do this."

"You kidding? I been waiting all my life for a hostage like this one. Play my cards right, I leave here in a helicopter, end up in Aruba."

"It never ends that way."

"Nope. But if I'm going down, it'll be fighting."

Kelly chewed her lower lip and silently cursed Rodriguez for being such an idiot; the bartender, for being completely insane; and herself, for not leaving the FBI a few months ago. Only fifty-one FBI agents had been killed on active duty in the entire history of the Bureau. One of those had been her former partner. If she contributed another, she might as well turn in her badge tonight. "You really want that? Hostage negotiators, snipers, lasers on your chest? It'll get messy."

"Will it get me on TV?"

The bartender was smarter than he looked, and didn't sound scared. Not a good combination. Kelly decided to try another tack. "There are two shots in there—that's if you had a chance to reload. How far do you actually think that will get you?"

"Far enough."

The sound of running boots, then chatter as the responding officers explained the situation. Out of her peripheral vision she caught a flash of blue. Kelly spun, finger beside the trigger, but someone caught her hand. She let out her breath when she saw Phoenix SWAT lining up behind her, out of sight of the door. The commander leaned close and asked, "How many?"

"One that I've seen. Double-barrel shotgun, assume it's fully loaded. Agent Rodriguez is on a chair about three feet to the right."

The commander issued a series of complicated hand signals to the rest of the team. He put a hand on her shoulder, motioning for Kelly to move behind them and out of the way. She shifted down the line.

"Hey lady, I'm getting lonely in here."

She glanced at the commander, who nodded. "I'm still here," she responded.

"You know, I always had a soft spot for redheads. Maybe you should come in, get down on your knees and show me what you can—"

The rest of his thought was sliced off by an explosion. Kelly twisted her head away, seeing stars. The SWAT team swarmed the room on the heels of the flashbang, barking commands. Kelly waited, braced for the sound of gunfire. A full minute passed, the smoke slowly dissipating. Finally, the commander stuck his head out. "All clear if you want to come in."

Kelly entered the room. The bartender was on his belly, hands cuffed, tears streaming down his face. It would be a while before his vision and hearing returned to normal. *Shame that the damage wasn't permanent,* she thought, quickly examining Rodriguez. He was tied to a chair, suit and shirt streaked with blood. His face looked like someone had worked it over with a bag of nickels. Considering this crew, maybe they had. His head lolled to the side. He was conscious, but barely. She knelt beside him and untied his hands,

"Agent Rodriguez."

One eye squinted open.

"There's a bus outside, I told them to bring in a stretcher," the SWAT commander said.

Kelly nodded her thanks. "Did you get anything out of them?" she asked Rodriguez.

He made a strange sound, choked and garbled. It took her a second to recognize it as a laugh.

"That's all right. I'll see you at the hospital." She got out of the way as two paramedics rushed in a stretcher. She could press for more details after he'd been treated. Rodriguez looked like crap, but the kind of crap that was survivable. Hopefully he'd have something. From the look of things, they hadn't intended to keep him alive. No reason for them not to talk freely. At least if he'd over-heard something, the afternoon wouldn't be a total disaster.

Kelly stepped outside as the bartender was being led to a paddy wagon packed with his cohorts. "Not him," she called to the officer.

He turned, puzzled.

"He rides in a car alone. And I want him kept separate from the others at holding."

The officer shrugged. It was the same guy who looked at her disparagingly when he arrived as backup. "Not a problem." He led the bartender to his squad car, making sure to knock his head on the frame as he pushed him into the backseat. The bartender grunted but didn't say anything.

Kelly turned back to the SWAT commander. "You got this?"

"Sure. Worst of it's over, now we just secure the site. We'll get some patrol officers to handle it."

"Great. I'll give my statement at the station. Then I want to start on the interviews."

"Looks like it'll be a long night, huh?"

"That actually sounds optimistic," Kelly tossed back as she headed to her car.

Fourteen

Jake lay on the bed in his hotel room, hands crossed behind his head, remembering the last time he saw Kelly. She'd come up to New York for a visit, one of their typical morning train up Saturday/evening train home Sunday weekends. Never enough time, but at least he got to fall asleep with his arms around her for a change. After indulging in too much paella and sangria at a Spanish restaurant in the West Village, they decided to walk back to his place. For late May it was unseasonably warm, a mini heat wave, and the magnolia trees were in full bloom.

Kelly's dress was as red as her hair and she was laughing at something he'd said. She was framed by the glowing margins of a streetlight and he couldn't help himself, he gathered her in his arms and kissed her. Usually she'd never tolerate that, she hated public displays of affection. But that night she'd had enough wine to make her tipsy and she melted into him, his hands on the smooth silk of her waist, her fingers in his hair, one of those times when a kiss was so much more than the meeting of lips. It was as close to a perfect moment as he'd ever gotten.

His phone rang, shattering the reflection. He checked the caller ID: Syd.

"Hey," he said. "Find anything on Parrish or Krex?"

"Not a damn thing."

Jake heard a garbled loudspeaker in the background. "Where are you?"

"JFK. I'm flying out to meet you."

"Yeah?" Jake sat up and set his stocking feet on the floor. "You sure?"

"I'm sure that if I spend another day alone in that office, I'll be tempted to take a diver off the roof. Seriously, we need to hire a secretary." Syd paused before continuing, "Besides, I'll have my laptop and cell phone. No need for me to be chained to a desk."

Jake grinned. "I didn't realize the decorators got around to installing the chains."

"Funny guy. You okay with this?"

"Sure, I could use the company. Another day with Randall and I might be tempted to take a diver myself." He was going to ask what she saw in the guy, but let it drop. "I was wondering how long you'd tolerate being an indoor cat."

"Yeah, well. It was worth a try. Where do we start?"

"Tomorrow I'm cruising by a biker clubhouse in Stockton—the warden's file says Dante Parrish hung out there before he got arrested. Figure some of his old prison buddies might be hanging around."

"I'm sure they'll be thrilled to talk to you." Syd scoffed.

"Probably not. But you, on the other hand, they're gonna love."

"I do have a way with a Harley."

Jake laughed. "I'll bet. Anyway, we might find someone Parrish pissed off who knows where he is."

"Sounds like a plan. I'm on the red-eye, meet me at Oakland Airport around six tomorrow morning."

"You got it, boss. Enjoy the middle seat."

Syd snorted. "Please. Like I'd fly anything but first class."

Jake's reply was cut off. He caught himself smiling as he hung up. Syd reminded him a lot of his first girlfriend, Lana, a feisty girl who grew up on a ranch and could rustle a calf or win a beauty pageant, depending on what the occasion called for. She'd been exuberant, passionate…pretty much the antithesis of Kelly. Jake shook his head. He knew that Kelly wasn't thrilled about his new business partner. He first met Syd when she infiltrated a smuggling ring that was trying to utilize his former boss's ships. Sure, she was damned attractive, but he'd never viewed her as anything other than a friend. And he was smart enough to know that a relationship with her would probably follow the same track as all his earlier ones: six months of intensity before the crash and burn. At his age, he preferred stability.

Jake stood and stripped out of his clothes, glancing at the clock. It was just after nine, still early, but tomorrow was likely to be a long day. He called Kelly to say goodnight, got her voice mail again, and hung up. Moodily, he gazed back up at the ceiling.

The Phoenix police chief closed the door and joined her at the observation window. "Is there a skinhead convention in town?"

"Apparently," Kelly said, crossing her arms over her chest. They both watched as the detective tried again.

"Why did you attack Agent Rodriguez?"

"John Harper, Private, 54687."

"I gotta say, you're making a big mistake. All the other

guys are rolling, you're going to be left holding the ball. Time for you to smarten up."

The guy stared levelly at the wall opposite, as if the detective wasn't even there. "John Harper, Private, 54687."

The detective shifted in his chair to gaze at them through the one-way glass and shrugged.

"What is that crap?" the chief demanded.

"Far as I can gather name, rank and serial number," Kelly said with a frown.

"What, he's former military?"

"Nope." Kelly nodded toward the file on the table. "Lifer, in and out of prison since he was fourteen. So I'm guessing that's his prison number."

"So what the hell?"

Kelly shook her head. "I don't know. They seem to think they're some sort of military group."

"Under whose orders?"

"I'm guessing the bartender, Patrick Croll. He seemed to be in charge when I was there."

The chief eyed the skinhead. "This connected to the Morris thing?"

"Maybe. Rodriguez was following up a lead related to that 911 call."

"The tip on the stash house?"

Kelly nodded.

The chief shook his head. "Boy, you folks love to make our lives harder. We find the gun that killed Morris in a house filled with scumbags, along with a pile of artillery that would make bin Laden blush. But no, you gotta bring skinheads into this."

"They beat Rodriguez up, and were probably going to kill him," Kelly pointed out. "Doesn't seem like they're exactly innocent."

"Lady, I don't want to tell you your job, but someone named Rodriguez walks in there, it's a toss-up whether they'll kill him for being Mexican or being a Fed. Doesn't mean they know jack-shit." The chief held up a hand to silence her. "Things are different down here, especially after what happened to Duke. Can't go strolling into a place like that, counting on a badge to save you. Shit, I wouldn't go in with anything less than a SWAT team."

Kelly stopped herself from retorting that Rodriguez wasn't supposed to go in alone. Regardless of how she felt, she wouldn't rat him out to Phoenix P.D. She wouldn't even tell McLarty unless she had to.

The chief was watching her out of the corner of his eye. Inside the room both detective and con had settled into an uneasy détente. The chief leaned forward and rapped on the window. The detective stood, clearly relieved, and gathered up the papers on the table.

"You see their files?" he asked Kelly.

"Sure, I skimmed them."

"Notice what they all had in common?" He leaned forward. "Drugs. Every last one of these guys has gone down for possession or intent at least once in their miserable lives."

"So?"

"So the MS-13 squad is encroaching on the skinheads' turf, and they decide to send a message by ratting out their stash house. The Morris gun being there was a coincidence."

"Maybe," Kelly conceded. "But look at this guy. Does he strike you as a rat? Seems to me they'd settle it another way, not get the police involved."

"They use us as much as we use them," the chief said darkly. "Anyway, Agent Jones, I spoke to ASAC McLarty today, told him you were almost done here."

"You had no right to do that," she protested.

"I can't afford to assign officers to a task force that could drag on forever, not when I've got three punks we can charge with this. Especially since they probably did it." He shot her a pointed look. "I also don't have the man power to save G-men who get in over their heads."

Kelly bit her lip, determined not to rise to the bait.

"So wrap this up, Agent Jones."

"I'll see what I can do," she finally replied.

Seemingly satisfied, the chief left the room. Kelly watched as Harper worked his jaw, gaze still locked on the same spot. She'd already spent an hour with the bartender. He recited the same litany, the only difference being that he leered at her the entire time. The captain was right, of course. The 911 call was already a tenuous connection to the Morris case, and extending it to what happened at the bar was insanely circumstantial. But something about it nagged at her, especially considering the way these guys were behaving. This level of organization was unusual for low-level convicts. It was hard to shake the sense that someone out there was manipulating them. Up close the case looked airtight, but the farther away you got, the more it stank.

Her cell phone buzzed and she glanced at the screen. It was Jake. She repressed a pang of guilt. She hadn't returned any of his calls today. Partly because she didn't feel like explaining everything that had happened, it was still too fresh. But more than that, lately the distance between them felt like a gulf, and not just because they lived separate lives in separate cities. When they spent so much time apart, it was sometimes hard to remember what they had when they were together. It almost felt like a different life, one she'd read about but hadn't actually lived. In a way this separation made it easier for her to compartmentalize. When she was at work she immersed herself in her cases, then with Jake she tried to set all that aside. For some reason, the prospect of eventually combining the two was terrifying.

With a sigh she powered down her phone. It had been a long day. Given some time to ponder the true meaning of the three strikes law, maybe one of these guys would cave. If not, she'd have to come up with something else.

Kelly debated stopping by the hospital to talk to Rodriguez, then decided he'd already been through enough for one day. And the truth was she was so tired and angry, she didn't trust herself to stay professional. He'd put a lot of lives at risk by not following protocol. Chances were he'd be too sedated to talk anyway. Better to get a goodnight's sleep, then she could deal with him in the morning.

Dante perched on the edge of the couch, hands on his knees. He'd only been in Jackson's house once before, on another late night visit. That time, though, he'd been bringing good news. It was much more difficult to enjoy the opulent surroundings with Jackson raging around the room.

"Explain to me again how these orders were misinterpreted."

"I—"

"Didn't you instruct them to be discreet when they made that call?"

Dante shrugged. "Yeah, sure. I told them to go somewhere no one knew them. Somewhere in a spic neighborhood."

"And why, exactly, did they not follow that order?"

Dante wiped sweat off his forehead with the back of his hand. Never in his life had he felt so helpless. And incredibly guilty, even though he personally had done nothing wrong. These were his men, and Jackson counted on him to make sure they executed every stage of the mission perfectly. They'd failed him, so he'd failed Jackson. "They got lazy."

"They got lazy!" Jackson roared, emphasizing each word. "This was the most important part of their mission. But they used the pay phone directly outside the bar?"

Dante said feebly, "They said there aren't many pay phones anymore—"

"And they're right!" Jackson jabbed a finger into Dante's chest, and he winced. "*You* should have provided them with cell phones. Untraceable, disposable phones. Why didn't you?"

"I figured that's what they'd use." Dante said in a small voice. "I told them how important it was—"

"So you trusted them to figure that out for themselves?"

Dante simply nodded.

"And that's why I'm disappointed with you, Dante. A leader never leaves a single decision to the men beneath him. He dictates their every move, their every action. Success on the battlefield depends on it. Is that clear?"

"Yes, Mr. Burke," Dante said, after a long pause indicated he was meant to respond.

"Good. About that other thing, is it in process?"

Dante nodded. "They should be in Houston by dawn."

"Excellent." Jackson waved a hand, dismissing him. Dante paused on the threshold.

"Sir, Sergeant Croll wants to know who their lawyers are."

Jackson's eyes narrowed. "What lawyers?"

"It was something I'd promised them, sir. Since you told me they'd be covered…" Dante's voice trailed off under the force of Jackson's gaze.

"That coverage was intended for active cells that accomplished their goals."

"Yes sir, but considering, you know, what they did..." Dante focused on the floor. "It would keep them from shooting off their mouths. Not that they would," he added hurriedly. "But if they knew you were looking out for them, they'd have even less reason..."

He raised his eyes to find Jackson regarding him coldly. One thing he'd learned in three years of working for the man, he did not like to lose, and this definitely fell into the loss column.

"Get them someone. But make sure it doesn't lead back to me."

"Yes sir." Dante quickly left the room, barely breathing until he'd crossed the threshold.

JULY 1

Fifteen

Jake fought through the traffic idling curbside. He spotted Syd standing at the end of the platform, dressed entirely in black. It took another five minutes to get to her. He popped the trunk and she threw her bag in, slammed it shut, and practically dove into the front seat.

"So how was first class?" he asked, noting the flush in her cheeks. Clearly she was excited about something.

"Mediocre. They didn't even have warm nuts." She pulled off her sunglasses and leaned over to punch an address into the GPS. He caught a whiff of shampoo as a strand of her hair brushed his face.

"Hey, I already got that—" he protested, but she cut him off.

"Change of plans. We got a hit on the GPS signal from Madison's game console."

"No shit?" He raised an eyebrow.

"I know. I didn't think it would amount to anything, but had one of my guys tackle it anyway. And lo and behold, it pinged late last night. Got the message from him when I landed."

"So we know where she is?"

"Well, we know where the DS Lite was. It stopped transmitting a few hours ago, so we need to hurry. Should be there in less than an hour unless you drive like a granny."

"I drive just fine." Jake snorted. To prove it, he veered across two lanes of traffic, darting onto the on-ramp for 880 North. "So are we calling in the cavalry?"

"No need. I've got a team ready."

"Yeah? That was quick."

"I put them on standby when Randall called. Figured since she was taken from SFO, she might still be in the Bay Area."

"Not bad, partner," Jake said grudgingly.

"They'll have vests and sidearms for us."

"You sure about this? If things go south, there could be a lot of fallout…"

"Believe me, I trust this team a hell of a lot more than some Feds who've never been outside Hogan's Alley. If she's still alive, we'll get her."

"All right," Jake said, despite a twinge of unease. He'd never been a stickler for the rules either, but like most former operatives Syd followed a completely different code. For them, rules didn't exist. And he was more than a little concerned about what she considered a crack team. "So where am I headed?"

"Benicia. I've got to make some calls to find out if everything is ready, so shut up and drive. I'll tell you more when we get closer."

Madison pressed her ear to the door. She'd been up most of the night waiting for it to fling open again, terrified of what that asshole was going to do. She was pretty certain they were going to kill her.

In both hands, Madison clutched the metal tray they brought her meals on. It was old, rusty around the edges, with *Olympia Brewing Company* in fancy scrawl above a painting of a lady in a hat. It had always struck her as incongruous, especially now. Usually Lurch came to take it away, but last night he'd never rematerialized. She wondered if he couldn't face her, knowing what was about to happen.

The tray was a flimsy weapon, but better than nothing. She planned on waiting in the shadows beside the door. When it swung open she'd launch herself forward, try to catch him square across the face. Hopefully startle him enough to make a break for it. It was a long shot, and she knew it. It didn't matter how many push-ups she did, he'd still easily overpower her. But maybe she'd buy herself enough time to get above deck. She had to try. And if it turned out they were in the middle of the ocean, she would jump overboard and drown. That was still preferable to whatever sick torture he had planned.

After the man stormed off she'd heard arguing. It sounded like just the two of them, but it was hard to tell with the echoes and distortion. She pictured Lurch standing with his head down, getting yelled at. For some reason that hadn't made her feel better.

Nothing but silence for hours now. Usually they brought breakfast right around dawn, but based on the fragments of light seeping into the room it was already late morning. Madison wondered what the hell was going on.

Footsteps. She inhaled sharply, pressing harder against the door. Someone was coming. It was impossible to tell who, since each step resonated against the metal floor. Madison realized she was hyperventilating, the tray shaking in her hands, and she fought to calm down. This was it. She had one shot at getting out of here.

She stepped back into the shadows, listening to the sound of the latch being unbolted, metal grinding against metal. Her knuckles were white, blood pounded in her ears. She braced herself as the door slowly swung open.

It felt like an eternity passed before a silhouette crossed the threshold. Madison leaped forward with a slight cry, swinging the tray with the full force of her weight behind it.

A grunt: she'd miscalculated. It wasn't the other man, but Lurch standing there. Instead of the face she had caught him in the chest. He caved backward. Her eyes widened as they met his. He looked confused. Regaining her senses Madison lunged past him, tripping over her feet. She caught herself from falling and raced down the corridor. Lurch yelled something but she didn't pay attention, didn't focus on anything but running as hard and fast as she could.

After a second Madison's brain caught up to her feet and she realized the corridor was ending. A narrow hallway branched left and she took it. She sped past small doors molting gray paint; no time to check them, she'd have to hope that the way up was obvious, a ladder or a staircase. She was suddenly overwhelmed by a desperate desire to see the sun. Tears flooded her eyes and she shook her head to clear them.

The hallway dead-ended in another corridor. Madison skidded to a stop. No sign of an exit in either direction. She chewed her lip, wondering if she should have checked the doors.

Suddenly, Lurch appeared at the far end of the hall. Even from here she could see his features twisted with anger. She whirled and sped in the opposite direction, praying to herself, "Please God, don't let him catch me, please…"

The door facing her was latched with a heavy metal bar. She almost slammed into it, caught herself, and strained to lift it. She could hear Lurch pounding toward her. The latch fought her efforts, and she cried out in frustration. It suddenly gave with a shriek and she yanked the door open, almost crying with relief at the sight of a ladder.

Madison scrambled up, panting. She was in a narrow tube that seemed to go on forever, at the very top she could make out a hatch. She felt the ladder shift and glanced over her shoulder. Lurch was at the bottom. For a large man he moved surprisingly quickly. He was only two stories behind her and gaining fast.

Madison tried to quicken her pace but her arms and legs shook from the effort. Looking up, she had another forty feet to go. She prayed the hatch wouldn't be locked.

"Madison!"

She jerked at the sound of her name and nearly fell. A small voice in her head perversely noted this was the first time Lurch had spoken to her since the airport. She focused all her energy upward: thirty feet left. Her heart was battering her rib cage. Sweat poured down her face but she didn't dare wipe it away, her hands were already slick with it. Twenty feet. She yelped as one hand slipped off a rung and she dangled, almost tumbling backward. Lurch was closer now, less than fifteen feet away. She gritted her teeth and swung the hand back up, gripping with all her might. Gathering herself, she resumed her climb.

She reached the hatch. Madison pressed against it, arms shaking. It didn't budge. Once again she strained. With a slight groan, the hatch swung up and out.

Madison felt a hand swipe at her ankle and kicked it away. Gasping, she hauled herself out, slipping off the ridge at the top and landing in a pile on the deck. Lurch's head poked out behind her. She scrambled to her feet and spun, running again, not caring where she went as long as it was away from him.

Acclimated to the shadowy bowels of the ship, Madison was blinded by the dazzling sunlight. Squinting, she stumbled repeatedly on detritus strewn about the deck. She could still hear Lurch pursuing her, but it sounded as though he'd slowed, and a ray of hope shot through her chest. The air was fresh, salty. She was outside. She might even get away.

Her eyes finally adjusted, and she realized she was careening toward the edge of the deck. The railing was ten feet in front of her. Madison whirled, scanning in the opposite direction. Her heart sank. The boat was moored in the middle of a string of others. Off in the distance past the farthest turret, the shimmering brown of land. But no way to get there, at least not that she could see. And it looked too far to reach by swimming. She stood for a moment, gasping.

"Stop."

Madison spun around. Lurch was stumbling toward her, clutching his belly, nearly bent double. Her lip curled—at least the bastard was suffering as much as she was.

"No way off," Lurch said, shaking his head. He advanced toward her, one arm outstretched. "C'mon, now…"

She shook her head, backing away until her heels hit cold steel: the side of the boat.

He beckoned with his fingers. "It's okay, I promise."

"Go to hell," Madison said. She glanced back, then climbed up on the lip of the gunwale. She swayed slightly, arms flung out for balance.

Lurch's eyes widened with surprise as he shouted, "Don't!"

Madison ignored him. Tears streamed down her face as she turned and dove forward.

Sixteen

"Knock, knock." Kelly rapped tentatively on the door.

Rodriguez held up a finger and she frowned. He was on his cell, sitting up in bed with a notepad on his lap.

Kelly waited irritably for him to finish. Most of the night she'd tossed and turned, debating what the captain had said. She'd never been one of those agents who took the easy way out, dismissing inconsistent information just to get a case over and done with. She liked to think the victims deserved more. In spite of everything she clung to the belief that her job was to seek out the truth, even when it was inconvenient.

But as dawn broke, she decided to blame Morris's murder on the MS-13 stash house crew. The Phoenix P.D. would be happy, her boss would be happy, things in the media would settle down. Despite the decision, she still couldn't sleep. Kelly lay there watching early morning sneak through the worn drapes in her hotel room, wondering what she was turning into. She didn't know herself anymore.

She shifted her attention back to Rodriguez. He looked like hell. His face was swollen almost twice its normal size and crisscrossed with ragged black stitches. His nose pointed left, and a gauze bandage stuck out from the shock of hair on his right side. She felt a surge of sympathy. Jerk though he was, she wouldn't have wished that much abuse on anyone.

He clicked the phone shut with a snap and said, "Who do you love?"

It looked like he was trying to grin through the pulp that was now his face. Kelly arched an eyebrow. "I've got to be honest, you still don't top my list."

"Well, that's about to change."

"You've been working?" Kelly asked, dubious. "On pain meds?"

"Told them not to give me any," Rodriguez said. He shifted slightly, then winced. "See?"

"That seems a little extreme. You were badly injured."

"Let's just say I'm not someone who can take pain meds." He avoided her eyes.

"Oh," Kelly replied, surprised she hadn't known Rodriguez was a recovering addict. That information should have been in his file.

"Anyway—" he cleared his throat "—I heard the assholes from the bar weren't talking. So I spent the morning tracking down the owner."

"That was smart," Kelly admitted grudgingly. "Who is it?"

Rodriguez held up a finger. "That's where things get interesting. That dive bar has a paper trail a mile long. Dead-ends at a shell company."

"Really?"

"I got a friend at the IRS to do some legwork for me. If you sort through all the subsidiaries and parent companies, there's one corporation at the top. Hard to find since it was registered offshore, but what can I say, my friend owed me a favor. And we got lucky."

"So who owns it?"

He plowed on. "The Acme Lounge was initially bought by a group called Lion's Share. Shell company, there's nothing else there." Clearly Rodriguez had done a lot of work on this, and wanted to present every detail so that fact was not lost on her. Kelly repressed the urge to sigh. "Lion's Share is owned by Diamond Tooth, which is a division of Fiddle and Flute…"

"Fiddle and Flute?"

Rodriguez held up a hand. "Wait, it gets better. Anyway, five or six other dummy corps, then I got to the pièce de résistance." He held up the notepad.

Kelly leaned in to read it, then shook her head. "Omega? Never heard of it."

"Really?" He looked startled. "Not a fan of the business section, huh?"

"Why would I read the business section?" Kelly furrowed her brow.

"Because you can't retire on what the Bureau pays you, that's for sure. Gotta invest on your own." Rodriguez shook his head, then winced again. "Damn, I can't blink without hurting. Omega is one of the largest corporations in Arizona. They own a big chunk of the Southwest, everything from communications to mining. And guess who the CEO is?"

"I haven't a clue."

"Jackson Burke. One of Duke Morris's closest friends and a major contributor to every campaign run by an immigration reform candidate. He personally footed the bill for that proposition in Texas that would have mandated immediate deportation for anyone without a green card."

Kelly vaguely remembered something about that, but to be honest she didn't follow the news closely unless it related directly to her cases. "So you're suggesting that Burke had Morris killed, and pinned the blame on a Salvadoran street gang?"

"That's exactly what I'm saying."

"But why? Especially if they were friends? It sounds crazy."

Rodriguez shrugged. "Maybe he is crazy. Or maybe when that proposition failed, he decided to try a different approach. Flame public sentiment against illegals, try to force a bill through that way. I hear the Senate resuscitated that immigration reform measure today."

"Still. It's hard to see the head of a major corporation ordering executions."

Rodriguez snorted. "You kidding? Those guys are ruthless. The Iraq War was all about Blackwater and the oil companies. They got the government to do their dirty work for them."

Kelly didn't answer. She was never one for conspiracy theories, and there were a lot of holes in what Rodriguez was postulating. But it might warrant more investigation.

"I almost forgot to mention." He tapped his pen down the names on the list. "Featherwoods, The Sackett Corporation…a lot of these terms are associated with white supremacists."

"Seriously?" Kelly frowned. "Why be so obvious?"

"Probably a little inside joke, an offshore bank wouldn't examine the documents closely. And like I said, these companies don't actually do anything, they only exist to shift money around."

Kelly crossed her arms, thinking. After a minute she said, "So can we get a line on what else those companies are involved with? Buildings they own, that sort of thing."

Rodriguez cocked his head to the side. "Good idea. Maybe we find something else that proves they're dirty."

"Exactly. Because this is all good work, Rodriguez."
He appeared to flush at her praise, but it was hard to tell
with the bruises. "But for us to accuse a CEO of murdering a senator, we're going to need a hell of a lot more."

"Yeah, I got you." Rodriguez glanced back at his pad.
"So I'll call my friend back, see if she can find everything
filed under these companies."

"Perfect. I'm going to take another crack at your
buddies from the bar."

"Give them my best." He smiled tightly. "And by that
I mean if you get a chance, kick the shit out of them."

"That's not really my thing, Rodriguez." Kelly smiled
wryly and stood, awkwardly patting his leg. "Get some
rest. You look terrible."

"Gee, thanks." He leaned back against the pillows and
closed his eyes. "Maybe I will take a nap."

She was almost at the door when he called out, "Hey,
Jones?"

"Yes?"

"Finally feels like I have a partner."

She opened her mouth to reply, but he was already
snoring.

Randall lay on his side, hands tied behind his back,
ankles knotted together. He had no idea where he was.
They'd placed a sack over his head that smelled terrible,
like it used to hold dead animals. Initially he'd gagged
and almost vomited, but caught himself. These guys
probably wouldn't keep him from drowning in his own
puke. They'd knocked him out with an injection, and
when he came to, the distinctive white noise of a plane
surrounded him. Now he jostled from side to side. Had
to be in a car, or maybe a truck, since the floor felt rough
beneath him.

Still, he was alive, that was saying something. Randall wondered what the hell they wanted. He'd already given them everything they'd asked for, and obviously couldn't provide information from outside the facility.

And Madison—what had they done with her? Probably already dead, he thought with a sinking in his gut. He'd failed her. He should have gone to the FBI as soon as she was taken, told them the truth and suffered the consequences. Now he'd condemned them both.

He started crying, sobs muffled by the sack. The sound of a truck panel sliding up stopped him. Light seeped through the coarse material, and he squinted.

Someone barked a command and Randall was dragged to his feet. They lowered him roughly to the ground and he landed hard on one knee. He yelped as someone yanked him up by the elbow. The sack was ripped away.

"Hope you had a nice ride." It was the guy with the shaved head who had initially recruited him, wearing that same smug grin.

"What the hell is going on?" Randall demanded, voice quavering. He was in an enormous warehouse the size of an airplane hangar. A few feet away he saw a makeshift laboratory, complete with a glove box and remote control panel. A dozen yards farther, three large flatbeds lined up as if in formation. A group of men encircled him, all huge, bald and menacing.

"Got another job for you, Grant."

"Fuck you." Randall said. Despite his fury, it came out sounding weak. "I'm done helping you."

The man's bushy eyebrows shot up. "We still have your daughter."

"You've probably already killed her."

"Why would we do that when we still need her?" The

man cocked his head to the side. He had an unnerving smile, as if he was wondering how Randall would taste.

"So show me some proof." A glimmer of something behind the man's eyes. Randall stood taller. "I said, you want my help, prove that my daughter is still alive."

The man's eyes narrowed. One of the other thugs lurched forward, but stopped when the first raised his hand. "Sure, why not. Meanwhile, you can get acquainted with our little project."

"Food first. I haven't eaten since you grabbed me. And I've got to take a piss," Randall said, emboldened by their concession.

The man examined him for another moment, as if amused by the show of bravado. After a minute he said, "Hulk, take him to the head."

A blond guy with a ridiculous handlebar moustache shoved Randall forward. His eyes locked on something clipped to Hulk's belt: a dosimeter, used to measure radiation levels. The first circle was tinted, showing a measurement of 5 rads—still in the normal range. As Randall was marched toward a small door, he swept his gaze across the trucks, realization suddenly dawning. Dear God, they wanted him to help build a dirty bomb. And he was the one who had provided the radioactive materials. If handled correctly, there was enough iridium to render a major city uninhabitable for years. Hell, more than years—decades.

Randall's jaw tightened. Whatever happened to him and Madison, here he drew the line. And if he was going to die anyway, he planned on taking these assholes with him.

Seventeen

Jake strapped on his vest, checking out the rest of the team under lowered eyelids. Four men who all had that Delta Force look, close-cropped hair and cold eyes. Probably former Special Ops soldiers who survived the fighting in Afghanistan and Iraq, finished their tours and decided they were done with the military. That's what his brother tried to do, after more than twenty years of active service. What they didn't realize was that life and the experiences that came with it weren't things you could just walk away from. Most of them ended up returning less than a year later, either reenlisting or working for a private sector company like Blackwater that offered a real paycheck. Or, apparently, with The Longhorn Group.

"Any of you done hostage rescue before?"

They all raised their gaze in unison. He practically expected them to bark, "Sir, yes, sir!"

The one closest to Jake, a kid who couldn't have been more than twenty-five but looked like he ate nails for breakfast, said, "My unit was in Afghanistan for two tours, sir. We did more than ten snatch and grabs."

"Yeah? I thought only one hostage total had been rescued in Afghanistan."

They exchanged glances. "One that you heard of," someone muttered.

Jake ignored the jab. "So how many of those were considered successful missions?"

"They were all successful, sir. That doesn't mean everyone survived."

One of the other guys grunted a laugh. They went back to checking their gear.

Jake made sure his HK USP .45's clip was full and that he had two backups. He wasn't crazy about this plan. Without doing any recon they were going in blind. There could be two guys holding Madison, or twenty. They might be dealing with a couple of hack ex-cons or well-trained mercenaries. And they didn't even have time to get the lay of the land.

Twenty minutes earlier Syd had left to requisition a boat. Jake heard a dull roar in the distance and saw her at the helm of a Zodiac, skirting the waves. She'd originally wanted to approach as a dive team to maintain silence and the element of surprise, but Jake wasn't keen on the idea. It was going to be hard enough getting on the boats without having to deal with thirty pounds of dive equipment as well as the rest of the stuff they needed. When she announced the change of plans, he'd gotten a few glances from the Delta guys. He shrugged it off. Didn't matter what they thought of him. The important thing now was to get Madison out alive. If they hadn't killed her already.

They were on the outskirts of Benicia, about forty miles northeast of San Francisco. Jake gazed across the water. Suisun Bay was a ship graveyard, where decommissioned naval vessels were stored until someone decided what the hell to do with them. Dubbed "The Mothball Fleet," everything from Liberty ships to destroyers were tied side by side in daisy chains. Proud warriors of decades' worth of wars, they were now rusted and fading, all but forgotten. Apparently someone had remembered them. It was the perfect place to stash a hostage. Barely monitored and protected from prying eyes thanks to their distance from shore. And once aboard, you were in the ultimate defensible position. It wasn't a location someone like Mack Krex would have come up with on his own, that was for sure. Jake wondered again who the hell they were dealing with.

Syd waved them over. One of the Delta guys grabbed the bowline, holding it while the rest of the team passed their gear into the boat. Syd kept the engine running. As they climbed in, the boat rocked and sank almost to the gunwales. Syd was dressed the same way they were: gray camo, armor, weapons at both hips and an ankle holster. Her blond hair was tied back, cheeks flushed with excitement. "Let's go," she said.

They were approaching from the far side of the bay, to lessen the chances of being spotted. They'd debated going in street clothes, hiding the weapons until they were on board, but decided against it. Not many people would believe this group was out for a pleasure cruise.

Jake clutched a rope strung along the port side and watched the ships grow larger. It was hard to ignore his growing apprehension. He chalked some of it up to the usual nerves before an operation, but partly it was also the sense that this had spun out of his control. Syd was clearly holding the reins now. Even though this had been her case to begin with, her personal connection, he wasn't sure he liked that. She seemed to be enjoying herself a little too much, especially considering what was at stake.

There were eighty-four vessels total, strung together in clusters ranging from nine to eighteen. And Madison could be on any of them. If the GPS signal was still active they could have pinpointed her location, but even from this proximity Syd wasn't getting a read. It could take them all day to search, risking discovery by the Maritime Administration guards who periodically patrolled. All in all, Jake figured they had a hundred to one chance of everything turning out okay. Not the kind of odds he'd bet a life on.

They neared the first string of boats. Everyone stiffened, straightening slightly in their seats. They were about a nautical mile offshore. The water was flat and gray around them, matching the hulls. The sheer size of the boats was awesome. They rose out of the bay like giant monoliths, cold and impersonal.

"How the hell do we get on board?" Jake asked.

"I'm going to anchor at the far side, we'll throw a line up and climb," Syd responded. The rest of the team nodded as if this was something they did twice every day. Jake groaned internally and wished he'd spent more time in the gym. He wasn't exactly in rope-scaling shape.

Syd eased the Zodiac around the port side of the last boat in the chain, the farthest point from shore. She was careful to stay in the shadows. Jake had to hand it to her, she was good. Impetuous but careful, an odd combination. As they rounded the stern, Jake caught a movement. He squinted against the reflection off the water, raising a hand to his eyes.

"Holy shit," he said.

Syd followed his gaze. In the next line of boats a hundred yards away, they saw a small figure racing across the deck of a destroyer. A larger, lumbering man was in pursuit. Syd raised a set of binoculars to her eyes.

"That's her!" she said, throttling the motor. "Looks like it's game on, boys!"

* * *

Madison felt like her chest was about to explode. When she jumped off the ship, she hit the wooden block separating the boats hard, almost falling into the water below. She edged along it, then stood and gathered herself, vaulting a four-foot gap to reach the deck of the next boat. She landed funny, twisting her ankle. She rolled and clutched it, gasping in pain. Lurch's head popped into view less than ten feet away. His initial expression of shock quickly transformed to rage, and he clambered over the railing, prepared to make the same jump. Madison scrambled to her feet and ran.

She'd had to repeat the maneuver twice already, bracing herself before jumping, praying she wouldn't miss and drop into the chasm between the boats, hitting the icy water stories below. She didn't look down, focusing instead on where she needed to land. Her ankle throbbed with each step but she ignored the pain. She didn't let herself think about what she'd do when she reached the final boat. The shoreline still looked impossibly far away, and she'd never been a strong swimmer. But she wasn't going to give up now.

Madison heard a loud thud and swiveled, hopping awkwardly on her good foot to take some of the weight. Lurch had nearly missed the last jump. He was hanging from the wooden block by both hands, fingers flexed as he struggled for a purchase. He looked at her, eyes wild. "Madison! Help!"

She took a step toward him, then caught herself. What was she, insane? If she helped save him, he'd kill her. Already she could see him straining, trying to haul one leg up and over. She turned away. Another dozen feet to the next jump. She took a deep breath and started running again.

* * *

No one spoke. The roar of the engine would have drowned out their words anyway. Syd was alongside the ship where they'd seen Madison. Unfortunately the looming hull blocked their view of what was happening on deck.

Syd pointed two ships down. "We board there!" she yelled. "By that time she'll have reached us."

"Unless she falls first," Jake said, eyeing the gap between the ships. Jesus, the kid had some nerve. He wondered how she'd gotten away. They'd only seen one guy chasing her, so maybe that was all they'd have to deal with. It was almost too much to hope for. Hard to believe someone who had organized the rest of this operation so well would only assign a single guard.

Less than a minute later, Syd had maneuvered the Zodiac alongside their target. The rest of the team was ready; one of them already held a grappling hook with a rope attached. He balanced carefully as Syd cut the engine and they drifted. Aiming, he spun it twice in a circle to build momentum before releasing it. The rope flew up, unraveling as it went. It cleared the gunwale and he tugged until there was no slack. After leaning back to test it with his body weight, he nodded to the others. It was a stirrup line, Jake noted with relief, a sort of rope ladder used for scaling buildings. A hell of a lot easier than trying to muscle his way up with jumars. One after another the team climbed.

Clearing the gap between the ships was becoming increasingly difficult. Madison was tired, and her ankle throbbed. Running, she kept most of the weight on her good foot, glancing off the toes of the other and ignoring the twinge. But to jump she had to use both, and it was hard to land without at least bumping her bad ankle.

She took a deep breath and focused on the opposite deck. Bent her knees and launched herself in the air. The same terror in her belly as the gap opened up beneath her, a hundred-foot drop to icy waters, seconds that felt like minutes as she waited to plummet downward, cartwheeling off the hull…then she was clear of the gunwale and hit the metal deck hard, trying to catch herself on one foot. But this time she tripped, and something snapped. Her left foot hung off to the side at a strange angle. Frustrated, Madison pounded the deck with her fists, willing herself not to black out.

Her head reeled when she tried to sit up, and she awkwardly shifted onto one hip. She eased to her knees and pressed back on the ball of her good foot. Madison straightened slowly, but in spite of her precautions the injured foot shifted and she gasped in pain. There was a roaring in her ears as she forced herself to stand, this time balanced entirely on her right foot. She hopped forward one step, then another. Tears streamed down her face but she kept going. Another hop. The approaching footsteps slowed. She made it three more feet before an arm wrapped around her from behind.

"Stupid bitch," Lurch said in her ear.

"She didn't make it this far," Jake said, scanning the deck. He hadn't heard a splash, but it was a big fall, he might not have. He peered across the decks of the other ships but couldn't see anything.

"All right. I want to fan out, clear each deck before we go on to the next boat," Syd said, keeping her voice low. "Remember, objective is to retrieve the girl alive."

The men spread out. Jake crossed to the far side of the ship and climbed up on the cable rigging. He scanned the waters below. Aside from seagulls bobbing and the gentle slap of waves against the hull, there was nothing visible. He waved to Syd, indicating that he was going on to the next boat. She shook her head vigorously, but he ignored her.

"Jake, hold back," Syd's voice crackled from his waist. Damn, he'd nearly forgotten about their MBITRs. They each had a Multiband Inter Team Radio clipped to their vests. Syd had ordered them to maintain radio silence until they got a lock on Madison's position. Jake decided this was the perfect time to heed that request and turned his volume knob off.

He cleared the gap in a single leap, landing in a crouch on the three-foot wide wooden block separating the boats, then vaulted again to land on deck. He straightened slowly, gun ready, scanning from side to side. It was amazing how that training came back, years later he still moved instinctively when the situation called for it.

He moved forward as silently as possible, although he had to assume the kidnappers heard the Zodiac approach. He cleared the first turret, checking quickly to see if anyone was hiding behind it. The deck appeared empty. Jake heard a hard thud on the deck behind him, glanced back and saw two other members of the team. They fanned out around him, weapons drawn and held at chest level.

They were about to jump to the next ship when Jake heard a sound. It was dull and muffled, but definitely came from below. He caught Syd's eye and motioned down. She followed his hand, nodded that she understood and exchanged a series of elaborate hand signals with the others.

They were on a Fulton class submarine tender. As a teenager Jake had gone through a brief obsession with naval warships, probably since living in central Texas made the ocean seem as remote as the moon. He'd flirted with the idea of entering the navy, maybe even becoming a SEAL like his older brother. When he discovered that diving made him claustrophobic, he turned to the FBI instead.

But he could still picture the layout of this ship. There would be twelve ways to go below deck. Syd and one member of the team headed for the far end of the ship, and two others tackled the middle of the boat. The last Delta guy appeared beside him. Jake thought his name was Maltz, but introductions had been quick.

"You want to go first?" Maltz murmured.

Jake really didn't, but damned male pride made him nod. He yanked open the door. A blast of air from inside, cold and dank. The sweat under his vest immediately chilled and he repressed a shudder. It was pitch-black. He switched on his flashlight, held it next to his gun the way he'd been taught—training again, he thought. Sometimes being turned into a mindless robot was something to be grateful for. He tried not to think of a crypt but that's what the must and cold reminded him of.

He descended the metal steps to the berth deck as silently as possible, Maltz at his heels. It had been a long time since he'd done anything like this, and sweat seeded his brow despite the cold.

Jake reached the bottom of the staircase and swept his light across the hallway. Shadows leaped away from him. Maltz's light crossed his, illuminating the far wall. They were in a long, narrow corridor. Another hallway branched off to the left. Their flashlights only penetrated a few feet into the gloom.

He felt a tap on his shoulder. Maltz was gesturing down the hall. Jake was a little unclear on the hand signals but it looked like he wanted to split up. Not Jake's favorite course of action, if ever there was a perfect set for a horror movie, this was it. But the ship was enormous, it could take hours to search it. He nodded acquiescence and Maltz slipped toward the stern. Jake steeled himself and walked forward.

Another hallway branched off to his left, the middle corridor bisecting the ship. He debated for a minute. The hallway he'd been following was empty, no places to hide. It was mainly used to get quickly from the bow of the ship to the stern. Here, on the other hand, every few feet a door was set in the wall. Heavy steel, rust chewing through the gray paint. *Crew quarters,* thought Jake. He cocked his head to the side, listening. If someone had grabbed Madison, they'd probably holed up somewhere below deck. And the only way to find them was to check each room.

Jake faced the first door on the left. Three deep breaths before he decided he wasn't getting any more ready, might as well get it over with. He threw the door open and braced his shoulder against it. Quick sweep of the room, left to right, then behind the door. Nothing but a broken chair and metal bunk bed frames welded to the wall.

"One down," he said quietly, closing the door behind him. He followed the same drill with the door opposite: quick sweep, all clear, nothing but junk the navy hadn't bothered selling for scrap.

Jake was halfway down the hall when he heard a shout. The ship's acoustics distorted it, he couldn't tell if it was male or female. He darted back to the main corridor and strained his ears…another yell, garbled, and he suddenly remembered the radio. He spun the volume dial and heard Syd barking out instructions.

"Syd? Where are you?"

She was speaking rapid-fire, other team members chiming in. Jake was about to throw the radio against the wall in frustration when footsteps pounded toward him.

He spun. Maltz was running, talking into his radio. As he passed Jake heard him say, "Op tango objective princess located? Say again."

"What's going on?" Jake asked, falling in step beside him.

Maltz shook his head and quickened the pace, their flashlights shining frenetic beams of light down the dark corridor. Jake hustled to keep up.

They were almost at the bow when shots rang out.

Madison huddled in the dark, tears streaming down her face. The despair was crushing. She'd come so close to escaping, only to fail. Plus her left leg was in agony, it was hard not to scream from the pain.

After grabbing her, Lurch slung her over his shoulder like she weighed nothing. Madison battered at him with her fists, but he laid one hand on her broken foot and she almost passed out.

"Be good," he snarled, "or I'll make it worse."

At that moment they both saw people on the next ship. Her heart leaped, thinking she might be rescued after all. Lurch swore and dragged her downstairs. They were crouched in a tiny room, smaller and darker than the one she'd been held in before.

She tried to choke back her sobs, but the weight of her failure combined with the pain from her ankle made it nearly impossible.

"Shh!" Lurch said, breathing heavily in her ear. His hand gripped her arm tightly.

Dust disturbed by their entry still whirled in the air, tickling Madison's throat. She coughed.

"Jesus," he hissed. "What, you want to die?"

"You're going to kill me anyway," she choked. "Don't pretend you won't."

"If I was going to kill you you'd already be dead," Lurch said. "I could have tossed you overboard, shot you in the head." She caught a glint of light off something, realized he was showing her a gun. "I'm trying to save you, dipshit."

"The other guy…"

"Ralph was always an asshole," he muttered. "Hated that guy."

"Where is he now?" Madison asked after a minute.

"Dead." The word was hard, flat. Lurch seemed a little surprised by it himself.

"How?"

"Doesn't matter. But the rest of them are coming. You want to live, you'll stay quiet."

Madison tried to sort out what was happening. "So you're trying to save me?" she asked, puzzled. "Why?"

"I didn't sign up to kill no kids," Lurch said. "Now shut the fuck up, or you might change my mind."

She hunkered down, nearly overwhelmed by this new knowledge. *Signed up for what?* she wanted to ask.

A sound in the corridor outside. Madison pressed herself farther back into the shadows. She heard Lurch suck in a gulp of air, then his gun clicked. *This was insane,* she thought. After everything that had happened, she was going to die in a shoot-out.

The door slid open an inch. A slice of light penetrated the shadows. Madison's heart still pounded so hard people onshore could probably hear it. A second passed, then the door eased shut again. She released her breath, relaxing, and felt Lurch do the same. He leaned in to say something.

The door was suddenly flung wide. Madison flinched as light blinded her. Lurch dragged her to her feet. Something pressed against her temple and her heart sank. He'd been lying about saving her, she should have known better.

The light lowered an inch, enough for her to make out two figures.

A female voice ordered, "Drop it!"

Lurch's voice was full of surprise when he asked, "Who the fuck are you?"

Jake tore down the hall after Maltz, who quickly outpaced him. He seemed to have an exact read on where the shot originated. They passed another corridor, then Maltz darted down the next one on the left. Jake followed, adrenaline providing a burst of speed. Suddenly Maltz stopped dead. Figures blocked the entrance to a room. Jake's flashlight caught on blond hair, then a camouflaged back. Inside, someone was crying. He took another step forward, arching his head to see inside…

"We're here for Madison," the woman said. Madison stiffened at the sound of her name and felt Lurch shift behind her, the cold press of the muzzle easing up.

"Who sent you?"

"Her father. Just let her go." The woman sounded sure of herself. Commanding. Madison blinked at the mention of her father. She tried to place the voice, but it was completely unfamiliar.

"You the Feds?"

"No. Friends of the family."

The term was so incongruous, Madison laughed. It was the wrong reaction. Lurch moved suddenly, dragging her with him. Then an explosion, impossibly loud in the confined space. She swiveled in time to see Lurch cave backward as if punched. His arms swung out in front of him, as if grasping for the second shot. He hit the wall before slumping to the floor. Madison touched her hand to her face and it came away sticky.

Blood, she thought, fainting.

"Is it her?" Jake asked, realizing immediately how inane the question was. Of course it was Madison, who else could it be? "Is she okay?"

"She's fine," Syd said. She crouched beside the girl, using her sleeve to wipe off her face.

Jake peered past them toward the crumpled form in the corner. One of the commandos was checking for a pulse. "Dead," he said with finality.

Madison was crying, probably from the shock. Jake shoved past the two men blocking the door and knelt beside her. "Madison. It's going to be okay now," he said, trying to sound soothing. The words bounced off the metal walls, echoing back at him. "You'll be okay."

Madison collapsed against Syd, shoulders heaving. Her ankle was at a strange angle, probably broken; other than that, she appeared dirty and shaken but otherwise unscathed. Jake released a breath and slumped down, head in his hands. They'd found her, and she was alive. Chalk one up in the win column for The Longhorn Group. He reached for his cell phone to call Randall with the good news.

There was a commotion at the door. Jake glanced up to find that the other team members had vanished. Voices down the hall, the sound of arguing. Quickly regaining his feet Jake stepped back into the corridor.

"Who are you people?"

It was a middle-aged man dressed in a uniform that sagged around his knees. He held an enormous SureFire tac light in one hand, the other was raised as if warding them off.

"Stand down!" Jake ordered, noting the commandos'

raised guns. "For Christ's sake, stand down. It's just the MARAD guard."

It took ten minutes to sort out the situation, and another twenty for the medevac chopper to arrive. The MARAD guard had muttered about jurisdiction and losing his job. Syd took him aside, and whatever she offered calmed him down. Probably money, Jake thought.

Syd climbed in the chopper with Madison, headed to the nearest E.R. for her ankle to be examined. The paramedics administered a sedative. Tears still streamed down her face but she had finally stopped wailing. Her expression was unnerving, though. Jake wondered if she'd really be okay, there was no telling what those guys had done to her over the past week.

Audrey wept when he called, tears that sounded oddly bereft despite the good news. He couldn't reach Randall, left three messages on his cell and at work before giving up. The rest of the Delta team slipped away in the initial confusion, per Syd's orders. She didn't want them involved. Jake protested that they were going to have a hell of a time explaining the situation as it was, allowing their employees to leave the scene would only make matters worse.

"I got it covered," she'd said, nodding toward the MARAD guard.

More police boats were arriving. Jake slumped against the rail, watching as a swarm of uniforms slowly climbed the rope ladder. A dead body below deck, and here he was carrying three weapons of questionable legality. *Jesus,* he thought, shaking his head. He'd assumed that most of their cases would occur on foreign soil. Abroad, a few well-placed bribes let you avoid this sort of situation. He'd used that to his advantage while working for Christou.

But here he was left holding the bag, forced to explain to Benicia P.D. what the hell had happened. He'd be lucky not to get thrown in jail. Syd had left him with the number of a local defense attorney just in case. At the moment, that was small comfort. At least they'd gotten Madison back alive.

Jake's cell rang and he checked the number, smiling before clicking it open. "Hi, honey," he said. "How was your day?"

Eighteen

Kelly clicked the phone shut, exasperated. She was still trying to process everything Jake had said, something about a kidnapped girl, a mothball fleet and a dead kidnapper. Then the offhanded remark that she might have to post bail if things didn't go well. Not exactly a stellar beginning for The Longhorn Group, she couldn't help thinking. She knew Jake well enough to assume he was glossing over details that might upset her. It was one of the things that gave her pause, this ability to play things fast and loose when it suited him. He epitomized moral relativism; in his opinion any action was justified as long as it produced the desired end result. Above and beyond the other circumstances surrounding his dismissal, it was this quality that ultimately kept him from fitting in at the Bureau.

Almost a year ago Jake had tagged along on one of her cases. There was a pair of serial killers terrorizing the Berkshires. They escaped across the Canadian border with Jake at their heels. He was out of contact for a full day, and Kelly nearly went out of her head with worry. Soon after his return, one killer was found duct-taped to the hood of a car. The other turned up dead weeks later in the woods outside Montreal. The surviving killer confessed to the murder. He was currently serving life without parole, and the case was closed. It was that case that provided the first black mark on her career, but Kelly had long ago made peace with that.

However one question still niggled at her: Where was Jake when that murder took place? Could he possibly have witnessed it without interfering? She suspected that if he thought it served justice, that's exactly what he would have done. At the time Kelly decided she didn't want to know the extent of his involvement. After all, she'd just agreed to marry him.

Now, the initial glow of the engagement long faded, Kelly decided it was time for him to explain exactly what happened. She was sitting at the gate waiting for her plane to board. Rodriguez had uncovered a string of businesses filed under the same tangled web of parent companies, mostly located in Texas. They'd narrowed the list down to a few that looked promising, and Kelly booked a flight to San Antonio. As far as her boss knew, she was tying up a few loose ends, and would catch a connecting flight to D.C. the following day.

"Hey, partner."

Kelly glanced up, startled from her reverie. Rodriguez stood there, clutching the handle of his carry-on as if it were the only thing keeping him upright. If possible, he looked even worse than he had in the hospital that morning. The bruises had darkened into a mottled mask of green and purple, and stitches strained against his still-swollen features.

"Jesus, Rodriguez! What are you doing here?" Kelly jolted to her feet, trying to help him sit. He waved her off with annoyance and plunked down beside her. A young woman glanced up from her iPod and took in his appearance. She gathered up her things and shifted down a row.

"Guess I'm not making any friends on this flight, huh?" he asked ruefully.

Kelly caught the strain of pain in his voice. "You're supposed to stay in the hospital for another few days."

"Not according to our government-issue health plan. Docs gave me the okay. I look like hell, but there's nothing they can do for bruised ribs, and they can't reset my nose until the swelling goes down." He turned sideways. "I'm thinking of going with the 'Jude Law.' What do you think?"

"I think you should be resting." She eyed his ticket. "That better not be for San Antonio."

"Hey, I thought we'd reached a new level in our professional relationship," he sounded wounded. "Besides, this is my lead."

"You're insane." Kelly gestured to him. "I can't let you slow me down."

"Wouldn't dream of it." He straightened a leg carefully and grimaced. "I'll be fine. Got enough Advil to get me through. Hell, I could probably run a marathon if I had to."

"ASAC McLarty doesn't know you're doing this," Kelly guessed. His eyes confirmed it. "I'll call him, say you're not following orders."

"And you are?" he said pointedly. "I spoke with Phoenix P.D. They seem to think the Morris case is wrapped up with a bow. So I'm guessing you haven't filled McLarty in on the details of your Texas layover."

Kelly clenched her jaw. Rodriguez was right, she'd led her boss to believe the case was as good as closed, but persuaded him to hold off on the press conference. At the moment, she was as off the grid as Rodriguez was. A year ago she would never have considered such a move. But since she was already viewing her FBI career in the rearview mirror, it hadn't even given her pause. Which made her more like Jake than she cared to admit.

Rodriguez caught her expression, mistook it for guilt, and extended a hand. "Listen. You don't rat me out, I won't tell on you. Deal?"

Kelly eyed the extended hand, eyes narrowed. *Rat* was an odd choice of words. She wondered if he knew about the rumors. After a minute, she shook.

"All right, then." Rodriguez peered around. "Do I have time to grab a slice before boarding?"

Randall worked carefully, holding the blowtorch at arm's length. Beads of sweat ran down his face, both from the weight of the protective suit and lead apron and from stress.

They'd assigned the largest and most dangerous-looking man as his helper. Randall tried to refuse, inspiring a flash of pure relief on the guy's face before they were told it wasn't optional. Thor was supposed to make sure Randall did what he was supposed to. Not that he would have a clue if something was wrong, Randall thought disdainfully. He obviously had as much experience with low-level radioactive waste as he did with an Emily Post manual.

Thor stood at what he must have assumed was a safe distance, approximately twenty feet away. Close enough to intercede if Randall made a break for it. His nickname was so ridiculous that even under the circumstances Randall couldn't glance at him without wanting to chuckle. Not that there was much funny about the situation.

Low-level radioactive waste came from sources as

varied as hospital medical equipment and the density gauges used by building contractors. Few people were aware of how much radiation they came in contact with on a daily basis; it would probably terrify them to know. But even direct contact with most low level waste wouldn't have immediate dire consequences. For that reason, until 9/11 that form of waste disposal was at best loosely regulated and monitored on a state-by-state basis.

More dangerous waste materials, like plutonium from spent fuel rods, were consolidated at a few sites in Nevada and Texas. The government generally made sure they were safely stored in specially designed water-filled basins or dry casks, and closely monitored them. Although sometimes even those safeguards failed: some high-level waste remained in boron pools right next to the reactors generating it.

After 9/11, the government finally clued in to the fact that some waste, though categorized as "low-level," could prove lethal in a dirty bomb. Which explained Randall's promotion: his job was to oversee the transfer of low-level radioactive waste to a few secure facilities. So he'd spent the past two years making sure that for the first time since the Manhattan Project, everything was accounted for. All but the three items he'd redirected here.

Before Randall started, the U.S. Nuclear Regulatory Commission estimated that every single day of the year, approximately one source of low-level radioactive waste was lost, abandoned or stolen in the United States. In Texas alone, between 1995 and 2001 more than one hundred and twenty-three items fell off the grid. The most hazardous were industrial radiography-related sources, a potential source of gamma radiation. In one high profile case known as the Larpen incident, three industrial radiography cameras were stolen after a bankruptcy judge refused to provide money for their safe disposal. The cameras were recovered after the Bureau of Radiation Control issued a statewide press release and one of the thieves, fearful for his own safety, turned himself in and told authorities where to find them.

Something far worse happened in Brazil in 1987, when scavengers looting a defunct hospital came across abandoned teletherapy equipment. Fascinated by the deep blue light the cesium chloride emitted, they stole it, then sold it to a junkyard owner who planned to fashion it into a ring for his wife. His young niece painted herself with the blue powder dust scraped off the source. Other relatives used it to mark crosses on their foreheads. In what became known as the Goiânia accident, 249 people total were contaminated. Twenty people were hospitalized, four of whom died (including the junkyard owner's wife, niece and two workers who initially hammered open the lead casing).

In the aftermath of that incident medical facilities learned their lesson, keeping a tighter lid on used equipment. However one industry remained notoriously lax: oil production. X-ray radiography cameras were used to inspect oil and natural gas pipelines, making sure they'd withstand extreme stress. More technologically advanced cameras were constantly becoming available, and the older ones were discarded. Buried deep in the core of those cameras were gamma radiation sources, most commonly iridium-192 and cobalt-60. You could block other forms of radiation by simply holding up a cloth. But thanks to their short wavelength, gamma rays could penetrate skin. Exposure for even a brief period almost guaranteed a painful death.

Which was why Randall was being so careful. In addition to a heavy-duty protective suit and apron, he was using a respirator and wearing heavy gloves and boots. Thor was clad in a similar outfit; Randall was surprised they'd managed to find one in his size. Randall was using a blowtorch to remove the source material from the camera's lead container. The cameras he had diverted were Philips 160 kV constant-potential X-ray systems, designed to inspect large oil and gas pipes. Hence the need for the flatbed trucks—the housings were enormous, which guaranteed that camera operators worked at a safe distance from the X-rays.

The box holding the iridium wasn't large, but thanks to the lead casing it was extraordinarily heavy. Once he got the case open, there would be temporary exposure to the source material until he transferred it to the other container. He kept checking the dosimeter clipped to the outside of his suit. It was still within normal ranges, although far beyond what a human should sustain on a daily basis. The dots marching up the badge ranged from 5 *rads,* the lowest level of radiation exposure, to 100 *rads,* or "your skin is about to bubble and fall off." Right now the dot marking 5 *rads* was completely black. It was a good thing he wasn't planning on having any more kids.

The thought reminded him of Madison. Randall wondered if she was still alive. His bumbling attempt to secure proof of life had failed miserably. He cringed at the memory of posturing in the cracked bathroom mirror, thinking he'd shown them. The minute they brought him back into the main room, any illusion that he had control over the situation vanished.

"So? Where's my proof of life?" he had asked, trying to remember everything Jake told him. *Be tough, they clearly need you more than you need them,* Jake advised. *Seize control of the negotiation process, don't let them dictate all the terms.* And by the way, your daughter is probably already dead, was the addendum, but he knew Jake hadn't dared say it aloud.

"Someone wants to talk to you," the bald man in charge said, handing him a phone.

"Dr. Grant?" The voice was deep, with a distinctive twang.

"I want proof that my daughter is still alive."

There was a pause before the man spoke again, sounding bemused. "Oh, you would, would you?"

"If you want my help, I want proof." Randall tried to sound forceful, self-assured, but his resolve was wilting.

"Let me make something clear to you, Dr. Grant. At the moment, you and every member of your family live and die at my discretion. And that includes Bree and Audrey."

"Bullshit. They're somewhere safe, you can't get to them."

"Oh, you mean your mother-in-law's place in Massachusetts? She has a hell of a rose garden."

Randall's blood ran cold. He'd been a fool to listen to Jake and Syd, he should have hidden them better. Of course it would be child's play for someone with access to the inner workings of the facility to uncover their whereabouts.

"I'm sending you a text," the voice said.

Randall pulled the phone away from his ear and squinted at the image. It was pixelated by the cheap camera, but he could still discern the outlines of his mother-in-law's house. And Audrey's VW was parked in the driveway.

A tear snaked down his cheek as he pressed the phone back to his ear.

"I have men stationed nearby who can be at the house

in under five minutes. And they won't kill them quickly. Those men with you now? They're civilized compared to the ones I sent." The sound of a throat clearing, then the man asked, "So I'm assuming we'll have your full cooperation?"

"I'll need tools," Randall responded dully.

"Rest assured, Dr. Grant, you'll have everything you need. Now put Dante back on."

Dante. The bald leader had a name now. Of course, if they weren't bothering to conceal their identities, obviously the minute he finished the job he was a dead man.

He glanced at Thor, who absentmindedly scratched himself. Randall was to transform the materials into a radioactive dust that would spread a cloud of death when the bombs detonated. Someone else was constructing the bombs, he had no expertise in that field. But he knew radioactive matter. For the past two decades it was all he'd studied. He could recite the properties of each isotope, knew the half-life of every source. And chances were Thor didn't know an isotope from an isobar. Randall might not be able to stop this group without putting his family in horrible danger, but he could diminish the fallout from what they had planned. Literally.

Randall bent to his task again. Despite the media hysteria in 2002 when Jose Padilla was accused of trying to build a dirty bomb, fashioning radioactive material into a dangerous weapon required expertise. Initially, the worst casualties would be the same as any bombing: people in the immediate blast vicinity would be annihilated by the explosion. Then iridium would be dispersed in a toxic cloud. Depending on wind speeds and other conditions, a huge area could be contaminated by gamma radiation. Few people would die initially, but over the long term anyone exposed was at risk of developing cancer or other genetic mutations. The area itself would be deemed uninhabitable, and the cleanup costs could be in the billions.

And that was what made a dirty bomb so effective. Called a "weapon of disruption," as opposed to a weapon of mass destruction, the greatest danger would be from panic. If detonated in a major city, containment and decontamination of thousands of terrified victims would present an enormous challenge. Survivors of the blast might be trampled in the aftermath.

Transportation issues presented the largest impediment to unleashing a dirty bomb. Although the term "suitcase bomb" was coined after the Padilla case, unless a bomber used a specially lined container, he would probably die of severe radiation poisoning before reaching his target. And that container would be far too heavy to carry. Plus, they weren't the sort of thing you ordered off eBay.

Judging by the preparations across the warehouse, Dante already had that covered. The other men were converting metal drums, lining them with overlapping sheets of alloys. Probably not enough to prevent all traces of radiation from leaking out, but it would stop detectors from going off at every firehouse and police station they passed. And once the bomb exploded, those metal sheets would turn into lethal shrapnel. Randall had to hand it to them, they'd thought of everything.

Randall returned to his task. Inside the lead box he maneuvered robotic hands, watching the monitor carefully. One claw held a file, carefully scraping off chunks of iridescence. Never in his life had he felt so helpless, responsible for the lives of not just his family but so many others. Scrape, scrape. He was finally going to achieve the fame he'd always aspired to. He'd be known as the man who helped engineer the single worst day in the nation's collective history. And there was nothing he could do to stop it.

Nineteen

"Didn't figure you for the religious type," Jake said, slipping into the pew behind Syd.

She half turned, grinning at him. "I'm hiding out."

"Yeah, I get that." He examined his hands. Audrey and Bree Grant had arrived at the hospital an hour earlier and were rushed straight to Madison's room. He'd caught some of the reunion while standing guard in the hall outside. Flanking him were two Benicia cops. He got the feeling they were more interested in keeping an eye on him than protecting Madison. The local P.D. hadn't been all that satisfied with his story, and the discovery of another body on the ship didn't help matters. But no one had pulled out the handcuffs yet. Jake assumed the bigwigs downtown were still trying to make sense of it.

He sat back and crossed his hands behind his head. The hospital chapel was small, three rows of pews facing a crucifix. The whole place seemed like an afterthought. Outside twilight sifted through the smog, tinting the concrete in shades of tangerine and magenta.

"Still no word from Randall?" The shadows made it hard to read Syd's face.

Jake shook his head. "Nope. Talked to his coworker, Barry. Randall left work early yesterday, said he had a bug. Probably just couldn't handle being there."

"Strange that he's not picking up." Syd leaned forward, and he saw the concern in her eyes. "I'm worried."

"I was going to check out his apartment. That is, if you've got this under control."

"I'll come with you." She stood.

Jake balked. "Benicia P.D. feels strongly that at least one of us should stick around. Otherwise I get the feeling charges might be filed."

"Not going to happen." Syd waved a hand. "One phone call and it's taken care of."

"One phone call, huh? You're not working for the Agency anymore, remember?"

"They still don't want me getting frog-marched through some podunk P.D. Trust me, if an arrest warrant goes out with my name on it, it gets handled."

"So what if it has my name on it?"

Syd shrugged. "Dunno. Guess we'll find out."

"Not comforting, Syd," Jake said. "Maybe I will stay."

Syd laughed. "I'm kidding. It'll be fine, trust me. We'll check on Randall, then head straight back. They won't even know we're gone."

Jake debated for a minute, then sighed. "All right. Let's go tell your boyfriend how you saved the day."

"He's not my boyfriend," Syd grumbled, but followed him out into the night.

Neither of them noticed a battered sedan at the rear of the parking lot. A pair of bald men sat low in the front seat, watching their departure through binoculars.

"This is bullshit," Rodriguez said.

"It's not bullshit."

"So we flew all the way to Texas to park outside a warehouse?"

"We don't go inside without a warrant. And right now, no judge in his right mind would give us one," Kelly retorted.

Rodriguez made an exasperated sound and collapsed against the headrest, sulking. They had requisitioned a bu-car from the San Antonio field office. It had an oddly tangy aroma from the spray used to cloak stale cigarette smoke. The odor was nausea-inducing when the windows were rolled up to use the air-conditioning, but the alternative was sweltering with them open. It was even hotter here than in Phoenix, and dustier, if such a thing was possible, Kelly thought. Her shirt was soaked through, and she wished she'd taken off her jacket before getting in the car.

The argument wasn't helping matters. They'd circled the warehouse when they'd first arrived. Like the bar, the windows were painted black from the inside, doors locked. Rodriguez had picked up a rock, but Kelly managed to stop him in time. She might be willing to bend the rules, but she drew the line at breaking and entering.

So they'd returned to the car and sat, tucked in an alley between two other warehouses that offered a clear view of the building. After an hour passed uneventfully Rodriguez got itchy and pressed his point.

"This isn't accomplishing jack-shit," he grumbled, rubbing his less-swollen eye with a thumb.

Kelly had to agree. She'd been expecting a place where criminal activity was apparent, maybe another bar. The list Rodriguez's friend gave them only provided addresses, with no indication of what type of business was at each location. This was probably a huge waste of time, Kelly thought, glancing at her watch: 4:00 p.m. She'd already basically closed the case, and it didn't seem like there was anything to see here. Still, they should give it another hour.

"We should go to the next address on the list. It's not far." Rodriguez glanced at the printout in his hand. "Five miles, maybe."

"I say we give this some time. If nothing happens by five, we'll head there."

"Then what? There are twenty others on the list. Do we fly around and sit outside all of them?"

"Depends."

"On what?"

"On whether or not anything happens here. If it does, we can put other units on those buildings. But like you said, right now we got nothing. And we're not going to get much inter-departmental support based on that."

Rodriguez muttered something under his breath in Spanish.

"Wow. You're fun on a stakeout," Kelly said.

"I don't mind a stakeout if I'm prepared for it," Rodriguez shot back. "If you'd said, 'stakeout,' I would have brought some sodas. Maybe some chips, too. And a piss bottle."

"That's disgusting."

Rodriguez shrugged. "Hey, the soda's gotta come out somewhere."

"Bear in mind I didn't want you along in the first place," Kelly said.

"What, and let my partner go in without backup?" She threw him a sharp look, and he turned away, muttering, "Just because I got jumped once doesn't mean I'm useless."

Kelly chose not to reply. A pall descended over the car.

Faded paint on the side of the warehouse advertised *Franciscan Interiors, Makers of Fine Furniture,* but judging by the inactivity, it was everyone's day off. They faced the only entrance. To the far left a flight of stairs led to a door, on the right was a loading dock. They were in the outskirts of Laredo, Texas, a stone's throw from the Mexican border. The warehouse was set in an industrialized area, hunched buildings all worn the color of sand. Most sported For Lease signs, which explained the general air of stagnation. Laredo was one of those places economic booms avoided.

"We met once before, you know," Rodriguez said, breaking the silence.

"Oh, really?" Kelly said, only half listening as she fiddled with the radio. She'd been unable to find anything but country and Mexican rock stations, and if she heard one more song by Los Lobos she was going to tear her hair out.

"During that case on the college campus."

Kelly straightened and looked at him, trying to remember. Once another coed had been snatched, a slew of agents and other law enforcement officers swarmed the university to assist in the search. "Did you work with Morrow?"

"A little. Great guy. And I was with Jake at the boathouse when he found you."

Kelly flinched. Despite the warmth of the day a chill swept over her. "You must have been fresh out of the Academy," she said, fighting to keep her voice normal. She hated to admit it, but that case still gave her nightmares.

"I'd been in about a year." Rodriguez opened his door. "I'm going to walk to that bodega at the turnoff. You want something?"

"No, I'm good. Thanks," Kelly said. She watched him limp away.

Kelly froze at the sound of an approaching engine. In the rearview mirror she saw Rodriguez duck into the dusty scrub lining the alley. She slid down in her seat and hoped they wouldn't be noticed.

It was a navy truck with a white shell on the back. No name on the side, two guys in the front seat. Kelly wrote down the license plate as they parked at an angle outside the Franciscan warehouse. Both wore cowboy hats and sunglasses, jeans and tank tops. They walked to the door, unlocked it, and stepped inside. More big white guys, like the ones at the bar. Of course, they could be furniture makers, but something made her doubt it.

The passenger door opened and Rodriguez slid inside, carefully easing the door shut so it wouldn't click.

"Welcome back," she said wryly.

"Watched pot never boils, right? Should have left sooner," Rodriguez said. "So can we go in?"

"Not unless you saw some evidence of illegal activity that I missed."

Rodriguez tapped a finger on the dashboard. "Then what now?"

"Now we wait," Kelly said calmly. "At least we know the warehouse is being used for something."

"Maybe they'll come out with guns," Rodriguez said hopefully. "Or drugs."

"Or a machete and a sign saying, 'We Killed Duke Morris,'" Kelly said. "But I'm not holding my breath."

What they did come out with was far more interesting. Ten minutes after entering they rolled up the metal door, revealing the loading dock. They backed the truck in and popped the hatch on the shell. Kelly watched as they dragged an oversized duffel bag out. Hard to tell from a distance, but it looked like a body.

"That doesn't look legal," Rodriguez commented. "Call for backup?"

Kelly debated. She hadn't contacted the Laredo cops yet, figuring it was best to keep this visit quiet until she knew if they were onto something. But the last thing they needed was a repeat of the bar debacle. "Give me your cell," she said, holding out a hand.

He passed it to her.

Kelly dialed 911 and motioned for him to be quiet. "I'd like to report a break-in. Three-thirty-six Muldoon Avenue. That's right. Thanks." She handed the phone back to Rodriguez. "Five minutes," she said.

"Not bad," he said begrudgingly. "'Course, now we get to explain to a trigger-happy deputy why two FBI agents are responding to a robbery on their turf."

"We happened to be in the area working a case," Kelly said.

"And if it comes back to us?"

"It won't come back to us. Worst-case scenario, it comes back to you."

"Hey—"

Kelly grinned. "Relax, Rodriguez. I'm doubting Laredo P.D. has the technology to trace a cell call. Besides, if they get a good arrest out of this, they won't be complaining."

"You better be right."

Ten minutes later a cop car with *Laredo Police* on the door rolled past. Two cops got out, one young and lean, the other older and stocky. *Abbott and Costello,* Kelly thought. They parked in front of the loading dock. The younger cop sauntered over, ducked his head in and called out.

"Wow. Looks like a real crack team," Rodriguez said.

Kelly furrowed her brow. Their behavior was odd. The older cop leaned against the hood of their car, arms crossed in front of his chest. Not exactly how most units would respond to a B and E call.

One of the cowboys emerged from the building, the younger cop at his heels. He strolled over to the police car. The older cop straightened and shook his hand. They exchanged a few words, then the cop bent double. Kelly's hand tensed, ready to go for her gun, until she realized he was laughing at something the cowboy said.

"Oh, shit," Rodriguez said. "Now what?"

The younger cop had obviously noticed their car and was headed straight for them. The other two watched him. The cop's hand rested by his holster.

"Jones!" Rodriguez hissed.

The cop ducked low to peer in their car window. His eyes were concealed behind tinted Ray-Bans. "Get you folks to step out of the car, please."

Kelly kept her hands in view as she slid out, saying, "FBI. I'm going to reach for my badge."

The cop nodded slowly, watching her. Rodriguez kept his arms up.

She handed over her credentials and he examined them. "You're pretty far from home, Agent Jones," he said, handing them back.

"We're following up a lead on a case," Kelly said.

"Funny, at roll call they didn't say anything about Feds coming to town," the cop said. His hand was off his belt but he still looked wary.

"I didn't want to trouble your department until I found out whether or not it was a solid lead," Kelly said, reading off his name tag, "Officer Rowe."

"So I don't suppose you know anything about a 911 call." The way he said it wasn't a question.

"Nope," Rodriguez answered.

The cop's gaze shifted to him. "I'm guessing you're a Fed, too?"

Rodriguez moved to hand over his ID, but the cop waved it away. "That lead have anything to do with what happened to your face?"

"Not directly," Rodriguez grumbled.

"Then it's got something to do with this alley?"

"Actually, with that warehouse," Kelly said, nodding toward it.

"Yeah? Well, Travis and I patrol this area all the time. Everything there looks good. Just checked it out myself."

"Really? Because about ten minutes ago Agent Rodriguez and I saw two men loading a suspicious item in their truck."

Rowe turned and waved over the cowboy. He approached slowly, jaw working a piece of chewing tobacco. His eyes skittered over both of them before returning to the cop.

"Hey, Jim. Got some federal agents here think you're up to no good," Rowe said, making it sound like a joke.

Jim laughed weakly. "That right?"

"Yup."

"What was in the duffel bag?" Kelly asked.

Jim shrugged. "Supplies."

"Supplies for what?"

He glanced at Rowe as if seeking approval before saying, "Carpentry. My brother and I are contractors, use this place to store our stuff."

"Seems like a lot of space for a few hammers and nails," Kelly noted.

Rowe and Jim exchanged a look. The cowboy shrugged.

"Then you won't mind if we take a look around?" she continued.

Jim's mouth opened and closed a few times, then he spit a long stream of tobacco juice in the dirt at their feet.

"Jones," Rodriguez protested as she started walking toward the building. Kelly didn't turn back, and after a minute he fell in step beside her. "Are you sure this is a good idea?" he said in a low voice, glancing back.

Kelly could hear Rowe and Jim following them. "You have a better one?"

"There are four of them, and the cops are armed. I say we go back to the car, get the hell out of here. Check out the other address."

"We're on their radar now," Kelly said. "Watch my back and we'll be fine."

Rodriguez muttered something about being dumped on the other side of the border, but she ignored him. Crooked or not, she doubted any cop would risk two dead FBI agents turning up on their watch. For all Rowe knew, their boss had their exact coordinates.

Kelly placed her hands on the loading dock and hauled herself up. Rodriguez muttered something about his injuries, and Jim went to unlock the side door. While she waited, Kelly let her eyes adjust to the dark. The inside was cavernous, large enough to house a 747. The entire room was empty save for a circle of chairs. Two small Quonset huts were hunkered down against the far wall.

"Offices," Jim said, following her gaze.

"So only you and your brother use this place?" she asked.

"Rent was cheap," Jim said, following her as she crossed the warehouse floor.

"Lots of empty places around here," Rowe explained.

"You know the owners?"

Jim shrugged again. His head was tilted forward, hat shielding his eyes. Kelly reached the first office. The walls were lined with posters of nude centerfolds. A tire calendar displayed a topless woman perched on a stack of whitewalls. No desk, just a few bare cots on the floor. Kelly wrinkled her nose. The scent of urine was unmistakable.

"We sleep here sometimes," Jim offered up lamely.

"Piss here, too?" Rodriguez asked.

Kelly could hear the tension in his voice, knew he was thinking the same thing she was. Whoever had slept here, it wasn't the cowboys. "Where's your brother?" she asked.

"Other office, doing some paperwork," Jim said. "I came out to see what Luke wanted."

Rowe stiffened. "So you two are friendly," Kelly noted.

Rowe shrugged. "Part of my regular rounds."

Kelly nodded as if that was the most natural thing in the world and crossed to the opposite office. The door opened before she reached it, blocked by the other cowboy. *Not much of a family resemblance,* she thought to herself. This guy was larger, thicker through the shoulders. He still wore his hat.

"Agent Kelly Jones," she said, extending a hand.

He shook it reluctantly. "Jethro Henderson."

"Mind if I take a peek?" she asked.

Jethro shrugged and stepped aside, tucking his hands in his pockets. The other hut was similar to the first, with the exception of the mattresses. Posters on the walls, a battered desk.

"Not a lot of tools," she commented.

"Keep most of 'em in the truck," he said warily.

Rowe stood at her shoulder. "So looks like you're about done here," he said with finality.

"Soon as I check the truck," Kelly replied firmly.

Something passed between Jethro and Rowe. Kelly thought she caught a small nod, but couldn't be sure.

"That okay by you, Jethro?" Rowe said slowly.

"Feel free." Jethro tossed her a set of keys.

Kelly unlocked the back of the truck and lifted the gate, then struggled to lower the rear hatch. She flushed slightly, feeling amused eyes on her back as it slammed down harder than she'd intended. She reached forward, tugging the duffel bag toward her. It was heavy and only moved a few inches.

"Give you a hand with that?" Jethro asked, appearing at her elbow.

She waved him off. "I got it." She unzipped the bag and opened it. Inside was a stack of tools. She sifted through to see if anything was hidden underneath, but only encountered more metal. Kelly withdrew a pair of tongs and held them up. "What's a contractor doing with tongs?"

Jethro tensed, but after a moment let out a small laugh and said, "You got us. After a long day, we throw a barbecue." He held out his wrists. "Want to cuff me now?"

Rowe laughed with him. Kelly's eyes narrowed. "Thanks, I'll wait."

"Just pulling your leg, ma'am," Jethro said, still smirking. "No need to get all riled."

Rowe followed them back to the car. The other cop watched from under the brim of his hat as they passed. Rowe opened Kelly's car door, then shut it behind her.

"Thanks for the assistance, officer."

Rowe nodded, watching as they pulled away. Kelly drove in a slow circle around the parked police car, heading for the interstate a few blocks away.

Rodriguez shifted in his seat, clearly irritated. "What the hell was that?" he asked.

"What do you mean?"

"You didn't ask them about the corporation. Or what the mattresses were for."

"I'm thinking they weren't going to tell us. Not even if we asked nicely."

"Still—"

"And we're out of our jurisdiction, in the middle of nowhere." Kelly gestured to the bleak surroundings with one arm. "Four of them, two of us."

"But something is going on there."

"Definitely." Kelly steered onto the on-ramp. "The question is, what?"

"Coyotes, maybe, smuggling people in? Someone was using those mattresses." Rodriguez winced and adjusted the seat belt over his bruised ribs. "We're close to the border."

"Maybe. But then their affiliation with Laredo P.D. doesn't make sense."

Rodriguez peered out the window, thinking. "Plus that doesn't jibe with their poster."

"What, all the pinups?" Kelly rolled her eyes. "That seemed pretty typical."

"Not those, the one in Jethro's office. The Statue of Liberty behind barbed wire."

"Didn't see it."

"I recognized it. Texas Minutemen."

"One of the vigilante border patrol groups?"

"They would say, 'True Americans.'" Rodriguez smirked.

"So why would they be keeping people in the warehouse?" Kelly furrowed her brow. "And what's the link to the skinheads from the bar?"

Rodriguez shrugged. "Common interests? Hate groups have doubled in membership in the last decade. They gave a symposium on it at the Academy last year. Internet makes it easier for them to link up with each other, and immigration has been a rallying cry." He shook a fist, saying, "Send them back!"

Kelly cocked her head at him. "You know the strange thing? I can't tell if you're serious or not."

"Why, because I'm Mexican?"

"Yes." She pulled into the high-speed lane to pass a slow moving truck. After a minute she added, "Emilio and his grandmother seemed to bother you."

"That's because they're part of the problem, getting involved with a gang that ruins lives and communities. And then they refuse to report a crime or assist an investigation. Pisses me off."

"You can hardly blame them, if talking ends up getting them deported."

"Yeah. But it's not exactly what they teach in Citizenship 101." Rodriguez paused, examining a scab on his knuckle before continuing. "Hey, I'm all for reform. Too many illegals die each year trying to make that border crossing."

"So you support building a fence?"

"I would if I thought that would work. But anyone who thinks a Mexican can't handle a ladder hasn't hired a paint crew lately."

Kelly tried to figure out how to frame the next question. In conversations like this she was always afraid of accidentally saying something that might be perceived as racist. Eggshell territory. "But you're second generation, right?"

Rodriguez's knuckle was bleeding again. He tucked it in his mouth and spoke around it. "You're thinking I'm a hypocrite for saying they should reform immigration now, after my family got in. But it's different. In the eighties, there were less than two hundred thousand illegals entering the U.S. every year. Now there are closer to a million, mostly from Mexico. Too many people for a country whose resources are already limited. And recent immigrants aren't assimilating. I'm an American, everyone in my family considers themselves American. But some people want to have it both ways."

Kelly mulled over a response. She hadn't given immigration much thought before this case. Her relatives had all arrived in the early 1900s, long enough ago that she took her American heritage as a given. Someone whose roots went less deep might fear the hold was more tenuous. Which meant new arrivals were perceived as a threat. "Anyway," she said, "immigration seems to be the only link so far. Duke Morris's murder, the attack on you, the warehouse being used for something illegal that the police are in on."

"Makes sense."

"You think? I was going to say it all sounds pretty circumstantial." *Much easier to blame it on a Salvadoran gang and get on with my life,* Kelly thought, repressing a yawn. The scene at the warehouse had taken it out of her, she felt like she'd run a marathon.

Rodriguez glanced at her. "So what next?"

What she really wanted was to get a room at the next hotel, close the blinds, and sleep for three days. Kelly passed a Holiday Inn and watched sadly as it receded in the rearview mirror. "We check out that other warehouse. Maybe it'll tell us more about what the hell is going on."

"Awesome." Rodriguez said, satisfied. "And screw the warrant. We go in first."

Kelly didn't answer, but thought that this time she might let him.

Madison tried to scream but a hand clamped over her mouth, stifling it. A man's face hovered above her. She lashed out, striking him with her arms and one good foot, tears rolling down her face. She'd escaped the boat, only to have something happen here in the hospital. *What the hell was going on? Where were the guards?*

Suddenly, her mother appeared over the guy's shoulder. He was one of her rescuers from the boat, Madison realized, overcome with relief. Her mother shoved the guy aside and whispered in her ear. "It's okay, sweetheart, you're safe. But we have to go."

"What? Go where?" Madison asked, confused, craning to see if Bree was still in the chair beside the bed. She was gone. "Where's Bree?"

"Already outside, honey. Please, Mr. Maltz is saying we need to hurry." Her mother looked anxiously over her shoulder at the guard. He was standing by the door, peering down the hallway.

"I don't understand. Aren't we safe here?" Madison started to shake.

Her mother rubbed her arms. "It's just a precaution. We'll be okay, I promise."

"Shift change," Maltz said, voice flat. "It's time."

"We have to go now, Maddee." Her mother held out a pair of baggy sweatpants she'd brought from home, as if Madison was a toddler and needed help getting dressed. Madison glanced at the guard, then held the back of her gown closed with one hand and let her mother pull on the pants. She'd cut off the left lower leg to make room for Madison's cast.

"What about my medicine?"

"I have pills in my purse." Her mother smiled weakly, clearly trying to be reassuring. "They were going to release you tomorrow anyway."

"But I thought the police wanted…"

"It's time." Maltz held out a wheelchair, and without thinking Madison lowered herself into it. The hallway was empty, lights dimmed. She heard some chatter at the nurse's station around the corner, a bark of laughter. He was leading them toward the stairs, not the elevator, she realized.

"My ankle. I can't…"

"I'll carry you."

"What? No—"

"Madison, please be quiet!" Her mother's voice was low but urgent. For the first time Madison realized that she didn't sound drunk. She hadn't heard that clarity in months.

Maltz soundlessly opened the door to the stairwell and wheeled her in with one hand. He put on the brakes and scooped Madison up. She felt awkward, embarrassed. She couldn't figure out what to do with her arms, putting them around his neck was too weird so she ended up crossing them over her chest.

The stairs exited on the far side of the parking lot, away from the ambulance dock. A white van idled at the curb. The panel door slid open, and another guy reached for Madison. Something about the entire situation felt wrong. She wondered why her mother assumed they could trust these guys. If her father had sent them, why hadn't he shown up yet? But she saw Bree already inside, tucked between two of them, her face drawn and scared. Madison swallowed hard and let herself be pulled in. They maneuvered her onto the long banquette lining the rear of the van. Maltz helped her mother inside and closed the door. Madison noticed they kept the headlights off until they were out of the parking lot.

"Where are we going?" she asked after ten minutes of silence. She'd never been in this part of California before, everything was unfamiliar.

"Somewhere safe," Maltz said.

"Is my father meeting us there?" She saw her mother exchange a glance with Maltz. "What?"

"Nothing, honey. It's just—"

"Dad's missing," Bree interrupted. "That's why we had to leave."

"So it's not over," Madison said. Fear tightened a noose around her neck. She struggled to breathe.

"Calm down, honey." Her mother bent forward, reaching awkwardly to stroke her hair. "I'm sure he's fine. We're just being extra careful."

It wasn't fine, and Madison knew it. She shook off her mother's hand and let the tears come as the city lights receded.

A half mile back, a sedan followed them through every turn.

Twenty

"This is ridiculous. There's nothing here." Jake threw a stack of papers back on the table. They'd spent the past few hours tearing apart Randall's apartment. The more time passed, the more it looked like Randall's departure hadn't been voluntary. They both knew it, though neither had said it aloud.

"He must have told you something. You practically lived together the past few days," Syd said.

"Not exactly. Most of the time I was driving all over God's green earth looking for Mack Krex," Jake grumbled. He plopped down on the couch and wished a coffee place were still open. He'd already ransacked Randall's cupboards and found nothing but tea. "What kind of guy doesn't drink coffee?" he muttered, checking his watch. Midnight already. He experienced a momentary flash of irrational rage at Randall. They rescued his daughter, and then the guy disappeared. Jake knew it was their own fault. It should have occurred to them to keep better tabs on Randall, but still. Everything about that guy was bad luck.

"Randall drinks it, but he doesn't make it himself. He's hooked on lattes."

Something triggered in Jake's brain. He lunged to the kitchen and fumbled through cabinets.

"What the hell?" Syd asked, hands on her hips.

"The mugs. That was how he got info in and out, something about coffee mugs." Randall had three of everything: plates, mugs, utensils. Apparently he didn't do a lot of entertaining. Three travel mugs with the facility logo lined the shelf above the plates. Jake grabbed one and twisted the bottom. Nothing happened. He strained harder, but it didn't give. "Damn. Maybe if I had a knife…."

"Or maybe it takes some finesse. Randall wasn't exactly he-man," Syd said, reaching out and taking it from him. She held it to the light and examined it. Removed the lid and scanned the inside. After turning it over in her hands, she pressed on a spot beneath the handle. The bottom popped off.

"Impressive," Jake said.

"What can I say? Spy stuff." Syd grinned. "But bad news. There's nothing in here."

Jake grabbed the other two and repeated the trick, opening the bottoms. Empty. "Maybe there's another compartment." Jake tapped one on the edge of the counter.

Syd raised an eyebrow. "It's a coffee mug, Jake, not a cryptex."

"So he gave them info on flash drives. Let's check those again."

"I've checked them all twice. They're blank, if there were files on them they've been erased."

Jake set the mug on the counter and looked at her. "You knew this guy. Where would he go?"

"With his daughter missing?" Syd shook her head. "Nowhere. Whoever kidnapped Madison probably has him."

"Why not grab him in the first place then? Saves them a step."

"They needed his access to the facility. And now, apparently, they don't. He must have handed over whatever he was supposed to get for them."

"Shit," Jake said, remembering their last conversation, the look in Randall's eyes after he watched the video of Madison being tortured. "So they probably killed him."

"Probably. Unless they still need him for something."

Jake examined her. "You don't seem too torn up."

Syd met his gaze. "I gave up on mourning people, Jake. Once they're gone, they're gone, nothing you can do."

"That's…" Jake tried to think of something to say that wouldn't hurt her feelings.

"Cold? Maybe. But in my line of work, I learned to distance myself." Syd shrugged, seemingly unperturbed. "Besides, Randall might be fine. He's a smart guy, you never know."

Jake looked around the apartment. He hated to admit it, but suddenly being here with Syd was creeping him out. Her tone was unsettling, monotone and flat like she was a pod person or something. More than anything he wished he was in bed with Kelly, arms wrapped around her waist. Preferably naked. "So you want to call it a night, head back to Benicia? They probably noticed by now that we're gone."

"Hell no. We haven't even scratched the surface yet." Her eyes roved the walls. "Tons of places he could have hidden stuff."

"You need help?"

"Nah. Crash out on the couch, if I need you to move I'll wake you."

She didn't have to ask twice. Jake kicked off his shoes,

swung his feet up, and covered his eyes with one arm. Within a minute he was dead asleep.

Syd watched him while she rubbed her neck with one hand. She sighed, then went to her purse and extracted her tools.

Randall glanced at Thor. He'd been dozing on and off all day. Honestly, he couldn't blame him. Spending hours watching radioactive material get filed into a fine dust wasn't anyone's idea of a good time. He'd initially made an attempt to be vigilant, watching warily as Randall extracted the core material, shuffled slowly across the warehouse floor and placed it in the lead box. But once the real work had begun, he'd quickly lost focus.

Which suited Randall's plan perfectly. He waited until Thor's head dropped to his chest, then gave it five minutes. Everyone else was on the far side of the warehouse playing poker. Occasionally tempers flared and Dante intervened, but by and large the men were left to themselves.

Randall took a few deep breaths. He had to get this exactly right for his plan to succeed. He thought for a second of his girls, and in spite of himself, Audrey. The last vacation they took together, to the Big Island of Hawaii. Their marriage was already in its death throes, and most of the trip was marred by spats and recriminations. But there had been one night when their car broke down as they returned home after sightseeing. Initially it was business as usual: Audrey enraged, as if the car's failure was somehow his fault, Madison and Bree silent and stiff in the backseat. But the tow truck driver dropped them at a restaurant while the car was being fixed, and it turned out to be one of their best nights together as a family. Dinner was served on a patio perched on the sand, so close to the water the girls joked their table might get sucked out to sea. He and Audrey drank mai tais, and she developed a case of the giggles. They watched the sunset and munched on coconut shrimp while Madison and Bree fidgeted and chatted the way teenagers do. Everything that night had been wonderful. In fact it was the last perfect moment he'd experienced.

It was enough, Randall decided. He hadn't achieved everything he'd hoped to accomplish with his life, there was no Nobel on his mantel, no theory named after him. Funny how insignificant those things seemed now. He just wished he could have his family together one last time.

Thor stirred in his sleep, head reflexively bobbing. Randall waited for him to still, then took a deep breath. With a solid kick he knocked over the lead case.

It hit the ground with a loud thump. A cloud of fine shimmering powder scattered across the floor, settling into the ridges like chalk dust.

"Shit!" he said loudly.

Thor jerked to his feet. It was startling how quickly he came to life. "What?" His eyes widened at the dust on the floor, and the small cloud above it. He instinctively took a step back.

"It spilled," Randall said, raising both hands help-lessly.

"Holy shit!" Thor yelled, loud enough to draw the attention of the card players. Two of them stood, and another sauntered over.

Randall pulled off his dosimeter, held it up in one hand. "It's black," he said with finality.

Thor tore off his own, dropping it when he saw the same color. "No, no, no!" he moaned, backing away. "The fuck did you do!"

"What's the problem?" It was Dante, eyes cold. Thor

appeared incapable of speech. Dante registered the shock on his face and glanced at Randall, who still held his dosimeter.

"It spilled," Randall said.

"No shit." Dante crossed his arms over his chest.

Randall shrugged, trying to look blasé. Every cell in his body was screaming at him, fight or flight instinct on overdrive. It wouldn't make a difference, the damage was already done. As soon as that hatch opened he'd condemned Thor and himself to death; at least he'd be taking one of them with him.

Curious, the other men joined them. When they saw the powder, a murmur rose up. They backed away, close enough to hear but twenty feet from the spill.

Fools, Randall thought. They might not die, but they'd been contaminated.

"I told you to watch him," Dante said calmly.

Thor was beyond reason. He spotted a streak of blue on his pants leg and tore off his clothes, stripping down to a pair of boxer briefs.

"We need to get to a decontamination unit," Randall said calmly.

"Not going to happen."

"Thor," Randall said. "We need to get to a decontamination unit. They can save you."

His words penetrated. Thor's head whipped around to Dante. "I want to go."

Dante shook his head. "No."

"You'll be dead in a few days otherwise," Randall said, then raised his voice to make sure they could all hear him. "You'll all be dead unless we get to a decontamination unit."

A buzz rose up among the other men. Randall heard his words repeated and saw the fear in their eyes. Emboldened by it, he squared his shoulders and turned to face Dante. "You know there's still time to save them."

"They knew the risks," Dante said forcefully. But he glanced back over his shoulder.

"Fuck this. Doc, where's the closest place?" Thor snarled, drawing himself up to his full height.

"Where are we?" Randall asked quickly, hoping he'd respond without thinking.

"Outside Houston," Thor said without hesitation. Dante's eyes half closed with disgust and he swore under his breath.

"There's the Texas Medical Center. Right near Rice University, south of downtown."

"You're not leaving," Dante said.

"The fuck I'm not. Hey, you don't want to die, get in the van," Thor called to the others. He gathered up his boots in one hand and walked toward the van parked near the door.

"You're as good as dead already," Dante said. "They won't be able to save you."

Thor stopped dead, shifting his eyes to Randall. "I'm the expert," Randall countered. "Trust me, they can save you."

A blast by his ear. Randall cringed, hands jerking up protectively. Everyone froze. Everyone except Thor, who stumbled forward as if pushed. The second shot caught him in the back of the head as he fell. He landed hard, blood pooling around him.

Dante had already spun, holding the gun with both hands at shoulder height, military-style. "The rest of you were too far away to get sick. Strip off your clothes and we'll shower off one at a time. You'll be fine."

"He doesn't know what he's talking about," Randall said. "He's lying to you."

The men glanced back and forth between them, trying

to decide who to believe. Dante pointed the gun at Randall as he growled, "Shut the fuck up."

Randall shrugged. "Go ahead. Saves me a few painful days."

Dante shook his head. "I mean it, Grant. I'll have them bring your family here so you can watch what happens to them before you die."

Suddenly, two other men peeled off from the group, bolting for the opposite end of the warehouse. Dante watched them run. The others remained where they were, shuffling uncertainly. At the door the men glanced back, as if surprised by the lack of a reaction. Dante kept his gun leveled on the others. The door closed behind them. A second later there were two loud reports, followed by a scream. Then one last shot, and silence fell.

"No one leaves," Dante said firmly.

"Your dosimeter," Randall said, pointing at it. The lower circles had filled in, he was one shy of Randall's reading.

Dante glanced at it and half smiled. "I'm like you, Grant. Never expected to make it out of here alive." He marched back to the remaining men and said a few words. One of them nodded, the others examined the floor. After a minute, they filed off toward the bathroom. Dante watched them go, then reholstered his weapon. "Nice try, but nothing stalls this mission. Back to work."

"But—"

"Scrape this powder off the floor and get it back in the case. And I want the other cores finished by tomorrow. Any more accidents, your family pays. Got it?"

"What, no shower for me?" Randall said with forced bravado. In truth he was near tears. His plan had failed, and now he'd be dead within a week. He'd hoped the men would panic and rise up against Dante, enabling him to escape. At least he would've been able to save his family and let the FBI know about the plot.

"We both know it's too late for you. You're the expert, right?" Dante said snidely. He turned and walked away, calling back, "I mean it, Grant. Anything else goes wrong, we kill your wife and kids."

Kelly was having serious second thoughts. Rodriguez struggled with the door's dead bolt, swearing under his breath.

"I used to be able to do this in under a minute," he said, smiling apologetically.

Kelly raised an eyebrow. "Really? I must've missed that training seminar."

"Misspent youth. Anyway, I'm out of practice."

"I'm thinking maybe we should try to get a warrant…" Kelly said, glancing around. This area was less deserted than the other warehouse district. Despite the late hour a few trucks were still parked outside other buildings. She hadn't seen anyone around, but you never knew. An arrest for breaking and entering would definitely hasten her exit from the Bureau, and she wondered if subconsciously she was hoping the decision would be made for her.

The sound of pins clicking, and Rodriguez turned the knob. Kelly unclipped the top of her holster and put her hand over her Glock.

"Stay behind me," she said in a low voice.

"Not a problem."

It was pitch-black inside, the only illumination filtered moonlight from windows set far above. Kelly clicked on a flashlight, keeping the beam low to the ground. The layout was similar to the other warehouse, two smaller huts in the rear of the building, a large open area up front. Except this time, the space wasn't empty.

"What the hell?" Rodriguez whispered. A flatbed trailer held an enormous float decked out in the colors of the American flag, with slogans splashed across an eagle.

Kelly didn't answer, gesturing for him to stay behind her while they searched the warehouse. She checked the first door—instead of an office it housed a line of portable toilets. The smell rising from them was rank. The doors had been removed, and Kelly held one hand over her nose as she quickly scanned down the line. All empty.

She turned to find Rodriguez looking as puzzled as she felt.

"What do you—"

A sound from the other hut. Kelly motioned for him to be quiet. She crossed the warehouse floor quickly, staying to the left of the door, out of range in case whoever was on the other side was armed. She waited for Rodriguez to join her. He was breathing hard, even in the dim lighting she could see he looked pale. Pushing himself too hard, she thought. He should probably still be in the hospital.

He nodded at her, weapon drawn.

"FBI! Open the door and show me your hands!"

"Jones," Rodriguez said, motioning at the door with his Glock. Kelly glanced down. A padlock latched the outside. She frowned. Whoever was inside was not there voluntarily.

"Can you get that one open?" she asked.

"Step back," Rodriguez said. Kelly slipped behind him. He fired a single shot.

"Jesus, Rodriguez!" Kelly hissed. "That wasn't what I meant."

He shrugged. "It's a Master. Tough to break in to. Would've taken forever."

Kelly gritted her teeth and undid the latch. She yanked

the door open, stepping back while she scanned down the sight. Eyes stared back at her, the whites bright in the gloom. Kelly took a tentative step forward, then another. Her flashlight beam caused them to squint; some shielded their eyes with their hands. The smell was a hundred times worse than the toilets across the hall, and Kelly fought an involuntary urge to retch.

Rodriguez called out something in Spanish, and a series of voices answered, tripping over each other in their desire to be heard. The mass of people stood. Some pressed toward the door.

"Alto!" Kelly yelled, keeping her weapon up, hoping that was the right word. "Tell them not to move."

Rodriguez spit out another stream of Spanish, his voice heavy with authority. A few grumbles, but the people stepped back.

"See if you can find the lights," Kelly said.

Rodriguez vanished. Kelly kept her weapon raised. She didn't know what she'd do if they rushed her, there were too many to stop and no one appeared to be armed.

Suddenly, the lights clicked on. Kelly blinked with the others: after the dusky half-light, the glare was startling. The room was no more than ten-by-ten feet, but at least twenty people were crammed inside. Most were in their twenties or thirties, but a few appeared to be teenagers. Filthy, as if they had gone months without bathing, a fine layer of grime rendering them nearly indistinguishable.

"Jesus," Rodriguez said, reappearing at her side.

"Ask them why they're here," Kelly said. The room issued a palpable sense of misery, as if long after they left the walls would still be laden with it. She couldn't even imagine what would be worth subjecting yourself to these conditions.

Rodriguez asked what sounded like a question, and one of the men replied. Rodriguez motioned him closer, and they spoke in low voices for a minute. The man waited, watching with imploring eyes, while Rodriguez came over to explain.

"A coyote brought them here, a white man," he said. "Guaranteed he'd be able to slip them past *La migra* and the Minutemen. But once they got here, they were told they'd have to stay. That the coyotes had a plan for them to slip away during a parade. Only then would it be safe. Someone comes by once a day to give them food and take them to the toilets."

"A parade?" Kelly knit her brow, turning back to the main room. "So they're waiting to be brought out of here on a float? That doesn't make any sense."

Rodriguez shrugged. "Fourth of July is coming up, I'm guessing the float is for that. Maybe their coyote thought it would be easier to have them slip away in a crowd."

"They could just drop them in a Latino neighborhood in San Antonio," Kelly said, shaking her head. "Doesn't make sense."

"Yeah, you're right." Rodriguez frowned. "Plus that doesn't explain how the good ol' boys at the other warehouse tie into it. Why would Minutemen be coyotes?"

"It is kind of perfect. They know the border better than anyone else," Kelly pointed out.

"Yeah, but most of those guys would pay to shoot a Mexican. They're fanatical about it."

"You're right, it's strange." Kelly eyed the float. It looked garish in the austere surroundings. Here she was trying to tie up loose ends, and instead she kept adding more threads.

"What do we do with them?" Rodriguez asked. A few of the immigrants had crowded in the doorway and were watching them silently.

Kelly hated what she was about to say, but knew there was no other option. "You have to explain that we're going to lock them back in until their handlers come. As soon as they hear the doors open, I want them to make as much noise as possible."

"You want to be able to claim exigent circumstances," Rodriguez said.

"It's our only way in, especially if Laredo P.D. is working with them."

"What makes you think they'll come? If they think their operation has been compromised, they might take off."

"We rattled their cage. I'm guessing someone will come by soon to check on things, maybe even move them to a new location," Kelly said. "And I'm willing to bet it'll be our favorite Minutemen brothers."

"And if you're wrong?" Rodriguez asked, voice hard.

"Then we call the ICE." He didn't respond, eyes focused on the ground. Kelly examined him. "We're still the law, Rodriguez."

"Yeah, I know," he responded after a minute.

Kelly considered reminding him of what he'd said earlier, about the flood of people being a burden the country couldn't sustain, but she didn't have the heart. Things that were good in theory changed when you faced a couple dozen hungry, desperate faces. Kelly didn't like the thought of deporting them any more than he did, but she had no other option. She had to use them to snag the coyotes, so she could finally figure out what the hell was going on.

"I'll go explain," Rodriguez said, avoiding eye contact as he turned back toward the room. "But they might take some convincing. I suggest you keep your weapon drawn."

* * *

Dante couldn't stop scratching his arm. He could swear a rash was forming. He checked his dosimeter for the hundredth time. Still black, all but one circle filled in. He had showered twice, scrubbing so hard his skin was sore. It didn't help.

Damn that Grant, he thought, lip curling. Bastard had to complicate things by playing the hero. Dante had never been a fan of this phase of the plan, in fact he'd repeatedly said there was too much room for error.

It had been a bad few days. First the loss of the girl, and two of his best men with her. The arrests at the bar, the contamination of the warehouse, then having to waste Thor and the others. Now the rest were too spooked to be reliable. His army had been badly decimated. Dante could get more—the network was large, and one phone call would muster reserves. But he'd handpicked the men who were closest to the operation, and look how that was working out. He decided to stick with who he had, using fear to keep them in line. *That was the problem with cons,* he thought irritably. *They had no sense of honor.* Jackson was right, they were only suited to be grunts on the ground.

Dante's cell phone rang. He squinted at the number, then clicked it open. "Yeah?"

"We got 'em at a house outside Winters, California. What do you want?"

Dante thought for a minute. A vision of Grant's face crossed his mind, cocky and gloating after the spill. "Take 'em."

"You sure?"

"Yeah. And the girl, the young one? She goes first." A long pause. "There a problem?" Dante snarled, scratching at his arm again.

"Well, sir…there are four guards. And they look…"

"Yeah?" Dante said impatiently.

"They look like they know their shit, sir. I'm just saying, it's the two of us."

Dante rubbed his eyes with his free hand, thought it over. "All right. I know some guys near there." He glanced at his watch: Jesus, nearly 3:00 a.m. "I'll let you know when they're coming. Don't leave your position. And if they start to move again, call."

"Yes, sir."

"Don't fuck this up," Dante warned. "And when you kill the girl? Tape it. I got someone here should see that."

Dante hung up the phone feeling uniquely satisfied. He probably should have run the revised plan past Jackson, but he always hated to be bothered with details. And after the shit Grant pulled today, he needed to face some repercussions. Dante smiled as he imagined showing him that video. He'd see who the smart one was. And if Dante's boys did him proud, it would be the sort of death no father would ever want to witness.

JULY 2

Twenty-One

Jake blinked a few times, still half-asleep. He frowned. The light fixture above his head dangled precariously from a cord, swinging slightly in the breeze through the window. Outlet covers were scattered across the coffee table. The fan in the kitchen canted at a crazy angle. Syd sat cross-legged on the living room floor, papers spread in an arc around her.

"Morning, sunshine," she said without looking up.

"Man, I slept hard. What time is it?"

"After nine."

"Really?" Jake sifted through the mess for his watch. "Dang. Thanks for letting me sleep." He looked up. "You weren't at this all night, were you?"

Syd shrugged. "I grabbed a few hours."

She was intently perusing the papers in her hand, brow furrowed. Jake watched for a minute, repressing a yawn, before asking, "You find anything?"

"Yup."

"Great." He swung his legs to the floor and leaned over her, elbows on his knees. "Where'd he hide them?"

She pointed sheepishly to the filing cabinet. "In there."

"Wow, you spies really are something."

"Shut up," she said. Deep circles hooded her eyes. Despite that, whatever darkness had been in her last night appeared to have receded. She was once again cheerful, happy-go-lucky Syd. "I forgot I was dealing with a civilian, gave Randall too much credit."

Jake thought that was a bit harsh under the circumstances, but decided not to comment. "So what are they?"

"His bank records." She held them up. "Randall made four large deposits in the past year."

"How large?"

"Large enough to pay off his lawyer and buy this dump." She glanced around. "With some left over."

"Son of a bitch. He was involved."

"Looks like it."

"You okay?" He examined her.

"You kidding? I'm mad as hell." Syd snorted. "Bastard gets his daughter snatched, then calls me for help. I've got half a mind to call off my men."

"Don't do that," Jake said, thinking of how small Madison had appeared in the hospital bed.

"I won't. But don't think for a minute this is pro bono anymore. I'm transferring these funds to our account ASAP."

"You can do that?"

"One phone call." She winked at him. "Don't worry, Jake. I wouldn't do it to you."

"Remind me to switch to an offshore account as soon as I get home."

"Only slows me down, doesn't stop me," Syd teased.

Jake thought about her half of the company's start-up money, then decided he probably didn't want to know. "So can you trace back the deposits?"

"I can't, but I'll put one of my guys on it. Hopefully he'll have something by this afternoon."

"Okay." Jake yawned and stretched. "I'm going out for coffee."

"Great. Be quiet when you come in, I'm going to crash in the bedroom."

Madison pushed the crust of her sandwich around the rim of the plate until she caught her mother's look and stopped. She sighed and buried her chin in one hand. It was funny, twenty-four hours ago she would have killed for some company. When her mother and sister showed up at the hospital they'd all clung together, crying and talking over each other in an outpouring of emotion. After arriving at the farmhouse last night they all crowded into the same queen bed. In spite of that Madison slept fitfully. The slightest noise sent her bolt upright, her heart in her throat. Her mother stroked her hair and wiped the tears away. And Madison would slowly drift off, only to have it happen again an hour later.

By this morning they'd fallen back into their habitual state of silence. Bree sat by the fireplace reading a book. And her mother had become her shadow. Madison knew it was because she loved her and was afraid of losing her again, but for God's sake, they were in a two-bedroom farmhouse. It wasn't like there was anywhere to go. The commando boys, as she'd taken to calling them, wouldn't even let her look outside. But still her mother hovered as though she might slip through a crack in the floorboards and vanish. It was starting to become seriously annoying. The TV only had three channels, there was a VCR but the movies were really old and lame. And that was it. What she'd do to have her DS Lite back again.

"How long do we have to stay?" Madison asked again.

Her mother shot her a warning look, but she didn't care anymore. Nothing about this felt right. They'd had an army of cops at the hospital earlier, why hadn't they asked to be protected by them? Cops would put them somewhere safe, she'd seen it on TV. For all they knew, these guys could have been in on it from the beginning. This might be part of the whole plan. Madison had pointed that out when they'd first arrived, but her mother had shushed her.

"But what makes you so sure Dad hired them?" she'd asked.

"I just know," her mother had said, avoiding her eyes.

The commando boys kept glancing at her in a way that made her uncomfortable. If her dad had hired these guys, what was to prevent someone from offering more money to get them to switch sides? Just in case, she'd palmed one of the steak knives from the drawer and tucked it inside her cast. It was uncomfortable, pressed against her bare skin. But it was something. More than she'd had last time, at any rate.

The one who appeared to be in charge, Maltz, returned from the bedroom. He tucked a cell phone in his pocket and avoided their eyes. An hour ago one of them had returned from a trip outside visibly agitated, and since then there had been lots of whispered conversations.

"What's going on?" Madison asked.

"Nothing, miss," he said.

But within five minutes they were moving pieces of furniture, blocking the few windows. Maltz marched in with an armful of guns and dropped them in the middle of the living room floor.

"Sweet Jesus," her mother breathed. They both stared as he went through the pile, performing some kind of check on each.

Madison heard an engine gunning, and watched as they backed the van up to the door. "What the hell is going on?" she asked, hobbling up to Maltz. He'd produced a pair of crutches, but she hated using them.

Maltz eyed her. Clearly he wasn't comfortable around kids, or maybe humans in general. He wasn't much taller than her but he was thick, ropy muscle lending him an air of solidity. He had light blue eyes and dusty-blond hair cropped close to his scalp. Under other circumstances, Madison would have probably thought he was cute. Apparently he realized she wasn't getting out of his face without a response. "We've got company," he said simply.

Madison's lungs deflated as though someone was squeezing them. Once again she pictured the clamps being fastened on her bra and she started to shake. "The same guys?" she asked.

"I think so." Maltz awkwardly patted her shoulder. "You're gonna be okay," he said. "We won't let 'em get you again."

Madison didn't reply. She went and curled up next to her mother on the couch. Audrey's arms wrapped around her and Madison let herself be held, rocked back and forth as she watched the preparations through a stream of tears. One of the men had found some boards and they started nailing them over the windows. The sound of the hammer drove it home: this was never going to end. They had her father, and pretty soon they'd have the rest of her family, too. Madison wanted to scream but instead buried her face in her mother's chest. As Audrey hummed a tuneless song, one by one the windows were covered and the room slipped into darkness.

Twenty-Two

"Chip?"

Kelly shook her head. Rodriguez crunched noisily. "Haven't had these since I was a kid," he said happily, shaking the bag in her direction. "I didn't even know they still made them."

"That's exciting," Kelly said wryly.

"Hey, anything to lighten the mood."

Kelly shifted in her seat. She had to go to the bathroom again, but the nearest one was almost a mile away on a parallel road. It was nearly noon and the other ware-houses had a steady stream of trucks to and from their loading ramps. Their parked car hadn't attracted any attention yet, but she was nervous. The other warehouses could also be harboring illegal activities. For all she knew, there could be a posse assembling to string them up, and they were out here all alone. With every passing hour, her doubts about the plan grew. And Rodriguez's incessant chatter wasn't helping.

So far she'd been mistaken in her assumption that the cowboys would race to check the second warehouse. She and Rodriguez had spent the night in the car, taking shifts sleeping, and no one had appeared. Maybe Rodriguez was right, and the close call yesterday caused them to shy off. Kelly had agreed that if no one showed by noon, she'd call ICE. Rodriguez bet her fifty dollars that she'd be making that call, and they shook on it. She felt guilty leaving those poor people inside with no food or water. When she conceived the plan she'd expected to wait a few hours, max.

Kelly examined Rodriguez out of the corner of her eye. His face was the manifestation of a mood ring, with every passing hour a new shade was revealed. She had to admit, she was impressed with the way he was handling himself. The bar incident was a debacle, but since then he'd proven surprisingly devoted to solving the case, almost to an extreme. Under similar circumstances, she'd probably still be in a hospital bed.

"You sure you don't want one? They're almost gone." He held the bag out again, and this time she grabbed a handful.

"Thanks." Kelly popped one in her mouth and promptly gagged. "Oh my God!" she choked.

Rodriguez laughed and handed her a soda. Kelly took a gulp, swished it around her mouth, and spit out the window. "What is that?"

"Pork."

"That does not taste like pork," Kelly said, eyeing the remaining chips skeptically.

"Depends on what part of the pig you're used to eating." Rodriguez laughed at the shock on her face. "Easy, Jones. I'm messing with you."

"I'm never trusting you again." She sniffed, dumping the chips back in the bag.

"Please. Like you trusted me before?" Before she could craft a response, he shook his head and looked out the window. "It's okay. I've heard the rumors."

"So are they true?"

"Which ones?"

"That you ratted out your last partner," Kelly said. "Let's start with that one."

He shook his head, turning back to the bag.

"C'mon, I'm sure there's plenty of gossip about me," Kelly said, tapping his elbow.

"You bet there is."

Kelly wasn't expecting such a strong response. Now in spite of herself, she was curious. "If you want me to trust you, I need to know the truth."

"Is it so hard to believe I did a great job on my last case, and the promotion was based on that?" Rodriguez grumbled.

"You're twenty-seven years old," Kelly noted. "You'd have to find Jimmy Hoffa for that kind of bump at your age."

"Maybe I did."

Kelly raised an eyebrow. He glared back at her, then shrugged. "Fine. I ratted someone out, but it wasn't my partner."

"Who?"

"My boss. He buried some evidence on a case. I found out, told his SAC. Long story short, the FBI couldn't afford another black eye. He took early retirement, I was given my pick of divisions."

"Huh." It made sense, Kelly thought. Last thing the Bureau needed was a high profile officer dragged through the mud. And they'd definitely do whatever it took to keep Rodriguez happy. After working there for more than a decade, she recognized that the FBI could be every bit as dirty and political as a major corporation. Still, she tried to do the best job she could. Sometimes she even felt like justice had been served. Less and less lately, but sometimes. "Okay."

"Anything else?" Rodriguez asked, jutting his chin out.

She ignored his confrontational tone. "Are you a hermaphrodite?"

"What? They're not saying that."

Kelly laughed at his expression. "No, but it's a good one. Want me to start it?"

"I can promise if you did, my fiancée would hunt you down. And she's scary, trust me. Those boys in the bar wouldn't have stood a chance against her."

"I was surprised to hear you were engaged," Kelly said.

"What, I'm not a catch?" He grinned.

"You're so young to be getting married."

Rodriguez looked bemused. "Tell my mother that. She's been on me to get hitched since high school. You're engaged, too, right?"

"Sort of," Kelly mumbled.

"Have you sort of set a date?"

"Not yet. We're working out some…technicalities," Kelly said, wishing he'd change the subject.

"Don't wait too long, we had to sign up for the ballroom a year in advance. Me, I can't wait. August 31, back in L.A. It's gonna be off the hook. You and Jake should come."

Rodriguez sounded excited, and Kelly guessed that "off the hook" was a good thing. She shifted in her seat. "So what are they saying about me?"

"Ah, I was just trying to get under your skin, *chica.*" Rodriguez turned his attention back to the chips.

Kelly was about to respond when a familiar pickup appeared, rising and falling with the ruts in the road. It pulled into the lot in front of the warehouse.

Rodriguez elbowed her. "You were right."

"Damn straight I was. And you're out fifty dollars." She glanced at her watch: 11:59 a.m., right under the wire.

"How do you want to handle this?"

"Neither of them was carrying before, but that doesn't mean anything. I say we get them away from the truck, where they might have a shotgun. We know there aren't any weapons in the front of the warehouse. So after they go inside, we hit them hard and fast."

"Sounds good, boss." Rodriguez nodded.

Kelly looked him over. "You sure you're up for this?"

"I don't feel as bad as I look. Which is rare, usually it's the other way around."

Kelly decided they'd have to chance it. Jethro, the taller cowboy, was headed toward the door, Jim fast on his heels. "Let's go, quick and quiet. I don't want them barricading themselves inside with hostages."

Kelly got out of the car and bent double, staying low to the ground. She crossed the parking lot in front of the warehouse with long strides, gun drawn. As she got closer she overheard snippets of conversation, something about the Rangers' chances this season. Jethro was sorting through a key ring. Their backs were still to her. The sand muffled her footsteps and she steered clear of the gravel patches dotting the lot.

The door opened and Jethro stepped inside. Kelly waited until Jim had followed, then bolted up the stairs, catching the door as it was about to close. She glanced over her shoulder. Rodriguez was right behind her, eyes wide with exhilaration. She nodded at him, jerked open the door and slipped inside.

The cowboys sensed them and spun. Jethro darted a hand toward his belt and Kelly yelled, "FBI! Hands where I can see them!"

Jethro's hand stalled its descent. She could see him deliberating, and took three quick strides forward with the muzzle leveled at his chest. "I'd prefer to have you alive," she said, "but it's your choice."

His brother Jim already had his hands in the air. Jethro glanced at him, then slowly followed suit.

"On the ground, nice and slow," Kelly said.

"This is bullshit," Jim spat. "We ain't done nothin' wrong."

"Shush, Jim," Jethro said warningly.

"You kidding? Doesn't even matter, bitch. No one in this town is gonna charge us. You seriously think Luke'll put us behind bars? Hell, the folks around here think we deserve a medal, and they don't know the half of…"

"I said shut the fuck up!" Jethro growled.

"I'm not calling your buddy Rowe," Kelly said, digging a knee into Jethro's back as she fastened handcuffs around his wrists. "What we've got here is a federal violation."

"Fuck you," Jim said, kicking his legs at Rodriguez, who was bending to cuff him. "I don't want you touching me."

Kelly and Rodriguez exchanged a glance.

"Don't make me add assaulting a federal officer, that's another twenty-five years," Kelly said.

Rodriguez settled into a squat, hands clasped in front of him. "So, boys. How long you been coyotes?"

Jim snorted. "We're not fucking coyotes, you stupid spic."

Jethro snapped out his leg, kicking him hard in the shin. Jim yelped, then fell silent.

"Your brother has a lot to say," Rodriguez remarked. Kelly heard the undercurrent in his voice and knew the slur had gotten to him. "How 'bout you? You think I'm a dirty wetback?"

"Jethro Henderson. Colonel. TX-47928878."

"What?" Kelly asked, puzzled.

"Jethro Henderson. Colonel. TX-47928878."

His brother started chanting as well, changing name, rank and number, speaking with a slight lisp. Kelly and Rodriguez exchanged a look.

"Déjà vu, huh, Jones?" he said.

Jake clicked open his phone as he walked to the café on the corner. It was blazing hot outside, well over a hundred degrees. Hard to believe it was already July. He'd expected them to be married by now, and maybe even pregnant. Since he and Kelly were both older and didn't have much family, he'd figured they'd go to the courthouse and exchange vows there. Maybe they still would, he thought. Maybe this time apart had helped Kelly clarify what she was feeling, persuading her that it was time for them to move forward. Not that he was counting on that.

He dialed her number and got voice mail again. No missed calls, either, just a text saying she was following a lead and would call when she could. Jake debated leaving a message, then texted back *okay,* and shut the phone.

While Jake waited for his order to be filled he scanned the baked goods. Nothing looked appetizing, but his stomach growled and he realized he hadn't eaten anything since a mealy cafeteria sandwich the night before. He got three chicken wraps, figuring Syd would be starving when she woke up.

On the walk back he reviewed his last conversation with Kelly, and the reprobation in her voice. He knew they had different philosophies about how to work a case, and that if she joined The Longhorn Group that might become an issue. It could even end up widening the schism between them. But what was the alternative? Kelly had been miserable these past few months, conflicted about continuing with the Bureau. And even if she stayed there, she wasn't the type to settle happily into a desk job. She was smart and talented, she could probably do well at any career she set her mind to. But once you'd worked in the field, days spent sending faxes and filing memos were soul-crushing.

If they didn't at least end up in the same city soon, the distance between them would become far more than a physical obstacle. He was losing her, slowly but steadily, and had been even before the proposal. In all honesty, he was no longer sure that was such a bad thing.

He balanced the coffee and food in one hand while awkwardly opening the door to Randall's apartment with the other. Jake cursed slightly as liquid sloshed out of the top, scalding him. He glanced up to find Syd smiling. She had stripped down to a camisole and panties, sky-blue against her tan skin.

"I couldn't sleep," she said.

He started to speak, then the bag shifted and he lunged awkwardly to grab it, spilling more coffee.

"Here, let me help you," she said. Her hand lingered on his as she took the bag. She strolled to the kitchen, set it on a counter and bent to dig a dishcloth out of a drawer. She handed it to him, eyes fixed on his.

Jake wiped his hands, which were drenched with more than coffee. After a minute he said, "I would have gotten you a latte, but figured you'd be asleep."

"You're a sweet guy, Jake."

"Yeah, well—" He cleared his throat. "Any word from your friend?"

"Not yet." She took a step closer. "So we've got some time to kill."

Jake fumbled in his pocket for his phone and checked the screen.

Syd frowned. "I didn't hear it ring."

"It didn't but I—I'm expecting a call." Jesus, he was actually stuttering. When did he become such a moron? But then, he used to know exactly what to do in a situation like this. A few years ago he would have swept Syd into the bedroom the minute he saw what amounted to an open invitation.

"I've still got so much adrenaline in my system," Syd said, holding up her hand. Jake watched it hover in the air a foot from him. "Shaky. Not sure if I'll be able to sleep unless…"

"It's probably not a good idea," Jake said firmly, recovering himself.

She took a step closer. He could feel the heat coming off her. One more step and what little self-control he possessed would go right out the proverbial window.

A phone rang, and Jake instinctively fumbled for his. Syd's brow furrowed with annoyance. "It's not yours, it's mine," she snapped.

She grabbed her cell from the coffee table. "Yes?" Her eyes narrowed and she glanced at Jake.

"What's up?"

She raised a finger for him to wait. Jake tried valiantly not to notice her nipples through the filmy fabric.

"Can you defend it, or would it be safer on the move?" she asked calmly.

Clearly not her banker friend, Jake thought, settling on the arm of the couch. He sipped his coffee. From the sound of it, he might not have the opportunity for another nap. *Or for anything else,* he thought, as in spite of himself his eyes wandered over her curves.

"I think that's your best option." She listened for

another moment, then shook her head. "Not possible. But we can be there in an hour or so."

After another minute of listening, she shut the phone and turned to Jake.

"Trouble at the hospital?" he guessed.

"The Grants aren't at the hospital anymore. I moved them to a safe house in Winters last night."

Jake frowned. "When did we decide that?"

"I thought it was best, in case whoever took Madison wasn't done with her yet." She held up her hands at Jake's expression. "Look, it was Maltz's idea, and sounded good so I signed off on it. Then we got caught up here and I forgot to mention it."

It bothered Jake that she hadn't consulted him, but he decided that was a discussion for another day. In the future they'd develop a strict set of guidelines for how cases were handled. Maybe it was good they'd had this one to cut their teeth on. He was definitely coming away with a deeper understanding of what it meant to be in business with Syd. "So what's going on?"

"During a perimeter patrol Jagerson came across a parked car with two men camped out watching the house."

"Maybe they're locals."

"Maltz said that even in meth country these two stick out. No way they're local. And they seemed to be waiting for something."

"Reinforcements. Shit," Jake said. He ran a hand through his hair, still stiff from sweat.

"Looks like it." She brushed past him on her way to the bedroom. "We were pretty much done here anyway. We'll head up there to provide support."

"Do you have any other guys on tap?"

"Nope, those four were all I had in California. It'll take

a day to mobilize another unit and I don't think we have time."

"I don't like it, Syd. We don't know what we're up against."

She came out of the bedroom wearing a clean pair of jeans and a T-shirt, running a brush through her hair. "So what do you want to do?"

"Call in the Feds."

"Jake…"

"I'm serious. Whoever we're dealing with has some serious reach and resources. There might be fifty people coming to take the girl back. Against the six of us, I don't like the odds."

Syd sat on the couch, clamping a hair band between her lips and arching her back as she tugged her hair into a ponytail. Jake caught himself appreciating how this maneuver displayed her breasts and cursed under his breath. Now that his mind had gone there, it was stuck. "I don't want a swarm of Feds coming in and getting everyone killed," she said, wrapping the band around her hair.

"Neither do I. But if we all end up dead it won't much matter." Jake sensed she was wavering, and pressed the advantage. "Let me call a few people I trust. They can provide backup if this thing goes south."

"Fine, make the call." Syd stood and grabbed her backpack. "Let's get on the road, I told Maltz we'd be there in an hour. And don't forget the food."

Randall heaved again. The convulsions were so violent it felt as if his insides were being ripped apart.

Afterward he sat back, wiping his mouth and gasping. The rational part of his brain knew this was largely psychosomatic. The gamma radiation dose he'd received would induce nausea three to six hours after exposure, but it wouldn't make him this ill. But the stress of the situation combined with the knowledge that he had, at most, weeks left to live was affecting him.

A knock at the bathroom door. "Stop stalling, Grant," Dante growled.

Randall climbed shakily to his feet. He hauled himself over to the sink, splashed some water on his face, and rinsed out his mouth. The mirror above it was badly cracked, rending his face into a thousand fragments. Which pretty much matched how he felt.

Randall wiped his face with a rough paper towel and trudged back outside. Dante had been unable to find another volunteer for sentry duty so he was working alone. He'd been warned that if he tried to escape or dragged his heels, he'd be shot and his family would be raped and killed. Not that he needed the warning after the show of strength earlier.

As Randall worked, his thoughts focused on what he could expect in the coming days and weeks, the gradual deterioration of his body in the face of acute radiation poisoning. Vomiting was the first sign, followed by radiation burns to exposed skin. After that, a latent phase of five to ten days before he started shedding hair. The massive loss of white blood cells would weaken his immune system, inducing fatigue and leaving him susceptible to infection. If he survived that, the real fun began: uncontrollable bleeding in the mouth, under his skin and in his kidneys; sterility; internal hemorrhaging; complete destruction of bone marrow; gastric and intestinal tissue damage. Near one hundred percent fatality rate within fourteen days. Although chances were he'd take a bullet through the temple before much of that came to pass.

Randall pulled his suit back on, knowing full well that

he was kidding himself. He might as well strip down and wrap himself in cellophane for the good it would do. It was warm inside the warehouse even without the heat coming off the source, and sweat poured down his back, adding to the flu-ish symptoms. Randall pictured Audrey and Bree at her mother's house, sitting on the couch watching television, completely unaware of the threat outside their door. His darling Madison was probably already dead. He'd fucked everything up, and for what? A little money. He'd traded the lives of himself, his family and countless others for a grand total of $160,000. Pathetic.

His limbs felt heavy as he worked the robotic arms, trying to see through the tears behind his mask.

Twenty-Three

Jake clenched his jaw as Syd wove through traffic. They'd turned off the main highway onto a smaller two-lane road. Apparently Syd regarded the double-line separating them from oncoming cars as more of a friendly guideline than a mandate. Jake instinctively braced himself against the dashboard as she swerved blindly around a truck, skidding into the breakdown lane as a sedan bore down on them. Seemingly unperturbed, she jetted back across both lanes, ignoring the protesting bleats of multiple horns.

"Be nice to get there in one piece," Jake said tightly.

"CIA driver training. Best in the world," Syd replied, shooting him a look.

"I'm willing to bet your insurance company doesn't agree," Jake said.

"Relax. We're almost there." Syd glanced at the GPS then hit the gas, taking a curve at seventy miles per hour.

Ten minutes later they were a mile from the farmhouse. Syd slowed. An acrid smell seeped through the car vents.

"Maybe someone's burning trash," Jake said. Syd

didn't respond, steering onto an unpaved access road. The car bounced over sinkholes, tires kicking up gravel behind them. The smell of smoke was unmistakable now. Light glinted off a large object up ahead. When they got closer, Jake recognized it: the team's white van. The front was crushed, bumper wrapped around a fence post, windshield shattered. A thin trail of smoke wound out the window, curling and rotating as it ascended.

Syd stopped the car fifty feet away. Jake drew his gun and got out, staying low as he jogged forward. Syd darted ahead of him. They slowed as they approached. The stench here was terrible, sharp and tangy, burnt upholstery mixed with something else.

Jake checked the interior, popping his head up quickly: empty. He sidled around to the driver's side and yanked the door handle, letting it swing wide while he stayed out of range. He counted to three, then ducked his head inside. Someone had torched the interior. Broken glass on the passenger side, and the seat was smoldering. Jake winced at the smell.

"They used a Molotov cocktail to force them out of the van," Syd said. She walked further down the road, panning her eyes across the ground. "Skid marks and bullet casings. Looks like we missed the party."

"So you think they got them?"

"One of them at least," Syd replied. She was about fifteen feet away, standing beside a pile of brush. Jake trotted over to join her. One of the team members lay on top of a patch of rotting leaves. Half of his face was scorched, the rest of him unrecognizable. An assault rifle was still clenched in his hands.

"Burned alive," Jake said. "Jesus."

"He took a couple with him," Syd said softly. "Good man."

Jake followed her gaze. Ten yards down the road two bodies lay facedown, sprawled where they had fallen. He approached carefully, keeping an eye on their hands. When he got closer he saw the sticky pools of muddy blood surrounding them, their leather jackets riddled with bullet wounds. Just past them, two motorcycles lay on their sides at angles to each other.

"So where's the rest of the team?" he asked, glancing around. The surrounding countryside was eerily still. The sting of something burning still irritated his nostrils.

"Let's get to the house," Syd said briskly, turning to walk back toward the car. Halfway there she froze. "Hear that?"

Jake listened hard. "Thunder?"

Syd had already bolted for the car, barely waiting for Jake to dive into the passenger seat before gunning the engine.

"We can't rush in there without a plan," Jake said as she tore down the road.

"We don't have time for one. We're probably already too late."

Jake opened his mouth to argue, then froze as they rounded a bend. At a break in the barbed wire fence lining the access road, a narrow driveway led through a grove of trees. The driveway dead-ended at a building awash in a flame, consumed by a pulsing heat that produced the roaring noise they'd heard.

"Oh my God," Jake said. "Please don't let them be in there."

Around noon the tension in the house ticked up. The commando-boys were antsy, they kept rechecking things they'd examined a minute before. One of them paced until his buddy glared at him, raising an eyebrow in their direction. Then he sat down, knees jiggling. Madison wanted to scream. They were sitting here waiting to get attacked.

"Why don't we just leave?" Madison asked again. Her mother shot her a look. She ignored it. "This is nuts. If you only saw two of them, we could get in the van and drive away."

"They'll follow us. We're in a defensible position here," Maltz said. "On the road we're vulnerable."

"So we drive to the police station, tell them what's going on. They're probably looking for us now anyway, right?" Madison looked at each of them in turn. "They'll keep us safe."

"We're not sure we can trust them," Maltz explained after a long pause.

"The police? Are you insane? Mom, tell them." Madison crossed her arms in front of her chest and turned to her mother.

"Honey, these men seem to know what they're doing," Audrey said, though she sounded uncertain as she eyed the guy cleaning his gun for the umpteenth time. "I think we should trust them."

Madison snorted, grabbed her crutches and clomped into the bedroom. Bree was sitting on the bed, balancing a notebook on her knees as she scribbled. She looked at Madison but didn't say anything.

"What?" Madison said. "This is not my fault."

"I never said it was." Bree seemed preternaturally calm. "It's got something to do with Dad."

"I know," Madison huffed. She dropped onto the other bed and let her crutches clatter to the floor. "Why is Mom trusting these guys?"

Bree turned her attention back to whatever she was writing. She'd kept a diary for years, always hidden as if it held state secrets or something. But once they moved into the apartment and had to share a room, it was easy for Madison to find. The contents were disappointing, though—lots of stuff about boys and what Bree and her friends did every day. "These guys saved you, right? They have some experience with this stuff. We don't," Bree said with finality.

But Madison was tired of everyone acting like they knew better than her. She was the one who had been kidnapped and held for days. She knew what they were capable of. At the memory her hand automatically reached for her chest, and she swallowed hard to keep from crying. She kept her voice low, leaning forward as she said, "Yeah, but if they're only in it for the money, maybe the people who took me will offer them more. Dad's not rich. What's to stop them from handing us over?"

"It's not like that." Bree shook her head impatiently, as if Madison had said something ridiculous. Her short hair bobbed before settling back into place. "The woman in charge, the one from the hospital? She has a personal interest."

She said the word *personal* like it was something dirty. Madison's eyes narrowed. "Why would she have a personal interest in us?"

"Because she's dating Dad," Bree said without meeting her eyes.

Madison felt as though she'd been punched. Sure, her parents were divorced, but the thought of her dad with another woman was still awful to contemplate. She tried to remember her, could only recall a pretty but tough-looking blonde. She wished she'd paid more attention.

There was a noise in the distance, a rumbling like thunder. Bree sat up straight, eyes wide. Madison froze, pulse pounding in her throat.

"What is that?" she asked.

The door to the room flew open. Maltz was wearing a bulletproof vest and had a rifle slung across his back. "It's time," he said.

"Time for what?" Bree sounded scared. Madison started to hyperventilate, picturing herself back in that room, the man coming for her...

"Put these on." He tossed a couple vests into the room. Bree bent to pick them up and handed one to Madison. It was heavy, and Madison struggled to pull it over her head. She fastened the Velcro as tightly as it would go, but it was too big for her and stuck out on either side like wings. Bree's was similarly large and hung past her waist. *We look like kids playing dress-up,* Madison thought. Maltz examined them critically. "They'll do. C'mon, we gotta be ready."

Ready for what? Madison wanted to ask, but she was too frightened to speak.

Bree handed Madison the crutches and followed her into the main room, keeping one hand on her elbow. Their mother was sitting there, also looking ridiculous in a vest. Her eyes were wide, and seeing how frightened she was made it so much worse. The roaring had grown louder, it sounded like a swarm had surrounded the house. *Motorcycles,* Madison thought. They were in a farmhouse in the middle of nowhere, and it sounded like a hundred motorcycles were circling them.

One of the men peered through a narrow crack in the boards nailed over the windows. "I'm counting at least eight."

Maltz swore under his breath. "Assessment?" he barked.

"Looks like a gang. I see a few shotguns, some handguns. No carbines or semiautos. Firepower, but nothing too heavy."

"Okay. With any luck, we're dealing with amateurs."

Maltz turned to them. "Here's the deal. Dangel is going to drive the van away, drawing them off. We're going to head out the back and go cross-country. There's a river at the property line, then another few miles to the next house. If they tail us, we'll engage, but I'm hoping it won't come to that."

"That's it? That's your plan?" Madison asked, incredulous. "How the hell am I supposed to run through the woods? In case you haven't noticed, I'm in a cast."

"I'll be carrying you, miss," Maltz said.

"Oh my God." Madison turned to her mother. "Mom, don't tell me you're agreeing to this?"

Her mother continued staring at the floor.

"Any questions?" Maltz asked.

Bree stepped forward, voice strong as she said, "We're ready."

A minute later, something thumped against the far wall, glass shattering. Smoke drifted into the room. Her mother screamed. Maltz froze for a second, then nodded at Dangel, who jumped into the back of the van and climbed through to the front seat. A second later he revved the engine. As the van tore away from the house, Maltz slammed the front door.

"Everyone to the back," he ordered.

Madison clomped through the kitchen to the back door. Her mother and sister were already huddled there, eyes wide with fear. The other two men stood on either side of them. Their jaws were tight, and they avoided her eyes. Maltz appeared a second later. They all waited. Another thump, near the bedrooms. A wisp of smoke curled into the room, dancing up toward the ceiling.

"We're going to be burned alive," her mother said, voice strangely calm.

"Not if I can help it, ma'am." Maltz seemed to be waiting for something. One more smack against the wall by the kitchen, then the sound of motors retreating into the distance.

"They're leaving," Bree said.

Maltz motioned for them to step aside. He opened the rear door a crack and thrust his head out quickly, scanning from side to side. Seemingly satisfied, he slipped outside.

"What do we do?" Bree asked. One of the men frowned and motioned for her to be silent. A second later, the door swung wide and Maltz reappeared.

"It's time. Go, go, go!" he said.

One of the commandos raced out. Bree and her mother followed on his heels, Audrey tripping on the threshold. The other commando caught her and helped her to her feet. Madison was suddenly airborne.

"Hey!"

Her crutches fell to the ground with a clatter. Maltz had thrown her over his shoulder. He dashed off into the woods. Madison gritted her teeth, bumping against his back as he ran. She lifted her head. Flames were licking at the farmhouse, a line of them along the base. They climbed steadily as if alive, racing up toward the roof. She heard more glass shattering, then they dipped into a gulch and the house vanished from view.

Twenty-Four

"They're not talking," Agent Taylor said, handing her a cup of coffee.

Kelly smiled at him. "I figured."

"Getting a lot of that these days," Rodriguez commented. They were sitting on the warehouse's loading dock. Behind them, the building throbbed with activity. Agents from the San Antonio field office were interviewing the illegals. Jethro and Jim were waiting for transport to a federal detention facility. Despite repeated attempts at questioning, they continued to issue the same response.

"Yeah? I've never seen anything like it." Taylor shook his head. "Who else?"

"Bunch of skinheads in Arizona."

"Arizona? That connected to the Morris killing?" Taylor's eyebrows knit together. He was in his early forties, dark hair gelled back and a suit that had seen better days.

"We think so, but we're not sure," Kelly said.

"What's with the float?" Taylor jerked his head toward it.

"The Mexicans said they were supposed to ride in the parade next week, then slip off into the crowd."

Taylor shook his head. "This pair has Minutemen written all over them. Can't figure out why they'd be running illegals."

"We can't, either," Kelly said. "Have you had any trouble with them before?"

Taylor shrugged. "ICE will be here soon, they'll have more information. There have been scattered reports here and there, bodies found in the desert, rumors that some of these guys have gone vigilante. But nothing solid."

"Nothing you've pursued, you mean," Rodriguez said.

Taylor narrowed his eyes. "Like I said, that falls to the folks at ICE. But you know how it is down here. Locals are complaining that the fence isn't enough to stop them. But it's harder to make it across now, so more illegals try the desert. The number of them who die out there has sky-rocketed. They found ten young girls this week, they'd been dead a few days so there wasn't much left. And there's less and less money to do anything about it. I got a pal works the border, he's supposed to cover three hundred miles a night on his rounds. He stopped driving an ATV after nearly losing his head running into a trip wire the coyotes strung up. Then, if he catches anyone, he's supposed to stop them himself. Half the time they scatter or throw rocks at him. Maybe he gets one or two."

"And I thought we had a shit job," Rodriguez said.

Taylor nodded. "No kidding, they should get combat pay. And God help them if they stumble across drug runners, some of those gangs carry UZIs. So folks around here turn a blind eye to people doing something about it. The Minutemen refer to themselves as true patriots, claim they're keeping America safe for Americans." He jerked his head in the direction of the office. "My guess is these boys fall in that category."

"But their side business is running people across the

border? That doesn't make sense." Kelly's brows knit together.

Taylor shrugged. "Nope, you're right. And what's the connection to the Morris case?" She and Rodriguez didn't answer. He eyed them, then said, "So what's your next step, barring these guys talking?"

"There's another place to check in Texas," Kelly said. "Outside Houston."

"You got enough for a warrant?"

"Maybe, based on this bust. We could claim linkage, say we suspect a similar criminal enterprise is taking place since they're both owned by the same shell corporation."

"I know a friendly judge in that district. You want me to make a call?" Taylor offered.

"That would be great," Kelly said.

"Guessing you'll need backup, too," Taylor said, glancing at Rodriguez. "I gotta say, you look like hell."

"Thanks," Rodriguez said wryly.

"There are some good people in the Houston office, I'll see about getting them to tag along." Taylor glanced at his watch. "You catch the next flight, you could be there in a couple of hours. I'll try to have everything ready by then."

"Listen, we really appreciate the help," Kelly said, scrambling to her feet. "You sure you don't need us here?"

"Nah, it's all over except for the paperwork. But next time you kick up a shitstorm like this, I'd appreciate a heads-up first."

"Will do," Kelly said, neglecting to add that hopefully there wouldn't be a next time, at least not for her. "And if you wouldn't mind waiting a few hours to process our friends, we'd appreciate that."

"You want to make sure they don't warn their buddies

in Houston, huh?" Taylor grinned. "I think it'll take some time to get them to a telephone."

"Perfect," Kelly said. Taylor shook her hand, then headed back inside.

"So I'm guessing this means we don't get to sleep?" Rodriguez asked, stretching his arms above his head and yawning for dramatic effect. "Or have a decent meal?"

"Later. We need to jump on this before anyone gets wind of what happened here." Kelly felt a rush of adrenaline. They were onto something, she could feel it. And whatever was in Houston might provide the final piece that explained everything.

"Yeah, yeah. Duty calls."

"You don't have to come, you know." Kelly eyed him. In spite of his joking tone, he looked exhausted and there was a thread of pain in his voice. "I'll have backup."

"And miss out on seeing Houston? Never," Rodriguez said. He lurched clumsily to his feet, wincing. His limp seemed worse as she followed him back inside.

As they walked past the processing table that had been set up, Kelly avoided the pleading eyes of the illegals. They were being taken to a detention center, then in all likelihood would be shipped back across the border.

"Señora!" one of them called out. *"Por favor!"*

Kelly ignored them and kept walking. She tried not to think about all those bodies in the desert, the ones who had failed. In a few weeks, some of these people might be facing the same obstacles again, undertaking the long, deadly trek through the wilderness. Jethro glared as she passed him. He and Jim were shackled to chairs, a couple of agents standing guard over them.

Kelly's phone buzzed, the caller ID reading *ASAC McLarty.* Kelly hit the ignore button. She'd have to call her boss soon to get approval for marshaling Houston field office agents, and for the warehouse search warrant. It was a conversation she wasn't looking forward to. In fact, there was a good chance that by this time tomorrow, she would officially be out of a job.

"Motorcycles," Jake said. His voice was muffled, shirt pulled up over his mouth to filter the smoke. They were still a hundred feet from the house, but rolling clouds of soot swept through the trees, stinging his nose and tightening his chest. There was a line of bikes parked a few feet away. "Maybe that Stockton gang Dante hung with. You think the Grants were in there when it lit up?"

"I doubt it," Syd said, fumbling with her radio. "Otherwise the bikes would be gone. Dangel must've drawn them off with the van so that Maltz could get the others out."

"God, I hope you're right," Jake said, watching the fire lick the nearest trees. "This whole place is going to be destroyed if the fire department doesn't get here soon."

"Not likely. An area like this, it's probably all volunteer. Might take them an hour, minimum." Speaking into her radio, she said, "Maltz, this is Syd. Do you read?"

They both listened. Static poured out. Then the sound of Maltz's voice, choked and garbled.

"Can you make that out?" Jake asked.

Syd shook her head. "Nope, they must already be over the hill." She squinted past what remained of the house toward the river. On the farside, foothills lined the horizon.

"But on the plus side, it sounds like they're still alive," Jake said.

"Maltz, at least." Syd walked briskly back toward the car. "We need to find a road close to where they'll come out. Let's check the map."

Suddenly, she bucked forward. Jake heard the concus-

sion a beat later. He instinctively dove to the ground and
scrambled for cover behind the nearest tree. Syd lay
facedown ten feet in front of him. She wasn't moving.

"Syd!" he hissed.

Another shot kicked up the dirt a few feet away.
Clearly not all of the bikers had followed Maltz into the
woods. And one of them was a hell of a shot. Jake
checked his HK, making sure the safety was off and that
it held a full clip. The fire and smoke made it hard to see
and his eyes smarted from the heat, forcing him to squint.

He saw Syd's foot shift, and a wave of relief rolled
over him. Apparently the sniper witnessed the movement,
too, because the leaves next to her ankle jumped. Jake
gritted his teeth. Syd was wearing a vest, and flat against
the ground she presented a tricky target. If he ran out to
try and save her, there was an excellent chance he'd be
hit instead. But the alternative was letting the sniper take
potshots until one struck home.

Deciding, Jake fired a volley of shots, counted to five,
then sent another hail of bullets in the sniper's general direction. Without hesitation he raced from the tree line and
lunged for Syd, grabbing her ankle. He felt something hit
his calf. With an almost superhuman surge of strength he
swung her behind an enormous tree. Jake dropped down
beside her, breathing hard and clutching at his leg. He
patted it all over, then yanked up his cuff. Nothing: he was
unharmed. He sent a silent thanks to his guardian angel
and turned his attention back to Syd. She was lying on
the ground, unconscious.

"Christ, Syd," he muttered, checking her for bleeding.

Maltz dumped Madison on the ground near her mother
and Bree, then went to confer with the other commandos.
It felt like they'd been traveling for miles. They'd gone

up and over three hills already, sticking to orchards when they could, cutting through open fields quickly, everyone who could run bent double. They'd passed a few houses but Maltz gave them a wide berth, refusing to stop for help. When Madison asked why, he explained they didn't know the area well enough to know who to trust, some of these houses might even belong to the bikers. The thought gave Madison a chill. It was starting to feel like the whole world was chasing her, that she'd never be safe. She was beginning to believe they'd be running forever.

"You okay, honey?" her mother asked with concern, running a hand across Madison's cheek. Her teeth chattered through the words. She and Bree both looked frozen now that they'd stopped moving. Madison was the only one who hadn't had to wade through the fast-moving river. She wondered what time it was, her stomach was rumbling. She wished she'd eaten more at breakfast.

"I'm fine, Mom." She huddled closer, and her mother drew her in with one arm.

Maltz approached. "They're still on us," he said, voice grim. "A few have dropped away, but Fribush saw the rest about a mile back. Looks like they know these hills, and they have some tracking experience. So we better get moving."

"I'm so tired," her mother said in a thin voice. She didn't look well, eyes hollowed out, skin waxy. She probably hadn't slept much since Madison had been taken, and now she was being subjected to this.

"We're hoping it's not much farther, ma'am," Maltz said. "I'm trying to raise Syd Clement on the radio. She and Riley are meeting up with us."

"Then what?" Madison asked. "There are only two of them. How will that make a difference?"

Maltz crouched beside her. "Ready to go?"

Madison sighed, but let herself be hauled back up. Her mother and sister struggled to their feet, clearly bone-tired. They set off again, unconsciously falling into the same pattern: a commando in the lead, followed by her sister and mother, then Maltz and her. Jagerson brought up the rear.

They'd gone a few hundred feet when Madison heard a shout. She raised her head off Maltz's back and saw a glimmer in the trees where they'd just been resting. Another yell, then a shot was fired. Without any warning she was dropped to the ground.

"Looks like we're going to have to make a stand," Maltz said.

Twenty-Five

Randall watched, completely disheartened, as they loaded the last barrel onto a truck. It had been encased in a large wooden crate, identical to dozens of others still waiting to be loaded. A forklift maneuvered it into position, then slid it all the way to the back.

"Where does it go now?" he asked.

"Does it matter?" Dante was monitoring the packing, making sure the crate containing the barrel was completely buried behind the others. The other two trucks were already waiting by the door.

Randall rubbed his arm. He'd stripped off the PPE suit, acknowledging the inevitable. A long red burn had appeared, though whether it was an actual rash or due to his constant scratching was debatable. "You're going to kill me anyway," Randall said with detachment. "No reason not to tell me."

"No reason to tell you, either."

"I'm guessing you'll kill my family, too," Randall said.

Dante shrugged, his face unreadable. "We're not animals."

At this, Randall barked a laugh. Dante turned and

scowled at him. "Killing Americans isn't what we're about, Grant. The ones who died gave their lives for the greater good."

"The greater good? Do you even know what that means?" Randall shook his head. "You're spouting someone else's rhetoric."

Dante's brow darkened. "It's not rhetoric."

"Says the moron who probably couldn't use the word in a sentence," Randall scoffed. "Fine, don't tell me. Your bomb will never work, anyway."

"What?"

"It won't work." Randall shook his head. "Did you honestly think I'd help you, knowing you'd kill my family regardless?"

"What did you do?" Dante's eyes narrowed.

"Go to hell," Randall spat.

Without replying Dante whipped out a gun, took a step forward, and fired twice. With an expression of surprise on his face, Randall crumpled to the ground.

Dante watched blood pool around the ruins of Grant's head. A rumbling, and the first truck rolled down the ramp and out of the warehouse. His gut told him that Grant had been lying. He was too scared to fuck with them, knowing what they were capable of. He was just trying to make them think the plan wouldn't work. But still…if it failed, Jackson would have his head on a platter.

Dante caught up with the last truck as it was about to exit the building, swinging himself into the cab. He eyed the reflection of Grant's lifeless form in the side mirror. He had to admit, for a pinhead the guy had some balls. The question was, how far had he been willing to go?

"Syd?" Jake checked her pulse. There was a thin trickle of blood by her temple. He probed it—shallow, probably just a scrape from hitting the ground. She was still breathing, he could see the steady rise and fall of her chest. He lifted her shoulder carefully, turning her on her side. If she'd taken a bullet, it would have been in the back. They were both wearing vests, so unless it was armor-piercing it shouldn't have penetrated. No sign of blood on her shirt. He felt along her back, the contours of the vest hard against his hand.

She shifted suddenly.

"You okay?" Jake began lowering her down, but she batted his hand away.

Syd's voice was strained as she said, "That was, hands down, the worst extraction ever." She sat up stiffly.

Jake could have cried from relief. "Christ, you scared me."

"Thank God for Kevlar." She rapped her vest, wincing slightly. "Still feels like I got shot in the back, though. No blood?"

"Nope. If you want to strip down, I can double-check."

"Sounds like some good kinky fun. But we'll have to save that for later." Syd rolled her head from one shoulder to the other. "Our friend still around?"

As if in response, wood spit off the tree they were hiding behind. "We're pinned down," Jake confirmed.

"Fantastic. Any word from the others?"

Jake had completely forgotten about the radio. He glanced around but didn't see it. "I think it dropped when you got hit."

She gave him a hard look. "And you didn't retrieve it?"

"I decided to grab you instead," Jake retorted, a flush rising in his cheeks. "But the radio would probably be more grateful."

"More useful, anyway." Syd pulled herself up until she was leaning back against the tree. "Has he moved?"

"Not yet, as far as I can tell."

"Well, he'll be coming in soon, he knows he's got us. He'll look for a better angle on this side of the tree. We need to keep moving, distract him."

"I think he's got a laser sight. His aim was too good," Jake said.

"How many rounds do you have left?"

Jake checked. "Plenty, as long as we aren't here for a few days."

"All right." Syd checked her own weapon, moving awkwardly. "We should move."

Jake eyed her with concern. "You sure you can manage it?"

"Please. I once made it five miles with a bullet in my side. I can handle it." She shifted to a crouch, gun ready. "Let's head toward the river, we can split up there and trap him between us."

"That brings us farther from the car."

"We take care of him, then go back for the radio and call Maltz from the car." Sensing his skepticism, she laid a hand on his arm and said, "Trust me, Jake. I've been through worse."

Jake was having a hard time imagining a worse scenario. He'd never been pinned down like this. Despite his stint in the FBI and later work in private security, the past few days had presented the hairiest situations of his life. Maybe he wasn't really cut out for this new line of work. But he wasn't about to admit that to Syd, who unless he was sorely mistaken was thoroughly enjoying herself.

"On three," she said. "One...two..."

The crack of a rifle, and a yelp. They exchanged glances. "What the hell was that?" Jake asked.

Suddenly, a garbled voice. It took Jake a minute to

realize it was being filtered through a loudspeaker. He shrank deeper into the shadows of the tree.

"More hostiles?" Syd hissed in his ear.

"I don't think so." Someone was barking orders. Another exchange of fire, then silence.

"I still say we make for the river," Syd said in a low voice.

A figure approached through the trees, silhouetted hazy-blue by the smoke. Jake stiffened, tightening his grip on his gun.

The man shouted to be heard over the roar of the fire, "Jake Riley, get your ass out here!"

"Who the hell is that?" Syd asked. She looked stupefied.

"The fucking cavalry," Jake said, face splitting in a wide grin as he stood and emerged from the shadows.

"Thanks for coming," Jake said, shaking George Fong's hand as he took him in. The years had been kind to George. He still had that lanky surfer look, broad across the shoulders, lean in the hips, dark hair longer than Bureau specifications. Not surprising since he'd been raised in Hawaii, son of a Japanese mother and native father.

"You kidding? My life is dull now, I can use the excitement." George nodded toward the burning farmhouse. "Up to trouble as usual, huh? We found a couple good ol' boys with a sniper rifle. Don't suppose you'd know anything about that?"

Jake shrugged, and George's eyes narrowed. "Hey, it's not what you think," Jake said defensively. "I'm one of the good guys."

"Benicia P.D. doesn't seem to agree. They've got a BOLO out for you, something about a couple of dead guys on a boat and a missing girl?"

"It's not as bad as it sounds."

"Sure it isn't." George crossed his arms. A beam in the house collapsed with a thundering crack. "Nice handiwork."

"Not mine."

"Glad to hear it. Any bodies in there?"

"Not that I know of, but we didn't get a chance to check."

"We?" George raised an eyebrow.

Jake glanced back. Syd had finally come out of hiding and was approaching slowly, looking ready to flee at the slightest provocation. "This is my new partner, Syd."

George looked her over appreciatively. "Sure, the hot former-spy girl. Man, I might have to join this new company."

"We're not hiring yet," Syd responded, trailing her eyes over him, "but I'll certainly take it into consideration."

"Perfect. We'll be all set for our first sexual harassment lawsuit," Jake said, rolling his eyes. He hated to admit it, but the flirtation bothered him. Of course, women always took to George. It was one of the reasons they'd bonded—the two of them could walk into a Georgetown bar and have the pick of the place. He and George had gone through the Academy together, then split off into different field offices—Jake to Seattle, George to San Francisco. He was one of the few people Jake stayed in touch with after being expelled from the Bureau.

"I'd never sue such a lovely lady," George said.

"Jesus," Jake groaned. "So how many agents did you bring?"

"Three from the field office, since it was last-minute," George said, suddenly all business. "Just so you know, they're under the impression we're bringing you in."

Jake raised an eyebrow, and George shrugged. "Hey,

only way I could get any official support. Bureau rules. And even then I had to link it to the kidnapped girl." He glanced around. "She behind one of these trees, too?"

"We think they set off on foot, probably across the river. She's with three of my men, her mother and her sister," Syd said. She'd retrieved the radio and was tinkering with it. "Maltz, do you copy?"

The only response was static.

"And unless the kid joined a biker gang, it appears they've got company?" George asked.

"Definitely. We're not sure how many, though."

"Christ, Jake. I can always count on you to get my ass in a sling." George rubbed his chin. "All right. We'll head north on route 128, across the river. With any luck, we'll pick up their signal. I'll see if I can raise the locals to help."

"You sure the locals aren't the problem?" Syd asked skeptically.

"My, aren't we paranoid. You really are a spook." George grinned. "I assisted on a case up here a few years back. If it's the same sheriff, he's good people."

"We'll have to chance it, Syd," Jake said, gazing toward the river. "Madison can't walk, she'll be slowing them down. They're probably running out of time."

Twenty-Six

Madison covered her ears. It was like being in the middle of a war movie, but so much louder in real life. She'd had no idea guns were so deafening. She didn't know how anyone could stand shooting them.

The commando-boys had stashed her, Audrey and Bree behind a rickety shed on the outskirts of a ranch. There was a house a few hundred feet away, but despite the noise nobody had appeared at the windows—probably empty. They'd been headed there, hoping to find a working phone, when all hell broke loose. Maltz had ordered them to stay down while he and the other men handled the situation. That was what he'd called it, a "situation," as if this was all a big misunderstanding, not life and death. She had no idea how many people were out there trying to kill them, but it sounded like hundreds. The three of them huddled together, hands over their ears, terror in their eyes.

"There are too many of them!" her mother yelled as a spray of bullets sent a chunk of wood flying off the shed.

Bree spoke, but her words were overwhelmed by a rapid pounding that tore up the ground twenty feet away.

"We have to run for it," her mother said, eyes wild. "Get to the house, call for help."

"I can't run, Mommy," she said, tears streaming down her face.

"I'll go," Bree said.

It took a second for Madison to process the words and realize that Bree was serious.

"No, honey…risky…" her mother's voice was drowned out by another explosion.

Madison recognized her sister's grave expression, the same look of intense concentration that terrorized opponents during field hockey games. She reached out a hand to stop her, but Bree was already on her feet, running for the house.

She zigzagged crazily, bullets spitting up clods of dirt around her. It was amazing that Bree knew to swerve like that, Madison thought, impressed. She'd already covered half the distance. Madison had forgotten how fast she was, she'd been an all-star forward back in California but ditched field hockey after the move. Bree said the team at the new school was lame, they'd never win, but Madison figured she had another reason. Watching her slip through the trees, fast and sure-footed, it looked as though she would have dominated every game.

"Is she going to make it?" As her mother spoke there was a brief lull in the shooting, and her voice was overly loud. She sounded hopeful, and scared.

Madison didn't answer. She watched, riveted, as Bree vanished into another stand of trees. There was more cover now, she'd made it through the open field and only had ten feet to go. "She is," Madison breathed, hardly believing it. "She's going to be okay."

Suddenly a figure emerged from the shadows on Bree's left. Madison opened her mouth to scream a warning, but it was too late. The man lunged for Bree, driving her sideways with a long sweeping tackle. Madison felt her mother clutch her hand, heard her shrieking as they both watched Bree vanish beneath him.

"I'm getting really tired of warehouses," Rodriguez said in a low voice.

Kelly didn't answer, but silently agreed. They were in a cluster of warehouses on the outskirts of Houston that were nearly indistinguishable from the ones in Laredo. It made Kelly recall what Jake had said the other day, about always feeling as if he was getting off the freeway in the same place.

It was nearly four o'clock. They'd managed to grab the last two seats on a flight from San Antonio and landed a half hour ago. True to his word, Agent Taylor had wrangled a tactical unit from Houston to participate in the search. Not before Kelly got an earful from ASAC McLarty, however. Apparently the Phoenix D.A. had thrown a press conference announcing arrests in the Morris case, and the Bureau was happy to have everything tied up with a bow. McLarty was less than thrilled to discover that not only did Kelly suspect the Salvadorans were innocent, but that one of the nation's most prominent businessmen might be involved. He'd told her in no uncertain terms to tread carefully.

"You don't find anything, I want you on a plane home tonight," he'd thundered.

"And if I find something?" Kelly asked, unable to keep the challenge from her voice.

The only response was a dial tone. She suspected that no matter what happened, she probably couldn't count on a good reference from McLarty in the future. Which was a shame, since he was the reason she'd transferred to this unit. But when her case in the Berkshires went sideways, Kelly quickly learned there was only one job McLarty was interested in protecting: his own. She shouldn't have been surprised. During her tenure she'd served under her fair share of ASACs. But she'd thought McLarty was different. It was incredibly disheartening to have the wool ripped from her eyes.

Kelly stood back. The tactical unit was going in first, for which she was secretly grateful. Over the past few days she'd had enough busting down doors to last the rest of her life. Rodriguez looked moderately better after catching a catnap on the plane. She still felt like crap, and hadn't been able to reach Jake in California. She hated when they fell out of touch like this. The worst part was admitting that after a few days, she had to remind herself to call him. She suspected that wasn't a good sign.

Kelly shrugged it off, trying to get her game face on as the tactical team swarmed through the door. A series of calls echoed through the warehouse and bounced back to her and Rodriguez.

"Ready to see what's behind door number three?" Rodriguez asked, eyebrows raised.

"I'm hoping for a brand-new car," Kelly said drily.

"All clear!" someone yelled from inside.

Kelly reholstered her Glock as she entered. The warehouse was dark, solely illuminated by a dim bulb in the far corner. Suddenly, the lights clicked on—one of the agents must have found the switch. This warehouse was about double the size of the other two. On the near side of the room, a set of rickety card tables had been pushed together and were surrounded by folding chairs. Beer bottles, empty chips bags and decks of cards littered the surface and the surrounding floor.

"Tire tracks," Rodriguez noted. "Something big came through here."

"Definitely," Kelly agreed.

There was a pile of clothes in the center of the room. Two of the tactical team officers knelt beside it. The rest of the warehouse was bare.

"Uh-oh," Rodriguez said.

Kelly crossed the distance quickly. As she got closer the clothes resolved themselves into a body lying in a pool of congealed blood. Two more steps and she could make out what was left of his face. He was in his mid- to late-forties, tall and thin. He was wearing jeans and a button-down shirt.

"Dead." One of the officers glanced up at her. "You know him?"

Kelly shook her head. "No ID?"

"Not on him. We'll check the rest of the place, but who knows…" He shrugged helplessly. "You should see those back rooms, they're a mess. Looks like they had a small army camped out here."

"Doesn't look like a skinhead, and he's definitely not Mexican," Rodriguez said.

"Minuteman, maybe? And there was an altercation?" Kelly said.

"We'll get a team out here to dust for prints, have the ME give us a time of death," the officer said.

"No rigor, so not long ago," Kelly said.

"Unless it already passed," Rodriguez remarked.

"He looks too good for that. In this heat, no AC, even in a sheltered area he'd be in much worse shape." Kelly wasn't a doctor, but she'd seen enough dead bodies to get a sense of these things. She wondered who he was, and why he'd been killed. She shook her head, frustrated. This case kept raising more questions than it answered.

"I want his photo run against missing persons reports filed in the past week."

"Just in Houston?" the tactical agent asked.

"Let's start there, then expand to the rest of the state."

"Look on the bright side," Rodriguez said. "We made good on the warrant. That should get McLarty off your back, at least for now."

"Maybe," Kelly said, distracted. There was something glowing twenty yards away, toward the rear of the warehouse. "What's that?"

Rodriguez followed her across the warehouse. Kelly knelt to examine the strange powder: it shimmered iridescent blue, almost seeming to pulse.

Rodriguez reached a finger toward it. Kelly grabbed his hand, stopping him. "Don't."

"Why not?"

"Didn't your mother ever say if you don't know what it is, don't touch it?"

Kelly waved over the head of the tactical unit. He trotted toward them, slowing when he saw the powder.

"Holy shit," he said in a low voice, stopping a few feet away.

"Can we get a—"

"Everybody out! Now!" he hollered, turning and circling a finger in the air. At his tone the rest of the unit froze, then retreated for the exits.

"What is it?" Rodriguez asked, sounding scared. He took a few steps back, tracking it. His footprints glowed phosphorescent.

The agent noticed. "Sir, I'm going to ask you to remove your shoes without touching them. Then we go outside and wait for a Hazmat team."

"Shit, are they ruined?" Rodriguez looked down, panic seeping into his voice. "I love these shoes."

"What do you think it is?" Kelly asked the tactical commander. They watched from twenty feet away as Rodriguez gingerly pulled off one shoe with the toe of the other, then beat a path to them in his socks, careful to avoid the small puddles of blue.

"Not exactly sure, ma'am. All I know is if it glows, we go. Standard procedure."

"How long until we can get a crime scene unit in here?" Kelly asked, following him to the door.

He shook his head. "I got a feeling," he said grimly, "that this is going to be a hell of a lot bigger than one dead guy."

Twenty-Seven

Maltz had his back pressed against a tree. He could see Fribush and Jagerson behind a tractor about a dozen yards to his left. Jagerson had taken a hit. He was clutching his leg while Fribush bent to examine it. They were pinned down. There were two, maybe three hostiles at twelve o'clock, about twenty yards away from him. Another two at ten o'clock, aiming at Fribush and Jagerson. The rest had either fallen behind or were holding their fire, though he doubted these amateurs would be that smart. So far they'd been tentative—a good spray of fire was enough to send them diving for cover. But Maltz was running out of ammo, and they knew it. They were getting bolder, advancing. Dangel had never made it back from the van run, which meant he was probably down, and if Jagerson couldn't be moved, Maltz didn't love the odds of them completing this mission. To be brought down by a group of hacks would be the ultimate insult, he'd prefer to swallow his gun. And he hated the thought of these rednecks getting hold of the girls and their mother, even if they were the biggest collective pains in the ass he'd ever had the pleasure of dealing with.

Where the fuck was Syd? he thought, checking his radio again. It spit out a stream of static, and he cursed silently. If he made it out of this alive, he was definitely upgrading, this subpar civvy shit was worthless. He tried transmitting their position via Morse code again, compressing the talk button, hoping someone out there was paying attention.

"We got her!" A voice yelled. Maltz's heart sank. He craned his head around the side of the tree, careful to stay out of the line of fire. A guy in a leather vest with scraggly hair was dragging one of the girls—the older one, without the cast. Crap. Maltz wondered where the other two were, if they'd been smart enough to hide.

"Stop shooting or I kill the bitch!" the guy yelled.

Maltz braced himself against the tree trunk. His rifle was specially equipped with an infrared laser, allowing him to see exactly where the shot was going, even at a distance of a few hundred yards. He sighted down his rifle: Bree was an inch too tall, just blocking a perfect head shot. Maltz gritted his teeth, mentally willing her to move to the side, duck down, something. She stumbled slightly and his finger tensed, but the guy yanked her up again. They were fifteen feet away now. If he had a good opening, there was no way he could miss. The girl stumbled again, and he had a clear shot. Maltz steadied his aim, braced to squeeze the trigger...

"Wait! Please don't hurt her."

Maltz squeezed his eyes shut in frustration as the mother emerged from the shadows, hands held high. *Jesus,* he thought, shaking his head. *Civilians.*

The scraggly guy's head pivoted, ruining the angle, and Maltz sighed. Another figure appeared, hopping on one leg—the youngest. *Fucking perfect time for a family reunion.*

He glanced over to Jagerson and Fribush. Fribush shrugged and indicated that he didn't have a clear shot, either. Maltz clenched his jaw as the guy gathered the women in front of him. "All right, assholes, stop shooting or I'll start."

Maltz hadn't fired a shot in a few minutes, and neither had his men, but he figured this wasn't the time to point that out. A pro would have demanded they throw down their weapons and show themselves; the fact that he hadn't meant they still had a chance. He signaled for Fribush to keep a line on the guy. If Maltz could draw him away from the women, into a position where Fribush had a clear shot...

"I'm coming out! Don't shoot!" Maltz yelled, leaning his rifle against the tree. The guy's head swiveled, searching for him. Maltz took a step forward, still obscured by the shadows. He had a Glock 19 tucked in a holster behind his shoulder. If necessary he could access it quickly.

He heard voices approaching and took another step forward, breath tight in his chest. He hoped the rest were still leery of getting too close, otherwise they might be doomed.

"Bunch of crap you put us through," the scraggly guy griped, "crossing the river and shit."

"Yeah, well." Maltz stepped to the side, and the guy tracked him. Untrained adversaries tended to follow with their bodies as well as their eyes, an instinct that only served them in dealings with other amateurs. One more step to the left and Fribush would be able to pick him off without risking the women. "Just doing my job."

"Who the fuck hired you?" The guy shifted as Maltz took another step, turning with him. *Good,* Maltz thought. *Just one more foot...*

A sudden noise, from the direction of the house. They all froze. The guy reacted a second after Maltz, spinning to face it, opening himself up....

They didn't end up needing the radio to find Maltz and the others, all they had to do was follow the gunfire. It bounced off the hills, sending them down a few wrong turns as they tried to pinpoint it. They were backtracking, and had reemerged on the main road when a cop car tore past, blazing lights and sirens.

"I guess someone dialed 911," Jake said.

"Sounds like World War III out there," Syd said. "Hope Maltz and his boys have extra ammo."

Jake hoped so, too. He was a little nonplussed by how calm she was. The hairier the situation, the happier and more at home she appeared. Something about that scared the crap out of him. George sat in the backseat, purportedly to keep an eye on them.

"Yeah, stay on this guy," he said into his radio. "And make sure your vests are on before you get out of the car."

Syd gunned it, hot on the heels of the cop car.

"The sheriff knows we're coming, right?" Jake asked.

George shrugged. "He should. But it might not be a bad idea to keep your hands in sight when you get out of the car."

"Get him to shut those damn sirens off," Syd said. "We gotta go in quiet."

George glanced at Jake and raised an eyebrow. Jake shrugged. "What the lady said."

"Okay, boss." George conveyed the message to his team in the other car and the sheriff. The sirens abruptly stopped. Another cop car appeared behind them.

They crossed a bridge over the river, bouncing over a cattle grate on the opposite side. The sheriff's car took a sharp right onto a narrow lane that turned out to be a driveway. He wrenched the car onto the shoulder a few hundred feet from the house. Syd pulled in next to him, and the other cars followed suit.

A lanky guy in a sheriff's uniform and hat climbed out, tucking a rifle over his shoulder before approaching. His eyes narrowed slightly at the sight of them behind George. "Good to see you again, Agent Fong." He shifted his gaze to Jake, then Syd. "You the folks kicked up this shitstorm?"

"That would be us," Syd said. "We've got a family out there, mother and two teenage girls."

"Alone?"

"Three of my men are with them."

The other FBI agents, two men and a woman, joined them. Everyone was wearing their vests, faces tight. Jake recognized the air of expectation. There was a palpable rush of adrenaline before a fight, when you were dreading it and itching for it, all at the same time.

"So I'm guessing you're in charge here?" the sheriff asked George.

George glanced sidelong at Syd, then stepped forward. "'Fraid so. Looks like a biker gang is after them."

"Sure, the Rogues. Been trying to run them out of town since I got the job. You want to take them off my hands, you've got my blessing."

"How many are there?" Syd interrupted.

The sheriff shrugged. "Eight, maybe nine now. Busted a few for a meth lab a while back, so they're serving time."

"Corcoran?" Jake asked.

"Hell if I know." Sheriff shrugged. "And don't much care."

There was a break in the gunfire, and they all cocked their heads. "I'm guessing that's our cue," George said.

"I'll take the lead, the rest of you fan out. Remember," he said, looking directly at Jake, "we only shoot if they pose an immediate threat."

Jake wanted to point out that warning was more appropriate for Syd, but when he turned to see if it had sunk in, she was already gone. He could make out her blond hair ducking into the trees.

George shook his head. "Okay, head for the house. It sounds like the worst of it is up there."

A sharp crack split the silence. Maltz instinctively dropped to a crouch, his right hand snatching the backup weapon from its holster. Another shot, and the scraggly guy's gun went off as the side of his head exploded. He staggered a few feet before dropping. In response, a volley of shooting poured from the woods.

"Down! Get down!" Maltz waved frantically at the women, who had frozen in shock. The older girl reacted first, flattening herself to the ground, followed a second later by her mother and sister. Maltz watched as they covered their heads. Over the barrage he could hear them screaming.

A figure appeared by the farmhouse and Maltz leveled his gun, ready to pick him off. Something about the shape stopped him: the guy was wearing a baggy windbreaker. Feds, had to be. Syd had come through after all.

The sound of gunfire retreated. Reenergized, Maltz spun and pursued it through the trees. Shadowy figures dodged ahead of him in an all-out rout. Someone was coming up behind him, running hard. He spun and spotted Syd.

"About fucking time," he said. She grinned in reply, dropping to one knee and squeezing a few rounds off at the heavy guy puffing away from them.

The guy dropped his gun, raised his hands in the air and waved them. "I surrender!" he yelped.

"Christ," Syd said, shaking her head at Maltz. "Civilians, right?"

Madison sat beside Bree. Her mother stood at her shoulder, wringing her hands and emitting a long, unbroken moan. Bree was so pale, her breath coming in short rasps. Madison couldn't remember ever feeling so scared, this was worse than the boat, worse than the house burning down around them. Her sister might die, and it was all her fault.

"It hurts," Bree said, breathing hard, teeth clenched.

"Try to relax," the man said soothingly.

Madison recognized him from the hospital, his name was John or Jay or something like that. He gently cradled Bree's injured arm, carefully shifting it from side to side as he examined it. He eased up Bree's shirtsleeve, pulling slowly where blood plastered it to the wound. She winced, hissing out through her teeth.

Madison had to turn away at the sight of the nasty hole in Bree's arm, it looked like someone had carved through the skin all the way to the bone. She fought the reflex to retch, heard her mother saying, "Oh my God, oh my God," over and over again.

Madison focused on the dead man fifteen feet away. For some reason the gore didn't bother her, it was like looking at a Halloween dummy from a cheesy haunted house. And she was glad he was dead, she thought with a flare of anger. She wanted them all dead, everyone who had chased her and taunted her and sent her fucking e-mails pretending to be a great guy. She wanted everyone involved with this dead and gone, then maybe she could go back to her normal life and pretend none of it ever happened.

"It passed right through, which is good," the man said. He looked at her mother as if weighing her, arrived at some conclusion and turned to Madison instead. It was only then that Madison realized she was crying. He mistook her tears of rage for sadness and said, "Don't worry, kiddo. It's gonna be all right now."

Madison didn't answer. He handed her something, and she gazed blankly at it. It was a piece of cloth.

"Keep pressure on the wound, okay? I'm going to check the sheriff's car for a medical kit. Ambulance should be here any minute."

Madison let him place her hand on Bree's arm. She kept her eyes averted, trying not to see the steady trickle of blood flowing around the cloth. The man trotted back a second later holding a white box.

"Got it," he said, kneeling beside them again. He drew out a few items before gingerly lifting her hand. "This is going to burn for a second, but I want to get it clean," he said clumsily.

As Bree's howls erupted, Madison squeezed her eyes shut and clamped her hands over her ears, trying to keep from screaming herself.

Jake felt shaky. It had been a long time since he'd administered medical attention to someone, and the last time hadn't exactly been a success story. But with any luck the kid was going to be okay, it looked like the bullet went straight through. It was hard to tell with all the blood, but it didn't even appear to have nicked the bone: probably a ricochet from that final barrage. Luckily the bullet had already slowed, energy dissipating, by the time it hit her. Still, the mother moaning and Madison's jagged expression—they got to him. Jake took a deep breath, glancing back at them. The ambulance had finally arrived, and they were climbing in after the stretcher. George was going to follow to get their statement. He wanted Jake and Syd to meet them at the hospital, "In case I still need to bring you in," he'd said, only half-jokingly.

Jake was bone-tired. All he wanted to do was lie down in the back of the car and go to sleep for a few days. His phone rang. Without checking the number he answered.

"There you are," Kelly said warmly.

Hearing her voice made his eyes smart with tears. He chalked it up to exhaustion. "Yeah, sorry I've been un-reachable." He looked around. The dead guy was being zipped into a bag, and the remaining bikers sat on the ground in a semicircle, hands zip-tied behind their backs, waiting for the paddy wagon. The ground was covered with spent bullets and casings. He couldn't even begin to sum up the situation, so instead asked, "How are you?"

"I've been better. If I never go into a warehouse again it'll be too soon."

"Yeah?" Jake said. Syd emerged from the trees, Maltz by her side. They were discussing something in low voices, glancing at the Feds. Jake's eyes narrowed. Syd didn't have the look of someone who planned on making herself available to the authorities.

"…and now they won't let the techs in, not even to print him."

"Who?" Jake asked, tuning back in.

There was a long pause. "Is this a bad time?" Kelly said coldly.

"No, I mean…yeah, it is, kind of." He struggled to come up with a way to explain the last few hours. "But I'm listening. I miss you so much."

The words rang hollow, even to him. "It's been busy here, too," Kelly said stiffly. "And now I've got another body to deal with, but McLarty still won't get us a warrant for Burke. Apparently he was just named Morris's replacement in the Senate, and it wouldn't be 'politically appropriate' to question him."

"Jackson Burke, the businessman?" Jake asked, confused. "You think he killed someone?"

"I think he's involved somehow. All the shell companies tie back to him, and the building I'm outside right now has some sort of glowing powder all over the floor. They made us leave, and Hazmat won't let me inside to see the body. God knows how long it'll take to ID him under the circumstances."

Syd finished up her conversation with Maltz and walked over to Jake. She stood a few feet away, arms crossed over her chest, clearly impatient.

"Hey listen, Kel, I've got to go."

"All right." She sounded almost relieved. "When are you heading back to New York?"

"Not sure yet, we've got some loose ends here." He considered mentioning that his next call might be from a prison cell, then figured he'd cross that bridge when he came to it. "Good luck with the ID."

"Thanks."

Jake heard the hopelessness in her voice, and wished he could put his arms around her. He started to say so, but she'd already hung up. He tucked the phone in his pocket with a pang of guilt and faced Syd. "Let me guess. You're not planning on meeting everyone at the hospital."

"No, I'll come. But Maltz and his boys aren't keen on being fingerprinted."

"Shocking," Jake said, watching as Maltz and the remaining commando loaded their injured friend into the back of Syd's rental car. "What about getting that kid some medical attention?"

"Maltz says they'll handle it. Earns them a bonus, unfortunately." Her eyebrows knit together. "I'm hoping he pulls through, otherwise we'll owe a bundle. Dangel's death already puts us in the red."

"Wow," Jake said. He couldn't even begin to think of an appropriate response to that. "We're a little short on cars, then, since the van is out of commission."

"I know. I was thinking of dropping them off. Can you catch a ride with George?"

"And you'll meet us there?"

"Sure I will." She playfully punched his arm. "A little faith, Riley. You and I are stuck with each other."

"Okay. The hospital is in Sacramento. You have the address?"

"Oh, I'll find it," she said breezily. "Bye."

Jake watched the sedan pull away. The rest of the Feds were distracted, going through the scene, trying to piece everything together. The paddy wagon finally arrived and an agent herded the bikers inside. Jake turned to find George leaning against his car hood, watching him.

"So. Looks like she left you high and dry," George noted.

"She's meeting us at the hospital," Jake said defensively.

"Sure she is." George shook his head. "You can't trust the Agency or anyone it churned out. You know that, Riley."

"Well, I didn't have a lot of luck trusting the Bureau, either," Jake retorted.

George raised his eyebrows. "I heard you were engaged to someone from BSU."

"I am." Jake sighed. "At least, I think I still am."

"Wow. You make life in the private sector sound like a complete nightmare." George grinned. "Where do I sign up?"

"Depends. Are you really going to arrest me?"

George shrugged, surveying the scene. "As long as you can convince me this is exactly what it looks like, and the family backs you up, we can probably cut you loose. The sheriff is thrilled to have something to nail these jerks with, so that's a bonus. But I can't vouch for the Benicia P.D. They might still be touchy about you taking off with their star witness."

"About that." Jake lowered his voice. "I'm not sure it's over."

George's eyes narrowed. "How do you mean?"

"The husband originally hired us, and now he's missing. We still haven't figured out who snatched the girl, and every time we get her back, someone tries to grab her again."

"Shit, Jake." George rubbed his eyes with one hand. "And here I thought I might actually get to go home. Start at the beginning, and don't leave anything out."

Twenty-Eight

Kelly flipped over again and punched her pillow. Typical cheap motel-issue, the down kept separating until she was lying on nothing but pillowcase. She folded it double, but even then it only offered a small rise from the surface of the bed. She sighed. Sunlight was still leaking through the curtains and around the door. It was only eight o'clock, but she had gone to bed early to make up for the night before. Unfortunately her body clock was thrown off by all the traveling, and sleep was evading her.

Rodriguez didn't appear to be having any trouble—she could hear him snoring through the paper-thin walls. They were in a Motel 6 a few miles from the Houston field office. That afternoon they'd been moved progressively farther away from the warehouse as a multitude of hazardous material response units descended and expanded the perimeter. An ASAC Leonard from the Weapons of Mass Destruction Unit had shown up, face grave. For an hour he grilled her on every detail of their investigation. He was clearly dubious of the Jackson Burke link, but noted it down. And she hadn't been able to get any answers on when her dead John Doe would be processed. It was frustrating. For all intents and purposes this was her crime scene, but she'd been squeezed out of the loop. They were practically treating her like a civilian.

Finally, irritated by the vague responses and brush-offs, Kelly had conceded defeat. At a local Denny's she'd picked at a sandwich while Rodriguez tore through a stack of pancakes, then they'd checked into the motel. ASAC Leonard had promised to call as soon as he knew anything. Kelly checked her phone again, resisting the temptation to throw it against the wall when it showed *No new calls*.

The stilted exchange with Jake still bothered her, too. They were supposed to be getting married, but the past few weeks they'd had a hard time getting through a five-minute phone conversation. She tried to tell herself that a lot of couples weren't great on the phone. But the truth was over the past year and a half, they had spent more time on the phone than in person, and this strain was new.

Maybe it was the cases they were working on. This one was getting under her skin, and she was always distracted when that happened. And it sounded like Jake was having a similar experience. He usually shared every detail of his day-to-day activities. It was odd to have that suddenly shut off. She could tell he was constantly searching for things to say that wouldn't violate someone's privacy. But if this was how things would be once his business was up and running, how would they handle it? She pictured them sitting in silence at the dinner table every night, occasionally saying, "Please pass the salt." And a second later realized that after her brother was murdered when she was eight years old, that was exactly how family dinners were at her house. The thought of returning to that was awful to contemplate.

Kelly threw off the covers, flicked on the television and tuned to CNN. An image of Jackson Burke appeared on-screen, and she turned up the volume.

"…honored to be asked to serve the great state of Arizona in this time of terrible need. The murder of my good friend Duke Morris by a criminal gang of illegal immigrants aptly shows the danger he fought against his entire career. Our borders remain porous, thanks to a president and congress who are unwilling to stem the tide of violent offenders for whom it's become a virtual highway for drugs, weapons and prostitutes. These are the people putting needles in your kids' hands. These are the people ruining communities with drug wars and drive-by shootings. They're stealing our jobs, and in the process our nation. I pledge to continue Duke's work, devoting myself fully to…"

Kelly dialed the volume back down, irritated by the flood of rhetoric. What was Burke's game? Could he really have been involved in Morris's murder? He'd ideally positioned himself to assume the Senate seat. If Burke had run against Duke Morris in an election, they were like-minded enough to split the conservative vote, something the Arizona GOP wouldn't have supported. Still, murdering a friend to steal his job was cold, and there weren't any guarantees that Burke would be appointed. Morris's wife could have taken office until the next election.

Kelly flashed back on her, an anxious woman whose hands fluttered as she spoke, and realized that was unlikely. Mrs. Morris didn't appear stable enough for a spot on the PTA. And all the groups she'd run across in the past few days, from skinheads to Minutemen, shared an anti-immigration stance. Blaming an MS-13 offshoot for Morris's murder had forced the immigration issue back into the national consciousness.

Kelly powered up her laptop and searched for information on Jackson Burke. There were numerous photos of him at fund-raising events, arm in arm with celebrities, politicians and business magnates. Also, the text of a few keynote addresses, one given at his alma mater and the others at business conferences. They were all fairly mundane, focused on the future of various industries, with no overt references to his immigration stance. Interesting that the GOP had chosen him to fill the seat. Granted he was a major fund-raiser, hosting events for candidates—including Duke Morris—at what the society pages termed his "palatial estate" in Scottsdale. But Burke hadn't held any chairmanship positions or run for elected office prior to his appointment.

Kelly sat back and thought for a minute. Her stomach grumbled, chastising her for not eating more at dinner. She dialed Leonard again but was sent straight to voice mail, and she hung up without leaving a message. Kelly considered calling Jake, but decided not to. She knew it was childish, but the way he'd behaved, distracted, barely listening to her…he should be the one to call and make up for it.

Kelly powered down her computer and stretched her arms above her head, trying to ease the stiffness in her neck. After the pace of the past few days, it was strange to be stuck with nothing to do. She ran over the case again in her mind, and decided to make one last call.

Her friend Mark had left the Bureau for a job with the Southern Poverty Law Center a few years earlier. He'd said that he wanted to leave before all the idealism and faith in mankind was sucked out of him. At the time she figured he was being melodramatic, but he might have had the right idea. Maybe that was the problem, she'd overstayed her welcome.

After a few tries the switchboard routed her to an extension. She left a message for Mark, hung up, and was surprised when almost immediately her phone rang.

"Kelly! Can't believe you called, it's been years!" Mark said.

Kelly smiled. It was nice that someone actually sounded happy to hear from her. "Hi, Mark. Listen, I'm in the middle of a sticky case right now, and thought you might be able to help out."

There was a pause. Mark's tone had shifted when he said, "So much for catching up, huh?"

"No, I didn't mean… How are you?" Kelly asked awkwardly.

Mark laughed. "It's okay, Kelly. I should've known better, you're not the type to call for a chat."

Kelly wanted to protest, but he was right. Since Mark had left the Bureau she'd barely thought of him. And not only had they been close friends, they'd even briefly dated. She wondered what that said about her. "I'm really sorry, Mark."

"No problem. So what's going on?"

"I need to know more about different anti-immigration groups—skinheads, Aryan Brotherhood, Minutemen."

"Technically these days we refer to them as hate groups," he said. "And this is for a case, huh?"

"It is. Why?"

"There have been some interesting rumors flying around the Web lately. Nothing too serious, but the chatter has definitely ticked up on some of the sites we monitor. One guy made a reference to something big brewing, and immediately got flamed by everyone else."

"And that's not normal?"

"The big claims are, but the flaming was surprising." Mark sounded pensive. "Usually they love to get each other all riled up, kind of feeding off the hate. But they clamped down on this, went so far as to call the guy a liar and a troublemaker. Pretty out of character for that site. Made me think there might really be something in the works."

Kelly flashed back on the blue powder. "Could any of the groups you monitor pull off something major?"

"Hard to say. Back in the nineties, a few redneck Klansmen almost succeeded in blowing up a natural gas processing plant in Texas. If one of them hadn't got cold feet and gone to the Bureau, the explosion could have taken out hundreds, maybe thousands of people." She heard the sound of typing in the background. "Can you tell me why you asked about those groups specifically?"

Kelly weighed what she could say without compromising the investigation. "There might be a connection between some ex-con Aryan Brotherhood members and some of the border militia guys."

"Crap. That's not good. What people don't realize is that while hate groups have doubled their membership in the past decade, you people," Mark's voice turned harsh as he said, "have completely dropped the ball."

"I'm sure that's not true—" Kelly protested.

"It is," Mark interrupted. "The attack on 9/11 initiated a complete reallocation of resources. Now you ignore the domestic militias we were all so afraid of in the nineties, instead it's all about foreign nationals on our soil. When the truth is, we're more likely to see another Oklahoma City before another twin towers."

"Why has the membership doubled?" Kelly asked, trying to refocus him. That was one thing she'd forgotten about Mark, he went from zero to rage in seconds flat.

"Anti-immigration has been the great unifier," Mark said, catching himself. His voice was more controlled as he continued, "And the Internet made finding like-minded recruits a hell of a lot easier. The good news is that, by and large, these people are all talk. They love to rant and rave, but when it comes down to actually doing anything about it, most of them are too disorganized."

"But?" Kelly asked.

"But what we worry about is the possibility of someone smart and charismatic bringing all these disparate groups together."

"Like an American version of Osama bin Laden?"

"Exactly like that." Mark spoke in a rush, excited. "Imagine survivalists, skinheads and Minutemen. All heavily armed, all willing to fight. It would be like your own personal mercenary army. And if you had money to back it up, well…"

"Well?" Kelly asked when he didn't continue.

"Let's just say it would be really, really bad. People take for granted the stability of our country, but the truth is there isn't a nation on the planet completely immune to a coup attempt. Given the right circumstances, someone could seize power and overthrow the Constitution."

"That sounds a little far-fetched," Kelly said.

"Does it? In the last decade alone there have been more than thirty coup attempts worldwide. Thirteen of those succeeded. Our government has only been in power for two-hundred years, not long at all in the grand scheme of things. The Romans ruled in one form or another for nearly a thousand years, and look what happened to them. And the people assigned to defend us, the National Guard and most of our military units, are currently overseas. At the moment, the United States has a very limited homeland defense."

"Still…" Kelly tried to think of an appropriate response. Much of what he was saying was true, but the thought of a bunch of skinheads taking over the government still sounded preposterous.

"Still nothing. All it would take was some sort of cataclysmic event to coalesce people. Remember that 9/11 could very well have gone another way. Rather than rallying behind the president, people could have blamed him for not keeping the nation safe. And imagine the outcome if that had happened, and people took to the streets."

"You were born in the wrong era, Mark. Should've been a '60s radical," Kelly teased.

His voice lost some enthusiasm as he said, "Maybe you're right. I know you can't tell me much, but please, if you learn anything…"

"I'll call. And, Mark, let's keep this between us, all right?"

He hesitated before saying, "All right. But if things are in motion, I expect a phone call."

"Definitely." Kelly hung up and thought about what he'd said. She turned back to her laptop and enlarged a photo of Jackson Burke. He was wearing a tuxedo, the portrait of well-fed contentment, mouth half-open in a laugh. "An American bin Laden, huh?" she said, examining it. "You don't look like someone who'd enjoy spending time in a cave."

Madison sat next to Bree's hospital bed, picking at her cuticles. Ironic that twenty-four hours earlier Bree had been sitting beside her. The guy who gave her first aid was right, Bree would be fine. She had conked out while they were bandaging her arm. Madison envied her. She'd never been so tired in her entire life, but every time her head nodded she jerked awake. It would probably be a while before she slept through the night again, if ever.

The doctors had examined her leg and changed the cast

since it got beat-up during their escape. Her lungs had checked out fine, too, although they felt tight from the smoke. The nurse said that would probably go away in a day or two.

Madison glanced at the door. Her mother was talking to one of the FBI agents. For some reason she felt less safe having them as guards. The commando-boys had been scary, but that made them seem more effective. Her mother had her arms crossed over her chest and was examining the floor tiles, nodding occasionally while the agent explained something. She looked old, Madison suddenly realized. Her mother used to be so pretty, back when she and Dad were still together.

The agent left and her mother remained there for a moment. She turned to find Madison watching her and suddenly straightened, forcing a weak smile.

"Any news about Dad?" Madison asked, as her mother leaned in and smoothed the covers over Bree.

"Not yet, sweetie. But they're checking planes and trains to see if they can track him down. I'm sure he's fine."

She can't even make that sound believable, Madison thought. It was just like when she told Madison they'd never get divorced. Then three months later, boom. "What about his credit cards? Are they checking those?"

"Yes. I think so." Her mother slumped into the other chair. "They know what they're doing, Maddee. They'll find him if…"

"If what?" Madison pressed.

"If he wants to be found."

Madison processed that. Her mother was implying that maybe her father hadn't been taken by the bad guys, maybe he'd left on his own. But he'd never leave without them. Her mother, maybe, but he'd take her and Bree along. Wouldn't he?

"We should try to sleep for a bit," her mother said. "The nurse said the bed in the next room is empty. Would you like to lie down?"

"I can't sleep."

"Well, I'm going to try." Her mother used the arms of the chair to push herself up. "If you need anything one of the agents will get it, okay?"

"Okay."

On her way out she placed her hand on Madison's head, then bent and kissed her. It had been a long time since she'd done that, and Madison's eyes filled with tears. "It's going to be okay, honey, I promise," she said in a low voice before leaving.

Madison sank deeply down in the chair. The only thing she was sure of was that nothing was going to be all right, ever again.

JULY 3

Twenty-Nine

Jake started awake. He had dozed off while leaning back in a desk chair with his feet propped on a conference table, and they'd slipped to the floor. He shook his head to clear it. Syd was sitting across the table smirking at him.

"Comfortable?"

"These chairs were designed by sadists," Jake complained, trying to stretch out a kink in his back. George had appropriated office space from the Sacramento field office, and told the two of them to stay put while he dug up information on Randall Grant. Jake had tried to convince him to let them go to a motel, but George made it clear it was the office or a holding cell. And frankly the way his eyes lit up when he mentioned the cell gave Jake pause. "Did you get any sleep?"

"Yup." Syd pointed down. "Stretched out on the floor."

"Really?" Jake eyed it dubiously. The rug was of questionable vintage, covered with old coffee stains.

"It beats a cave in Pakistan where they're burning dung for fuel."

"I suppose." He checked his watch: 5:00 a.m. They'd

been here for nearly twelve hours, and his stomach was rumbling. Even cafeteria food sounded good at this point. He should call Kelly back, too, now that things had settled down. It was 7:00 a.m. in Texas. She was probably already awake. But better to talk to her on a full stomach, he reasoned. "You up for a trip to the mess?"

"I got the sense we weren't allowed to leave this room." Syd raised an eyebrow.

"And that's stopped you when?"

"Good point. Let's go."

George opened the door as they were about to step out. "Making a break for it?"

"Just heading down for some food," Jake said. "We're wasting away in here."

"Doesn't look like it would kill you to miss a meal," George joked, eyeing Jake's stomach. "Desk work has done you in, my man."

"Bullshit. I'm still at my fighting weight," Jake said defensively, trying not to be obvious about sucking in his gut.

"Not you, my dear, you're perfect." George winked at Syd. "Anyway, you might want to hold off on the prison break. I've got news about your boy."

"Yeah?" Jake's heart sank. George's humor sounded forced.

Syd sensed it, too. "Bad news," she said flatly.

"Yeah, I think so." George opened a file and slid out a photo. "This your guy?"

Syd looked at it first. Without commenting, she simply nodded, then handed it to Jake. Typical morgue photo, the flat light made it look black-and-white even though it wasn't. It was Randall Grant, all right. Someone had shot him at point-blank range near the temple. Death must have been mercifully quick, if there was such a thing.

"Crap." Jake handed it back. "Where?"

"Texas. When I accessed his fingerprints from the lab, I saw that another field office had matched them this morning. Made a few calls, but they're not releasing any information yet."

"Meaning what? They don't know who killed him?"

"Meaning, I get the sense they're dealing with something big down there. Mobile units were called in, and they're raising the threat advisory level to orange, maybe even red on the basis of this."

"Just because a scientist was killed?" Syd asked, puzzled.

"This guy Randall was a physicist, right?" George asked. "And you think he might have been smuggling nuclear info to the wrong people?"

"Maybe." Syd turned it over in her mind. "But how did he end up in Texas?"

"No sign of him on any of the plane manifests."

"Maybe he didn't fly commercial," Jake said. "Was there anything that might clue us in to what he was doing?"

"Like I said, my compadres in the great state of Texas aren't talking." George glanced at Jake. "But I was thinking you might have an in."

"Why would Jake have an in? He never worked there," Syd said.

"No, but his fiancée is the one who found the body."

"What?" Jake took the form back and scanned it. It was a basic FBI FD302 report. Kelly's name popped out at him. He flashed back on what little she'd told him about the case, something about Jackson Burke and a strange blue powder. "Oh, shit," he said.

"Call your girl," George said, nodding toward the phone on the desk. "And let's see if we can figure out what the hell is going on."

* * *

Dante watched as the lead-lined barrel holding the bomb was lowered into the center of the float. There had been a screwup with the one meant for San Antonio—the yokels in charge of the warehouse got snared in some FBI sting. He shook his head. Man, it was hard to find people you could trust these days. And he hated that their failure reflected poorly on him, at least in Jackson's eyes. He needed to make sure that from here on out, everything went smoothly.

Dante still couldn't believe the FBI had found the Laredo warehouses. Now he'd have to come up with a fresh crop of illegals to man the float. That was one thing Jackson was absolutely adamant about—there had to be immigrants, especially Mexicans, tied to the initial blast. Not a serious problem, Dante still had Minutemen willing to serve as coyotes. The trick was getting another float ready in time. Thank God he'd kept the construction materials in a separate warehouse.

Dante watched as his guys wrapped white, red and green streamers around a wire-mesh frame. He had to grin at the incongruity of it. Who knew the arts and crafts program at Corcoran would come in so handy one day?

His phone buzzed. Dante checked the number, then snapped it open. "Do you have them?"

"Sir, this is Curtis Clay."

Dante frowned, searching his mind. Remembered a beady-eyed little guy, sidekick to one of his boys in California. "You're not supposed to have this number."

"Yeah, I know, but…Jonas told me to call if something went wrong."

Dante's lip curled. Sure, everyone did each other in prison, but the ones who kept it up on the outside—he could hardly stomach the thought. The only reason he'd tolerated Jonas was that he was smart and took orders without giving him shit. "So?"

"So—" Curtis cleared his throat. "Jonas never came home last night, then I saw something on the news about a big bust over in Winters. Buncha bikers, and it was right near where you sent him." There was a note of accusation in his voice. "He said he'd be home by dark."

Dante could have sworn he heard sniffles. "Yeah, well, maybe he got smart and threw you over for some pussy."

A pause, then Curtis whined, "They said some of them were dead, too. But they're not saying who."

"What about the bitches?"

"What bitches?"

"The ones Jonas was supposed to pick up." Dante closed his eyes and fought the urge to hurl the phone against a wall. Shit, if this was true, he was down more men. And Jonas had been part of the next phase of the plan. He didn't have anyone else in the area he could trust with it. He should have known better than to call in the Rogues. Dante had never been keen on using bikers, they were too loosely organized, too likely to narc when they got caught. They were probably singing right now. He went over what they knew, trying to remember if any of it pointed to him, or worse, to Jackson.

"They didn't say anything about that on the news."

"Fuck the news. I want you to call around, find out what the fuck is going on. I want to know where they were taken, and what happened to the women in the house." Dante started composing a list in his mind. He needed to get in touch with one of his soldiers on the inside, make sure the biker pricks got the message that anyone who talked would suffer. Winters P.D. probably didn't have their own jail, and even if they did, wouldn't want to risk locals overrunning it. So that meant they'd be stowed in either Vacaville or Davis: Vacaville if he was lucky, he still had a good network there. Worst-case scenario they would have been driven to the federal pen in Sacramento. It would be harder to get to them there, but not impossible.

If the news was covering this, the Feds probably stashed the girls in a safe house somewhere. Weighing what had happened, Dante decided bothering with them was no longer worth it. They'd been bad luck, ever since the girl was snatched shit started rolling downhill. And they were so close now, he couldn't risk fucking things up any worse. Plus, with Grant dead, the only reason to mess with his family would be to exact revenge on his corpse. And for that he could wait. Feds wouldn't be watching them forever.

Creeper came out of the office, motioning for his attention. Dante held up a hand to indicate he needed one more minute.

"You got that, Curtis? I want to hear back from you in an hour, max, and I want a fucking hell of a lot more than what you saw on CNN." He clicked off without saying goodbye and looked at Creeper. "What?"

"They found the guy."

"What guy?" *I'm surrounded by a bunch of fucking morons,* he thought.

"The scientist guy, you know…" Creeper shuffled his feet.

"What, in Houston?"

"Yeah. Feds are all over it. Thought you'd want to know." He beat a retreat back to the office, clearly spooked by the expression on Dante's face.

Dante still clenched the cell phone in one hand, squeezing it hard. He barely saw the progress on the float.

He recognized this feeling, it was the one you got when a job was about to go really, really wrong. He'd had it that day in the bank, right before the off-duty cop pulled his piece and he wound up in Corcoran as an accessory to murder. If the Feds had the warehouse, the minute they saw the powder they'd know something big was in the works. And then they'd be shutting down every interstate, every bridge. He shook his head. One day away. They were so close.

He reviewed the list in his mind. He needed to get the other drivers on the phone and check their status. If it came down to it, he'd revise the plans. That was what separated a great general from a mediocre one, according to Jackson: the ability to adjust to changing circumstances on the battlefield. Dante took a deep breath. In the end, it would all be okay. He'd make sure of it, even if he had to drive a fucking float himself.

Thirty

Kelly awoke to the sound of pounding on her door. Blearily, she rolled over and checked the time: 8:00 a.m. She'd finally dropped off to sleep well past midnight. Her laptop sat open beside her on the bed, screen saver pulsating green. Next to it was the motel notepad on which she'd scrawled notes about Jackson Burke.

"What the hell, Jones. Are you alive in there?"

It was Rodriguez. She sat up slowly, straightening her blouse, wishing she'd changed out of it before falling asleep. It had been her last clean one, and now it was a wrinkled mess. "One minute." Kelly checked herself in the mirror on the way to the door and frowned.

"Jesus, I was about to get a battering ram." He looked her over. "Finally got some sleep, huh?"

"Not enough. What's up?"

"They got an ID on our guy."

"Yeah?" Kelly quickly skimmed the faxes he handed her. The dead guy was a nuclear physicist from a DoD research lab. That was a far cry from the extremists they'd been rounding up so far. But it didn't bode well for the powder.

Rodriguez read her thoughts. "I talked to someone on the Hazmat team. He said we should get checked for exposure. McLarty set something up at the hospital downtown, and we're supposed to head there ASAP. But since we were only in contact for a few minutes, and they got us out of our clothes and shoes, chances are it wasn't too bad."

"Meaning what, we lose all our hair?" Kelly tried to sound flippant, but the gravity of what had happened suddenly struck her. She thought of Jake, how he'd handle the news. A small, cold part of her wondered if he'd even care.

Rodriguez tried to match her tone. "That happens, I'm filing for full disability." He ran a hand through his buzz cut. "People would kill for this head of hair. And I want compensation for those shoes. This case has been hell on my wardrobe."

"Did Leonard have any theories on why they killed this guy Grant?" Kelly asked.

"Not for his clothes, that's for sure." She raised an eyebrow, and he dropped the tone. "Oh, we're being serious now. Leonard still isn't telling me jack-shit. But after we swing by the hospital, I'm thinking we head back to the warehouse, see what we can rustle up."

"You're that eager to expose yourself again?"

"I just want to find out what the hell is going on," Rodriguez said. "This is our case, it was our lead that got the ball rolling. I say we fight to get back in there. Can you get McLarty to back us?"

"I can try, but you're his golden boy."

"Please, Jones." Rodriguez shook his head and grinned. "Everyone knows you're his favorite."

Kelly flushed. "He has a funny way of showing it. Give me a minute to get ready."

"Sure. Might want to run a brush through that hair, too," he said pointedly, eyeing her scalp.

An hour later Kelly shifted in a chair as a technician drew her blood. "I didn't realize you could test for radiation exposure this way."

The technician focused on the syringe. "It's a relatively new procedure, but probably the quickest."

"And what if I received a serious dose?" Kelly asked.

"The doctor will be with you in a minute to explain," the technician said. She avoided eye contact on the way back to the waiting room, which Kelly took as a bad sign.

Rodriguez was already slumped in a chair drinking a can of apple juice. His raised his hand in a halfhearted wave. "Did they give you some juice? It's free."

"They didn't." Kelly turned back to the technician. "Was I supposed to get some juice?"

"We usually only give it to people who might pass out, but if you want some…"

"No, that's fine." Kelly sat in the chair next to Rodriguez. "Fear of needles?"

He flushed. The bruises on his face were finally fading, although his nose remained noticeably off-center. "The week I've had, I can't really afford to lose more blood. They tell you it'll be at least twenty-four hours until the results come back?"

Kelly nodded. "The doctor is supposed to come discuss our options."

"Antibiotics, antiemetics and potassium iodide. Worst-case scenario, we'll need a bone marrow transplant."

"Who told you that?" Kelly raised her eyebrows.

"Read all about it on the Internet last night. That pill they gave you before was potassium iodide. Keeps your thyroid from absorbing radioiodine. 'Course, if we were exposed to a different kind of radiation, we're screwed. Until they get the results back, they can't do anything." He stood. "So let's go."

Kelly looked at him. His jaw was set, and he seemed determined. He was probably right. The doctor would tell them to wait for the test results, and they'd deal with the consequences then. She nodded. "Let's go."

"You talk to McLarty yet?" Rodriguez asked as they strolled back to their car.

"I was going to call him on the way. I needed to power up, my phone died last night." In the car she pulled it off the cradle. Almost immediately, it rang. She recognized Jake's number and picked up. "Hi."

"Jesus, Kelly, are you okay?"

Sure, now he was concerned, she thought. "I'm fine. We're leaving the hospital, they should have the test results in a few hours."

"Okay. Are you heading to the warehouse now?"

"I am, actually," Kelly said, puzzled.

"Great. I'll meet you there."

"What? Where are you?"

"In Houston. It's a long story, but it looks like our cases overlap."

"What are you talking about?" Kelly struggled to process what he was saying. How could a K&R case in California have anything to do with the Morris killing?

"Look, it's a long story. I'll see you soon."

"What was that all about?" Rodriguez asked.

"I have no idea. But my fiancé is here, he said something about our cases overlapping."

"Great. Can't wait to see Jake again." Rodriguez steered them onto the highway and gunned the engine. "Maybe he can tell us what the fuck is going on."

* * *

Jackson Burke sat in front of a row of mirrors. This was an important appearance, an interview on a national political talk show the day after his Senate appointment. He needed to look just so, and with an eye to that had carefully chosen his wardrobe. The conservative blue suit—nice but not his finest, so he wouldn't alienate his base. A red tie, no stripes, a little wider than was currently fashionable. And of course the ubiquitous American flag pin. He'd instructed the makeup girl to eliminate the pouches under his eyes and even out his skin tone, but not to make him look like a dandy. He knew exactly what people expected from their politicians, it was all about attention to detail. Look trustworthy, and they'll trust you. Don't come across as too slick, throw in a few folksy expressions, and they'd be eating out of your hand. He'd spent a lifetime crafting his image and building his position as both a major donor and tried-and-true standard-bearer for the state party. When it came to naming Duke's successor, there was only one logical option. There had been a few hours of panic over rumors that the governor was considering some spic state senator. But one phone call reminded the governor who had buttered his bread through countless campaigns. Now it was finally time to reap the benefits of all he'd sown.

Of course, he could have run against Duke in the next election. But that raised the risk of splitting the party vote, not to mention alienating Duke and his supporters. No, this had been so much more elegant. This way Duke's legacy lived on, he became a martyr to the cause, and his supporters were now Jackson's. Everyone won. And after tomorrow, he'd not only be leading Arizona, but the nation, as well. Everything he'd said yesterday at the swearing-in ceremony would appear prescient: he, and only he, knew how to protect the American people from the danger on their borders. He'd already crafted his speech for the aftermath, pointing out how the administration had failed to stop the flood of terrorists, criminals and prostitutes who were destroying the American way of life.

People would be afraid, probably even more frightened than on 9/11. And he was fully prepared to capitalize on that fear. Years' worth of failed legislation could be pushed through Congress in a matter of weeks, if the Patriot Act was any indication. The president, already facing a disenchanted electorate, would find himself sliding in the polls as he was gearing up for reelection. And if everything went as planned, there would be an appropriate challenger confronting him, someone who had developed a reputation for steadfastness and strength when America needed it most. Sort of the Giuliani model, but without the tawdry affairs.

Jackson's phone rang, and he frowned at Dante's number. The man was turning out to be such a disappointment. Though Dante was infinitely more capable than the scum he ran with, and had mustered support in arenas that he could never have accessed otherwise, the string of recent failures proved what he had always suspected. Once trash, always trash.

Jackson answered on the fourth ring. "Yes." He listened, and the frown deepened. A PA appeared at the door and held up five fingers. Jackson nodded to show that he understood, waiting until she was out of earshot to say, "This is very bad news. How did they find it?"

As he listened a red flush rose up his neck, tainting his makeup. "You're right, under the circumstances we need to reconsider the targets. We'll switch to the backup sites. Make it happen."

Jackson hung up and drummed his fingers on the

armrest, blood pressure climbing. He fumbled in his jacket pocket for a bottle of pills, popping one in his mouth. As his pulse stabilized he focused on his breathing, eyes closed. It was going to be okay. He'd been very careful, and hopefully Dante had, too. Nothing tied him to that warehouse, and according to Dante it would take the FBI days to sort out the situation anyway. By then it would be too late.

The PA reappeared and Jackson hopped down from the chair, practicing his easy grin as he followed her down a long hallway to the set. In a way, this might be for the best. The new targets were not obvious ones, which meant he wouldn't have to worry about last-minute security measures. And after all this was over, he'd send Dante on a well-deserved vacation—one he'd never return from.

Jackson rolled his shoulders once, waiting for the applause to begin before bounding onstage to shake the host's hand. *No one can stop me now,* he thought, raising both arms to the crowd and letting their approval wash over him.

Thirty-One

Kelly scanned the scene. The perimeter now encompassed a full half mile around the warehouse. They had passed through two checkpoints to get within one hundred yards of the building. The entire warehouse had been covered in plastic sheeting, and the parking lot was bumper-to-bumper mobile labs and office units. It was like a small city had been raised within the past twelve hours. Dozens of people hurried from trailer to trailer, most wearing full Hazmat suits and masks, looking like so many moths fluttering around a bulb. It was madness, Kelly thought, taking it all in.

"Jesus," Rodriguez said, almost reverently. Kelly guessed she wore the same expression of befuddled awe. In all her time with the Bureau, she'd never seen anything quite like this. It drove home the enormity of what they had stumbled across.

Someone directed them to one of the many trailers, and she stood on the threshold. It was packed with people, a solid mass of bodies. Leonard leaned against a desk on the far side of the room, flanked by two other agents in matching suit pants and windbreakers. He was in his mid-fifties, taller than average with a beaklike nose and dyed hair. Against the opposite wall, facing him, stood Jake.

Kelly was surprised by a sudden welling of emotion. All the events of the past week caught up with her, and she had to restrain herself from rushing into his arms. As if sensing her, Jake turned. A slow smile spread across his face and he crossed the trailer in two long strides, elbowing people out of the way. He grabbed her in a tight hug and kissed her hair.

"Hey, babe. I missed you," he whispered.

Kelly let herself relax into him for a moment before becoming aware of everyone's stares. She stiffened and pulled away, managing a weak smile.

"So you two know each other," Leonard said drily.

"This is my fiancé," Kelly said, self-consciously running a hand through her hair.

"We were discussing what a strange coincidence that is." Leonard's face had hardened, as if he'd like nothing better than to slap handcuffs on her wrists.

"So has there been a break in the case?" Rodriguez asked, crowding in behind her.

Kelly stepped forward to give him room, at the same time surveying the rest of the crowd. She recognized Syd, who issued a nod along with her usual look of dismissive disdain. Another agent, an Asian man, stood next to her. The mood in the trailer wasn't friendly.

"You could say that. Apparently the vic hired these people," Leonard said, pronouncing it as though their status as people was in question, "to find his daughter. Then he disappeared."

"Where's the daughter?" Kelly asked, turning to Jake.

"Fine. At a hospital in Sacramento with her mother and sister."

Leonard's cell rang and he made a show of turning

away, as if privacy was possible under the circumstances. "Agent Leonard."

They all stayed in place as if frozen, waiting for him to finish. Kelly felt Jake's arm wrap around her waist, his thumb stroking her side through her shirt, and she repressed a shiver. Now that he was here, all of her doubts about their future seemed silly.

Leonard hung up.

"Well?" Syd asked.

"I'm afraid everything about this investigation is on a need-to-know basis," Leonard said dismissively.

"This is my investigation," Kelly said fiercely, taking a step forward.

"Was. Now it's being overseen by a joint task force, under the umbrella of Homeland Security." Leonard eyed her coolly. "You don't like that, take it up with your boss. He signed off on it."

"C'mon everyone. Let's take this down a few notches," the Asian agent said. "We're all on the same team."

"Not really," retorted Leonard. "Unless I'm mistaken, those two—" he pointed at Jake and Syd "—are civilians."

"Civilians who have information about your vic, and might be able to shine light on what's going on," the agent continued calmly. "And I'm guessing time is short. We play nice, everyone wins."

Leonard opened his mouth to reply, but Syd cut him off. "I know what Randall was working on. What he might have given them."

Jake snapped his head toward her. Interesting, Kelly thought, that Syd hadn't shared that information with her new partner.

"We're already working on…"

"Getting that information? From the facility?" Syd

snorted. "Good luck with that. I'm guessing they're so busy trying to cover their asses right now they've buried you in red tape."

Leonard looked peeved, but shrugged. "So? What's the connection?"

"Randall was in charge of making sure all low-level radioactive waste was transferred to a few high security facilities. My guess is, he was paid to reroute a few of them. That jibe with what you found inside?" Syd jerked her head toward the warehouse.

"Maybe," Leonard said noncommittally.

"Randall was a trained physicist. If they were trying to construct, oh, say, a dirty bomb—" Leonard stiffened visibly at the word, and Syd flashed a smug smile "—they'd need someone like him to provide access to radiation sources. So they kept him at the facility, and kidnapped his daughter when money wasn't enough to persuade him. Then they grabbed him for the second phase, to process the raw material. That fit your scenario?"

Leonard shifted, glancing at his partners before saying, "It fits."

Kelly recognized the look in Jake's eye. She'd only seen him that angry once before. "And you figured this out when?" He asked evenly, the accusation plain in his voice.

Syd waved him off. "Relax. It came to me on the flight, once George told us what they found here."

"Thanks for the input," Leonard said. "Now if you'll excuse me, I need to get back to work."

"What, that didn't help?" the Asian guy asked.

"Oh, it helped. But how the material got here isn't the issue right now."

"You want to know where it's going," Kelly said,

suddenly understanding. The entire case flashed through her mind: the illegals, Jackson Burke, the float. "And I think I know."

Every eye turned to her.

"How the hell would you?" Leonard said. "Agent Jones, you know too much about all this for my comfort."

"Maybe because she's good at her job," Jake said, stepping forward, fists clenched.

Kelly flashed him a look, and he stepped back. "Like I said, it's my case, I just didn't know what we were following. But now…" Something dawned on her, and she froze.

"Well?" Leonard said impatiently.

"What's the date tomorrow?" she asked, turning to Rodriguez.

"The fourth." His eyes widened. "Oh, shit. The Independence Day parades."

"Exactly." Kelly nodded. "That's why there was a float in the warehouse with the illegals."

"Yes, that occurred to us," Leonard said drily. "It's the most logical date for an attack."

"So you'll be checking parade staging areas?" Kelly asked, deflated by his response.

Leonard barked a laugh. "What, all of them? We know they had multiple tractor trailers in the warehouse, they could have driven the bombs hundreds of miles by now. Based on the vic's time of death, our best guess is they pulled out twenty-four hours ago. That gives us a range of nearly twelve hundred miles."

"Jesus, they could be almost anywhere in the country," Jake said.

"Wait," Syd said. "Bombs? Meaning there's more than one?"

Leonard glanced around at them, seemed to decide something, and nodded. "Inside the warehouse we found iridium, the main component in radiography cameras. They have a few industrial uses, mainly oil pipeline inspection. Once we got that info, we matched up deliveries to facilities, and it turns out—" he glanced at Syd "—three trucks were rerouted on the twenty-ninth by our vic. Each held one camera. And each camera has enough raw material for a dirty bomb. Based on the tire tracks, we're looking for three semis, and maybe that many bombs. Or they could have consolidated the material into one bomb, or spread it among dozens. We have no idea."

"Jesus," Jake said. "How many people could one of these bombs take out?"

"Depends," Leonard said. "The initial blast wouldn't be as strong as a nuclear explosion. But in a major city, a bomb goes off and people hear *radiation...*" His brow darkened as he said, "It could induce mass panic. Plus the fallout would pollute the area for months, or years. Cleanup would be in the billions."

"It could cripple the country," Kelly said.

"And make 9/11 look minor by comparison," Leonard concluded.

"So you're looking at likely targets," Syd said.

Leonard nodded. "Unfortunately, there are parades in nearly every major city tomorrow, and a hell of a lot of minor ones. Some of the parades require registration permits for floats, some don't. And there's no way we can cover them all."

A pall descended over the trailer.

"So what do we do?" Jake said after a minute.

"We're already doing everything we can," Leonard said, ushering them out. "So thanks for the help, and we'll be—"

"I have a lead you can follow up on," Kelly said. "But in exchange, I want to stay on this case."

* * *

Dante tensed as they approached the checkpoint. Looked like a standard agriculture stop, but now that the Feds had found the warehouse, it could mean almost anything. Creeper was driving, and he glanced at Dante.

"Be cool," Dante said. Creeper got his nickname by being so notoriously unflappable it creeped people out. He'd killed a family of five once, then made himself a sandwich and watched TV before leaving. Dante figured on a run like this, the most important thing was to have someone who wouldn't get flustered by a speeding stop. Plus Creeper had a license to drive these rigs.

One of the cops let through a white Toyota and waved them forward. Creeper eased the eighteen-wheeler between the orange cones. The cop motioned for Creeper to roll down his window.

Dante gnawed on the inside of his lip, rankled by the cop's attitude. *Typical CHP asshole,* he thought with disdain. *Always power-tripping.* Another cop appeared on his side of the truck. He made a show of grinning, even waved and said, "Morning, officer."

"Where you boys headed?"

"San Diego," Creeper said.

"Yeah? Coming in from where? Looks like you got a full load back there."

"Drill bits, headed for China," Dante said. There were, in fact, crates half-filled with drill bits, to compensate for the added weight of the lead-encased barrel the bomb was stored in.

The cop examined them for another minute. Dante could practically see the wheels spinning in his head. Obviously he and Creeper weren't upstanding, law-abiding citizens; any cop worth his salt could smell that. But then, plenty of truckers had done time. Not a reason to stop them.

Please don't inspect the truck, Dante thought over and over, a litany in his head.

"You folks mind pulling over? Think we'll have a look inside," the cop at Creeper's window said.

Creeper said, "Yes, officer," and drove to the shoulder where another cop waited with a clipboard. Dante's pulse raced, and he fought to keep the tension from showing in his face. He glanced over at Creeper, who still wore an impenetrable mask. But his knuckles were white on the steering wheel. They were so fucking close now, too. They were the final truck in a caravan that originated in Houston. Over the past two days they'd driven a hard line north, then west, covering more than one thousand miles. They'd stopped to check preparations at each site, then moved on, their numbers dwindling until only he and Creeper remained. Somewhere around Tucson it occurred to Dante that in the past few days he'd seen more of the country than he had the entire rest of his life. Most of it by night, of course, but still. It was something.

And now this could be it, Dante thought. A traffic stop that ruined everything and sent him to death row or worse, Gitmo. The Feds claimed to have closed it, but that was probably a lie like everything else they said. Shit, being penned in with a bunch of towel heads would be worse than death.

Calm down, Dante told himself. Unless they dug past three rows of crates, they wouldn't encounter anything suspicious. And like most cops, they were probably lazy at heart.

Creeper leaned forward, reaching for the piece under the front seat. Dante grabbed his hand, stopping him, and shook his head. Too risky. If things went south, Dante would handle it from the cab. In which case he'd probably be leaving Creeper behind, but no need for him to know that.

Creeper climbed out of the truck cab and went to unlock the back. Dante sat there, legs jiggling up and down. He heard the panel door slide up. A scraping sound, wood on metal—they'd moved one box. The crates were heavy as hell, though, he'd made sure of that. Dante could picture them shining a beam over the wooden crates, trying to peer into the depths of the truck. *Good luck,* he thought. *Now let us go.*

The sound of the door sliding shut again, a clank as it latched. Dante released a breath he didn't realize he'd been holding. Creeper said something, and one of the cops laughed. A second later Creeper climbed back into the cab. The cop, face split wide in a grin, waved them back onto the highway. Dante watched the roadblock diminish in his side mirror, until they went over a bump in the road and it vanished completely.

"What did you say to him?" Dante asked, breaking the silence.

"Who?"

"The cop. Why'd he laugh?"

"Told him it was about time the Chinese had to deal with something stamped *Made in Texas,*" Creeper said.

It was the longest sentence Creeper had uttered in the four years he'd known him, which was startling in and of itself. But that, combined with the fact that he'd made a joke, and to a *cop,* no less…Dante processed that, then cracked up. "Jesus, Creeper. Didn't know you had it in you."

Thirty-Two

"Christ. It's like looking for a truck in a truck stack," Rodriguez muttered as he scanned through the printout with a highlighter.

"Tell me about it," George complained, rubbing his eyes. "I might need glasses, this is giving me a headache. Jake, you wear glasses?"

"Nah. Not an old man yet," Jake replied.

"Fuck you," George said good-naturedly.

The three of them were ensconced in the trailer adjoining Leonard's, scouring tax returns from the shell companies linked to Jackson Burke. A search of the remaining warehouses on Kelly and Rodriguez's list had already been completed—the lead she'd used to stay assigned to the case. But unfortunately nothing had turned up. No more strange powder, or any evidence of radioactivity at the sites. Leonard had another team digging through the shell companies' real estate holdings, but so far they hadn't found any outside the list. Rodriguez's friend at the IRS had been thorough.

That left them working the transportation angle, trying to track down semis. Problem was, Jackson's corporation owned a lot of legitimate businesses that used trucks to ferry goods and materials around the country. Any of the trucks could have been diverted from their usual routes to deliver the bombs.

Working on the theory that a major purchase, like a truck, would serve as a deduction, Jake, George and Rodriguez were going through years' worth of depreciation forms. There were at least fifty trucks claimed so far, and they were only halfway through the stack. No way they could issue an APB on all of them, not without Burke finding out. And the Bureau was insisting they keep a lid on things until there was more concrete evidence. Jake suspected nothing would convince them short of the new senator showing up on Capitol Hill with a vest bomb.

ASAC Leonard had begrudgingly agreed to Kelly's terms, which included keeping Jake on the case. He wasn't happy about it, but Kelly had insisted. The trade-off was that Syd was escorted back behind the yellow tape. Jake suspected Leonard hadn't put his foot down because he knew he could assign Rodriguez, George and him the scut work. They'd been at it for hours now, and even though he'd never admit it to George, his eyes were swimming from the lines and bars of standardized IRS forms. They noted down the make and model of each truck and the company that purchased it, then ran that information through the DMV database for a plate number. Not that they'd be using registered license plates, as Jake pointed out. Leonard dismissed the complaint, which confirmed Jake's suspicions.

"I think we're going about this all wrong," Rodriguez said, pushing back from the table.

"Yeah?" George asked. "You want to switch off, handle the DMV queries for a while?"

"Hell no. But I was thinking…if Burke is trying so

hard to cover his tracks and smear some illegals for this attack, wouldn't he take every precaution to make sure the trucks couldn't be linked back to him?"

"Maybe. But they were purchased through shell companies, and it's hard to prove he's involved with those."

"Hard, but not impossible. My contact found out in less than twelve hours. She's good, but you know that if this goes down, they'll have teams tearing apart every aspect of it for months."

"You're right," George said. "And at that point, even a hint of an association with the attack would destroy him. That's probably why there wasn't anything in the other warehouses. Burke used one of his own for the nitty-gritty of the assembly, but for the rest of it, he could rent a different space. That way it wouldn't link back to him if things went south."

"No politician would risk it," Jake agreed. "So what are we thinking? He rented the trucks? Paid cash, maybe?"

"Can you even do that?" George asked. "I thought you needed a special license to drive those."

"You do," Rodriguez said slowly. "But he probably wouldn't use drivers linked to his company, either." He drummed his fingers on the tabletop. "He's been using ex-cons and skinheads to do his dirty work. Maybe he recruited some of them?"

"Good theory," George agreed. "Gotta be some truck drivers in that group. Question is, how do we track them down?"

Jake jerked upright. "Dante."

"What?"

"Dante Parrish. The Corcoran warden mentioned him as someone high up in the Brotherhood leadership, but Syd and I didn't get around to tracking him down." Jake shuffled through some papers. "We got the lead on Madison, then Randall disappeared and I completely forgot about him."

"Okay. But if Syd had trouble digging something up, why would we have better luck?" Rodriguez asked.

George shrugged. "Hey, we got the resources of the entire U.S. government at our disposal. It's worth a shot. Why don't you call Syd? Maybe she found something out and forgot to tell you."

"Yeah, maybe." Jake dialed her number. He'd been meaning to check on her anyway. He knew that getting escorted off the scene must've smarted. Syd wasn't ac-climated to being told that her security clearance was insufficient.

She picked up on the third ring. "Hey, I only have a sec. The plane is about to take off."

"What? Where are you flying?" Jake said. "I thought you went back to the hotel to sleep."

"Hard to sleep when we've got a bombing to thwart," she said archly.

"Syd…"

"Relax, I won't get you in trouble. Just tell your girl-friend I headed back to New York in a huff."

"Is that where you're going?" Jake asked. "Back to the office?"

"Not exactly."

Jake shut his eyes. Why was every woman in his life so bullheaded? "Syd, this is nuts. If you figured some-thing out, tell me and I'll let them know. We could have a swarm of agents on this."

"Not big on swarms. I work best alone. You of all people should know that, Jake."

"Shit." He knew that his chances of swaying her were slim to none. He could rat her out to Leonard and have her tracked on a flight manifest, but he squirmed at the thought. They were partners, even if he was the only one who seemed to get what that meant. And besides, thanks to her former profession, she probably had a drawerful of identities on hand. It was unlikely she was traveling under her real name. Although in retrospect he wondered if he was even privy to that information. After all, what kind of parents named their girl "Sydney"?

He sighed, then said, "All right. I need to know if you dug up anything on Dante Parrish before we got sidetracked."

There was such a long pause Jake wondered if he'd lost the connection. "Nice one, Jake. Totally forgot about our friend Dante," she finally said. "Huh. You're right, if we could track him…"

"We're pretty sure he was tied to Madison's kidnapping, right? So if he's part of the larger plot—"

"Then he might know where the trucks are headed. It's a long shot, but maybe. Wish I could help, but my sources came up dry."

"Maybe we'll have more luck. And, Syd?"

"Yes?"

"Be careful, okay?"

"You know me, babe."

"Yeah, that's the problem," Jake muttered to the dial tone.

"So we're trying to track down Dante Parrish?" George asked.

"Yeah. Syd didn't have any luck, but maybe the long arm of the U.S. government will." After all, Jake thought, the FBI likely had databases she couldn't touch. "And while we're at it, let's see if we can gain access to prison records. I want the names of any Aryan Brotherhood gang members who did time with Mack Krex and Dante Parrish. Maybe some of them have licenses to drive big rigs."

"Probably a lot of them do," George said, cocking his head to the side. "It's a pretty common job for ex-cons. Bosses don't care if you killed someone, long as you didn't do it while driving."

"Well, it's worth a shot, right?" Jake pointed out.

Rodriguez shrugged. "Hell, I'll switch out one mindless search for another. At least this one doesn't involve tax forms. Doing this made me realize I forgot to file this year."

"And you call yourself a government employee," George said.

"Hey, what they're paying us, we shouldn't even have to file. That should be a perk of the job, you ask me."

"Amen to that, brother."

Jake watched them tap knuckles. "All right. I'll call the prison since the warden knows me. You two start on Dante. Anything you can find on him would be helpful."

"Including an address?"

"That, and his exact location on a GPS." Rodriguez snorted. "Sure. We're on it."

Jake watched as they set to work with renewed vigor. It wasn't much of a lead, in fact it might prove to be more busywork. But at least it was their own busywork. And if they found something, he was not above rubbing Leonard's face in it.

"No, I understand completely that there's no official organizer. Still, you must keep track of—" The agitated voice erupted in another stream of accusations, and Kelly winced, holding the phone away from her ear. "I'm afraid you misunderstood me," she said when he finally trailed off. "We have no interest in interfering with your right to free assembly. We're just trying to find out if you have a list of participants—"

There was a renewed tirade about McCarthyism and witch hunts. When he invoked Abraham Lincoln, Kelly said, "Thanks for your time, sir," and hung up.

Leonard glanced at her. "No luck, huh?"

"Same as the rest of them." Kelly leaned back in her chair. She had spent the past few hours calling parade organizers in cities under the Houston field office's jurisdiction, asking for the names of everyone who had been issued a permit for a float. Unfortunately, by and large the parades were ad hoc affairs. Sometimes it was even hard to determine if anyone was in charge.

Kelly had to admit, she was happy Jake and the others were in the other trailer. It would have been distracting having him here. She'd had to fight for him to stay, but figured she'd rather have him where she could keep an eye on him. Especially after the way he'd behaved during her Berkshires case. And separating him from Syd, who had an even weaker moral code, was a critical part of her plan. The best way to make sure he didn't do something reckless was to keep him close by. Ideally, one trailer over. She, Leonard and three other agents were manning the phones in this trailer. Every other field office nationwide was doing the same thing, trying to procure lists of participants in Fourth of July parades.

Unfortunately, they were encountering a number of obstacles. Some parades were issued a single permit that covered the entire event. Other cities authorized individual permits, but were more than happy to include any float that showed up at the staging area. And the organizers rarely knew where the floats were arriving from; they were constructed everywhere from people's driveways to the streets on the morning of the Fourth. It was a mess.

"They'd probably be a lot more cooperative if we told them why we needed to know," Kelly pointed out.

"What, and start mass panic?"

"It wouldn't hurt to tell people to steer clear of the parades tomorrow," Kelly said.

"We tell people to skip the parades, they're going to want to know why," Leonard argued. "You're basically suggesting we tell every city in the country to cancel Independence Day."

"Why not, if it saves some lives?"

"Because it won't make a difference. If the bombers get wind of the fact that we've figured out their plan, they could drive into a populated area and detonate this afternoon. Our best chance is not to let them know we're on to them."

"I don't think we're making much progress," Kelly said.

"Look, Agent Jones." Leonard glared at her. "We've got agents on the ground tracking down as many floats as they can find, in addition to driving around every major city with radiation detectors. We've called in the National Guard and every law enforcement officer available. Tomorrow they'll be reporting to staging areas at dawn, checking each entry. We've spent a long time preparing for something like this. We've got it covered."

Kelly couldn't help saying, "Like you had Katrina covered?"

Leonard's voice was edged with irritation. "We're not FEMA, Jones, and this isn't the first major bomb plot we've encountered since 9/11. We've dealt with this scenario before, and prevented it from happening. And remember, you're free to leave at any point."

Kelly set her jaw. Leonard had adopted a tone she hated, the old, *you don't know what you're talking about, useless female* voice. It triggered something in her memory. "Where's Burke right now?"

"He's still in D.C. But we've been told to steer clear of him for now. Legal is sorting through the paper trail between him and the shell companies. If they come up with a definitive link, they'll arrest him. Until then, he's officially not a suspect."

"Phoenix," Kelly said suddenly, eyes widening.

"What about it?" Leonard had turned back to his files.

"It's one of the targets. Has to be." She could have kicked herself for not thinking of it earlier. If Burke planned on using the attack as a springboard to jettison himself to the next level of political power, he'd need a valid source of righteous indignation. And if an attack happened in his district, he'd be poised to take full advantage when disaster struck.

"You think he'd take out his own constituents?" She had Leonard's full attention. His shaggy brows knit together.

"Getting back to Hurricane Katrina," she said, raising an eyebrow at him. He rolled his eyes, but kept listening. "Could anyone outside the state have named the mayor of New Orleans or the governor of Louisiana before? And suddenly they were all over the news. That's what Burke wants, to develop a following for his pet cause. And if one of the main targets was his home base…"

"He'd have that in spades," Leonard said slowly. As he lifted the phone receiver, he pointed a finger at her. "Mind you, this doesn't mean we're saying he's connected."

"Of course not." Kelly shrugged. "Maybe we got an anonymous tip."

Leonard grinned as he dialed the Phoenix field office. "For a pain in the ass, you come in useful sometimes, Agent Jones."

Syd waited by the curb. Less than a minute after she rolled her bag into the taxi zone, a large black Suburban pulled up, Maltz at the wheel. She threw her bag in the back and climbed into the passenger seat.

"Thanks for coming down here."

Maltz shrugged. "You're the boss. Jagerson is still recovering, so I've got Fribush and Kane with me."

Syd glanced back at them. She'd worked with Fribush before. She didn't know anything about Kane but he looked capable enough. Aside from slight variations in height and hair color, Special Ops guys were basically replicants: same body type, same square jaw, same army/navy surplus attire.

"Kane's local," Maltz said. "He thinks most of the floats are assembled in the warehouse district south of town. Figured we'd start there."

"Sounds good," Syd said, leaning back in her seat and closing her eyes. She'd been trained to go for a week straight with less than an hour of sleep a day. Consequently, she could drop off nearly anywhere, at anytime. She'd passed out at takeoff and woke up as the wheels touched ground, but still felt groggy. Just because she could do it didn't mean she enjoyed it.

"How are the Grants?" Maltz asked.

My, he was chatty today, Syd thought, surprised. "I have no idea," she said. She didn't. In fact she'd completely forgotten about them when the FBI made it clear her services were no longer required. And now, with Randall dead, that connection had been broken. "Why do you want to know?"

Maltz shrugged. It was hard to tell with his perpetual ruddiness, but she could swear he was blushing. "They seemed like nice girls. Nice family," he said

"I guess," Syd said dubiously, thinking of Audrey. *Nice* wasn't the first word that came to mind, but then she hadn't spent much time with them. Maybe they were nice people to flee through the countryside with. Anything was possible, she supposed.

"You got everything?"

"Most of it," Maltz replied. "Kane's got a good base of supplies."

"Good," Syd said, relaxing back in her seat. As she watched the passing landscape she ran through possible strategies and scenarios in her mind. The desert sun outside the window burned hot, reminiscent of the countless other sand-blown cities she'd driven through over the years. This one was notably less exotic, however: Phoenix, Arizona.

She was surprised Phoenix hadn't occurred to the others. It hit her the minute Burke's name was mentioned. Of course he'd target his hometown—it was the natural choice. In the trailer she'd waited for it to dawn on the Feds. Obviously they didn't have as much experience with warlords and ambitious generals, since they kept droning on about warehouses and driving radiuses. She'd almost told them, but after the brush-off they'd given her, decided against it. She knew how to stop one of the attacks. And perversely, she decided to help. Hard to say whether this was a knee jerk reaction to being told she was useless, or something else. Maybe it was because as an operative, she'd frequently been forced to stand by and do nothing while all sorts of terrible things happened, since there were "bigger issues at stake." She'd always hated that expression, it usually meant a slew of innocents were about to draw their last breath and no one really gave a shit.

So here she was, then. Syd Clement, former spook, on a mission to save Phoenix from becoming even more of a barren hellscape than it already was.

"I'll go in first," she said, turning to Maltz. "Check each one out. If I need you, I'll give the signal to move in."

"You sure? We could split up, it would go faster."

"If you got what I asked for, this shouldn't take long at all," she said, glancing at her watch. Nearly 3:30 p.m. Syd closed her eyes and said, "Wake me when we're close."

Thirty-Three

"Bingo," Rodriguez said.

"You got something?" Jake crossed the room and leaned over his shoulder. There was an image on his computer screen.

"That's Burke, you moron," George said.

"No shit, Sherlock. But check out who's behind him," Rodriguez retorted.

It was a society picture from a formal event. Burke had his arm around someone identified as a prominent lobbyist, who apparently was no stranger to Botox. And in the background, on the edge of the frame, was a hulking beast of a man. It was hard to tell from the angle, but…Jake compared it with Dante's mug shot. It was him all right. Square head like a pit bull, shaven bald, looking wildly uncomfortable in a suit a size too small. "When was this taken?" he asked.

"A year ago, at a GOP fund-raiser."

"Any idea what Dante was doing there?"

"I say we call this lobbyist and ask."

"We could fax this over to his office, let his secretary have a gander…"

"For all we know Dante is his secretary. And the higher-ups don't want Burke to get a whiff of this yet." Jake looked at them. "Do we run this by Leonard?"

"Fuck Leonard," Rodriguez said forcefully. "Great thing about lobbyists is that they love getting calls, day and night."

"I knew there was a reason I liked you, Rodriguez." Jake cracked a smile. "Sorry, George, I have a new favorite agent."

"I'm all torn up about it." George rolled his eyes. "Please, promise me you'll tread carefully. I'm not cut out for the private sector."

It took all of ten minutes to track down the office number for the lobbyist in the photo, and another five to convince a beleaguered staffer that they needed to speak with him immediately. After outlining what the administration thought of lobbyists who didn't help the FBI in matters of national security, and how that reflected on pork barrel spending for their clients, a cell phone number was produced.

"Who wants to make the call?" Rodriguez asked, holding up the receiver.

"Dibs." George put it on speakerphone. The lobbyist answered on the third ring. From the sound of things, there was a full-scale party going on in the background.

"Hello, Mr. Jeffers, this is Special Agent George Fong calling from the FBI. Your name came up in the course of an investigation, and I was wondering if you could help us out."

"What? My name?" Jeffers voice veered quickly from alarm to a practiced honeyed tone. "I'm sure there must be some mistake. Let me give you the number for my attorney—"

"The investigation actually involves a third party, sir. All we need is for you to identify a man in a photo."

A long pause. "Well, I suppose that would be—"

"We'd really appreciate the help, Mr. Jeffers. I'm sending it to your phone right now."

Rodriguez sent the photo, and they waited. Jeffers maintained a running monologue, most of which revolved around damn cell phones and how tricky they were to operate. Rodriguez rolled his eyes, and Jake made a motion for him not to laugh. "Ah, this…this is Jack Burke," Jeffers finally said. "Just became a senator, you know, after that tragedy with—"

"Right, we know. I'd actually like you to identify the man standing behind Mr. Burke on his left."

"Oh, all right." Jeffers sounded inordinately relieved that the investigation didn't involve a new senator whom he probably had high hopes for. "That guy. I can't remember his name, he's just Jack's bodyguard," he said dismissively.

"I didn't realize Mr. Burke needed a bodyguard," George said carefully.

"Oh, well, I'm sure he doesn't. My wife and I assumed it was one of Jack's eccentricities, he's quite a character. He took him to a few events. You're right, though. As I always say, you only get mugged at those parties by people like me." He laughed heartily.

"Thanks for your time, Mr. Jeffers. And if you'd please keep this conversation private for the moment—"

"Oh, absolutely, absolutely." His voice dropped to a conspiratorial whisper. "I have to say, I'm not surprised to hear the bodyguard's in trouble. He seemed…rough around the edges, if you know what I mean. I was surprised Jack hired him, he usually has excellent taste in people."

"Clearly," George said, before hanging up.

"Nicely done." Jake clapped George on the shoulder.

"Bodyguard, huh?" Rodriguez said. "Wonder if that means he was on the official payroll."

"If he was, it's under a different name," George said. "I went through all the records, there's no Dante listed anywhere, not even under the shell companies."

"So is it enough to take to Leonard?" Rodriguez asked. "It's a link, but if they're not willing to smear Burke, maybe they won't use this, either."

"Something tells me they won't have any reservations about throwing someone like Dante under the bus," Jake scoffed.

"Even if it tips off Burke?"

"Screw Burke. At this point, he should know we're breathing down his neck. I say we make sure they plaster Dante Parrish's face across the networks," Jake said forcefully. The two agents exchanged a glance. "What?" he demanded.

"It's just…at this point, we should let the Bureau decide how they want to manage things," Rodriguez said, looking uncomfortable.

"Rodriguez is right, Jake. They might want to keep the search for Dante on the down low. If Burke gets backed into a corner, he might detonate early."

"Et tu, George?" Jake said.

George shrugged. "I got a job to keep, man. And nobody wants those bombs going off."

"All right, fine," Jake said, defeated. "Let's head over to the big people's trailer."

Kelly opened the door of the trailer and was startled to find Jake poised to knock, with George and Rodriguez behind him.

"Hi," he said. "How's it going over here?"

"All right, I guess," she said cautiously. "Did the truck search turn anything up?"

"Um, we decided to go in a different direction."

"Jake…"

"Trust me, you're going to like what we have to say."
He glanced past her shoulder, where Leonard was tucking
his computer into a case. "Going somewhere?"

"Phoenix, actually. We figure since it's Burke's
district—"

"Oh my God," George interrupted. "You're right, it's
the perfect target. Can't believe I didn't think of it."

Rodriguez groaned at the mention of Phoenix.

Jake gave Kelly a hard look. "Let me guess—invited
guests only. And we're not on the list."

Kelly shifted uncomfortably at the hurt in his voice.
"You said you had something?"

"Can we come in?"

Leonard muttered something under his breath, then
waved them in impatiently. "What is it?"

"Wow. You really weren't expecting us to come up with
anything, were you?" Jake grinned. "Nice to be appreciated."

"Cut the shit, Riley. I don't have time for it. Our plane
takes off in a half hour. If you've got something, spit it out."

Jake glared at him. Kelly half expected him to storm
out of the trailer. But after a long second, he handed over
a stack of photos, saying, "Your printer sucks, by the
way. That's the best resolution I could get."

"Who the hell is this?" Leonard asked, holding up the
top picture.

Kelly examined it: a mug shot of a skinhead. He didn't
look like any of the guys she'd arrested in Arizona, but it
was hard to be sure.

"Dante Parrish," Jake said. "Burke's bodyguard."

"And I care about this why?" Leonard demanded.

"Because we're pretty sure he was involved in the kidnapping of the Grant girl. And now it turns out he's linked

to Burke." Jake shrugged. "But hey, if we're bothering you, we'll head back to the kids' table."

"It makes sense," Kelly said slowly. "To get the Aryan Brotherhood on board, Burke would need someone to bridge the gap. He wouldn't have been able to make those connections on his own."

"I'm willing to bet if you look, you'll find photos of Burke with someone involved with the Minutemen, too," Jake said, jabbing the photo with one finger, "and probably some biker gang. But right now, we got this guy."

Leonard flipped through the stack, settling on the one with Burke in the foreground. "Okay," he said finally. "It's something. I'll put it out on the wire."

"That's it?" Jake asked.

"Yeah, that's it. Now, I've got a plane to catch." He turned to Kelly. "You coming, Agent Jones?"

"One minute."

"Fine. But any longer and we leave without you."

Leonard glowered at Jake as he pushed past. Kelly saw Jake's jaw go rigid and put a hand on his arm. "Don't."

"What?"

"I know that look."

"He would've deserved it." Jake grinned, but his eyes remained serious. "And I don't love that you're flying into a city with a bull's-eye painted on it."

"That's why I was going to call you from the plane," Kelly said, but at his expression she backtracked. "That was a joke. A bad one."

"You should know better. Jokes aren't your thing."

"Apparently," she agreed, running her hand up to his shoulder. George and Rodriguez moved a few feet back to give them some privacy. "Leonard isn't much of an outside-the-box thinker. And I want to stop at least one of these attacks if I can. If we catch whoever is in charge in Phoenix, they might know where the other bombs are."

"They won't." Jake shook his head. "Classic cell structure. There probably aren't many people who know the whole plan. And only a few will be able to connect it back to Burke. He's had a long time to plan this."

"Still, I've got to try."

"This is a hell of a last case," he said, avoiding her eyes.

"Tell me about it."

Without warning he pulled her in tight to his chest. "I love you, Kelly. Don't get hurt," he whispered fiercely into her hair before letting go.

"I love you, too," she said, managing a weak smile before trotting to the waiting SUV.

Thirty-Four

"**P**ull over," Syd barked. Maltz obliged, screeching to the side of the road. Fribush and Kane jolted forward but didn't say anything. Syd ran her eyes over the low buildings. They were south of Phoenix, in an area dominated by abandoned warehouses and factories that had seen better days. The first three stops had been fruitless, just a bunch of people clambering over makeshift floats festooned with cheap-looking red, white and blue bunting. The entries ranged from floats with a "love your local farmer" theme, complete with fake orange trees, to papier-mâché tributes to the Declaration of Independence. It all struck Syd as horribly pedestrian, but she complimented their creativity profusely before moving on. They'd been at it for nearly two hours, and she could feel the team's spirits flagging. If they didn't turn up anything here she'd break for a meal. She needed them sharp in case the shit hit the fan.

But first, there was one last place to check. An older man at the last site had mentioned driving by a float being assembled farther south. And bingo, within a hundred yards of the place her dosimeter went bananas.

At her tone, Fribush and Kane straightened. "What do you want to do?" Maltz asked.

"Circle once, not too slowly."

Maltz obeyed, swinging the SUV past the open entrance to the warehouse and continuing toward the rear. Syd kept her face relaxed while she studied the building. The nose of a red truck poked out the door. The familiar tacky patriotic bunting around the cab, a crisp new American flag mounted across the grill. One man visible by the door, most likely keeping watch. No way to know how many others were inside. The main exit was partially blocked by the truck. There was a narrow alley between that building and the one next door; it didn't look like any doors opened onto it. Around back, a door was set in the wall next to a battered Dumpster, probably an emergency exit since there was no handle. Not good, that meant it might be alarmed. Syd couldn't see any windows, either; whoever chose the site knew their job. Which didn't leave a lot of options for her team. At least there were no visible cameras. She waved for Maltz to drive down the block while she turned it over in her mind.

"What do you think?" he finally asked.

"You and I go in the front," Syd said, "using the cover we discussed. Fribush and Kane check the back to see if they can get in quietly. If they can, signal me via cell and we'll use the flash bangs, throw them off enough to pin them down."

"And if the back is locked?"

"Same plan, but on my signal we blow the door. I don't want them heading out the back while we take the front. There are other cells out there, we don't want them to know a target has been compromised."

"Wouldn't hurt to do a more thorough recon," Maltz said uncertainly.

Syd shrugged. "I don't think we have time. The drive-by might have already spooked them."

Fribush and Kane got out of the SUV, removed two duffel bags from the hatch, and trotted toward the rear of the building. She waited until they were in position, then nodded at Maltz. He pulled a baseball cap down low over his eyes and circled back to the front. The man inside the door stepped out as they approached. Maltz parked at an angle, discreetly blocking the truck, nose slightly out in case they had to leave quickly. Syd pulled out her ponytail and ran a hand through her hair. As she stepped from the car, she flashed the lookout a hundred-watt smile.

He was young, no more than twenty-five, tough and stringy-looking. Definitely not the first team, Syd thought— strictly benchwarmer material. Whoever assigned him lookout duty figured it was something even he couldn't screw up. But she was about to prove them wrong.

"Hi there!" she said, letting her accent shine through. She jutted a hand toward him.

He reflexively shook her hand, jaw slightly agape. Maltz stood right behind her. His HK was tucked inside a many-pocketed photographer's vest, and around his neck hung a digital camera that harbored a 9mm and a huge flash designed to blind and disorient.

"I'm Gail Jones, from the *Arizona Republic?* We're doing a story on the parade tomorrow? You know, the sorts of things people are doing to prepare, what Independence Day means to them…" She laid a hand on his arm. "Human interest. We've taken shots of almost all the other floats, and would love to include yours. Did you go with a red, white and blue theme? Or something else?"

"Umm…" he stammered.

She brushed past him into the warehouse. It was

stifling inside, the heat had been trapped by the cheap metal roof and the air appeared to shimmer. Syd fanned herself with one hand as her eyes darted around the interior. Another man was adjusting something on the truck bed. He straightened at the sight of her and frowned. No one else visible, but it was hard to make out the depths of the warehouse in the dim lighting. She caught movement by the back door—Fribush and Kane.

"Hey, lady, you're not supposed—"

She swiveled to face the kid, who had a look of growing alarm in his face.

"I really love this, your whole melting pot theme. Haven't seen anything like it yet. Do you mind if we take a few pictures?"

"No pictures!" The other man jumped off the float and ran toward them, waving his arms forcefully. *Head of the local cell, I presume,* Syd thought. Maltz raised the camera.

She pasted her best startled look on her face. "But really, what you've done here is so great. Why don't you all gather in front of it. One shot and we'll be out of your hair. This could be the lead—"

"Get the fuck out," the guy snarled, skidding to a stop directly in front of her. He was average-sized but had a hard look to him—prison, or maybe the army, Syd thought. Shit. And he was clearly the brains of this particular operation.

He glared at her, then his gaze shifted to Maltz. His eyes suddenly narrowed, and Syd knew they'd been made. "Flag!" she yelled, digging in her purse for her gun. She fumbled it and cursed.

All hell broke loose in the warehouse. Maltz's camera flashed, blinding her, followed immediately by the sputter of rounds being squeezed off. Something sparked to her right, and Syd instinctively dove in the direction of the flatbed, commando-crawling until she was underneath it. She got behind one of the wheels just in time to see the kid drop, felled by Maltz. The other guy had vanished.

Shouting erupted from the rear of the warehouse. Syd panned the darkness quickly, eyeing through the sight on her HK. The yelling was coming from behind a door to a partitioned-off area. It slammed open and a spray of bullets pocked the floor and walls. There was a sudden bright light and piercing noise. Syd jerked her head away, wishing she had a free hand to plug her ears. The flash bang was hell in an enclosed space.

Everything was muffled, as if sounds were crawling to her ears through glue. Maltz was fifteen feet away, aiming his gun at something she couldn't see. She was rusty, since diving for cover it had taken her thirty seconds to process the scene and react. Not good. If she was still with the Agency, that alone would have been grounds for dismissal.

A sudden rumbling, then a lurch. For a second Syd experienced the disconcerting sensation that the warehouse was moving away from her, then realized it was the tires as the truck headed out the door. She rolled in time to avoid getting squashed and lay as flat as possible, watching the tow lights blink red. A collision, the grinding of metal muted by her temporary deafness as the truck shoved their SUV aside as if it were an errant toy. She jumped to her feet. Maltz was already behind the wheel when she scrambled in. One side of the SUV was badly scraped and dented, but it looked driveable.

"Fribush and Kane?" she asked, breathless.

"It looked like they had it handled." Maltz peeled out after the truck. "Bastard just missed me, had a 9mm subcompact in his jeans. By the time I reloaded he was in the truck cab."

"We've got to stop him," Syd said, watching as the truck fishtailed, the flatbed whipping in a wide arc as he spun onto the main road.

"We can try," Maltz said, jaw set. "But I gotta be honest, a car versus a big rig, I don't love our chances." He glanced at her. "You want to call the cops?"

Syd chewed her lower lip. She hated the thought of it. But if that truck made it downtown…she dug in her purse for her cell phone. "Stay as close as you can without riding up his ass," she muttered as she dialed.

Jake picked up on the third ring. "Hi, partner," she said.

"Hey," he said. "How's Phoenix?"

"How did you know?"

"Call it a lucky guess. So, did you find the guy?"

"We did, actually." Syd watched as the truck nearly took out a Honda Civic. It swerved up the on-ramp to Route 10, headed north toward Phoenix proper. "One slight problem, though. He's got the bomb on the road."

"Jesus, Syd."

"I was thinking you have a better shot at getting the police to respond. Coming from me, it might get dismissed as a crank call."

"Go figure." Syd heard Jake talking to someone in a low voice, then an exclamation in the background. "All right, George is handling it. I'll stay on with you while he patches us through to dispatch. What exit are you closest to?"

"He just passed Exit 155." Syd watched smaller cars struggle to get out of the way, several of them nearly colliding with each other. Maltz swerved around them, managing to stay fifteen feet back from the truck's tail. It was surreal watching the float whip around, the Statue of Liberty canted sideways by the rapid turns, streamers tearing away and wafting back on the breeze. Syd wondered where the bomb was—inside the main statue?

It would make sense, especially if someone had a funny sense of irony. "You're pissed, aren't you?"

"*Pissed* isn't the right word. I'm just wondering what it is about me that sends women running toward a bomb," Jake said cryptically.

Syd decided that didn't bear a response. She called out the next few exits as they blew past them. The truck was gaining momentum. She watched nervously as their speedometer crept past ninety, then a hundred. Horns blared in their wake, but the truck cleared a straight swath.

"Uh-oh," Maltz said suddenly.

Syd saw it at the same time: the highway swept up a bridge in a long arc, and there were brake lights ahead. Rush-hour traffic. "Shit," she said.

"Yup," Maltz agreed.

"Jake, he's driving about a hundred miles an hour, and he's about to hit traffic," Syd said.

There was silence on the other end of the phone. "The nearest unit is still a few minutes away," Jake finally said. "They're setting up roadblocks at the exits, but it doesn't sound like he's going to make it that far."

"Definitely not. This is going to get ugly." Syd turned to Maltz. "Flip around and get us the hell out of here."

Maltz nodded, slowing down. The truck plowed forward as if the driver was oblivious to the danger ahead. "C'mon," she breathed. "Slow the fuck down. Don't do this."

They had almost decelerated enough for Maltz to turn the SUV around when the truck started climbing the bridge. Two cars skidded into each other as the drivers took too long to react. The screech of brakes, crunch of metal. A horn blared, then was cut off as the truck slammed into the wall of slower vehicles at the top of the ramp, scattering them like metal jacks.

"Crap," Maltz said. They watched in silence as the truck moved inexorably forward, slowing incrementally like a knife carving through butter. It hit the Jersey barrier on the shoulder of the bridge. For a second it appeared as if the concrete might hold, but the weight of the truck plowed through it. The cab suddenly vanished from view as the float pitched high in the air.

"Stay low!" Syd said, diving into the backseat.

Maltz spun the wheel in a tight turn, flipping them around. Their tires got caught in the loose gravel on the side of the road and spun helplessly.

"Maltz, get back here! It's too late!" Syd grabbed at his arm, trying to drag him into the backseat where they'd have more cushioning.

He didn't respond, just ground down on the accelerator until the SUV jerked free and fishtailed, spitting pebbles. He gritted his teeth as he floored it. Syd instinctively braced herself against the back of the seat. In her heart she knew it was already too late.

Everything seemed to slow down. Maltz shouted something and her cell phone emitted tinny sounds from the front seat, but Syd couldn't make them out. Her hands covered her ears, her eyes squeezed shut as she waited for what seemed like forever.

Then a flash so bright it penetrated her closed lids, followed by a roar of sound and a wave of heat, and the world vanished in a roiling cloud of darkness.

Thirty-Five

"Syd? Syd!" Jake shouted into the phone. He spun around. "The call got dropped. I'm redialing, tell dispatch to hang on…"

George and Rodriguez were staring at him, dumb-founded. Jake had been relaying Syd's information to George, who conveyed it to the police dispatcher in Phoenix. There was a burst of chatter from the receiver. George looked at it; his arm had dropped to his waist when Jake started yelling. He raised it back to his ear. An expression of horror spread across his face. After listening for a minute, he squeezed his eyes shut and said, "All right. Good luck."

He hung up. Jake stared at him. "Jesus Christ, George. Why'd you hang up? Syd will—"

George shook his head. "The bomb went off, Jake. Dispatcher had to go, they're mobilizing special teams to the area."

It was hard to speak, but Jake forced the words out. "How bad?"

George sat down hard. "They don't know yet. They're sending in a crew to check for radioactivity, but…"

His voice trailed off. Jake shook his head. "Damn it, Syd. What did you do?"

Leonard glared down at the ground. "Why the hell are we still circling?" He motioned one of the other agents to the cockpit. The agent walked up the aisle hunched over, his head brushing the ceiling.

Kelly watched Leonard tap his heel restlessly against the floor. They were in a private jet, commandeered from an oil tycoon who apparently owed the government a favor. Shame that given the circumstances she couldn't enjoy the trip. Contrary to the depiction of countless TV shows, there wasn't a private fleet of planes available for FBI agents. They nearly always flew commercial, in coach.

The agent returned from the cockpit.

"Well?" Leonard asked.

The agent leaned over and said something in a low voice. Kelly strained to hear. He had gone completely pale, which she took as a bad sign.

"Jesus Christ," Leonard hissed.

"What?"

"It went off," he said bluntly, digging out his cell phone. "They're not letting any planes in or out. Whole city has gone into complete lockdown. Governor called in the National Guard, and the Phoenix field office is scrambling."

"Oh my God," Kelly peered out the window. The smog appeared denser to the south, but there was a nearly impenetrable layer everywhere. She pictured gamma rays coursing out in all directions, invisible but deadly, sliding over the sleek face of office buildings and skimming across benches in playgrounds and parks. "How many dead? Are they evacuating the city?"

"I'm about to find out." Leonard finished dialing and

settled back in his seat, looking blankly out the window. Kelly could see other airplanes circling at various altitudes, waiting to be redirected. She caught herself chewing her lower lip, an old habit from when she was a kid, and forced herself to stop.

After a clipped conversation, Leonard hung up. "Explosion was caused by a crash on the I-10. Thankfully they were still on the outskirts of town, so collateral damage is limited. Not many houses, mostly office buildings that closed early for the holiday. The initial blast zone…" He shrugged, raising both palms faceup. "Hard to say. They're guessing no more than a hundred casualties. Took out a section of the highway, emergency crews are waiting to go in."

"And the radiation?" Kelly asked.

"We should know the levels soon. Luckily we had a mobile unit driving around already, and some readers installed on government buildings downtown. National Guard is setting up mobile decontamination centers. They're telling people to stay in their houses unless they were in the immediate blast zone, which will have to be evacuated. Not much wind, which helps."

"What the hell made it go off?" Kelly wondered, gazing out the window.

Leonard's face hardened. "Damned if I know. Maybe something spooked the bastards." His eyes flicked over to her before shifting back to the window. He still seemed suspicious. Kelly tried not to take it personally. "It'll be a while before they sort things out. Right now they're focusing on treating victims and keeping the public calm. The rest we deal with later."

"So are we landing?" Kelly asked.

"No point now. I doubt he planned on triggering all of them in Phoenix."

Kelly shook her head. "No, that wouldn't make sense. If he wanted to create panic, it would be good to spread it out. And if other cities were involved, the link to Burke would be less obvious." She rubbed her eyes, suddenly exhausted. They had arrived too late. And despite Leonard's proclamation that it could've been a lot worse, it was bad enough. Up to a hundred people, possibly more, were already dead. "Has Burke made a statement yet?"

Leonard shrugged. "I have no idea. Even if this was part of the original plan, he'd have to wait a few hours to make it look good." He jabbed a finger at her. "If he was involved, and I'm still not conceding that he is."

"He is," Kelly said sharply.

"Fine. Any idea where he sent the other bombs?"

"No one's turned anything up?" Kelly asked.

Leonard shook his head. "They've found property owned by Burke everywhere from Albuquerque to Little Rock. Parades in every major city in between. They're sending teams to check each site, but like you said…"

"The building might not even be connected to him this time. He only needed the space for a few days, so he could have paid rent, or they might be using an empty building for the setup." Kelly was suddenly immensely relieved that Jake was still in Houston. With a concentration of agents from every department with an acronym, it was probably the only city safe from an attack.

"He might even be considering New York or Chicago," Leonard said.

Kelly shook her head. "I don't think so. If he's trying to galvanize a base, he'd target people who are already concerned about immigration. Those other cities are at too much of a remove."

Leonard's cell rang again. He picked up and listened

to a stream of chatter on the other end. "He's sure?" He asked after a moment. It was hard to tell whether it was good or bad news. "Fine. We'll join them." He snapped the phone shut. "A California state trooper recognized the photo we put out on the wire."

"Dante Parrish?"

Leonard nodded. "Routine agriculture stop on Route 8. Dante was a passenger in a semi. Cop remembered because they checked their cargo. Said something seemed off."

"But they didn't find anything?"

Leonard shook his head. "That was someone from the San Diego field office. He got the sense they didn't look very hard."

"So you think Dante headed to San Diego with one of the bombs?"

Leonard eyed her. "It would jibe with your theory. San Diego's got some serious border issues."

"Lots of bases there, too, which makes them an even better target," Kelly said thoughtfully. "It would look like an attack on the military."

"If your theory is correct," Leonard reminded her.

"If it's not, and you have something else to go on, by all means…" Kelly said.

He examined her for a long moment. "Could be L.A., too."

"Could be, but then why wouldn't he stay on Route 10 from Texas?" Kelly asked.

She could see Leonard weighing it, not wanting to admit she was right but unable to come up with an alternative. "Fine," he said after a minute. He shifted his attention to the other agent. "Tell the pilot to take us to San Diego." He turned back to Kelly. "But I'm putting Los Angeles on high alert, too."

"Good, you should," she said. "Along with every other major city in a border state."

As Leonard placed a series of calls, Kelly found herself remembering the confusion on 9/11. Rumors abounded: that more planes were hijacked, that the U.S. was retaliating against Afghanistan, that a land invasion was imminent. At the time she'd been stationed at the New York field office, which had been as bad as everywhere else. Maybe they were right about trying to avert panic by not telling people the truth. But Kelly hated the thought of letting everyone head to tomorrow's parades, lawn chairs and umbrellas their only defense against a toxic bloodbath. "Now that one of the bombs has gone off, are they going to warn people?"

"That's above my pay grade," Leonard said, looking out the window. "The president will decide."

The plane tilted sharply left as the pilot shifted course. The dusty desert landscape below looked apocalyptic. Kelly gazed blankly down as mountains rose and fell, chasing shadows cast by the setting sun until everything faded to black.

They sat in silence for the remainder of the flight.

It was hard for Jackson Burke to maintain his characteristic poise. He felt like a kid on Christmas. Everyone wanted to shake his hand and tell him how refreshing it was to have "new blood" around, although they hastily added that it was so sad about poor Duke. Jackson always agreed, the appropriate amount of sober reflection in his voice as he reiterated his dedication to upholding Duke's legacy. They ate that up, and it always eased the awkward moment. Yes indeed, he had a bright future. And it was about to get a hell of a lot brighter.

Of course, he'd been attending parties like this for

years. But always as a donor, spending the bulk of the event engaged in what he referred to as "rich people small talk." How Aspen was just not the same anymore, the disgraceful increased luxury tax on jets, which countries were currently best for offshore accounts. The usual.

But tonight was a whole new experience. Even the rubber chicken dinner tasted better. Everyone in the room sought him out, pressing for their own pet earmark. Jackson nodded and made promises he never intended to keep, trusting that tomorrow's events would sweep all that pettiness aside for the foreseeable future. It was his issue everyone would suddenly care about, his issue that Congress would devote itself to solving. And if the president refused to go along, sticking to his coddling policies in complete disregard of the will of the American people…well, a lot of things could happen then. The next presidential election was right around the corner.

Jackson was almost at the door, headed home for an Ambien-induced good-night's sleep so he'd be fresh for the morning's events, when he was waylaid by one final glad-hander. He looked familiar, and Jackson tried to place him. Definitely a lobbyist, something to do with mining? He searched his brain, and a name materialized as the man extended his hand. "Jeffers! Great to see a friendly face in this jungle."

"Absolutely, absolutely. And congrats on the new job!" Jeffers leaned in without releasing Jackson's hand. "You won't be forgetting us little people now, will you?"

Jackson clapped him hard on the shoulder, relieved to skip the Duke Morris mourning dance. "I could never forget you, Jeffers! And of course I appreciate your continuing support."

"Sure, sure. After all, you're barely in and it's time to start running again, right?" Jeffers said jovially.

Jackson responded with gravitas, "Of course, I haven't decided on running yet. This is just a favor I'm doing the governor, out of respect for Duke."

"Sure, sure," Jeffers repeated, and Jackson was suddenly annoyed with him. The clod was acting as though he already had something on him. And there was simply no way that was true.

"If you'll excuse me, it really has been a long day."

"I'm sure it has." Jeffers lowered his voice. "I was happy to see you left your bodyguard back in Arizona. Especially after the phone call I got earlier this evening."

Jackson frowned. He had taken Dante to a few events to impress him and gain his trust, passing him off as personal protection. But after the wooing he'd explained that they couldn't appear publicly anymore, better to keep a low profile. Why would Jeffers remember him? "Sorry, what phone call?" he asked, careful to keep his tone neutral.

Jeffers leaned in conspiratorially; Jackson could practically taste the bourbon on his breath. It smelled like he'd had an extra helping of the crab salad, too. "The one from the FBI. They said not to tell you, but after all these years of friendship I figured I owed you a heads-up. We Arizonans have to stick together, right?" He straightened and shook his head. "They had a picture of you and him, said he was a 'person of interest.' So sad, when you find out nasty things about employees. Even with background checks, you can't be sure these days, can you?"

"No, sadly, you can't," Jackson agreed stiffly. He hoped the shock wasn't registering on his face. The FBI had somehow connected the dots, from the warehouse to Dante, and from Dante…to him? It wasn't possible. He'd been so careful, set up so many intermediaries.

Jeffers was still regarding him closely, a look of

victory in his eyes. "Anyway, thought you should know. I'll be in touch soon about that new copper mine." And with a final wink he was gone.

Jackson took a moment, waiting until his breathing steadied. He felt as though he'd been punched. This could ruin everything. If they proved a link…he wondered if they had tapped his phone. He'd only used a prepaid cell when calling Dante or the other captains, but he'd seen on television that they could even monitor those if they wanted to.

He ran a hand across his forehead and it came away wet. He headed for the door, no longer in the mood to talk to anyone, but froze on the threshold. Where should he go? Would they be waiting for him outside the town house he'd rented? Would they haul a U.S. Senator past the cameras in handcuffs? Everything was crumbling, years' worth of work and planning, all down the drain because he'd taken Dante to a few parties. The entire fragile coalition he'd devoted nearly a decade to building, spawned as he watched the trial of Timothy McVeigh, thinking if only he'd been smarter, and had some money to back his vision up. Imagine what he could have accomplished, instead of looking like a nut job McVeigh could have galvanized people. And then Jackson set out to do just that, slowly, carefully. Always covering his tracks.

The valet brought around his car as he pondered his options. He had a horse ranch in Virginia. Maybe that would be best. At the very least, it would take them longer to find him.

Deciding, Jackson turned onto the Beltway and headed south. He had an hour's drive ahead, plenty of time to come up with a strategy. And worst-case scenario, he had three bombs to bargain with.

Thirty-Six

Something intruded on her consciousness, an annoying repetitive noise that took a few seconds to identify. Car alarm, it was a car alarm. Jesus, why wasn't anyone turning it off? She could really use more sleep....

Syd groaned and opened her eyes, prepared to pull on her robe, run outside, track down the car's owner, and kill them. Or at least make them understand how socially unacceptable it was to own a car with an alarm that didn't shut off automatically. Especially since they weren't an effective deterrent anyway.

But she wasn't in her bed. It was hard to see, the air was thick with dust and smoke. She was in an unfamiliar car, stuck in the well behind the front seat. The roof had been crushed nearly down to her head. Syd scrambled to process it. Tel Aviv? Karachi? She coughed reflexively, trying to get her bearings. Suddenly, it all came back. Phoenix. The bomb. The shock wave had sent the SUV tumbling end over end. There had been fire and searing heat and...

Oh shit, she thought. Not just a bomb, a dirty bomb. Which meant she had to get the hell out of here. She knew the risks of contamination, and the longer she spent in the affected area, the greater the exposure.

And where the hell was Maltz? Syd raised her head a few inches, didn't see him. Okay, first things first. She shifted, working her right arm free from where it was pinned beneath the front seat. She wiggled the fingers, then bent the elbow—a little sore, but nothing appeared broken. Same with the left arm. Taking a deep breath, she eased her right knee up to her chest. It felt like her toes were wiggling, but it was hard to be sure. She pushed off the foot and winced—definitely bruised, but she didn't see any protruding bones.

It took nearly five minutes to complete the personal inventory. Scrapes from the broken glass, a gash on her right shin, and her ears were ringing. Other than that she seemed fine. Nothing she hadn't gone through before. As long as she didn't tear herself open trying to get out of the car, she should be able to hike out of the blast zone.

She pulled herself to sitting, knees against her chest, in the small space where the roof pressed down to meet the floor. A few more inches, and a jagged piece of metal would have eviscerated her. Looked like she was still lucky.

Unfortunately, the same didn't appear true for Maltz. Syd shifted slowly, contorting until she was on her knees, and squinted into the front seat. Empty. The front of the car had been completely crushed, like some giant monster had chewed it to a messy metal pulp. On the side of the car she was on, the roof had only been compressed halfway down the window. A few shards of glass clung to the frame. Syd yanked free a piece of shredded leather seat cover, wrapped it around her hand, and knocked the rest of the glass free. The opening was about six inches high—tight, but she should be able to make it. The only danger was a section of the roof that had been punched downward, creating a nasty-looking spike. Syd took a deep breath. As long as she stayed to the right side she should be okay. It was either risk it, or allow more radio-active particles to infiltrate her as she waited for help. And she was never good at waiting.

Syd took a deep breath before starting through the window. Her head cleared easily, the trouble came as she arched, trying to pull her upper body free. The cloud outside the car was thicker, hanging like a dust storm that was awaiting approval to proceed. Something caught her hip and Syd sucked in her breath at the flash of pain. Shit. She'd hit the spike. She tried to ease forward, but the sharp steel sliced deeper. She couldn't crawl free without impaling herself. Carefully, she lowered herself back into the car and checked her side. It was hard to tell in the dim light, but the scrape didn't look too bad. She pressed the piece of seat cover against it and frowned. What next? Night was falling, and the thought of sitting alone in the dark was almost unbearable. She would get through it, she'd been trained to handle anything, but still. It felt like she was the last person on earth.

Worse yet, that fucking car alarm was still going off.

No emergency crews yet, which wasn't surprising. First responders had probably been ordered to wait until radiation levels were measured. It was odd, though, that she couldn't hear anyone else. How long had she been knocked out?

"Hello?" she called out tentatively, before yelling, "Anyone there?"

Syd thought she heard grunting nearby, but her hearing was still out of whack from the explosion. She wrapped her free arm around her knees and hugged them to her chest, surprised by an overwhelming urge to cry. She couldn't remember the last time she cried, maybe when her mother died. It had been at least a decade.

"Get a grip, Sydney," she chastised herself.

A sound outside sent her hand to her hip before she remembered taking her holster off to look like a newspaper reporter. Syd hated being unarmed. She scoured the interior, groping under the seats before giving up. She'd have to trust that looters would be dissuaded by fear of contamination. And that she wasn't too messed up to fight if she had to.

A light shone through the window, and she squinted, turning her face away.

"Boss?" a voice asked.

"Fribush?" She could barely believe it. "How the hell did you find me?"

He held up a small device. "GPS. Sorry it took a while, we had to find alternate transportation."

Syd could have cried from relief. This was precisely why she'd put Maltz in charge: he could assemble a team so blindly loyal they'd march into a radioactive haze to find him. "I'm stuck in here. Can you get the door open?"

Fribush examined it, probing the frame with his flashlight before stepping back. She heard low voices, then he reappeared. "Hold tight, boss. We got something back in the truck."

A few minutes passed. She heard the sound of jogging feet. A section of the door eased away, protesting the treatment with a groan. After a minute, the lower panel popped out. Fribush extended a hand to help her. Syd carefully extricated herself, feet first, watchful of the jagged edges. Once free, she stretched her arms above her head. "Can't remember the last time I was this happy to be upright," she commented. "Thanks."

Fribush pointed toward the front seat with his crowbar. "Maltz in there, too?"

"No. Let's do a quick search of the area." Syd didn't state the obvious, that since he'd been ejected they would probably be collecting parts of Maltz to take with them.

Fribush got a look in his eye. He nodded and handed her a spare flashlight.

Syd pulled her shirt over her mouth to filter out the silt. It was impossible to see more than a foot in any direction. The flashlight beam was refracted by the sand in the air, which almost made the cloud more impenetrable. They'd landed well off the highway—thank God Maltz had gotten away from the bridge before the explosion, otherwise they would have hurtled down a forty-foot drop. The area they'd landed in was flat. Her beam picked out a saguaro rising like a ghostly sentinel, spikes collecting grimy flakes of dust. Brush dotted the landscape, grasping at her feet as she shuffled through it. Pieces of metal were scattered across the ground, some from their car, some from others. She came across another twisted metal frame, bent almost beyond recognition. Syd panned her light inside, but it was too late for the driver.

She heard a yell and hurried toward it. Kane was kneeling on the ground next to the highway blacktop. In front of him lay the mangled body of Michael Maltz.

"Is he…" Syd suddenly realized this was going to affect her more than she'd anticipated. She had initially met Maltz in Syria, and they had worked together a few times since then. The sad truth was that more than anyone else in the world, including Jake, he had probably been her best friend.

His leg was bent at a strange angle and his face was a mass of road burn.

"He's breathing," Kane said, checking his pulse. "But we need to get him in. Now."

She nodded. "Where's the car?"

Kane didn't answer. He and Fribush had already lifted Maltz. They moved at a full trot, Maltz bouncing slightly as Syd struggled to keep up. A green SUV was parked in the lot of a deserted office park. The steely facade was startlingly incongruous in the haze.

They drove fast, weaving around mangled cars that lay on their sides and roofs as if tossed by a giant tide that had receded. People stood at the side of the road looking bewildered. One raised an arm to flag them down, but they sped past.

"Jesus," Syd said, taking in the destruction. "How far does this go?"

"About a click," Fribush answered. "They're setting up a perimeter now. Probably take them a few hours to help these folks. They care more about containing the damage."

"How did you get through?"

Fribush didn't answer, but for the first time since he'd found her managed a small smile.

The haze was starting to dissipate and Syd gulped deep drafts of air, trying to clear her lungs.

"We heard on the scanner that they're setting up a decontam center at the state hospital. It's not far. We'll head there, get you checked out, too." Fribush shook his head. "All that talk after 9/11 about preparedness. They didn't prepare jack-shit."

"They never really thought it could happen here. Not like this," Syd said quietly. "They never understand what people are capable of."

Jake, George and Rodriguez sat transfixed by the TV monitor: aerial views of Phoenix from choppers; an enormous cloud shrouding the southern part of the city; interviews with people who had stumbled out of the haze. Survivors were dazed, clearly in shock, all dusted with a fine layer of silt, lending them an oddly uniform appearance. Reporters shouted questions at them as they were bundled in survival blankets and trundled into waiting ambulances. Emergency workers in the background wore grim expressions. Cops held out their arms, shepherding the reporters back. An excited babble of contradictory information. Depending on which channel you tuned to it was a terrorist act by al Qaeda, a gas tanker explosion, a chemical plant accident. Shots of the northern part of the city, a sheer wall of cars with personal items strapped to roofs and spilling out windows as people grabbed what they could and fled. Cell phone networks were overwhelmed by calls and servers were failing. The governor urged everyone to stay calm, claiming they had the situation under control. No one believed him.

"Jesus," George commented. "If it's already like this, imagine what'll happen when someone mentions radiation."

"They're probably waiting for the National Guard to arrive before announcing that," Rodriguez said.

Jake didn't say anything. He flipped from channel to channel, pausing whenever the camera zoomed in on one of the survivors. Rodriguez and George exchanged a glance.

"Riley, I'm sure Syd's fine," George said, not sounding sure at all.

"She was in the immediate kill radius," Jake said flatly. Which meant her chances for surviving the blast were slim to none. It was almost inconceivable that Syd, who seemed impervious to danger, could be taken out by anything. Even a dirty bomb.

"We don't know that. They were driving away when it happened," Rodriguez said weakly.

"We should go there. See if we can help," Jake said.

George shook his head. "No way. Airports are closed, they're not letting anyone in or out. Not even us."

"I can't just sit here," Jake said, running a hand through his hair. He couldn't remember ever feeling so impotent. Syd was in Phoenix, dead or dying. He hadn't heard from Kelly. The airport was only a few miles from ground zero, she might have been on the ground when it detonated. And he was sitting on his ass in a goddamn trailer in Houston.

"Nothing we can do, bro," George said sympathetically.

The door opened, and they all swiveled toward it. An agent from the Houston field office stood there. "Where's ASAC Leonard?" he asked.

"Not here," George said. "Why?"

"Dallas found something, they're asking for backup."

"Great. Tell them we're on our way," George said authoritatively, grabbing his windbreaker off the back of his chair.

"I thought Leonard had to clear…"

"It's fine. Get us transportation there, we'll take along anyone you can spare."

"I guess." The agent looked dubious. "But maybe I should run this past my ASAC."

"Go ahead. I'm willing to bet right now he'd say the more the merrier." George raised an eyebrow. "All on the same team, right?"

"Yeah, of course."

"So let's get to Dallas."

Thirty-Seven

Dante examined the float. Even he could see it was over the top. But then beaners weren't known for their good taste, so it was probably perfect. A papier-mâché version of the White House covered the barrel that held the bomb. It was surrounded by a desert panorama and photos of famous spics. He shook his head. It was almost too good. Rage welled up in him at the sight of all those brown faces. A few of his guys were going over everything one last time, checking the detonator, making sure the barrel was completely concealed. Tomorrow they'd stock the float with illegals, drive to the parade staging area, and wave bye-bye. Dante glanced at his watch, feeling a tremor of nervous anticipation. In a little more than twelve hours, America would be stepping back onto the right path. There was a cot in the office and he considered trying for a few hours of sleep, but he was too keyed up.

Dante could picture the Feds reviewing video camera footage from the parade route, the shot of the float going by, the bright flash...they'd make the connection, all right. And when they found out the truck was rented in

Mexico and driven across the Texas border a week ago, that would clinch it. It was genius. Jackson would make a big speech connecting Morris's murder to this new attack on America, and the government would finally do something about all the spics.

Growing up, Dante's favorite movie had been *Red Dawn,* about a Russian invasion of the United States. The truth was, America was already under attack. It was being invaded every day, slowly but surely, by people determined to steal everything. Pregnant women crossed the border when their brats were about to drop, just so they could be born Americans. Then they registered for welfare and food stamps. And now they were getting their own people into positions of power. It was like an ant problem, Jackson said: Give them a few morsels of food and the next thing you know they're walking away with your refrigerator. We put up fences, they dig tunnels. We ship them back, they show up in even greater numbers.

Dante had seen it often enough in prison, the spic gangs getting bolder every year. Back home they'd been expanding their turf; never content with a few square blocks, they tried to drive everyone else out of business. Well, he and Jackson were finally going to put a stop to it. Take America back for Americans.

He watched one of his guys adjust the fence in front of the White House and smiled. Tomorrow was going to be the greatest day of his life.

Kelly scanned the airplane hangar. Her thermal imaging binoculars showed fuzzy forms clustered in a few different areas. Some in the center of the room, probably working on the float, then a larger group in the rear corner. Based on the Laredo discovery, she was willing to bet those were more illegal immigrants being offered up as sacrificial lambs.

She lowered the binoculars. One of Leonard's roving radiation detectors went ballistic in this area, and they'd reconnoitered to make sure it was the right place. Sure enough, a group of skinheads was inside working on a float.

A dozen feet away Leonard was deep in conversation with the commander of an elite Hostage Rescue Team that had been brought in specifically for this infiltration. There were three FBI units surrounding the hangar. Unfortunately the building was located in San Diego proper, not far from the airport. Quick damage estimates brought the potential loss of life into the thousands if the bomb was detonated here. They had to do everything in their power to make sure that didn't happen.

The HRT commander hustled off and Leonard walked back to her.

"What do they think?" Kelly asked.

"Tough but not impossible," Leonard said. "Looks like at least fifteen people inside."

"Some of those are probably illegals."

"I know that," he said, sounding irritated. "But we don't know how many. And we can't chance that bomb going off. They might even be wired to detonate it."

The thought made Kelly sick. "So what's the plan?"

"They're going to storm in, full shock and awe."

"What does that mean?" Kelly asked.

He turned away. "It means there probably won't be any survivors."

"Oh my God." Kelly's hand went to her mouth.

"Fifteen lives versus thousands, Agent Jones. It's not a risk anyone is willing to take."

Kelly started to argue, but stopped herself. He was right. They couldn't afford to have this turn into another

Phoenix. But she had to wonder: If the innocent people inside were American citizens, would it have made a difference? "When?"

"About an hour." Leonard glanced at his watch. "It's 9:00 p.m. now. We're hoping some of them will be asleep."

Kelly thought about the Mexicans in Laredo who begged her to help them. She remembered Emilio, skinny legs sticking out from his shorts, his grandmother wailing. "What about Burke?" she asked abruptly.

Leonard eyed her. "He's in Virginia. They're watching him, but without more evidence we can't bring him in."

Leonard might as well have added that because Burke was rich and powerful, he'd get away with it no matter what, Kelly thought. They'd pin this on Dante Parrish and a few other underlings, and that would be the end of it. A hard knot of rage formed in her stomach.

Leonard tucked his hands in his pockets. "You've done good work here, Jones. I'll make sure your ASAC knows that."

Kelly didn't respond. She turned and walked back to the car.

Jackson Burke poured himself another finger of whiskey. He usually didn't indulge in more than one drink a day. The doctors had cautioned against combining his medication with liquor, and he hated to lose his innate sharpness anyway. Lord knew that tonight he needed it more than ever. But he was still reeling from the discovery that the FBI was investigating Dante. He'd spent the drive from D.C. reviewing everything that linked them together. He called his office and ordered security footage from the past few years erased from the hard drives. A few of his staff had met Dante personally, but always under the guise of his bodyguard. All their real meetings had taken place nights and weekends, when the building was empty.

And the others—what if they were tracked down, too? Only three men in the world knew enough to connect him to the plan. Jackson shook his head. He'd been so careful not to leave a paper trail. He called them on disposable cell phones, met in out-of-the-way places, and firmly insisted they refrain from their natural and unfortunate tendency to boast.

Had the FBI already tracked Dante down? He should be at the backup location in San Diego, making sure everything was ready. But perhaps he was in a small room somewhere being interrogated. The thought made his hands clammy. Jackson crossed the room and dug an un-activated cell phone out of his desk drawer. He juggled it for a minute, wondering who would answer if he dialed.

I should have known better, he chastised himself. A bunch of thugs and rednecks could never be marshaled into an effective force. They simply weren't capable of it.

Jackson slammed his fist on the table so hard the glass jumped. They were so close, and now his entire life might be snatched away. Jackson pictured himself in a cell, the walls closing in. It was too bleak to even imagine. They would paint him as the worst kind of traitor. Although given the right jury he might be able to make people understand….

Jackson flipped on the television to distract himself. It took a moment to figure out what was happening, he initially thought it was an action movie. A banner across the bottom of the screen read: PHOENIX BOMBING. His eyes narrowed as Humvees rolled past. Jackson turned up the volume and focused intently on the young blond newscaster whose voice betrayed excitement as she said, "The National Guard has moved us back another mile. They haven't told us why, but it's feeding speculation about what caused this explosion. As you can see—" she waved back over her shoulder "—there's a large, noxious cloud over the blast area, and some of the survivors are complaining of tightness in their chests. They've secured and evacuated an area over three miles wide…"

"Huh," Jackson said, sitting back with a frown. One of the bombs had gone off early. He wondered why. Phoenix was Jared's responsibility. He watched as a map of Phoenix appeared on-screen, with the evacuated area tinted pink. Didn't look like it happened at the warehouse, if CNN had the right spot marked. The truck, then—and if Jared was driving, that would eliminate at least one of the links to him.

Jackson took a slug of whiskey, feeling better. His home phone rang. He eyed it as though it might leap off the table and bite him. After three rings, he picked up.

"Senator Burke," he said, trying to sound authoritative.

A hesitation, then a voice said, "Senator? It's Chad."

Chad. He thought hard, came up with a lanky, pock-marked kid who escorted him around the Capitol yesterday. Chad Peterson, his new assistant. Of course. "Yes, Chad. What can I do for you?"

"I'm sorry to call you so late, Senator, but you weren't answering your cell, or your Georgetown line, and we…have you seen the news, sir?"

Jackson's eyes shifted back to the television. "I just turned it on. I still can't believe it." Which was true. All that careful planning, and now the timing was shot to hell.

"I know this must be a shock to you, sir. I hope everyone you care about is okay."

The sentiment took him off guard. Of course everyone

was okay. He'd ensconced his mother in a Santa Barbara spa yesterday, and there really wasn't anyone else worth caring about. But he tried to adopt the appropriate note of gravitas as he said, "Thanks so much, Chad. I'm praying that they are."

"I'll pray, too. My parents…the cell towers are jammed, so I can't get through."

"Well, I'm sure they're fine," Jackson said, put off by Chad's sniveling tone. If he wasn't arrested tomorrow, the first order of business would be finding a new assistant. Chad was clearly not built for pressure situations.

Chad took a deep breath, gathering himself before saying, "The thing is, um…we're getting a lot of calls from the media. They're wondering if you have a statement. Since it's our district."

"Oh." Jackson experienced a rush of excitement, followed quickly by anger. Of course he had a statement prepared, the perfect response to this crisis. He'd spent months honing it: two concise, carefully worded pages that struck the perfect note of sorrow, empathy and strength. But did he risk reading it now, when the FBI might show up and haul him away midsentence? "Let's wait for morning," he finally said.

"Certainly, Senator." Chad sounded relieved. "I'll tell them."

"And Chad?"

"Yes, sir?"

"Don't ever call me on this line again."

Chad stammered an apology and hung up. Jackson sipped the last of his drink, watching the news jump between correspondents without gaining any additional insight. He reviewed different scenarios in his mind. If they didn't have Dante yet, they'd no doubt have him soon. The early explosion in Phoenix put a new spin on things. By now even the slowest FBI agent would have discovered the missing radioactive waste and realized there were probably more bombs in the mix. And after the warehouse raid, they would have made the link to parade floats. Jackson had to admit, due to their complete incompetence over border control, he hadn't given them enough credit. For them to have tracked down Dante was really quite impressive.

Clearly it was time to switch gears and send them something they weren't expecting.

He picked up the cell phone and dialed the code to activate it. Dante answered on the third ring. Jackson gave him the new orders, then called Dallas. After hanging up, he drained the last of the whiskey and settled back against the couch cushions. The trace of a smile illuminated his face as he watched the terror and confusion play out on-screen.

Thirty-Eight

Syd swallowed hard. The potassium iodide solution was repellant, but hopefully would alleviate any damage from the radiation. She'd also taken a frigid five-minute shower, then given them her clothes to destroy. She shivered in fresh scrubs. Her wounds had been cleaned and bandaged, then she was shunted aside as other, more critical cases arrived.

Syd made her way through the maze of tents. It was like every other field hospital she'd been in; this one was installed in a hospital parking lot to contain overflow and reduce the risk of contamination.

"Brings you back, don't it?" a voice at her elbow said. She turned to find Fribush.

"Yeah, it does," she said, knowing exactly what he meant. Could have been Mosul, could have been Tbilisi. A war zone was a war zone. "How's Maltz?"

He nodded toward the door. "They took him inside."

"Looks bad though, right?"

He shrugged. "Maltz has survived worse. I'm not counting him out."

Refreshingly optimistic, Syd thought. Especially for a Delta guy. "I need to make a call."

Without a word he handed her a phone. She dialed the number, feeling a little guilty for not calling sooner.

Jake answered on the third ring. "Riley here."

"Jake, it's me."

Relief flooded his voice as he said, "Jesus, Syd, I thought you were dead. What the hell happened?"

"I'm fine. Maltz…we're waiting to hear on Maltz."

"Christ." He laughed. "I honestly can't believe you're okay. Man, I thought…" His voice lowered a register as he said, "I was really worried."

"Well, I'm fine," she said, taken aback by the outpouring of emotion.

"There's a lead on another bomb, so we're on our way to Dallas. And Kelly sent a text, she and Leonard are in San Diego trying to stop a third."

"Oh." So they had the other sites covered. "But what about Burke?"

"No idea, they're still keeping us in the dark." His voice lowered as he said, "But George said it's gotta be solid before they'll arrest a senator. I get the feeling that he might skate."

"Really," Syd said, her voice hardening. Of course he'd skate. She'd seen it time and again, politicians shirking responsibility for terrible acts. No surprise there.

"Anyway, rest up for a few days. We'll meet back in New York when this is over to talk about things."

Interesting, Syd thought. Unless she was mistaken, the things he wanted to discuss didn't sound entirely business-related. Which would be fine by her. Jake was a bit of a Boy Scout by her standards, but it might be a nice change of pace. And she'd be doing him a favor, getting him away from that miserable fiancée. "Sure," she said. "See you there."

She handed the phone back to Fribush, who asked, "How you feeling, boss?"

"I'm fine."

"Yeah? Doctors clear you to leave?"

She shrugged. "Doctors have bigger things to worry about. Why?"

"'Cause you look like you've got places to go."

Syd grinned at him. "Remind me to put you on full retainer, we need more sharp guys."

Fribush tucked the phone back in his pocket and asked, "You got dental?"

"Get me some real clothes and make sure I'm on a plane by sunup, I'll throw in vision, too," she said. "Tell Kane to keep an eye on Maltz, and let's go."

Dante gunned the engine and impulsively kissed the cross that hung from a chain around his neck. The call had been unexpected, but not unwelcome. He'd been crawling out of his skin at the thought of waiting all night. What Jackson wanted was a better plan anyway. And he had specifically asked Dante to take charge of it.

Dante waited as one of his men rolled open the door at the end of the hangar. They were in a deserted airfield south of downtown San Diego. It had been the perfect staging area, no prying eyes to see what they were up to. It had taken less than an hour to shift the bomb from the float back into the truck they'd arrived in. The men had grumbled at the extra work, but perked up when he said they didn't need the spics anymore, so later they could take them to the desert for target practice. His boys deserved it after everything they'd been through. He was glad to hear that Jackson finally appreciated their efforts. It was pretty clear who the real patriots were in this organization.

Jackson was uncharacteristically warm when he wished him good luck. Funny, Dante could've sworn he even sounded a little drunk, which was unheard of. Jackson barely touched the stuff, said he preferred to keep his mind sharp. Dante had been impressed by the level of self-control that implied. He'd been sober himself since that day. But what the hell—maybe he'd have a drink to celebrate once this was over. Jackson would probably have some fancy champagne waiting. Maybe he even had a party planned.

Dante put the truck in gear and rolled outside. It had been a while since he'd driven one, but it came back quickly. And besides, he wasn't going far. The spot Jackson had in mind was less than fifteen miles away. He'd be there in twenty minutes, max.

He shifted the truck into second gear and turned onto the access road out of the airport. He thought he caught the glint of something in his rearview mirror, but when he looked again it was gone.

Dante shrugged it off. It was late at night, and after everything that had happened he was paranoid. This was almost over. Within the hour, his job would be completed. And then all he had to do was wait for the world to change.

"Shit, he's on the move," Leonard hissed. They'd dropped back in preparation for the HRT team to initiate their operation. Kelly watched a truck emerge from the hangar.

"That's not a float," she said. "Must be the truck they used to bring the bomb here. Is it still hot?"

Leonard held up a finger. He was on the radio, engaged in a heated back-and-forth with the HRT team leader, who wanted to know what the hell to do with his men. They had been on the verge of busting through the windows lining the upper story of the building, and were currently trapped on the roof. "Hold your positions until we figure out what's happening." He glanced at Kelly, then spoke into the receiver, "Was the truck hot?"

"Yeah, we got a reading off it on the way out. Hot as hell, but then it would be if it hauled the stuff here from Texas."

"What about the hangar? Are the radiation levels still high?" Kelly asked. Something occurred to her, but it wasn't an idea she liked.

Leonard looked annoyed at serving as intermediary, but asked.

There was a pause before the commander responded, "Not as high as before."

"It's in the truck," Kelly said.

"How do you know that?" Leonard demanded.

"The bomb went off early in Phoenix, so they must be deviating from their plan. Maybe Dante got wind of the fact that we're looking for him."

Leonard appeared unconvinced. "Maybe. Or they're trying to get rid of the evidence before the parade tomorrow."

"No." Kelly shook her head. "Burke is too smart. By now he knows it's only a matter of time before we track down Dante. I'm guessing he was sent on a suicide mission."

"We'll stop the truck, check it just in case," Leonard reasoned, picking up the radio again.

Kelly put out a hand to stop him. "You can't do it here. If it blows, it'll take out half of downtown. We need a better spot."

Leonard looked like he wanted to growl. "Hard to find a good spot if we don't know where he's headed. And I'm guessing if he sees a string of black-and-whites on his tail, he'll blow it then and there."

Kelly thought for a minute. "The border," she finally

said. "That's what it's all about for these guys. He's going to blow it somewhere near the border."

"That's nuts. Why would they punch a hole in the wall for illegals to pour through?" Leonard snorted.

"Maybe he's headed for the guard booths. Or it might be symbolic, to show that border patrol is ineffective. Either way, it's the most likely target."

Leonard picked up the radio again. "I want the CHP liaison to come up with a good spot to stop that truck, preferably somewhere unpopulated between here and the border. And I want all available units to converge on that spot." He signed off and glanced at her. "Happy?"

"I'll be happy when we stop him," she said.

"Women. Always so demanding." Leonard turned the key in the ignition and kept the lights off as they drove out of the shadows on the opposite end of the airfield.

"Where are we going?" Kelly asked.

"We're an available unit, aren't we? I want to be there when they take this guy down."

Jake, George and Rodriguez were a mile from the meet spot when an eighteen-wheeler whipped past, followed by a string of what were clearly unmarked cars.

"Uh-oh," Rodriguez said. "Looks like we're late to the party."

Jake whipped their car in a U-turn and joined the caravan, inspiring bleating horns from the other drivers.

"Better get on the radio and ask them nicely not to shoot us," he said.

George sighed, but radioed their Dallas contact and explained the situation.

"What'd he say?" Rodriguez asked.

George shrugged. "Said he's glad for the extra help. Apparently half their field office is still in Houston, and another bunch were sent to Phoenix. He's spread pretty thin."

"Probably a good idea to gloss over that Jake's a civilian," Rodriguez observed.

"Probably," George said drily.

"They got a plan to stop this guy?" Jake asked, eyeing the speedometer. It was at ninety and climbing. The rental car hadn't been built for high speeds, and it was all he could do to keep it on the road. If he pushed much harder, pieces might start falling off.

"Up ahead, at the thirty mile marker. They're going to blow the tires when he hits the roadblock. They want us to hang back in case he blows the bomb."

"That's the plan? Keep your fingers crossed and hope the truck doesn't blow up?"

"Hey, don't blame the messenger," George said. "I get the sense we're not dealing with the best the field office has to offer."

"Jesus," Jake said, shaking his head. "Where do they think he's headed?"

"The border. San Diego reported their guy bolting around the same time. They figure there's been a change of plans."

"That's what, three hundred miles from here? Four?" Rodriguez asked.

"Something like that," George said. "But he caught on to the tail almost immediately. Now they figure he's just running scared."

Jake tuned them out as soon as they mentioned San Diego. He pictured Kelly tearing down a similar road, pursuing a truck wired to take out everything in a mile radius. It was madness. Syd had barely survived, and here they were following in her footsteps. He remembered the panic in Syd's voice as the truck charged into traffic. When the line went dead, he nearly lost his mind. It was a normal reaction, he thought. After all, she was his business partner, and a good friend. But part of him knew it was more than that. He could have cried from relief when she called. It was like a clamp released from his heart.

Kelly, he reminded himself. He should be worrying about Kelly. Syd was fine, she'd be on a plane to New York as soon as the airport reopened.

"There's the twenty-five mile marker," George pointed out. "Time to ease up."

Jake slowed, watching the truck lights fade into the surrounding darkness. The other unmarked cars followed suit until they were at a standstill, a solid line of vehicles marching toward the horizon.

"What if he pulls off?"

George examined the map he'd dug out of the glove compartment. "No turnoffs between here and the blockade."

Route 35E had slimmed to a two-lane road, too narrow for the truck to turn around even if he wanted to. Jake tapped the steering wheel nervously with one finger. This was farm country, acres of fields rolled away from the road. Power lines were strung shoulder to shoulder like steel sentinels. A rabbit skittered across the blacktop, shuddering for a moment in their headlights before vaulting the last few feet into darkness.

Ironically, having a quiet moment to reflect rattled him more than anything else. Jake wondered how the Grants were doing, if they'd found out about Randall yet, and who told them. He tried to remember the last time he got a full night's sleep, or had a real meal. And now he was on a dusty Texas highway in the middle of the night, braced for an explosion. Madness.

"You think he's there yet?" Rodriguez asked, breaking the silence.

As if in response, there was a flash in the distance. The sentinels flared bright red.

"Oh, shit," George said.

Dante frowned into the side mirror. He hit the gas, bringing his speed up to eighty. The sedan followed suit. No doubt about it, he had a tail. Shit.

He was so close, too. Another five miles and he'd hit the turnoff into the housing development a few hundred yards from the border wall. All he had to do was park the truck, get out, and walk away. Then five minutes later: boom.

But they'd found him somehow. How was it even possible? Dante scratched the scruff where his hair was growing back. He and Jackson had spent so much time laying the groundwork for this plan, sketching out every possible twist. But things kept going wrong. He sighed.

Well, there was one last thing he could do. Taking a hand off the wheel, he felt in his pocket for the remote detonator.

"He's spotted us!" Leonard hissed, grabbing for the radio. "Who's the moron in the lead car? Back the fuck off!"

But it was clearly too late. Kelly watched the truck leap ahead. They were on the outskirts of San Diego, clusters of housing developments surrounding them. Thousands of people asleep in their beds, completely unaware of the danger.

"We have to stop him," she said.

"No kidding. Any suggestions?"

"Get him on the CB radio." She looked over at Leonard. "The truck must have one, right? Figure out what channel he's on, see if a negotiator can talk him down. Make sure they know his name."

Leonard barked the command into their radio. A minute later they heard the rustle of static, then a hostage negotiator hailing Dante. On the third attempt, a gravelly voice responded. "Yeah?"

"Dante Parrish, this is Agent Bennett with the FBI. Come to a stop and get out of the truck with your hands raised. You have my guarantee that no harm will come to you."

A pause, then they heard a low chuckle. "I think we're way past harm, buddy."

"Tell Dante that Burke gave him up," Kelly said.

Leonard shrugged, then conveyed the information on their private channel.

Another long pause before Dante retorted, "He wouldn't do that."

"How do you think we found you, Dante? He set you up to take the fall."

"I'm doing this for the good of the country," Dante replied.

Kelly grabbed the receiver over Leonard's protests. "A true patriot wouldn't kill innocent Americans, Dante. No one is going to blame the illegals now. They'll know it was you."

They were less than five miles from the border. The truck slowed.

"You know what's crazy?" Dante said meditatively. "My brother works a farm in Washington State. You know the government can track every cow from where they were born in B.C., all the way to the pen they're in now? But you can't find eleven million immigrants. Explain that to me."

On the other channel the hostage negotiator said, "He seems to be responding to her, so keep going. Try to keep him calm, use his name a lot. Make him understand he'd be killing real people."

"Us among them," Leonard muttered.

"It's a broken system, Dante," Kelly said. "No one's saying it isn't. But this isn't the way to fix it."

The truck ahead had slowed nearly to a stop. The nearest car paused a few hundred feet away. Kelly and Leonard were fifth in line.

"Do we pull back?" another voice asked over their channel.

"Hold for now," Leonard said, picking up the receiver. "We're at a safe standoff distance if the bomb is the same size as Phoenix."

"But if it blows…" Kelly said worriedly.

"I said hold. Keep going, Jones."

Kelly took a deep breath, thinking through what she was going to say. "We don't want another Phoenix here, Dante. A lot of people died there today, a lot of women and children."

"You don't understand." It was hard to tell if he was angry or despondent.

"Make me understand."

"They bring in drugs, and get kids hooked. They take our jobs. Pretty soon they'll be running the country. And no one's doing anything about it."

Odd talk for an ex-con, Kelly thought. Dante Parrish was hardly a paragon of American family values. Burke must be extraordinarily convincing. "But, Dante, don't you see this will only make them stronger? You'll be the bad guy."

"Careful," the negotiator cautioned on the other line. "That might set him off."

"I'm not the bad guy. Not anymore," Dante said defiantly.

"I'm not saying you are, but…"

Suddenly the door to the cab swung open and Dante appeared, hands raised above his head.

"Does anyone have a bead on him?" Leonard asked. "Tell me his hands are empty."

"Negative. He's got something, just can't see what it is," another agent chimed in.

"All right, initiate the jamming." He glanced at Kelly. "We're probably going to lose radio contact."

"Why?"

"Chances are he'll try to remote detonate. We're jamming all signals to block that."

"I didn't know you could do that," Kelly said, watching Dante fumble with something. He glanced back at the truck, puzzled.

"New technology, developed to combat IEDs in Iraq. Not foolproof, but we're up to a seventy percent success rate."

"Seventy is still pretty risky," Kelly said dubiously.

"That's why we wanted the truck out of city limits. But it looks like it's working," Leonard said. "Should we go round up our boy?"

Leonard opened his car door and drew his weapon. Kelly secured her vest before following. Within a minute a dozen agents were approaching the truck. Fifty feet away they fanned out in a semicircle.

Dante had his back to the truck, arms out as if surrendering. Kelly saw something in his hand, probably the detonator. Despite Leonard's assurances about the jamming, her breath was shallow and her skin buzzed with fear. She pictured the haze over Phoenix and imagined a mushroom cloud blooming around them. Her gun shook slightly, and she inhaled deeply to try and regain some calm.

"Dante Parrish, drop it and get on your knees," Leonard ordered.

Twenty feet away now. Dante appeared strangely

calm, the corner of his lip turned up in a sneer. Another
five feet, and Kelly realized he was saying something. She
strained her ears, listening. He'd slipped into a low
murmur. She caught the phrase, *I thank whatever gods
may be for my unconquerable soul...*

It took her a minute to place it. When she did, her eyes
widened and she froze.

Leonard turned to her, puzzled. "What's he saying?"

"Take cover!" Kelly yelled, trotting backward, keeping
her gun level. A single headlight illuminated Dante, arms
raised to the heavens as if preaching, head tilted skyward.
Leonard stared at her as if she'd lost her mind. The rest
of the agents were within ten feet of Dante, too close.
"He's reciting 'Invictus'!"

"What?" Leonard asked.

"Get everyone back!" Kelly yelled. "Move!"

Something dropped from Dante's hand.

Kelly spun, prepared to sprint. A surge of adrenaline
shot through her veins, but it felt as if she were moving
through molasses. Suddenly, a flash from behind set everything in stark relief, cars reflecting the glare. She was
lifted off her feet as if a giant hand had swept her up. Her
arms and legs pinwheeled as she flew. There was a clap
so loud she felt it in her bones, her head throbbed from
the concussion.

A roar, as if an entire ocean was crashing down on her,
and Kelly was whirled away.

Thirty-Nine

"Did it blow?" Rodriguez asked.

"The flash didn't look that big," George commented.

Jake didn't say anything. He was no expert, but George was right; the blast they'd witnessed was nothing compared to the Phoenix footage captured by a police chopper. That shock wave had knocked the helicopter out of the sky.

George got on the radio. "This is Agent Fong. What happened?"

They waited tensely for a response. A minute later someone said, "All good here. We've got two bad guys, bringing them outside the perimeter in case this thing is on a timer. Bomb squad is going to fly in some suppressant and dump it over the truck. But so far so good."

"What exploded?" Jake asked.

"Flash bangs after we blew the tires. These boys are practically bleeding out their ears." The agent on the radio chuckled. "We had them on the ground and hog-tied in under a minute."

"Nice work," George said. "Keep us posted."

"Well, that was anticlimactic," Rodriguez sighed. "Looks like they didn't need us after all."

"You kidding? I was not liking the possibility of being anywhere near a dirty bomb," George said. "Those things mess with your DNA. And I plan on sending little Fongs out into the world someday."

"God help us all," Jake said.

They all laughed harder than the joke deserved. Since arriving in California six days ago, Jake had existed in a tight knot of adrenaline and nerves. It was a relief to feel some of that release.

"One more down, anyway," Rodriguez said. "Wonder how they're doing in San Diego."

As if on cue, George's phone rang. "Fong here," he answered.

His face grew still as he listened. Jake and Rodriguez waited impatiently for him to finish. After a minute he said, "Right, I understand. Thanks for calling."

"Well?" Rodriguez asked.

George examined the dashboard. "They stopped the bomb in San Diego. Leonard had high-tech jammers block detonation."

"So what's with the face?" Rodriguez asked. "This is good news, right?"

George met Jake's eyes for a second before shifting back to the dash. A chill crept around Jake's heart.

"What is it," he asked, fighting to keep his voice level.

"Dante had a grenade, they think it was his backup plan to ignite the C4. It didn't work, but a bunch of agents were moving in to arrest him. Leonard and two others were a few feet away when it blew. They didn't make it. Another nine are injured, some critically. And Agent Jones…"

"She's dead?" Rodriguez asked.

"No, she's in a medically induced coma. Jake, they said it doesn't look good."

Jake's jaw set in a hard line. He whipped the car around and floored the accelerator.

"Maybe I should drive," George said.

"Jake, we haven't actually gotten permission to leave—" Rodriguez protested.

"Fuck permission," Jake snarled. "I'm getting on the next plane. Find out what hospital she's in."

July 4

Forty

Jackson Burke jerked awake. An empty bottle of whiskey lay beside him, the television was still tuned to Fox News. With a groan he rubbed his head. He didn't remember polishing off the rest of the bottle, in fact he didn't remember much after his conversation with Dante. The disposable cell phone sat on the end table next to his blood pressure medication. He'd have to dispose of it today, maybe bury it in the woods.

His eyes narrowed as a newscaster announced that the Phoenix bombing was being declared an "accident," and that contrary to rumors no chemical toxins were dispersed by the dust cloud. In fact, the governor was urging people to return to their homes. The camera cut to the governor at a press conference. Jackson snorted as his old pal Gary bleated on about the state coming together in the aftermath of this terrible tragedy, about how they'd all work together to rebuild, blah, blah, blah.

But could they be lying? Surely they would have tested the area for radioactivity. The emissions should have been significant. Jackson pondered it. Either the government

was willfully encouraging people to remain in an area
polluted by gamma rays, or something had gone wrong
with the bomb's construction. He clenched his hands.
Apparently Dante had let him down again.

Jackson frowned and kneaded his temples. It took a
minute to pinpoint what was nagging at him. Why
weren't they discussing San Diego and Dallas? Those ex-
plosions should be dominating the news. He flipped
through the channels, all were still spreading and discred-
iting rumors about Phoenix. Every major affiliate was
interviewing locals who had lost family in the blast. A
cement wall near the off-ramp was covered with photos
of missing relatives, serving as an impromptu bulletin
board.

Irritated by the sight of an obese woman whimpering
into a microphone, Jackson shut off the TV and stomped
to the desk in the corner. Grabbing his laptop, he stormed
back to the couch. The online news sites all had the
Phoenix incident as their top story, although most claimed
it was an accidental crash involving a truck transporting
crude oil. He finally located a link to San Diego. Around
dawn the AP reported a small explosion near the
U.S./Mexico border. Initially news crews leaped on it, but
a border patrol spokesperson announced it was just fire-
works, and the story quickly slid into the background.
Search as he might, he couldn't find anything about Dallas.

Jackson reflexively clenched his fists. So it had all
been for nothing. True to form the government was
burying it, making sure the event went down as an
accident. And there was a chance that both Dante and
Christian were alive and in custody.

Jackson felt a familiar light-headedness and his vision
blurred. Faltering to his feet, he lurched across the room,
grabbing the pill bottle on his second attempt. He wrestled

the top off, palmed a pill and tossed it in his mouth. He gagged as it caught in his throat. Jackson stumbled to the wet bar, stuck his head under the faucet and gulped some water. Standing and wiping his mouth, he immediately felt better. *Thank God for modern medicine,* he thought.

An instant later, an enormous pressure as if someone had reached into his chest and was crushing his heart.

Jackson tried to sit, but a spasm rocked him and he went down hard. Jesus, he'd never experienced pain like this before. Sweat poured from him, and his lungs compressed. He gasped for breath. The cell phone was still on the end table. He had to get to it and call 911...

A blond woman appeared above him. He blinked, wondering if he was hallucinating. She was dressed all in black, her feet on either side of his head. Jackson grabbed at her ankles, but she kicked his hands away. He opened his mouth to beg for help, but only a strangled gurgle came out.

She shook something. It made a happy sound, like maracas. "You looked stressed, so I replaced your pills with Nardil. Hope you don't mind." She knelt by his head, stroked his hair, and bent to whisper in his ear. "But you really should have mentioned the high blood pressure meds. All sorts of drugs don't react well with those. Especially if you've been drinking." She nodded toward the bottle on the sofa.

"Ple-ease..." he managed to grunt, imploring her with his eyes.

"Sorry, Mr. Burke," she said, strolling toward the door. "I'm fresh out of favors at the moment. Happy Independence Day."

Forty-One

Jake sat by Kelly's hospital bed, head in his hands. He'd had to fight to enter the ICU. In the end, George's badge got them through before Jake punched a nurse.

George stood by the window, gazing out at the setting sun. They'd taken the first flight out of Dallas, arriving in San Diego around noon. George periodically excused himself to field some calls, then returned with updates on the bomb investigation. Jake didn't even bother processing those, he just sat staring blankly at the motionless form on the bed. Kelly looked so small lying there. Part of him didn't believe it was really her, she looked too frail, her skin so pale it was almost translucent.

A hole had been torn in the truck by the force of the blast, but the C4 didn't ignite. Leonard died instantly, along with two other agents. Two more were touch and go. Apparently Kelly had shouted out a warning that gave the rest time to take cover at the front and rear of the truck, which shielded them from the worst of the explosion. All that was left of Dante Parrish was a shoe and a necklace. He'd spent his last moments reciting the same poem Timothy McVeigh read during his execution.

Kelly had been found nearly thirty feet away, one leg trapped under a hunk of metal from the side of the truck. She was suffering from massive internal bleeding. After the first round of surgeries they induced a coma and crossed their fingers. Every hour someone came to check her right leg, which produced a noticeably lower bump in the sheet than the left. There were murmurs about removing it, but when they tried to wheel her to surgery Jake almost had to be restrained. George talked the doctors into waiting. What was left unspoken was that in the end, the leg might be irrelevant. There was a good chance Kelly wasn't going to survive.

Every so often Jake broke the silence. Random childhood memories, past cases, how he pictured their future together. They said she might be able to hear him, but holding her hand, he knew it wasn't true. He kept stroking the ring he'd put on her finger, the canted edges of the ruby hard and cold against his thumb. He could feel it through her slender fingers—her hands were always so cold, even when it was warm outside—there was no one in there. Kelly's chest rose and fell, but she'd already checked out.

George reentered the room. "Burke's dead."

"What?" Jake looked up.

"They went to arrest him at his place in Virginia—after the guy in Dallas talked they finally got a warrant. Looks like a heart attack."

"That's convenient," Jake said. The bastard was lucky, because Jake had already planned on making sure he felt every bit of the pain Kelly was experiencing. A heart attack was merciful in comparison.

"And whoever prepared the iridium for the dirty bomb screwed up—it was packaged in such a way that it wouldn't disperse. So they've given the all clear for Phoenix." George rubbed his eyes as he spoke. He appeared to have aged years in the past two days.

"Randall," Jake said, thinking that maybe he hadn't given the guy enough credit. Despite everything, he'd made sure the bombs wouldn't wreak as much havoc as they could have.

"I'm headed to the cafeteria, you want anything?" George asked.

"Not hungry." Jake rubbed Kelly's hand again to warm it. The blip on the monitor kicked up. His eyes darted to it, but almost immediately it settled into the familiar rhythm.

"C'mon, just a banana or something." George paused at the threshold. "Doctors said there probably wouldn't be any change tonight. You might as well eat something, or try to get some sleep."

"Leave it alone, George," Jake said, more forcefully than he'd intended.

George raised both hands in defeat. "Fine."

He passed Rodriguez on the way out. Jake heard them exchange a low murmur, then Rodriguez entered, looking concerned.

He wished people would leave them alone. Jake wanted to bar the door and keep everyone out, stop them from poking and prodding her every five minutes. He imagined scooping her up in his arms, tucking her in the car and driving away. They could go to the beach—Kelly had grown up on the East Coast, she'd never seen the sun set over the ocean. He could give her that.

Jake couldn't shake the feeling that somehow this was his fault. If he'd refused to get the company involved in Syd's private bullshit, then maybe Kelly wouldn't be lying here. She would never have heard of Dante Parrish, wouldn't have been in San Diego, miles away from him, when that maniac set off a grenade. Part of him knew it was ridiculous, but the guilt was tough to shake. Plus he had to admit, the past few days he'd spent more time thinking about Syd. If Kelly didn't make it, he'd never be able to forgive himself.

Rodriguez was still standing by the door looking uncomfortable.

"You can go home, you know," Jake said without looking up.

"Yeah, I know," Rodriguez said, eyes locked on Kelly's inert form. "She was a great agent."

Jake wanted to throttle him for using the past tense. But he took a deep breath, nodded and said, "Yeah."

Forty-Two

Kelly rose and fell on the waves. Every so often a noise intruded, the background bleats and calls of enormous undersea creatures, but as the swell kicked up even that receded. It was so peaceful here, so warm. The long rays of a setting sun dusted her skin with traces of pink and lavender. Invisible arms wrapped around her, cradling her close.

The low murmur again. In spite of herself Kelly strained to hear. The voices sounded familiar, and she suddenly realized where she was. Growing up she'd replayed this day over and over in her mind, claiming it as the last remaining shred of what her family had been. But she hadn't thought about it in years. It was odd that it came to her now.

It was the day before her brother vanished. She was standing on a stool at the kitchen counter, helping her father make pancakes. Alex came in from taking out the trash, and their mother made him wash his hands before setting the table. Fingers still wet, he poked a finger in the batter she was stirring, flicking it at her. She yelled at him to stop, but he just grinned. Her father barked at both of them to be quiet, it was impossible to concentrate on flipping with all that racket. He was making her favorite, one large pancake with two smaller ones serving as mouse ears: "Mickey Pancakes," they called them. Alex usually claimed he was too old for them, but that day he ate without complaining. The smell of sizzling bacon mingled with fresh-cut grass. Her mother sat at the table, sipping her coffee and reading the paper. A typical weekend morning, like hundreds of others they'd shared. There was nothing particularly significant about it. If Alex hadn't disappeared the next day, it would have slipped into the patchwork of her other childhood memories, fuzzy and indistinct and frayed.

The image spun away from her on the next wave. She halfheartedly reached for it, feeling the warmth trail through her fingers. Kelly caressed it once, then released it with a faint sense of regret. It was too pleasant to resist. She let go of everything and floated away.

Author's Note

Books have their origins in all sorts of strange places. This one started with a late-night conversation over drinks, when a friend who works for the FBI mentioned that hate groups have doubled their membership in the past decade, but the level of surveillance on them has dropped significantly. All of the information and statistics contained in the text are accurate to the best of my knowledge. I did, however, invent the job that Randall holds; as far as I could determine, no one is currently overseeing low-level radioactive materials, and the U.S. government is not working to consolidate them in secure locations, despite the fact that many sources are lost or stolen each year. It's enough to inspire a serious case of insomnia.

As always, there are countless people to thank for their gracious assistance with my research. Any mistakes are solely my own. Dr. Sidney Drell helped me sort through the seeds of ideas to find one with the potential to sprout. Camille Minichino worked tirelessly through many drafts to ensure that a writer who truly can't tell the difference between an isobar and an isotope got the "radiation stuff" right. Robin Burcell helped with police procedures and terminology. Lee Lofland not only answered multiple niggling questions, he also directed me to Richard McMahan and Michael Roche, my "bomb squad" who helped me figure out what would and wouldn't work (and as promised, Mike, I left San Diego relatively unscathed). The real-life George Fong is even cooler than his fictional counterpart, and always patiently answers countless questions about FBI procedure and gangs, in addition to arranging my once-in-a-lifetime tour of Quantico.

Mark Potok of the Southern Poverty Law Center was kind enough to answer questions about the current status of hate groups in our country and some of the threats we face. Dr. D. P. Lyle always comes through with an innovative and undetectable way to kill someone (which inspires not just admiration, but a healthy dose of fear).

My beta readers, whose keen eye for typos and inconsistencies made each draft better than the last: David Gagnon, Kate Gagnon, Vickie Browning, Deborah Indzhov, Richard Goodman, Raj Patel. Everyone at the Sanchez Grotto for providing such a warm, supportive writing community and being excellent procrastination buddies: Raj (again), Shana Mahaffey, Alison Bing, Paul Linde, Diane Weipert, Sean Beaudoin, Ammi Emergency, Jeff Kirschner, and Whimsical Doggo Doug Wilkins, who makes it all possible. And of course the inestimable Kemble Scott, who always remembers my events in his newsletter (even when I have forgotten them) and has been a great friend, confidant and sounding board.

My fellow bloggers on The Kill Zone: Kathryn Lilley, Joe Moore, Clare Langley-Hawthorne, John Ramsey Miller and John T. Gilstrap, for always inspiring stimulating dialogue and tolerating my occasionally rambling, late posts. And my fellow Norcal Sisters in Crime and MWA groups have been invaluable resources.

Everyone at MIRA Books has been incredibly supportive, especially my editor, Lara Hyde, a tireless advocate who is a pleasure to work with (I realize that the same cannot always be said for me, and for that I'm sorry). At MIRA I also owe a huge debt to Valerie Gray, Margaret Marbury and Emily Ohanjanians. I'm grateful to the best sales team in North America: Don Lucey, Tracey Langmuir, Heather Foy and everyone else who works so hard to promote my books.

An agent is said to be a writer's best friend, and with the Philip G. Spitzer Agency that's more than just an expression. Lukas Ortiz has been a great friend and an amazing agent, and I'm guessing he's one of the few willing to answer his phone at 2:00 a.m. in Frankfurt when a pressing question arises. Luc Hunt has been an amazing source of advice and alternate titles, and a reliable set of eyes on each revision. Joel Gotler was kind enough to provide an education on the entire book-to-film process, and convinced me to make Madison a bit older than I'd originally intended.

I've been fortunate to have a slew of booksellers and librarians champion my books. I can't thank you enough for the support. This can be a difficult industry to navigate, and all of you made it so much easier.

The Egans (Joe, Uta, Caroline and Rick) always make Seattle one of the best stops on my tour. I highly recommend them for any and all book launch party needs, the spread they lay out is to die for. My Wesleyan partners in crime: Dave Fribush, Colin Dangel, Ty Jagerson and Dave Kane provided the perfect names for the "commando-boys" (in exchange, I'm expecting free drinks for life).

Last but never least, thanks to my family for their unconditional love and support, and almost saintlike patience for working weekends, constant complaining and general grumpiness. I really couldn't have done it without you.

JOSEPH TELLER

A speeding sports car forces an oncoming van off the road and kills all nine of its occupants...eight of them children.

Criminal defense attorney Harrison J. Walker, or Jaywalker, is serving a three-year suspension and having trouble keeping his nose clean when a woman seduces him into representing the killer, who happens to be her husband.

Struggling with the moral issues surrounding this case, Jaywalker tries to limit the damage to his client by exposing the legal system's hypocrisy regarding drunk driving. But when he rounds a blind corner in the case, he finds a truth that could derail his defense.

DEPRAVED
INDIFFERENCE

MIRA®

Available now wherever books are sold.

www.MIRABooks.com

MJT2691

P.D. MARTIN

IN KUNG FU TARGETED STRIKES
CAN KILL INSTANTLY...
BUT HOW?

Aussie FBI profiler Sophie Anderson is settling into her job in the L.A. bureau when she's pulled into a case like no other—the victim has had his throat literally ripped out. But what weapon could have caused such devastating injuries? And who is the John Doe?

As L.A.'s underworld rears its ugly head, Sophie will have to draw on her experience and her developing psychic skills to find a brilliant killer who's carved a trail of death in organized crime across the U.S. He leaves only one thing behind him—horrifying murder scenes.

The Killing Hands

*Available now
wherever books
are sold.*

MIRA®

www.MIRABooks.com

MPDM2639

NEW YORK TIMES AND *USA TODAY* BESTSELLING AUTHOR

ERICA SPINDLER

Nearly killed as a teenager by a hit-and-run boater, Jane Killian has everything to live for—especially now, as she and her husband, Ian, are expecting their first child.

Then a woman with ties to Ian is found brutally slain and Ian is the prime suspect. Determined to prove her husband's innocence, Jane starts to have doubts. When she begins receiving anonymous messages, she's convinced they're from the boater she always believed deliberately hit her and got away with it.

Now Jane must face the tormentor who knows everything about her—including her deepest fears, which he will use mercilessly until he sees Jane dead.

SEE JANE DIE

Available now wherever books are sold.

MIRA®

www.MIRABooks.com

MES2833

**FROM THE BESTSELLING AUTHOR
OF *THE MARK***

JASON PINTER

Am I my brother's keeper?

If I'd known I had a brother, I might have been. But he's
dead—shot point-blank in a rathole of an apartment,
wasted by hunger and heroin. Stephen Gaines, a man
with whom I shared nothing...except a father.

This stranger came to me for help...and I blew him off,
thinking he was just some junkie. Now I'm forced to
question everything I ever knew....

All I can do for Stephen Gaines now is find his killer—
and with the help of Amanda Davies uncover the whole,
hard truth.

**THE
FURY**

"A brilliantly conceived,
edge-of-your-seat thrill ride."
—*Chicago Tribune*
on *The Guilty*

*Available now
wherever books
are sold!*

MIRA®

www.MIRABooks.com

MJP2627

REQUEST YOUR FREE BOOKS!

2 FREE NOVELS
FROM THE ROMANCE/SUSPENSE
COLLECTION PLUS 2 FREE GIFTS!

YES! Please send me 2 FREE novels from the Romance/Suspense Collection and my 2 FREE gifts (gifts are worth about $10). After receiving them, if I don't wish to receive any more books, I can return the shipping statement marked "cancel." If I don't cancel, I will receive 4 brand-new novels every month and be billed just $5.74 per book in the U.S. or $6.24 per book in Canada. That's a savings of at least 28% off the cover price. It's quite a bargain! Shipping and handling is just 50¢ per book.* I understand that accepting the 2 free books and gifts places me under no obligation to buy anything. I can always return a shipment and cancel at any time. Even if I never buy another book from the Reader Service, the two free books and gifts are mine to keep forever.

185 MDN EYNQ 385 MDN EYN2

Name	(PLEASE PRINT)	
Address		Apt. #
City	State/Prov.	Zip/Postal Code

Signature (if under 18, a parent or guardian must sign)

Mail to **The Reader Service:**
IN U.S.A.: P.O. Box 1867, Buffalo, NY 14240-1867
IN CANADA: P.O. Box 609, Fort Erie, Ontario L2A 5X3

Not valid to current subscribers of the Romance Collection,
the Suspense Collection or the Romance/Suspense Collection.

Want to try two free books from another line?
Call 1-800-873-8635 or visit www.morefreebooks.com.

* Terms and prices subject to change without notice. Prices do not include applicable taxes. Sales tax applicable in N.Y. Canadian residents will be charged applicable provincial taxes and GST. Offer not valid in Quebec. This offer is limited to one order per household. All orders subject to approval. Credit or debit balances in a customer's account(s) may be offset by any other outstanding balance owed by or to the customer. Please allow 4 to 6 weeks for delivery. Offer available while quantities last.

Your Privacy: Harlequin is committed to protecting your privacy. Our Privacy Policy is available online at www.eHarlequin.com or upon request from the Reader Service. From time to time we make our lists of customers available to reputable third parties who may have a product or service of interest to you. If you would prefer we not share your name and address, please check here.

NEW YORK TIMES AND *USA TODAY*
BESTSELLING AUTHOR

ALEX KAVA

On the busiest shopping day of the year, some idealistic
college students believe they're about to carry out an
elaborate media stunt at the largest mall in America. They
think the jamming devices in their backpacks will disrupt
stores' computer systems, causing delays and chaos. What
they don't realize is that their backpacks are actually stuffed
with explosives ready to detonate by remote control,
turning them into homicide bombers.

FBI profiler Maggie O'Dell must put her own troubles aside
to help figure out what's behind this terrorist attack—and
try to keep her brother from becoming one of the casualties.

BLACK FRIDAY

Available now wherever hardcover books are sold!

MIRA®

MAK2651

www.MIRABooks.com

MICHELLE GAGNON

32539 BONEYARD   __ $6.99 U.S.   __ $6.99 CAN.

(limited quantities available)

TOTAL AMOUNT	$_____
POSTAGE & HANDLING	$_____
($1.00 for 1 book, 50¢ for each additional)	
APPLICABLE TAXES*	$_____
TOTAL PAYABLE	$_____

(check or money order—please do not send cash)

To order, complete this form and send it, along with a check or money order for the total above, payable to MIRA Books, to: **In the U.S.:** 3010 Walden Avenue, P.O. Box 9077, Buffalo, NY 14269-9077; **In Canada:** P.O. Box 636, Fort Erie, Ontario, L2A 5X3.

Name: _____
Address: _____ City: _____
State/Prov.: _____ Zip/Postal Code: _____
Account Number (if applicable): _____
075 CSAS

*New York residents remit applicable sales taxes.
*Canadian residents remit applicable GST and provincial taxes.

MIRA®

www.MIRABooks.com
MMG1109BL